Pillow Talk II

Selected Titles by Lesléa Newman

Fiction

Girls Will Be Girls
In Every Laugh a Tear
Every Woman's Dream

Good Enough to Eat
A Letter to Harvey Milk
Secrets

Poetry

Love Me Like You Mean It
Still Life With Buddy

Sweet Dark Places
Signs of Love

Humor

Out of the Closet and Nothing to Wear
The Little Butch Book

Nonfiction

SomeBODY to Love: A Guide to Loving the Body You Have
Writing From the Heart: Inspiration & Exercises for Women Who Want to Write

Children's Books

Heather Has Two Mommies
Remember That
Matzo Ball Moon

Saturday Is Pattyday
Too Far Away to Touch
Fat Chance (a novel)

Anthologies

Pillow Talk: Lesbian Stories Between the Covers
My Lover Is a Woman: Contemporary Lesbian Love Poems
The Femme Mystique
Eating Our Hearts Out: Personal Accounts of Women's Relationship to Food

Pillow Talk II

More lesbian stories between the covers

Edited by
Lesléa Newman

 alyson books
los angeles | new york

MANUFACTURED IN THE UNITED STATES OF AMERICA.

THIS TRADE PAPERBACK ORIGINAL IS PUBLISHED BY ALYSON PUBLICATIONS,
P.O. BOX 4371, LOS ANGELES, CALIFORNIA 90078-4371.
DISTRIBUTION IN THE UNITED KINGDOM BY TURNAROUND PUBLISHER SERVICES LTD.
UNIT 3, OLYMPIA TRADING ESTATE, COBURG ROAD, WOOD GREEN,
LONDON N22 6TZ ENGLAND.

FIRST EDITION: JULY 2000

00 01 02 03 04 **a** 10 9 8 7 6 5 4 3 2 1

ISBN 1-55583-519-8

LIBRARY OF CONGRESS CATALOGING-IN-PUBLICATION DATA
PILLOW TALK II : MORE LESBIAN STORIES BETWEEN THE COVERS / EDITED BY
LESLÉA NEWMAN.—1ST ED.
   ISBN 1-55583-519-8
   1. LESBIANS—SEXUAL BEHAVIOR—FICTION. 2. LESBIANS' WRITINGS,
AMERICAN. 3. EROTIC STORIES, AMERICAN. I. TITLE: PILLOW TALK TWO.
II. NEWMAN, LESLÉA.
PS648.L47 P56 2000
813'.01083538'086643—DC21   00-029987

CREDITS
"DIESEL DONUTS," © 1999 ILSA JULE, WAS PREVIOUSLY PUBLISHED IN *THE
MAMMOTH BOOK OF LESBIAN EROTICA* (ROBINSON PUBLISHING, LONDON, 1999).
REPRINTED BY PERMISSION OF THE AUTHOR.
"A FEMME IN THE HAND," © 1999 LESLÉA NEWMAN, FIRST APPEARED IN *GIRLS
WILL BE GIRLS: A NOVELLA AND SHORT STORIES* (ALYSON BOOKS, 2000).
REPRINTED BY PERMISSION OF THE AUTHOR AND PUBLISHER.
COVER PHOTOGRAPH COURTESY OF C.J. SCHEINER.

for me and my gal

Contents

Introduction

The girls are at it again! When I put out the word that I was putting out—another anthology of lesbian erotica, that is—I was amazed at the volume of manuscripts that appeared in my mailbox daily. The stories, like a couple of happy healthy dykes, kept coming and coming and coming. I am enormously proud to present hot off the press (and I do mean hot) this collection of twenty-six erotic lesbian short stories guaranteed to make you swoon.

What will you find between the covers? An anonymous subway encounter, a tryst with a movie star, a romp between two menopausal lovers, a butch/femme rendezvous. You'll find out what occurs when two straight girls decide to play "dyke for a day" and see how hot things can get when two lovers are trapped in the eye of a hurricane. You'll also watch what happens when lesbians answer personal ads, pick up hitchhikers, try to help out a friend, and visit the girl next door. As lesbians know, anything can and does happen once you find yourself between the covers.

The contributors to *Pillow Talk II* range from well-established authors such as Maureen Brady and tatiana de la tierra to up-and-coming writers such as Lisa Gonzales and Lauren Johnson. I thank all the writers who contributed to

Pillow Talk II as well as all the writers who allowed me the privilege of reading their stories. I also thank the wonderful staff at Alyson Publications, especially Angela Brown, Scott Brassart, and Greg Constante, for their support of this project.

Happy reading—and be on the lookout for *Pillow Talk III*!

Lesléa Newman
June 2000

She Makes Me Wanna
by Aya

"Meet me at the library at eleven," she said, then hung up. The dial tone hummed in my ear. My cunt tightened. Her voice, the click, the hum was like turning on my vibrator; my body responded accordingly.

I began to lay out what I would wear before I started my shower: a red sleeveless sundress, a white T-shirt, and brown leather sandals.

We take each other on mystery dates. Take turns being in charge of a secret destination or activity for the day. Today I am to be the one surprised.

When I plan a date for her, she wants me to take control. She doesn't want to have to think about what's going to happen or make decisions about whether it should happen. Sometimes I blindfold her and drive her what seems a long distance. When we stop she doesn't know if she's at my house, her own, or in a roomful of quiet strangers. One time I placed headphones over her ears, tied her to my oak bed frame, and let Usher's "You Make Me Wanna" curl into her, while *I* was all she could taste, smell, and feel.

On my dates I want to visit all my favorite places and fuck there. Places like the Pot Holes (a geological formation of narrow rock craters filled with cold spring water and deep

1

enough to swim in), the Quabbin Wilderness Preserve, the River Mill used book store, the balcony at the Unitarian church, and, today, the White-Stone Library. I want to make memories.

This morning, in preparation, I washed all over with a brush with stiff bristles on one side and a thick sponge on the other. Rubbing lightly scented soap into the bristles, I painted circular strokes of white lather onto my coffee-dark skin. Resting my foot on the side of the tub, I soaped between my legs. The sponge tickled my labia, grazed my clit, reminding me of her tongue and what was surely to come.

I was introduced to Logan O'Banyon at Gay Pride. I was thrilled to be in the company of the writer of the O'Banyon mystery series. My favorite title is *50 Ways to Kill Your Lover*. She was a dreadlocked member of the lesbian literati and a local celebrity. I've read everything she has ever written, not just because of her incredible writing style and her wonderfully twisted plot lines (although both are good reasons) but because I am a voracious reader. Post office work is not as hard on the brain as it is on the body. It leaves me plenty of time for reading when I've finished hauling everybody's mail around. I'm convinced my book-buying habits keep many of the smaller lesbian publishing houses afloat.

She said she had seen me around town but never had the opportunity to speak to me. Of course she has seen me; I deliver mail to most of the neighborhoods on the north side of town. Neither rain nor sleet nor gloom of night. *Right*. She said I was cute in my summer uniform. She liked the blue shorts and pinstriped shirts, my sensible black walking shoes. She thinks my short 'fro makes me look like a boy. I admit, I am somewhat muscled from the exercise I get on my route, but I'm no boy.

We started with dinner dates at the Sampan Pagoda. It turns out Chinese food is our drug of choice. One night as she was spooning brown rice onto her plate, I asked her how someone as fabulous as herself could be single and available. At first she furrowed her brow and lowered her eyes, then looked straight at me, "As a matter of fact, I was dumped for a younger dyke." Her voice grew softer, and she lowered her eyes again, "But it was my own fault. I spent too much time locked in my study, writing. She used to say it was like not having a girlfriend, and I guess she was right. When I wasn't writing I still wasn't a proper lover. I just wasn't as interested in sex as I should have been, as I had been when we first got together. Maybe that's what happens after you turn 50." She shrugged. "I don't get wet the way I used to. I wonder if I still can." Believe me, she knows the answer to that question now.

My story was kind of the opposite. I told her that at the end of this summer, I will be moving to Oakland to be with a woman I've loved long distance for three years. My soulmate. She was originally from Oakland and was here for graduate school. We met in a reading group and over time fell in love. She was the sweetest woman I had ever met, and in the sheets she was paradise. After a year of lustful secret meetings—secret because she was not out to her son—she moved back to California. Between visits, we carried on long distance. Hell, she could make me come *over the telephone.* I would have moved long ago, but she thought it best to wait until her son graduated from high school; then she thought I should wait until he was firmly ensconced in college. September will mark his second year at Gardener University. So you might wonder why someone starting a life with the woman of her dreams began a torrid affair just

3

before her new life would begin. Well, it's because I am on the verge of getting exactly what I've prayed for, because I am leaving a job that has become comfortable and easy, because I am leaving my family and people I've known forever, because I am leaving ex-lovers who have become friends, because it feels like a kind of death. I need this "thing" with Logan. Yeah, I'm going to California at the end of August, but I'm going with no regrets, ready to start anew, and I'll be damned tired when I get there.

Don't get me wrong; we didn't just decide arbitrarily to spend the summer in each other's arms. It kind of crept up on us and became a weird sort of defense mechanism, a defense against a broken heart, against the unknown.

We started spending time together, and we fit like a hand in a leather glove. Some of my running buddies got up a Friday night game of Spades, and Logan and I played partners. We were killing the other team on a regular basis. It was as if we were reading each other's minds. One night after a *serious* beating, my friend Laurie threw down her cards and said she wouldn't play if Logan and I were going to be partners every game—what a sore loser. After that game I was too tired to drive home, and Logan offered to let me stay the night at her house. She lay down with me on the fold-out couch, just for a little while—or so we thought. We talked in the dark until almost dawn. She told me about her "tickle spot," and I threatened to touch it. I told her about my sensitive ears, and she teased me by describing how she would touch them if I let her. We compared notes on former lovers' orgasms and how we'd brought them about. Logan, it turned out, was quite the rogue. She'd had several brief affairs with other authors and one-nighters with fans. Her life intrigued me.

4

While we lay together, she began touching me with light strokes as she spoke. I was getting very turned on. I started touching her back, and soon the talking stopped. That night we made love. Softly, quietly, being careful with each other, as if the other might break. We continued to see each other and have sex until it was clear a decision had to be made. Logan said she was getting ready to start a new novel and was not ready to begin a new commitment. I knew I couldn't stop the momentum I had begun when I bought that one-way ticket to San Francisco International.

We decided to spend July and August pleasuring each other in every way we knew. We agreed not to name what we were doing, not to say "I love you," and not to fall in love. It was all figured out. Logan didn't want a relationship. I didn't need a lover. We had eight weeks and five days until I boarded the plane in Hartford. What we do is not about love. We are just in it for sex.

🙒   🙒   🙒

Today, when I arrived at the White-Stone Library, Logan was standing near the front door, her hands in the pants pockets of her tan linen suit. She wore a gold silk blouse and black leather pumps that matched her attaché case. Her graying dreadlocks curled toward her collarbone and spread across her shoulders. When she saw me in my sundress, she said, "You look like a schoolgirl." I felt my cheeks burning, moisture forming deep in my cunt, sliding toward my swelling labia.

"Come on," she turned, and I followed her through the heavy library doors.

She leaned over the front desk, joking with a librarian. I

stood back and let her do her work. I heard her say something about the archives and research. The librarian's cheeks colored with a spreading flush as she fished in a side drawer, then handed Logan a gold ring that held two keys. I wondered what had made the librarian blush as I followed Logan to an alcove. My own cheeks grew hot as I imagined myself as one of a harem of concubines led to a pleasure chamber. Logan used a key to call the elevator marked FOR ACCESSIBILITY OR LIBRARY STAFF ONLY.

White-Stone Library was small. The basement and first floors were open to the public. The two remaining floors were for storage and archival research. Logan used a key to bring us to the third floor. In the elevator, she discovered I wore no panties under my dress. She reached under my clothes and cupped her hand against my dampened pubic hair and clit. She leaned into me, kissing my mouth hard, pressing me against the wall. I startled at the bell that signaled the passing floors, afraid the door would slide open and reveal her body pressed against mine, my dress pulled up around my waist.

When the elevator stopped and the door opened, she held me there, shivering in fear of being discovered. I peered over her shoulder into the dark room while she bit a hardened nipple through my dress, leaving a wet circle where her mouth had been.

The second key unlocked a Plexiglas door behind which hundreds of seemingly ancient books were shelved, a room within a room. Logan chuckled nervously as she locked the door behind us.

The room smelled like an attic, old and sweet but not musty or damp. The air was cool and dry. I recognized the climate control suspended from the ceiling with the dim fluorescent lights. I hoped a security camera wasn't hidden amid the technical-looking machinery.

Her heels clicked officially against a floor that looked fashioned from smooth stone blocks. Logan went to a long honey-colored table and set her attaché upon it. She opened the case and pulled out a thin blue flannel blanket and spread it on the floor. It wrinkled onto itself. Stepping back, she shook the blanket and guided its float so it was half beside, half beneath the table.

Logan turned to look at me, indicating with a tilt of her head for me to stand near the table. "Take off your sandals," she said. As I walked over the blanket, she removed her pumps, letting them fall to the floor with an alarming clatter. Without looking I knew she had followed me across the blanket. From behind, her arms came around me and hugged me, pulling me against her. Logan began to raise my dress over my head. I felt the linen against my ass, then the smooth silk blouse against my back as she pulled my T-shirt over my upstretched arms.

One of her arms curled around my thigh as her hand slipped between my legs. I half-heartedly tried to hold them closed. Her thumb gently stroked my clit while the side of her hand burrowed deep into my hot slick coulee. "This is one time when I could use another hand," she whispered into my ear before biting it, then licked where she had bitten. With her other hand she squeezed my knot-tight nipple between her thumb and forefinger. I might have laughed at her whispered wish, but my breath was caught in my throat behind an inhaled moan. She slid her hand from my crotch and made it obvious she was sucking my taste from her fingers. I stood naked with my back to her while viscous drops of my desire threaded their way down my thighs. I didn't turn when she stepped back, away from me. The only sound in the room was that of pants being unzipped, the rustle of silk being pulled over her head. I imagined her clothes folded neatly at the edge of the blanket and mine strewn haphazardly.

Logan's body spooned against mine as she cupped my breasts. She was naked, and I felt her belly, then her slightly scratchy pubic hair. She alternately kissed and nibbled my neck. Her hands held my hipbones as if to keep me still. I leaned back, closer to her, but she pushed me forward, bringing me closer to the table, and bent me over until my elbows and forearms rested on the smooth hard surface. She humped against me, miming penetration, rubbing her furry mons against my ass. Using her knee she opened my legs wider. Her finger slid along the groove that ended at my swollen clitoris. She tickled me with the soft pad of her fingertip while her other fingers seemed to hunt for a way to enter me at the same time. I groaned loudly and pushed against her hand, trying to help her fingers find what they were looking for and answer my body's plea for release.

Logan crouched between my legs and pushed them wider apart. I felt her mouth on me, sucking hard on my clit, then stroking it with her tongue. Her finger found its way to the tight rose of my asshole and threatened to push its way slowly in. She alternated sucking and moving the tip of her tongue quickly like hummingbird wings. I stretched myself along the cool tabletop, my breasts flattened against it. My hands searched for an edge that was out of reach. I was leaving this earth, stretching my body the distance from this room to heaven. The sweet-smelling wood pressed against my cheek. I couldn't tell if I felt her hot mouth on me or if it was her finger pushing its way into my pussy. It *was* her

8

finger…moving in and out, in and out…in, and then there were two…three. My voice begged, "Please, oh, God, please, oh…."

When her fist slid inside me, I put my hand over my mouth to stifle a scream, to keep my voice from echoing off the cement walls. As she drove herself into my willing body, I heard her hoarse whisper, like a mantra repeating, "Come on, baby. Don't leave me. Please, please, baby. Sweet darlin', don't leave me." Her dreadlocks whipped across my back. I was in the place between heaven and Earth when I felt myself tighten around her clenched fist. There was nothing but sensation and stars falling in the midnight sky. My beating heart was trying to wrench itself free.

I was crying hard as she lowered me to the blanket. She held me and rocked me as I whispered and sobbed "I love you" into her cheeks, her neck, her mouth. "I know, baby," she crooned in my ear. She stroked my hair and rocked me, curled in her arms.

I waited outside while Logan returned the keys, unable to stand in the lobby while women with small children passed me on their way to story hour. My once-smooth cotton dress was now wrinkled, suggesting it had been balled on the floor. I tried to tell by feel if my hair appeared mashed out of shape, if my brushed neck curls had become belligerent individual naps. Did I smell like the sex I'd just had? *God, she makes me wanna forget my California dreams and stay right here. Am I falling in love?*

Leaning against the building's warm bricks, I tried to imagine what it would be like to stay in this town as Logan's lover. Would it be a continuation of the feelings we had now? I saw us holding hands over dinner, then curled together in my bed. But what would I do while she barricaded herself in her study writing for days on end or touring the country? I have a life, a job, friends to keep me busy during those times, but a distant relationship is not what I want. Would she tolerate my calls to California to speak with the woman of my dreams while she was away? In my mind's eye I saw the airplane ticket receipt under my jewelry case and the packed U-Haul boxes stacked neatly in my living room. A totally committed one-to-one was what I wanted and what I was moving to California to get.

"Babe, do you need a ride home?" She was watching me from the doorway. How long had she been there?

Logan dropped me off in front of my apartment. I could tell by the way she held her body that she did not want to kiss me. At times like these I believe we are both afraid of how much we want each other, how much more we want of each other's lives, and how little time we have. We become afraid that if we let the other know how deeply we each feel the possibility of a future together, it would blow our fragile worlds apart. We're just not gonna do it. Our "thing" isn't about love; it's about sex.

In two weeks and a day, I'll go on to California and start a new life. She'll stay here in Massachusetts and write her book. We might stay in contact with each other for a while; we might not. I'll buy her book. I wonder if she'll dedicate it to me. Yeah, right. Either way, it'll be all right. I'm sure everything will be all right. Really I am.

Rebellious Streak
by Elizabeth Bachman

I've never been very good with dates, but I remember this particular day, September 17, the day it all started. I came home after work that Thursday to find Marte making my favorite dinner. One look at the lasagna told me something was up. She has made her lasagna for me just two other times. Both occasions were my birthday.

"Hey, Laura. Did you have a good day at work?"

"Did you forget to mail the payment to the telephone company, or has the cable been shut off?" I asked, reaching for a beer in the refrigerator.

"Neither," she said. "Don't be so damned suspicious all the time."

"OK, Marte. I'll just read the mail until you're ready to tell me." I sat at the kitchen table and separated my mail into two piles: bills and junk. Doesn't anyone write letters anymore?

Silence filled the room, and I could sense Marte's impatience with me. But I wasn't in the mood for twenty questions.

"Oh, I talked to Mother this afternoon. She's coming for a visit."

I started laughing. "Aha! Now your lasagna is justified. How long is she gracing us with her presence?"

"Three days."

"Well, I suppose I can stay at Josh's place for a bit." Josh was my coworker and the only other friend I had in Atlanta. "That will give you a chance to have some time alone with her."

"No!" Marte dropped the spoon she was using to spread cheese between the layers. "Laura, you can't leave. You *have* to be here."

"It was just a hopeful suggestion. I doubt your mom wants me hanging around the whole time." For as long as I can remember, Marte and her mother have been at war, mostly over Marte's reluctance to let her mother plan her life for her. I wasn't exactly savoring the idea of playing mediator.

"Well, actually, she's very keen on seeing you again."

"She is? I never got the impression she liked me much. Something about my hair always being messy and my clothes always being dirty." OK, so I was a tomboy when I was young.

"No, she always liked you. You had ambition. You made something of yourself."

"Yes, but I don't have the right kind of job, and I never settled down and had a family."

"Well, she understands that now."

"Understands what?" Suddenly my mail didn't hold the same fascination it did a few moments before. I began to feel I had missed an important part of this conversation.

"Well, you see..."

"What does she understand?"

"I just couldn't take it anymore! She never lets up, Laura. She started telling me about the son of a friend of hers that lives in Atlanta and getting us together and how it was high time I settled down, and I just snapped."

I have always been fascinated by how easy it is to read Marte's emotions in her hazel eyes. When she's mad her eyes flash bright green, and when she's happy they turn soft brown. All warm and inviting. The familiar bright green sparked in them now, the color that usually appears when she discusses her mother. "What did you do, Marte?"

"I told her I was never going to get married. That she had to know the truth. That I was gay!" Marte stared defiantly at me.

I blinked. It was all I could think of to do. Marte started spreading sauce over the lasagna. Finally I managed to find my voice again. "OK. You're gay. What was her reaction to that?"

"Actually, she took it a lot better than I thought she would."

"Wait. Aren't you afraid she'll try to fix you up with the *daughter* of a friend of hers now?" I couldn't help laughing.

"Well, no, not now." Her eyes grew soft and warm again as she looked at me, waiting for the realization to hit.

And it did. Understands now? Understands *now*? The laugh died somewhere in the back of my throat. Here I sat, in *our* kitchen, in the apartment we shared, getting ready to eat the dinner she was making for me. I was her roommate. If Marte was gay, where did that leave me?

"Marte! You didn't!"

"I had to. It was the only way."

"Oh, God. I'll bet she loved that. She probably thinks I corrupted you or something. I can't wait to hear what she thinks about that."

"Well, I suppose we'll find out when she comes. Her plane arrives tomorrow night at 7:30."

Marte and I have been best friends since we were children. When I left New York City and moved to Atlanta,

Marte decided I needed a roommate and moved there too. I think she just wanted to end her relationship with Jack once and for all, and moving away was the easiest answer. I thought she would stay with him forever. After all, her mother hated Jack. Considering that Marte seems to live her entire life as a rebellious statement against her mother, what could be better than staying with him? I suppose she was just too miserable to continue in it, even for her mother's sake. Marte is my best friend, and however she chooses to live her life is her own business. No matter how ridiculous I think some of her choices, I always try to back her up. There isn't much I wouldn't do for her. But this was pushing it.

"Laura, all you have to do is pretend we're lovers. And seem immensely happy. How hard can that be? They'll only be here for three days." Laura gave me another helping of lasagna. It was becoming less and less my favorite dish.

"They? Did you say *they*?" I felt the heartburn beginning.

"Sandy's coming too."

"Oh no. That's where I draw the line. I don't care if I have to marry Josh, I'm moving in with him tomorrow."

"Don't be ridiculous. It'll be a piece of cake. I've got it all figured out."

Sandy. Marte's kid sister. Sandy, who tagged along with us at every opportunity and never once failed to rat us out if we did anything wrong. I have always had an intense dislike for Sandy. Unlike Marte, Sandy has catered to her mom's every wish. She became a lawyer, married a doctor, and had two kids, all by the time she was 27. It was sickening.

I woke up the next morning, thinking the whole thing had been a dream until Marte stuck her head in the bathroom and told me not to be late that evening. "You don't

want to make a bad impression on your in-laws, do you?"
She giggled. I wanted to kill her.

I got home at a reasonable hour and immediately wished
I hadn't. Why didn't I go with my gut instinct and propose
to Josh? We could have been in Vegas by now.

I walked into my bedroom to change, and my mouth
dropped open. Nothing looked the same. It was all too sterile. Nothing personal in it. Not even my clothes.

"Marte?" I stuck my head around the corner, mustering
up as much calm as I could manage. "What have you done
to my room?"

"Honey, lovers don't have separate bedrooms, remember?" She batted her eyes and then laughed.

"Very funny." I walked past her into her bedroom. There
were all my things, neatly arranged, looking like they had
always been there. "We don't really have to sleep in here
together, do we?" I asked in disbelief.

"Well, really, Laura, what did you think? That my mother
and Sandy would believe we were a couple with separate
bedrooms?" She placed her hand on my shoulder. "It's just
for appearance's sake. I promise to behave like a perfect
gentleman." That smile again. Why is it so difficult to refuse
Marte a favor?

&   &   &

Nothing could have prepared me for what happened at
the airport. I was standing behind Marte (for protection?)
when her mother walked out the boarding door, saw us,
and broke into a huge smile. She hugged Marte and, to my
astonishment, hugged me as well.

"Hello, Mrs. West. It's nice to see you again."

"Now, please, Laura, call me Amanda. No need for formalities anymore, right?" She smiled even wider.

I wondered if I was supposed to hug Sandy too, but she alleviated my fears by not budging an inch and merely muttering a shallow hello. I returned it.

By the time we reached our apartment, I was all caught up on the family's happenings. So-and-so was engaged to so-and-so, this one had a new baby, that one was on her third. On and on and on. If Marte didn't have to concentrate on driving, I'm sure she would have jumped out of the car. I was too busy trying to figure out when "Amanda" would broach the subject of Marte and me. I decided she was going to handle it by ignoring it. I was wrong.

Halfway through a late dinner, Mrs. West turned to me and said, "So, Laura, Marte tells me you two are lovers." I nearly choked on my food as Marte laughed. "Is this a serious relationship or are you just going through a phase?"

"Oh, it's very serious, Mom. We moved down here to be together. Atlanta is very gay friendly, you know."

Unfortunately, her mother's eyes never left my face. Marte might as well have said nothing at all. They were both waiting for me to answer. "Uh, yes, that's right. It's very serious." I knew I didn't sound very convincing.

"You know, I've been after Marte to marry for some time now. What she needs is to settle down and find a good man to take care of her. I really wasn't expecting this."

"I know, Mrs. West, er, Amanda. But we're really quite happy together."

"What made you two decide you were made for each other all of a sudden, after all these years?" Cynicism and doubt dripped from Sandy's words. I was being cross-examined.

"Our lives have always taken different courses. I suppose it just wasn't the right time before. People change and grow and discover new things about themselves along the way." I could tell Marte was impressed with that answer by the way she looked at me. No doubt she had been trying to think of a good reason herself.

"Well, it's been a long day for us, and I'm sure the flight was exhausting for you. Let me show you to the guest room and let you settle in. We've got a lot planned for tomorrow," Marte said as she picked up a suitcase. I followed suit, trailing after her into what used to be my bedroom. I wondered what it was we had planned for tomorrow.

I woke up early the next day and set out on a quest to find bagels you wouldn't be embarrassed to serve New Yorkers. Not an easy task in Atlanta. As I drove down Piedmont Avenue, I remembered how awkward I'd felt getting into bed with Marte the night before. I chalked it up to the stress of the day. After all, it wasn't as if we'd never slept together before. Slumber parties when we were young, economy vacations that forced us to share a double bed. But this was different.

After we said our good nights, Marte had grabbed my hand and led me down the hall to her bedroom. All part of the act, of course. But I thought it was sweet. And she had been so attentive all through dinner, laughing at my dumb jokes, smiling affectionately at me. I wondered if she acted like that with all her lovers.

I finally made it home again, with a bag of less-than-perfect bagels, and found everyone sitting around the kitchen table drinking coffee.

"Ah, Laura, I've just been telling Marte what a wonderful job you've both done with the apartment. No doubt the books are all yours. My daughter doesn't go in much for academics."

Marte rolled her eyes. "That's right, Mom, I never did learn to read properly."

"Well, maybe if you had gotten a proper education, instead of majoring in art, you wouldn't be a clerk in a bookstore now," her mother said.

"Here we go again," Marte said as she put her head down on the table.

"I'm afraid you're going to be a little disappointed with these bagels, Amanda." I tried to change the subject.

"I was beginning to wonder if you decided to fly back to New York to get them. You've been gone forever," Marte said, kissing me on the cheek.

"Yes, Marte was just frantic over your absence. You'd think you never left her side before today," Sandy said.

"Well, we do try to spend the entire weekend together." I refused to let Sandy get to me.

æ   æ   æ

Marte wasn't kidding when she said she had a lot of plans for the day. She walked us all over town sightseeing. Later, while we were making dinner back home, I quietly asked her if it was her intention to exhaust the questions out of her mother and sister. She laughed and told me it was.

I began to relax a little as we ate. We discussed the sightseeing, the beautiful weather, Atlanta's cost of living. Even Sandy was polite, joining the conversation. Mrs. West asked me about my work, and Marte believably played the part of the proud girlfriend, telling her mother how important being a social worker is. I had to admit I liked hearing her gush on and on about me. But I should have known the scene was too perfect to last.

"What I'd really like to know is, what kind of a future do you envision having? It's not as if you two can marry or have kids." Apparently Mrs. West wasn't exhausted from the day's events.

"Why not, Mother? Lesbians have children all the time. Haven't you ever heard of artificial insemination?" There was almost a smirk on Sandy's face as she said this. "Which one of you is going to try that, or are you just going to take turns at it?"

"We really haven't discussed children." I had to put an end to this conversation.

"Why? Don't you want children, Laura?" I could see her mother using this as a weapon against Marte in the future.

"Yes, of course I do. But Marte and I don't think the time is right yet. We're still settling into this city."

"Don't worry, Mom. You'll be the first to know when we decide to have kids." Marte walked around the table and put her arm around me. "We've got plenty of time."

"Have you even thought about how hard it would be raising a child under these circumstances?" Sandy asked. "How he'll be teased at school and made to feel like an outcast?"

"How about we have our coffee in the living room? You can interrogate us more comfortably in there, Sandy." Marte looked as if she was about to blow a gasket. I had to say something.

"Sandy, we're not worried about raising children under 'these circumstances.' We know our children will be surrounded by enough love to withstand anything." Marte looked up at me, the green leaving her eyes, a warm brown spreading over them instead.

Mrs. West got up. "Coffee sounds wonderful. Let me help you get it, Marte."

❧   ❧   ❧

Marte and I went to bed early, worn out from the sight-seeing and dinner conversation. I changed into my usual sleep attire—an old T-shirt and cotton shorts—and climbed into bed. I heard the bathroom door open, then turned my head after a couple of minutes when I realized Marte hadn't come to bed yet. She was standing in the doorway, her hand on the frame, wearing a black negligee and striking a seductive pose.

"What are you doing?" I asked, my eyebrows as far up on my forehead as they would go.

"You don't like it?" she asked, pretending to pout.

I wasn't sure how to answer. Marte was indeed a beautiful woman. The nightgown was extremely short and complemented her long legs. And it was just transparent enough to confirm that she certainly had a beautiful body.

"Goodness, I believe I've rendered you speechless, Laura." She smiled even wider and sat next to me on the bed. "Do you need a cold washcloth on the back of your neck or something?"

"Don't you think you're carrying this charade a bit far?" I stammered, wishing she weren't sitting quite so close.

"Well, I might have to get up in the middle of the night again."

"And?"

"And go into the kitchen for a drink or something. Suppose my mom or Sandy saw me?"

I drew my eyebrows together, trying hard to figure out

what she was getting at. "What if they did?"

"Well, really, Laura. You'd think I'd go to sleep in something a little sexier than my old nightgown for my girlfriend." She looked exasperated.

"Oh," I said. "I get it. Let's get some sleep now." I reached for the clock. She sat there for another minute, watching me as I played with the alarm settings. Finally she got up with a sigh and walked around to the other side of the bed. I lay down, turned my back to her, and tried to go to sleep.

         ❧   ❧   ❧

Sunday was nearly as exhausting as the day before. You wouldn't think there could be so much to see in one city. But everyone was behaving themselves, and Marte could make just about anything fun.

We managed to get home at a decent hour and decided to sit outside in our little garden for a while. Marte and I were rather proud of it. It wasn't much, but it was all ours. The weather was beautiful for September, and we managed to have enough lounge chairs for everyone. I was starting to get comfortable when Marte announced she was going to make some iced tea. All of a sudden I found myself alone with her mother and sister.

"You don't really expect us to be happy with this, do you, Laura?" I should have known Sandy wouldn't let the occasion slip by.

"It's not that we're unhappy," Mrs. West threw a reproachful look at her younger daughter. "It's just that we're concerned. This isn't exactly an ideal lifestyle. For either of you. How can you be sure this is what you really want?"

Marte called from the kitchen, thankfully. I excused myself

with a sigh of relief. "Is everything all right?" she asked.

"It's fine. Now I know how it feels to be grilled in the Spanish Inquisition."

She laughed, patted my shoulder, and told me it was only for one more night. "It'll all be over soon, I promise. Now go back and tell them I couldn't find the sugar or something."

Our kitchen faces east, on the other side of the living room from the garden door. A rather large window sits between the two doors, and as it was a beautiful fall day, the window was open. I stopped dead in my tracks as I passed it. I couldn't see her mother and sister from where I stood by the window, but I could hear them just fine.

"Mother, it's all just ridiculous, this whole thing. I told you what I thought before we even got on the plane, and now you're going to have to admit I was right."

"Now, really, we can't be sure."

"It's all just a pretense, devised for your benefit. Marte has no intention of settling down yet, and she's tired of all your lectures. She'd say anything to stop them. Those two aren't lovers, and you know it. Come on, we're going right in there and make them admit the truth this instant!"

So much for Oscar-winning performances. I spun around and ran back to the kitchen to tell Marte what her sister had said, but as they approached, I realized there was no time. Marte turned toward me with a quizzical look on her face, and I did the only thing I could think of. I pulled her to me and kissed her. If that didn't shut her sister up, nothing would.

It seemed like hours passed while we embraced. The moment our lips met, I felt an electrical current run right through me. Before I could analyze the feeling, Marte's tongue slid into my mouth, searching for my own. I stopped analyzing and pulled her closer. It wasn't until I heard her mother clearing her throat that I came to my senses again.

I turned and looked at Sandy, who was bright red. Her mother said, "We thought you might need some help."

"Sorry, Mom. We got a little carried away looking for the sugar." A sheepish grin spread over Marte's face. After her family left the kitchen, she turned to me, her eyebrows slightly raised. "I heard them talking," I blurted out. "They thought we had made everything up so your mom would stop lecturing you about getting married." I sounded like an idiot. "Ah," was all Marte said before she picked up the iced tea and walked out of the kitchen.

❧   ❧   ❧

We all went to bed early that night. Marte came out of the bathroom wearing her old nightgown again, turned on the TV, and got into bed. What about the kiss? Should I bring it up? Should we discuss it? In the end, we just went to sleep.

Marte got up early the next morning to gas up the car before we had to leave for the airport. I stumbled into the kitchen to start the coffee. Her mother and sister were already there, dressed and ready to go.

I made some polite conversation about the weather being clear and the flight home probably being an easy one. I didn't hear the front door open as Marte returned.

"Laura, I have always liked you. Granted, you chose to waste your time working for the city, but at least you have some ambition. I can see you care for my daughter, but I'm worried. How do you know she feels the same? Marte has never been the settling-down type. She's never finished

23

anything she started. She has no career, no goals in life. She could leave you tomorrow and never look back. Do you know what you're getting yourself into?"

I felt something snap. What a lot of nerve she had! Marte was my best friend, and I'd be damned if anyone talked about her that way.

"You don't know the first thing about your daughter, Mrs. West. She is one of the kindest, most generous people I have ever known. I would do anything for her, and I know she would do anything for me. We have something you can never take away, not with all your meddling and needling." I felt the color rise in my face as I stared her and Sandy down. "Whatever she wants to do with her life is her business. I am in love with Marte, Mrs. West, and nothing you can say or do will change that. And I will thank you to stay the hell out of our lives!" The kitchen door opened, and I turned to see Marte standing there staring at me. All I could do was mutter an apology as I ran out of the room.

I heard Marte's car drive up about two hours later. I had been sitting on my bed most of that time, trying to focus on the events of the last few days, trying to figure out what to say. A few moments later Marte walked into my room and sat down next to me. I couldn't even look at her.

"I'm sorry," I said again, my voice sounding strange to me.

"What are you sorry for?"

"I shouldn't have talked to your mom like that."

"Don't apologize, Laura. I loved it. You know, no one has ever stood up for me like that before."

We sat there for what seemed an eternity, neither of us saying anything. I was afraid to open my mouth again. Afraid of what might come out.

"Laura," Marte finally broke the silence. "Not everything

you told my mother was an act, was it?" She shifted slightly, turning toward me. I felt her eyes on me, but I couldn't move, couldn't find my voice. All I could do was look down and shake my head. I knew every word I had said to her mother was true.

Marte put her fingers under my chin and gently lifted my head. Our eyes met, and for a second I thought I saw that familiar green flash into her eyes. Was she mad after all? "I didn't exactly lie to my mother either. Not completely."

"About what?" She had lost me.

"When I told her I was gay. I've never considered myself gay, not once, not even bi, but, Laura, I've been with a woman before. Twice, actually." She was talking very low, as if she were speaking to herself. "It wasn't my choice. I did it for Jack."

I wanted to leave. Get up and get away from this conversation. I knew what she was going to tell me. That she didn't want to go there again. That we had to resume our lives the way they were before. I couldn't bare to hear her say it. But her fingers were still on my chin, and her eyes were compelling me to stay.

"The first time we had been out drinking all night. Most of the details are a little fuzzy, but I do remember the highlights. We came home, and Jack started making love to me, getting me all excited. He whispered in my ear that he had invited someone over, someone he had met at the bar. I thought he was just making it up—until I heard a knock at the door, and a woman came into the bedroom. I started to protest, but Jack can be rather persuasive. I won't say I didn't enjoy it. But I put it down to temporary insanity. I had had too much to drink, and I was so worked up from the way he had been touching me. I did tell him afterward, though, that it would never happen again. He just smiled."

Marte had withdrawn her gaze—and her fingers from my chin—during all of this. She sat on the bed in front of me, staring down, her words coming very fast. "The second time wasn't exactly a surprise. We were out dancing when Jack spotted this woman. He told me he wanted to invite her home with us. I said I wasn't interested, but he wouldn't let it go. I finally gave up arguing with him. I wasn't nearly as drunk this time, and frankly I was nervous about the whole thing. I think Jack had talked her into it too, because it didn't seem like her kind of thing either. She wanted Jack. But we put on a little show for him."

"Why are you telling me this, Marte?" I finally asked.

Her eyes found mine again. I hadn't been wrong; there it was—that bright green spark. I tried to figure out what it meant.

"Because I want you to understand. I want to understand it myself. I really hadn't the slightest interest in either of those women. I don't remember ever looking at a woman before and feeling desire."

Desire. I thought I knew all there was to know about Marte. We had been through so much together over the years. I thought I had seen her in every possible situation: happy, sad, angry, indifferent. But I realized there was one emotion I had never seen up close.

"And then you kissed me." Marte paused, studying my face.

There it was, finally. That kiss. Should I tell her it was just an act? That I had just gotten caught up in the moment, in the pretense? I held my breath as she continued.

"Maybe I have felt this for a long time, Laura. Maybe it took my mother's visit to make me see things clearly, to know how I really feel. I tried not to think about it, to shake it off. But I haven't been able to think of anything else since that kiss. I found myself lying next to you last night, wanting to touch you. Wanting to know what you felt like. Wanting to take you in my arms and make love to you." Her eyes were so green that I was starting to feel a little dizzy.

"Tell me it was all an act, Laura. Tell me you feel none of this, that you want me to leave. Tell me you don't want to kiss me again."

I could have told her all of that, could have made everything the way it was before. But I was completely captivated by her.

She raised her right hand to my face, cupping my cheek gently with her palm, her thumb caressing my skin. Her left hand captured the other side of my face as she leaned forward. When our lips met I felt the electricity I had felt before. Her kiss was so tender, so exciting. My heart pounded in my chest as our tongues found each other, her hands pulling me closer. The kiss grew more passionate as her fingers entwined in my hair and my hands began caressing her back.

Slowly she pushed me down on the bed, our mouths still joined, drinking each other in. Her leg moved between my own as our bodies melded together. The sensation that coursed through my body was almost overwhelming. A low moan escaped my lips as her tongue found my ear, flicking inside. Our hands explored each other as she kissed me again, her tongue warm and soft in my mouth.

Marte looked into my eyes as her hands moved to the bottom of my sweater, almost daring me to protest. I smiled up at her instead as she pulled my sweater over my head. An intense heat began to work its way up from my toes as she leaned down and kissed my shoulder, her mouth traveling down to the top of my bra. Her mouth melted my skin as she kissed me through the lacy cotton. She reached behind me and unhooked my bra. I almost screamed when I felt her tongue against my nipple.

Her hand eased down to the top of my jeans, skillfully unbuttoning them. I turned my head, suddenly shy, as she worked the zipper down. I was almost embarrassed at how wet she had made me. But as her hand slid into my panties, she smiled at the discovery. She leaned forward again, kissed me, then put her lips to my ear. "I want to taste you," she whispered, exerting pressure with her fingers. My breath caught in my throat.

She slid off the side of the bed, kneeling between my legs. Grabbing the top of my jeans, she pulled them off, then did the same with my panties. I looked into her beautiful green eyes as her hands moved to my hips, beckoning me to slide toward her. Another wave of electricity hit me when she leaned her head down and kissed my damp curls, and I fell back against the bed as her tongue touched me, slowly licking. The strength of the orgasm took me by surprise as she pushed her tongue inside. I grabbed her hair and held on, feeling waves crash over me again and again.

I pulled her off her knees back onto the bed and held her in my arms, kissing her neck. I wanted to know all there was to know about this woman. Every detail that had escaped me over the years. I gently pushed her onto her back and sat on top of her, smiling down as my hands roamed over her stomach and breasts.

"Do you remember Mark Browning?" she suddenly asked. I gazed down at her, a bewildered look on my face, as I remembered my high school boyfriend. "He told me once that he never understood you, and it drove him crazy trying to figure out what you wanted. I laughed and asked him why he didn't just break up with you. He said, 'I would, but she's so damn good in bed.' " She started laughing. "I never thought that someday I'd be able to judge for myself."

"Honey, I plan on giving you plenty of opportunities to decide," I said before I kissed her deeply, capturing her tongue in my mouth. There was so much I wanted to explore, so much I wanted to give. I helped her out of her clothes and felt another surge of electricity as our bodies came together. I kissed my way down her neck, pausing for a moment to run my tongue over the hollow at the base of her throat. My tongue trailed down as I licked between her breasts, her breath coming fast now. She was deliciously wet as my fingers moved between her legs, stroking her lips. She thrust her hips toward my hand, trying to force it inside her. But I wasn't going to be rushed. I wanted to enjoy every minute.

As I moved my tongue to her left nipple, I ran my fingertip gently over her clit, barely touching it. She moaned loudly, digging her nails into my back. I let my finger move in lazy circles around her as I felt her clit grow harder and harder. I moved my finger down and inside her, feeling her muscles tense around it, feeling how hot she was inside. Slowly I began kissing her stomach, biting her gently as I moved down until I was kneeling between her legs, my finger still deep inside her. She bent her knees and opened her legs wide. She was so beautiful, the wetness glistening off her pink folds. I slid my finger in and out, slowly at first, then faster and faster. Each time I pushed into her, she raised her hips and thrust toward me. I was mesmerized, listening to her moan, watching her body move.

I looked into her eyes as I leaned forward, feeling her heat against my face. Another surge ran through me as my tongue dipped into her juices. I wanted to lap up every drop. She screamed out as I caught her clit between my lips, pulling and sucking it. I felt the muscles tighten around my finger as the orgasm rolled over her. I moved my body on top of her again, holding her close, feeling her body tremble.

"You know I'm in love with you too, don't you, Laura?" she softly whispered. I held her closer, never wanting the moment to end. We lay for a long time in each other's arms. I was listening to her breathe, her heart rhythmically beating, marveling in the wonder of it.

"Your mother will probably never talk to me again," I said, remembering what an idiot I had made of myself.

She laughed. "Want to know what Mother said?" I looked into her eyes, the color a soft brown now. "She said I'd be a fool if I let you get away. She thinks you're wonderful, Laura. She was impressed with your courage to stand up to her like that."

"You're kidding."

"No, really I'm not. I think Sandy wants to marry you too." We both laughed, then grew silent, then kissed.

Tyger! Tyger!
by J.L. Belrose

I'm lying on a pink blanket, offering my naked body to the sun, my dildo fixed firmly in my cunt. I'm squeezing on it like a baby sucking on a soother, the sun's heavy heat prowling around me. I imagine myself spread under a golden beast, a lioness. She thirsts for sacred rivers and prods my nipples with a rough and urgent tongue. Her ponderous she-lion head swings over my belly. Her eyes slit with delight as she sniffs my cunt. Her jaw quivers with desire.

But she defers her pleasure. She tenses, listens, turns her majestic head toward the house. Sounds inform her that Leah has returned from foraging the outer world. We hear her range through the house, boot-stomping, door-banging, until she charges out onto the dry cracked timbers of our deck, finds me sunbathing in the backyard. "Are you crazy?" she shrieks, and the jungle stiffens into eerie silence.

I roll my head slowly toward her and lift a hand to shadow my eyes from the sun. The sight of Leah makes me clench harder on my dildo. She's angry. She clamps her hands on the railing, arms ramrod straight from wrist to shoulder, as she glares at me from her platform. "Are you fuckin' insane?" she howls. "Somebody'll see you."

I smile serenely and shut my eyes to the sun's unblinking

stare. My hand slides down my belly to my clit. The waiting is over. I press my fingers to the hot sweet flesh, stroke, and dissolve into the jungle's savage pulse. Then, with a practiced thrust of muscles, I eject my dildo onto the blanket. "You are fuckin' crazy," she yells from the deck and slams back into the house.

I rest, pleased, then gather my blanket around me and, yawning, lazy with sun, negotiate the rough wooden steps. As I open the door, I see she's there, as I thought she would be, positioned in the hallway, blocking my passage. Her back propped against one wall, her boots jammed up to the other wall, her long, jeaned legs are angled across the hall. Her hands are tucked behind her. Her eyes, inscrutable onyx, crush mine and trigger in me the rippling aftershocks of orgasm.

I allow the blanket to loosen from my body. I step slowly, deliberately, across her legs, halting when my mouth almost touches hers. I say, eyes demurely lowered, "I waited for you. I waited until you were there."

I want to arch my back and rub cat-like against her, sliding myself down her body, stroking her with my face. I want to lick her feet. But she doesn't prompt me, so I move on, dragging my blanket behind me. "I waited for you *all* afternoon," I tell her over my shoulder as I pout my way into the bathroom.

I'm bending over the bathtub, testing the water from the tap, when she positions herself in the doorway behind me. I lean more forward, raising my ass, inviting.

"You've forgotten," she states, her voice a cool splash.

Yes, I suppose I have forgotten something. I know she's home earlier than usual, and there must be a reason, but I haven't tried to figure it out. "Mom's coming to dinner," she reminds me. I groan wretchedly, but she ignores my dramatics. She swaddles me in her let's-be-reasonable voice. "I thought, you being home all day, you might have gotten something ready."

Leah is always reasonable. As well as kind, considerate, responsible, and sane. It could drive me crazy. In my humble opinion, life stripped of adventure, devoid of fantasy, is boring. I step into the shower and visualize myself under a waterfall on a faraway planet where flowers, huge as houses, shine with the translucence of gemstones. The water, crystal pure ejaculate from the dyke-mother of the universe, splashes my face, cascades over my breasts and down my body. I relent. Leah needs me. "I'll take spaghetti out of the freezer," I shout across whirlpools of galaxies, "and I'll make a salad."

I towel-dry and apply lotion, soothing the glow of sun in my skin. I survey the clothes hanging in the closet and decide I'm a wood nymph, and nymphs, of course, don't wear clothes. I stroll down the hall to the kitchen. I jettison salad stuff from the fridge to the counter. I rinse, I chop, I slice, aware, as I work, of the huge striped beast slunk down on the floor behind me. It creeps closer and closer, until its hot breath swirls around my legs. Its massive tiger head nudges, pushes between my knees, forcing my legs apart. Its tongue rasps up the inside of my thigh. The tip of its tongue separates my cunt lips, finds my opening, and with soft steady pressure eases itself in. I lower my head, exposing the long soft curve of my neck to her teeth. She bites in sharp playful nips down from my ear, across my shoulder. From behind, her arms encircle me. Her thumbs and fingers pinch and pull at my breasts. I yelp, my nipples still tender from my afternoon's pleasure. "Open," she commands, "Stand still."

I tell myself to relax, submit.

"More," she whispers, and I obey.

"Tyger, Tyger, burning bright," I moan, as the beast's tongue twists inside me, fills me like a fist.

"Give it up," she growls, and I brace myself against the counter as tiger claws clutch at my belly, coaxing me down deeper onto the shaft inside me. Then a cry echoes up through my body as if from an ancient forest. The first saber-toothed tiger has roared at a pale young moon.

"What?" Leah calls from the bathroom.

"Nothing," I answer, hearing her tread down the hall. "I was singing."

She scans the undone salad spread over the counter, wilting. "How are you doing here?" she asks.

I pull a glistening carrot from my cunt. I rotate it slowly, examining it for traces of cream, licking off any I see. She's not amused. I hear suppressed panic in her voice as she says, "Please get some clothes on. Mom's going to be here any minute. Go! Go! I'll finish the salad."

I sigh, expelling all the breath in my body, and toss the carrot onto the counter. I flounce to the bedroom. I choose my leopard-patterned bodysuit and slither into it. I spike my hair with gel. I wonder if Leah's mother will say anything about the color. She's never seen it orange before.

I'm in the mood for makeup. I use liner to slant and extend my eyes. I add brown shadow and mascara. And more shadow. Finally, in the mirror, a leopard's eyes transfix my own. I look at my hands and know what I must do. I must extend the leopard spots from the sleeves onto the backs of my hands. With the eyeliner I draw irregular circles and fill them in with the brown eyeshadow. I look back into my mirror and see that my neck also needs spots.

I hear sounds of intrusion at our front door. Leah's mother has arrived. I sense monstrous vines of disapproval spreading over our floors, stretching up our walls, creeping across our ceilings. A monkey clings to the light fixture above my head and jabbers warnings.

On the pretext of getting tissues from the bathroom, Leah passes our bedroom door. "What the hell's taking you so long?" she hisses without stopping, without looking in. I begin applying my black nail polish, slowly, carefully, and allow it to dry thoroughly. Finally, satisfied with my appearance, ready to present myself, I leave my den.

Leah's mother is reorganizing our kitchen. The cupboard beside the sink has been disemboweled. Leah is reluctantly assisting in this activity. I'm embarrassed for her. I want her to say, "This is my kitchen. This is my home. Accept it. This is my mate. Accept her." But I know she won't. I sigh loudly. They stop. They stare at me. I smile demurely and wait.

I observe the mother's face solidify into contempt, but Leah's lips crimp together, sealing in laughter, and her eyes glitter. I'm reminded how much I love her. She says, "How excellent...showing Mom your costume. I haven't told Mom yet...about your new job...entertaining children...at birthday parties."

"I thought she had a skin disease!" the mother sputters. "God, she scared me!" She speaks only to Leah, but, mesmerized, she can't stop staring at me. Can't ignore me like she usually does.

She manages to turn briefly toward her daughter. "She's not going to sit at the table looking like that, is she?"

"I don't know," Leah says. "Ask *her*, why don't you?"

Leah's mother has never, ever spoken to me. In the nine years Leah and I have been together, her mother has never once addressed me directly. It's as if, by not talking to me, she thinks she'll somehow make me not exist. In the beginning I tried very hard to win her over, for Leah's sake. I thought, in time, I would at least earn some acknowledgment of my place in her daughter's life. But I won't. I know that now. And I don't care anymore. I just don't care.

But I rather like Leah's idea about my getting a part-time job entertaining at children's parties. In fact, I like it so much I think it might be true. I decide I should rehearse for it. Which means I can't answer even if I *am* spoken to, because I'm sure children know leopards can't talk. They do, however, sniff the air, particularly when they detect incursion upon their territory. They sniff at the intruder too, but they do it somewhat discreetly. They can, I determine, by cupping their paws, carry dishes to the table, but, of course, they can't use cutlery. Nor can they drink from cups. They slurp a lot. I discover too that they can't eat spaghetti without licking their paws almost constantly.

I'm much too preoccupied perfecting my act to look at Leah, but leopards have excellent peripheral vision, so I'm aware she's eating silently, concentrating on her plate. Her mother is silent too, sitting opposite me, not wanting to watch and yet compelled to. Her mouth wobbles as if she's about to speak, but she stops each time before she starts. She doesn't touch her spaghetti. She doesn't touch anything, not even her water. Not even the carrot sticks…which disappoints me profoundly. I'd placed them right in front of her, hoping she'd enjoy some.

Finally she turns to Leah. "Well…" she says, and her mouth opens and closes, opens and closes, like a fish finding its water mysteriously evaporated. I hope she's not having a heart attack. I almost relent. But I don't. I lower my head and lick my plate.

"Well..." she says again, and pushes away from the table. Leah gets up too and follows her to the door. I wait for Leah's litany of apologies to begin, but only silence throbs between them. Then my breath stops. Leah says words I have waited years to hear. "Mom," she whispers, "I really do love her. We're good for each other."

I lick my fingers. I want to purr. The mother retreats. I hear her promise as she steps out over our threshold that she won't be back "until things are different." And I know that means never. Things will never be "different" for Leah and me.

"That was quite a performance," Leah states, closing the door, then leaning against it. I lift a paw and playfully swipe the air. She doesn't smile. She regards me with carefully hooded eyes. She is wearing black. Her hair is black, smooth, sleeked back. Her arm, strong and sensuous, reaches out. Her fingers stroke at the light switch, and we are in darkness.

A shiny black beast, a panther, emerges from the shadows. Silhouetted for a moment by moonlight, in a stillness of power, she stands absorbing her freedom. Ravenous, her eyes burn bright. She crouches, leaps. She pulls her prey down into lush carpets. She rolls me on forest floors. I beg to be devoured, and, giggling, she feasts.

Flashing, Honey?
by Maureen Brady

First my love laughed at me for breaking a sweat on top of her as I pushed up to let a breath of air waft across my lobster chest, not sure if I was flashing or simply hotter than I'd been in years.

She traced the drips that ran down between my breasts, then cupped the breasts, puckered her lips to ask for a kiss, called me a hot tamale.

I stayed raised for another beat, skin melting, mind going under the heat, like it did sometimes on the subway in mid summer, to that place where I was one with it. Buddhist, though I wasn't a practitioner.

Desire stayed beneath the sweat, a precise fire residing below the passing burn, kindled by the tease of her mouth and the invitation in her eyes.

The wave gone, I dropped down to meet her chest again, cunt to cunt, belly to belly. Bliss—her softness, a steady heat up and down with a higher pitch below. A current strong enough to trip her breath. And mine.

I opened my eyes and watched her face as I pressed into her. She had a deep look of being in it, concentration, almost work, her eyes rolled upward, the center of her face narrowing down to grasp her feeling. She'd written a book in which there was a character who loved sex—didn't get enough of it—and sometimes thought that was all she'd really been created for. It went through my mind as I looked at her that she was this character and I'd had the good fortune to fall in love with her. And then I realized, of course, she was not that character. She cared about a great deal more—making up that character, for instance. Which was my good fortune too.

Within a few months of our meeting, she began to sweat too and stopped laughing. Nothing like lying in a bath of sweat in bed to meld a couple together. We joked about having our own furnaces. Actually not having them, being them. Often one of us set off the other in sequence, especially in the close proximity of making love. One steam engine catches up with the other, sets it off as in a relay race.

"You flashing, honey?" she asks me.

"No, you are," I reply, watching the flush rise in her neck, lifting my body apart from hers to give her a space to air in, since already her clothes are on the floor beside the bed.

It all started with a meal, of course. We'd taken a long walk by the river. Then she brought me back to her apartment and parked me upstairs in her loft area to watch the TV news while she finished cooking. As she repeatedly tasted her pasta sauce, I peered down to watch the verdict. She turned up her nose in derision. "It's not turning out well at all," she said, shaking in a generous sprinkling of parmesan cheese as an antidote. "I should have made you gumbo even though it takes days."

By the time the meal was ready, I was sliding into a state of dread. I had been around long enough to believe that people tell you right away about their failings; you only have to listen. I'd already spent a year with a woman who was a horrid cook, and when she'd ruined the first dinner she'd made me, I'd made the mistake of dismissing the failed meal as the result of an endearing case of nerves. Now

I lay up in the loft, semi-reclined on a rolled back futon, (which anyone could see must unfold into a bed), listening to this pert perimenopausal woman swear her sauce had gone astray, thinking, *You'd better watch out.* And then she was tossing up napkins, standing on a loveseat to hand me real silver, a couple of plates, a drink, a bowl of pasta, a salad. And ascending the stairs with the serving spoons.

I was amazed when my taste buds gave me an unequivocal yes. The sauce was heaven, both tasty and filling, and I was glad I hadn't run away before trying *it* and *her* out.

Dinner lasted. She'd gotten some pastries for dessert and made us some strong decaf. Our conversation was humming by then. We talked about coming out, or not quite coming out. I told her how it had taken association with a bunch of flannel-shirted radical feminists to walk me past the mark. "Goll-ee," she said, "I wish that had done it for me, but I've never been a joiner, and I was living in Paris then anyway." She had a more convoluted story. In. Out. In. Out. I pushed at all its angles, hoping she'd say "goll-ee" again, which she did with wide-open eyes as well as an accent on each syllable.

All through the talk I tried to imagine how I could get my hand to move over and touch hers, maybe hold it, maybe pick it up and kiss it to forewarn her I wanted to kiss her. We'd already bumped a number of times, as if we were two unbalanced people who now and again were prone to falling sideways. The air was charged in that way that makes you feel as if some special feelers are exuding from your body, and anywhere within six inches of her, *your* feelers can brush up against *her* feelers, and your hot spot sizzles and jangles. Why do we want to get so quickly to the next place when this magnified-aura thing is so rare and seems inevitably to go away when the newness wears off?

But I was, as I say, desperate to kiss her, now that I knew her pasta was nourishing. So the next time we came unbalanced, I awkwardly landed my head on her shoulder, and as she turned I moved my lips upward to hers rather than properly righting myself. The contact was like a super bingo, like when I won the triple jackpot on a slot machine—five hundred dollars for my little quarter—and the machine began singing, and, had it not been tightly anchored to the floor, it would have danced too.

A series of bingos followed—one when we took off our shirts and our eyes swept each other's breasts, and then we pressed our bare warm skin together. Our nipples screamed delight; our bellies fluttered. We murmured. Remarked on how well life was treating us. Murmured some more. And touched all the warm places again.

We delayed the final gratification until the next date—a night when I could cook for her. Scallops sautéed in a mushroom sauce over basmati rice. Fresh greens with my special dressing. Ben and Jerry's S'mores (low fat). Then, finally, we stretched out full length, naked and hot, and went at it.

Our bliss didn't foresee the near future day when we would stand and hug cunt to cunt; now it was only belly to belly, no touch below. From enjoying all those meals together. And preferring sex to exercise.

Our sex is excellent; our memories are not. We buy gingko biloba extract and forget to take it. And sometimes a week or so goes by and we forget how long it's been since we last had sex. Forget how fine and mellowing and bonding it is. Our age seems to have brought us to a contentment with it. Always before I was looking to make it better or find a partner who would make it better, get down further, read me,

41

desire me in the wildest way. Fifty seems to settle a woman to *what is* rather than *what might be*, which is a relief, I must say. The fantasy life no longer holds the energy. Can't compare to warmth and touch and reality, close attention, someone hallowing out your name.

We start real slow. At first I didn't like it that way. It was her choice. It threw me back to adolescence, to hours of making out with someone—a boy it was then—putting off the real act but staying hot for hours, making slick underpanties. Once I finally went "all the way," I sped up a whole lot, always felt, *Well, we're just going to do it sooner or later, so why not sooner?* That was a binge attitude, created by the long deprivation of being a late bloomer, then later by the fact that most of my relationships were short-lived, with long gaps in between, so whenever I started something up, I was desperately horny.

Now she holds me to a certain pace, and if I speed up she grabs my hand, puts it where she wants it, drops her voice, and drawls out like the Southern belle she is, "Don't rush. Here, do me like you do, slow." And I run my finger over her clit and keep going, plunge into her vagina, slide back out wet and run back up over her clit again, barely touching, almost like I'm more interested in the air above it than in that little bud that I know is going to grow like a bulb that's pulsed up with fluid and wants to go toward the sun. I do this run ten, twelve times until it feels as if I'm doing it to myself, my own clit rounding out, sending me the sensations of my warm belly skin, making me rub against her hip as I slide my finger back in.

I want her to say "faster, harder," but she doesn't. She's Southern through and through, just like that character in her book. She doesn't figure life will be any more solved when this act is over than it was before it started, so why not take her time?

I fly down to her face and wash my tongue around in her mouth—the heat there like the temperature in her womb. Cozy. Nearly hot as the furnace heat but more local.

I bring my body on top of hers, then move my cunt above my hand, which still travels as she has instructed, only now my clit energy follows right on top of it. And then I can't stand slow anymore and open her lips to me and press my clit against hers, pulling away for the tease that provokes her, then pushing in tight for the bead of light that streams out of one of us and beams into the other when we touch there.

She holds my Parker rolls, as she calls my buttocks; I hold her head, precious, feeling her sanctity neatly composed inside the pure round bones of her skull, despite the way in outer life she flies in all directions, chaotic and anarchistic. I pull at the roots of her hair, wanting to touch this essence of her as I ride her.

I ride toward the end of the Earth. Then I interrupt my ride to slither down between her legs, kick off the covers that want to bind my feet. I kiss her softness, her belly skin, the inside of her thighs where the skin seems to forget to age. I brush my hand across her garden like a rake uncovers the bulb that has just sprouted through the earth.

I get comfortable enough to settle in for a long feast. My tongue finds her bulb, draws it to raise, swell, pulse. She moans. I want to cry. She calls out. I go dizzy. She bucks and bays, and my own warmth rises further.

I go on top of her and ride off the end of the Earth. As the stars hit my body, I collapse fully into her and hold tight.

The Goddess of Heat has the good grace to stand by for a few moments. I wait for the next bath, knowing She will soon melt us further with sweat.

Anything for Her
Erin Brennan

It was Saturday night—date night—and I had high hopes for what Rosie had promised would be a night of fun and pleasure. "*An Affair to Remember*, the home version," she had called it. Her intention was to start with a romantic dinner, but dinner is never romantic for us because Rosie—my charming, athletic, fair-haired, blue-eyed, darling Rosie—eats like a slob.

"Can you pass the butter?" she asked between gulps of food, which she chewed loudly. I did so and watched as Rosie mashed her lasagna, salad, and a crust of bread together before shoving the whole mess into her mouth with great gusto. Watching her devour dinner with such joy was a sad reminder of how much Rosie loves to eat everything. Everything, that is, except me.

She lost her appetite for me months ago. We've been together twelve years, and we used to have great sex, so when she tries to fake it, I can tell. She can't make her heart pretend to pound and race or feign the drops of sweat she used to get between her breasts. There are possible biological reasons for why she doesn't get as wet as she used to, but she's lost her creativity too, her unique way of using nasty words to make irresistible suggestions. And the last time we made love, I glanced up from between her gorgeous legs and caught her looking at her watch. It was not coincidence that she finished just in time for *Law and Order.* She still loves me—my company, my loyalty, my cooking—and she wants to want me. I wish that were enough. I used to think I'd do anything for her, but lately I've been thinking about leaving. If that is shallow, so be it. I won't live without sex. For Rosie's peace of mind, I have quit smoking, cut back on alcohol, and stopped going to church, but I won't live without sex.

That's why she planned this special evening for two. It began with dinner by candlelight (lasagna from Ellie's Deli, but all service by Rosie), soft music (including our song, "It Had to Be You"), and my favorite wine (whichever white zinfandel is on sale). We were getting close to the good part—she was serving the orange sherbet—when the doorbell rang.

I mouthed to Rosie, "We're *not* home."

But she ignored me, looking expectantly at the door. "Hey, who's that?" she said loudly.

It was Lavinia, our new neighbor, the young woman with the old name. Lavinia is very cute in a Tinkerbell kind of way—bright eyes, toothy grin, slender body, and very short blond hair worn in a spike. She's 25, we've been told, but she looks more like 12. Maybe it's the enthusiasm.

"I'm so glad you're home." She said it very directly to me. In fact, she hurried by Rosie and approached me in such a rush that I braced myself, expecting her to jump in my lap.

"Please come over to my place," she whimpered, squatting by my chair. "Just for a little while?"

"Maybe tomorrow," I replied, almost sorry to disappoint her.

"I just need you right now so much," she pressed, sticking

out her lower lip. "I'm in the middle of this woman, and she's very interesting, but I can't get the waist right."

Rosie and I knew what Lavinia meant. She loves to draw, and she likes to get free advice from me. I teach art for adults at Springfield Junior College. So Lavinia was in the middle of *drawing* a woman.

"Rosie and I are having dinner, and—"

"It wouldn't take you long," Rosie interrupted. She even started clearing the table, a task she never performs, which took away my immediate excuse. "I'm sure Lavinia understands you could stay only a few minutes."

"You know it will take more than minutes," I retorted, angry at her for letting me go so easily, tonight of all nights.

Lavinia jumped to her feet, holding my hand. "Thanks," she said to Rosie. "I promise I won't keep her."

"See that you don't," Rosie warned. She walked us to the door and kissed me. It was a surprisingly sensuous kiss—her hands on my butt, her tongue in my mouth—and made more so by the fact that while Rosie kissed me Lavinia held my hand. It was as though they were competing for me; Lavinia pulled me out the door before Rosie had let go. But they were far too friendly for competitors, and Rosie released me with a big smile for the one who took me away.

"Let's go," Lavinia said gleefully. She clung to my hand as we walked to her house, all the way just one happy step from skipping.

Lavinia definitely has drawing talent. She is very good at picking out the single characteristic that makes something look the way it looks overall. As a teacher I should know a better phrase for that. Instead, I know many. I once gave three consecutive lectures based on the idea that art is more about recognition by the recipient than expression by an artist. Many of my students recalled that week on their class evaluations, creating many new euphemisms for "cruel and unusual punishment."

Lavinia stood close behind as I studied her sketch of a nude Michelle Madison. I had recognized her immediately, Springfield's own state amateur tennis champion, now a detective with the Springfield Police Department and the tallest strongest sexiest dyke in town. That's who Lavinia had on canvas—the woman I'd fantasized about endlessly and would never admit to wanting because a woman my age should desire more than broad shoulders, a firm round butt, and a mouth that looks like it could suck you from across the room.

Lavinia reached around me and waved a hand over Michelle's midriff in the sketch. "This is where it's so wrong," she observed.

"True," I agreed. Lavinia's sketch had captured Michelle's naked aggression, but it was nearly ruined by some kind of apparatus hanging from her pubes that I'd first mistaken for an ill-defined sex appliance.

"Michelle is a detective," I pointed out, not pretending I didn't know the subject. "She doesn't wear a waist holster."

"Sometimes she does," whispered Lavinia lasciviously. "Just for fun." She kissed my neck. Or was it a nibble? I thought maybe she didn't mean to—an oral accident. "The sketch is perfect here," she said, putting her hands on my breasts. "And here." This time she *licked* my neck, and my mouth fell open. She has the tongue of a cat. The familiar rough yet moist surface pulled my skin ever so gently. Of course, Lavinia's tongue is much bigger than that of the average domestic cat, and with it she licked my neck and ear while her hands roamed my body. My knees were instantly weak, and I was trembling. She started unzipping my jeans.

"I can't do this," I gasped.

"You're not doing this." Her giggle dissolved into a low friendly groan. "*I'm* doing it."

Her tongue going down on my butt did me in. I might have been able to stop before, but not after the wet kiss/scratch of her feline tongue reaching for those too-often-ignored back door spots. And then she was all over me—a phrase I'd not been entitled to use these past many months.

There are legends about what one woman can do to another woman's cunt. Those of us who have never experienced it will wonder, on dark angry nights, what it is like to be fisted by a stranger. An Amazon Orchid, something that kept a friend of mine humming for days, is still a mystery to me. But, as of tonight, I am acquainted with the joys of being licked by a woman who has the tongue of a cat.

Imagine the lingering tug of it; the effects of one rough lick are not gone before the next one begins. And the feral energy—her tongue is on you, in her mouth and on you again in fractions of a second. She does not tire.

Bang. I came, mumbling the words "I can't, I can't."

Lavinia had been kneeling between my legs while I leaned on her desk. Now, at the speed of light, she stood, slipped out of her clothes, and led the way to her couch. She kissed and fondled my breasts for a long satisfying time.

"Your tits are as good as a large pizza." She laughed and glanced up at my face. "So big I know there's gonna be enough for me."

I felt sick. How could I be doing this with her? And why did she have to mention food at this moment?

Lavinia managed an adroit acrobatic move that landed

her face between my legs and mine between hers. I eagerly found her cunt with my fingers, mouth, and tongue. And this time I was able to hold out a few seconds longer. She came before I did; I felt the vibrations of her moaning between my labia.

Surprisingly, she did not stick her butt in the air and meow. She did, however, jump to her feet and reach for the ceiling, stretching muscles, head to toe, in her thin young body. "So!" she pronounced meaninglessly as she picked up my pants from the floor and tossed them in my direction. She stopped to study her sketch on the easel, apparently so I could study her. I could smell her too, and she was redolent with the conceit of someone who had just scored too easily.

"So," she said again, quieter this time. "You and Rosie were having quite a little dinner tonight."

"We'd just finished," I observed inanely.

"And now we've just finished." She winked at me.

Rosie likes Lavinia. They met the day Lavinia moved in a few months ago and have been neighborly chums ever since. I've never bothered to tell Rosie I don't like Lavinia, but I don't. Having had sex with her didn't change that.

"When did you sleep with Michelle Madison?" I asked, accidentally making it sound like an accusation.

"Why, babycakes, I never kiss and tell," Lavinia teased. "Anyway, what makes you so sure I slept with Michelle?"

"You implied you had."

"Did I?" She grinned broadly. "Well, there's no crime in implying."

"It doesn't matter." I hurriedly finished buttoning my blouse. "I was just thinking about your sketch."

Lavinia dropped to the floor and sat at my feet, watching

my fingers as I relaced my ankle boots. "I really do admire you and Rosie for staying together all these years," she said. Her arrogance had vanished. She gazed sweetly into my eyes. "How do you do it?" She was such an odd creature. What on earth made her think I'd discuss monogamy with her now?

"Maybe Rosie just can't live without my fried chicken," I answered, but sarcasm didn't phase Lavinia.

"What's in it for you?" she inquired.

"Well, as you'll someday know," I stood and patted her head without affection, "it's nice to have your chicken appreciated."

I went into the bathroom, washed my face, and dried off, then did it again, and then again.

"Take a shower if you want," Lavinia called in to me, but I didn't. I just wanted to go home.

At the door Lavinia kissed me good-bye, and my shame did not one bit diminish my fascination with her tongue. It is the roughest, most powerful tongue I've ever known. We kissed for several minutes.

"Rosie loves you," she whispered.

"And I love Rosie," I whispered back, licking her tongue one more time.

"She and I came up with this idea together." Lavinia backed away from me and rested both hands on the door-knob behind her. "We did it for both of you."

"What are you talking about?" Nausea swept over me.

"To solve your problem, this rut you two were in. Rosie said even the kinky stuff didn't help anymore."

"*Kinky* stuff?"

"You know. Undressing in the garage. Doing it on the kitchen table. Bobbing for each other in the Webster Park fountain."

"Shut up!" I snapped.

Lavinia giggled. "You're right, it's not really all that kinky. And don't be mad at Rosie for telling me. She was asking for a favor, so she wanted to explain." Lavinia rolled her head to one side like a little girl. "And I did help, didn't I?"

What was there to say? How does one chat with one's neighbor on the notion of how having sex with her was simply domestic therapy—one session of eating each other, prescribed to cure frustration at home. Lavinia nodded knowingly at my bewilderment.

"You'll see. It'll be all better when you get home," she promised, closing the door and leaving me on her front step.

I walked home slowly, past the Littles' house, past the Coes', and up our driveway. With every step I took, I believed more certainly that Lavinia had told the truth. On reflection, there had been conspiratorial signs from Rosie and Lavinia over the past couple of weeks and especially earlier this evening. I recalled lingering looks they'd given each other, even winks and raising of eyebrows. They were already talking in shorthand too, the way old friends can because they've had so many long conversations. And Rosie didn't just let me go home with Lavinia tonight; she facilitated it.

But it was that Webster Park incident that sealed it. The garage and kitchen table things might be commonplace, but the fountain was our own secret. We'd snuck into the park late one night, against the law, and the indecency of actually getting into the water under Mr. Webster's statue had been surprisingly exciting. We had proceeded to grope and suck each other underwater to the point of exhaustion. But that was months ago. Whenever I've suggested returning, Rosie has declined, saying it was the kind of spontaneous event that cannot be repeated and is best kept as our fondly remembered secret. Apparently, Lavinia can now remember it with us.

So I'd simply done what Rosie wanted, as always. But what had she been doing? Thinking about what Lavinia and I were up to? Changing her mind?

She was standing by the stereo, punching in a CD program. As I came through the door, she turned off the lamp. Candles burned all around us, and Bette Midler's voice came over the speakers singing "Do You Want to Dance?"— my favorite slow song.

"How was the sketch?" Rosie pulled me into her embrace, and we swayed to the music.

"Lavinia has talent," I began, but said no more because Rosie's mouth was on mine. She maneuvered her thigh between my legs, her tongue filled my mouth, and her hands were everywhere at once. The woman was, praise be, all over me.

I doubted her, of course. Did she truly want me again, or was it just because I smelled of Lavinia? I doubted her, but I didn't stop her. Again and again, Rosie came at me with a passion she'd never shown before. She was literally hot to the touch and tasted both salty and sweet. Over the next couple of hours of dancing, fondling, and dirty talk, we both came twice, which meant I set a personal record for one night.

Eventually, we settled in bed, and Rosie was soon asleep, but she stirred when I got up.

"My plan worked," she declared huskily.

I grunted an ambiguous reply.

She opened her eyes and looked directly at me, seemingly wide awake for a second. Then she smiled, blew me a kiss, and scooted farther under the sheet, curling into the fetal position. "Good night, you."

"Good night, Rosie."

There was half a bottle of wine left from dinner. I took my glass and the bottle to our kitchen table, where I could open the blinds and look out at the night. We'll never talk about it directly, but we have solved the problem. Rosie realized she wanted us to mix a little, and she let me have the fun part. Should I feel guilty? It was her idea. Is it cheating when I do it for her?

I do hope Rosie is prepared for what she has started, because last week Michelle Madison invited me to stop by her apartment for a drink sometime. "Just you," she emphasized, knowing how hard it would be for me to say no. She gave me her number, and I kept it. Now I can use it. I choose that substitution—Michelle for Lavinia—and I choose to believe it will not be cheating. In any event, it's too late to believe otherwise.

Working Out
by Bridget Bufford

Too bad it's still cold at night; I'd like to put the top down. The Mustang's five years older than me and of a vintage too common to be classic, but it's a red convertible, almost irresistible. Holly had succumbed on the third date. "Terry," she said, "let me drive." I parked and walked around to the passenger door. Holly took off a little fast, popped the clutch, and barked the tires. I slid to the middle of this great bench seat and got more intimate than a bucket seat would ever allow.

We met at my favorite club, Minerva's. Tuesday night, the place was moribund, and this tall strawberry-blond goddess strolled in. Long legs, long hair; I flew to her like Icarus, circled that golden radiance. We danced four dances, and the goddess barely broke a sweat. I run and lift weights, and I was winded. I asked if she worked out and got her card: *Holly O'Brien, Certified Aerobics Instructor, The Body Zone.* "Come by and see me sometime," she said. I took her free introductory class three times.

The Body Zone is the biggest gym in St. Louis, a converted textile warehouse. I pull into the parking lot, get a spot near the entrance. It's Saturday, an hour from closing. Everybody's already gotten their workout in; those hard-earned buns of steel are garnering admiration in other venues, perhaps embarking on a different type of exercise. Not me—my night is just beginning. I grab my gym bag and bound into the lobby.

The Zone is also the most expensive gym in St. Louis. I joined a year and a half ago, during a three-month trial offer over the summer. When that expired, I quit. I can't afford the regular monthly charges, much less the initiation fee. Holly's been helping me out: I just say I forgot my ID when the gym is busy, and Holly lets me pass through. Tonight Holly's behind the counter, but so is Dave, the beefcake trainer. He's grinning, practically drooling; he never takes his eyes off her.

I conceal my driver's license in my hand and run the card through the scanner, which just beeps. "Still not working?" Holly asks, all innocence. I hold out my license, and she palms it. "Maybe we should just make you a new ID, Terry." She turns to the keyboard, enters someone else's code.

Excellent. I'm in the system. Holly's been letting me in with the driver's license ruse for two months now. It's risky, though; if caught, she could lose her job. We'd talked about making me a fake ID, but neither of us could figure out a way to falsify the payment. Last night I hit on a plan: Holly could go through the attendance records of lifetime members and find one who hasn't been in for a few months. Then she'd make a new ID for that account, with my name and picture on the card. The time is paid for; no one is using it. Nobody loses.

I pose for my picture with a big victorious grin. "I'll have this ID for you by the time you're done with your workout," Holly says.

Dave says, "I'll do it. You're closing. I don't mind." This

is great: Holly doesn't even have to make the card herself.

Before I change into my workout clothes, I take a quick shower. I want to be relatively fresh when Holly gets off. She leads two aerobics classes four evenings a week, and lately she's been working the desk until closing. I work days, painting houses; if I didn't lift, I'd never see her. It's been nearly a week since we spent the night together.

Hot water flows over me, the evening's first caress. Holly and I took a shower together at her place last Sunday. I ended up on my knees in front of her. She pressed her shoulders against the tiled wall, arched her hips forward; by the time she was done, the water on my back had turned cool. I shiver, in memory and hopeful anticipation.

Someone's humming over by the sink, a sweet familiar song I can't place. When I emerge from the shower in my towel, though, I find only a flushed young woman, sweaty from her racquetball date, and generic jazz on the sound system.

I put on my shorts and tank top, go upstairs to the weight room. Two Herculean red-faced men are at the squat racks. They bellow and exhort each other through "One more, push it!" The inclined abdominal board is hooked on the third rung; I climb onto the pad, secure my feet under the strap. The behemoths are reflected in the mirror, rising and falling as I curl my trunk, raise my torso again and again 'til the muscles burn and sweat gathers behind my knees. I fall back, take a few slow breaths. By the time I'm through with my abdominals, the guys are gone. I'm the only person here.

The lat pulldown machine has the wrong attachment. Since I'm short I have to stand on the seat to undo the clasp and suspend the longer bar from the cable. I hop down, take a wide grip, and sit. From arm's length I draw the bar slowly down, working the broad muscles of my back. I've always liked this exercise, the deep stretch as the weight pulls my arms overhead. Between sets, I find Holly's reflection in the mirror before me. She's still at the desk, flipping through an aerobics schedule, bored; I'll take care of that soon enough.

Bar dips next: I hoist myself onto the parallel bars of the rack, my body suspended between extended arms. I lower myself, controlled, then exhale and press up. Most women can't do dips. I crank them out like pushups, keeping time with the canned music. Panting, I jump down, wiping my sweaty forehead with the back of my hand.

Holly's reflection again, this time close. "Hey, girlfriend," I say and turn the wrong direction, disoriented by the mirrors. "You here by yourself?"

"Yeah," she says. "I'm closing, but I'm almost done. Hey, did you see those guys doing squats?"

"Couldn't miss 'em."

She tells me that they're linebackers; they play for the St. Louis Rams. Holly loves football; she was a cheerleader in high school.

"Looks like it's been busy," I say. "The windows are completely steamed up."

"It was a total zoo all afternoon. Everyone came in at once." She snags a leather jump rope from the floor and hangs it from the proper hook.

"You want to go out?" I ask.

"I don't think so; let's just go to my place and chill."

"Fine with me." I'll show her a better time that way. "Hey, can you spot me on the bench?"

"As soon as I'm done."

I grab a pair of dumbbells from the rack and face the mirror, curl the weights to my chest and lower them slowly, my elbows tucked to my sides. My biceps bulge, then lengthen. The sound system goes off; the sudden silence is eerie. My breath becomes loud. I can hear the switches snap as Holly turns off the overhead lights by the cardiovascular platform. I set the weights down like they're made of crystal.

That tune is in my head still, the one from the locker room. I do another set of curls to the slow meter, try to put words to it. *Amazing Grace, how sweet the sound/ That saved a wretch like me....* That's it. Haven't heard it in years; I don't know if I could remember all the words. The melody permeates my brain; I'm in for an evening of it.

My workout is done, except for bench presses. An Olympic bar sits on the two uprights that form the rack of the weight bench. The bar alone weighs forty-five pounds. I thread a ten- and a five-pound plate onto each end of the barbell, then sit and wait for Holly, feet up on the bench and my arms across my knees. A glance in the mirror confirms that the position displays my deltoids admirably.

Holly surveys the room. I picked up weights as I went, so it's already straightened. She shuts off the lights at the near end. "You don't mind, do you?"

"No, I can see." I point to the emergency lights by the exit.

"All right, let's get these done." She takes her place at the head of the bench. I lie down, whip out a quick set of ten. Holly scoffs. "Intensity, girl! You're working too light."

"I'm saving my energy for later."

She laughs. "How much can you bench?"

"More than this. Put twenty on either side." I hook my wrists behind the uprights and let gravity stretch my pecs. My legs fall to the sides, a provocative arrangement. I've always had a fantasy of making it on a weight bench. Sprawling on the narrow support, legs spread, the grunt and thrust and sweat; it gets me hot.

Holly slides forty pounds of plates onto the bar, then steps close. The hem of her gym shorts just touches the top of my head. I wrap my fingers around the knurling, a little in from my normal grip. Tighten the muscles behind my shoulder blades, take a big breath, and lower the bar to just above my nipples. Thrust it up with a grunt.

Holly helps position it on the rack. "Damn, Terry! That's more than I weigh. That's way over what you weigh."

"I weigh more than you'd think, for being short. We're probably about the same."

"Little as you are?" She looks dubious, but I'm not going to get into an argument over weight.

"Put on thirty more; I'll try again." That will be 175, more than I've ever done. Can't hurt to try it with a spotter.

Holly puts on two ten-pound plates. "Try this first. You want a lift-off?"

"Please."

She steps up to the bench. My attention is diverted—what I'd taken for a leotard is just a Spandex top tucked into shorts so loose I can almost see they cover nothing but flesh. I wasn't the only one thinking ahead. Holly grips the bar and tenses. "Ready?"

"Not yet."

She nods, eyes on the bar. My hand on her thigh startles her. Holly's definitely not wearing panties; curls brush against my knuckles. "Shit, Terry, what are you doing?" Her voice is edged with panic, low, but she doesn't move away.

"There's no one here." I cup my palm over that provocative little juncture where all the seams of her shorts converge, press gently upward.

"We're right in front of the window." Now she's whispering.

"No, we're not. Besides, it's steamed up. Nobody can see in." My thumb strokes the seam, persuading. "We can both get a workout."

Holly leans on the bar, takes a wide stance that brings her tantalizingly near. I slide my hand to her hip, draw her closer. Propped on my elbow, I can barely bring my face to her. I breathe against her shorts, then draw the cloth away and kiss the soft inner thigh. I reach for her breasts. Spandex restrains her nipples; a light persistent circling of fingernails brings them forth.

Half-reclining is a strain right after a workout. I hate to stop, but a tremor of fatigue wracks my left shoulder. I fall back onto the bench. "Come around to this side. I can't reach you there."

Holly looks to the window again. "You're crazy. I'm going to lose my job."

I knew she'd be like this. "Holly, we can't stop now. If I'm crazy, it's because of you." Holly gives me an "Oh, please" look, but I'm not giving up. She's stalling, twirling a lock of red-gold hair around her finger. "Just sit here in front of me a minute. At least give me a kiss." I sit up and lean back against the cold barbell.

Holly straddles the foot of the bench, places her hands on my shoulders. Is she going to reason with me, kiss me, or just hold me at arm's length 'til my passion falters? A drastic response may dispel her doubts. I stand, step close. Holly's hands fall to my waist. I entwine my fingers in her hair, dig my nails into her scalp until she shivers. Holly sits down, and I nip her neck, tarry at the soft spot behind her ear. Tip her head back, kiss her until her lips soften and her hands knead my hips and neither of us can breathe. Ardor prevails.

She lifts my shirt. Warm lips caress my nipples; her soft

touch brings a sweet ache to my groin. I take her hands. "Stand up."

She does, and I kiss her once again, slide down to the bench beneath her. Caress her thighs, urge her closer. Holly grips the barbell; I hope it is secure.

Her musky scent compels me. I slide two fingers inside her, curl them slightly, nuzzle the front of her shorts with my lips. "Wait," she says. She steps over me, takes off her top, her shorts, and sneakers. Gloriously nude, she straddles the bench again, shifts her stance to meet my eager tongue.

Her labia glisten, rich and swelling. I part the lips, point my tongue, find her clit. Her knuckles are white; she's gripping the uprights, her triceps taut. I relax my neck, the muscles of my jaw. My rhythm is established now; I realize that song is still in my head. *I once was lost, but now I'm found....* It almost makes me laugh, but that would be a crime right now. No point in fighting it; the tempo is right.

Sweat from Holly's thighs wets my shirt. Her breasts obscure a full view of her face, but I can tell she's looking up. Watching herself in the mirrors, I think. Ex-cheerleader, aerobics instructor—what else would she be doing? Back in high school, the cheerleaders sometimes practiced at the same time as the girls soccer team. I would look at them and dream of this very thing, even before I knew the finest feeling in the world is having some red-headed woman about to climax against my upper lip.

I can't stand it. I reach beneath my shorts, match the stroke of my finger to that of my tongue. *How sweet the sound...* Holly's breathing hoarsely. Each caress elicits a jerk of her hips. I try to lighten my touch, diminish the pace, but that crazy song compels me. *The hour I first believed...*

The weights rattle on the barbell; Holly shakes from her

foundations. Her hips grind into my face. A spasm rips through me, but when her left knee buckles, my hand gets pulled away, and I have to grab Holly to save myself. We tumble to the floor, me on top. She clutches my shoulders and bursts out laughing, tears rolling down her face. "Holly?" Now I'm whispering. "Are you OK?"

She wipes her eyes and laughs again. "You sucked the sense right out of me," she says. She's limp now, sprawled, arms outstretched. I curl against her side, stroke her beautiful bare torso, soothe her 'til her swollen eyelids flutter open. She smiles at me and starts to speak, then shoves me away. I hear it too—the elevator's moving. It stops at the lobby. In the mirror I can see the doors slide apart. A faint sweet song emerges, the same voice I heard in the locker room. "When we've been gone ten thousand years/ Bright shining as the sun...."

Holly leaps to her feet, then crouches. I grab her tangled clothes, throw them at her, untie the laces of her sneakers so they're ready to slip on. A middle-aged woman is pushing her cart of cleaning supplies into the lobby. By the time the woman shakes out a new trash bag, Holly is disheveled but dressed. Her eyes are huge, and her weird smile is just this side of a grimace.

"Lie down," she whispers.

"*What?*"

She shoves me onto the bench, repositions herself as spotter. "Ready?" she says loudly.

I start to laugh. Her glare pins me to the bench. I grab the bar, but there's no way. I wasn't sure I could lift this much the first time. "Holly, for crying out loud, I just got off."

She starts a lift-off. I tighten up in self-defense and manage to lower the bar to my chest without killing myself.

Limp with laughter, I can't budge it. I can barely breathe. Holly's ineffectual jerking bounces the 165-pound bar on my sternum, squashing me.

The cleaning woman runs past Holly, yells, "Grab onto the end of it!" Together they raise the bar to the uprights. I sit up, rub my chest, and erupt in another surge of giggles.

"You're lucky, miss," the woman says. "I came in a little early tonight."

"We were just going," Holly babbles. "I didn't think…I was closing tonight, but we were just…thanks so much."

"Yes, ma'am," she says. "You're welcome." She squats and reaches beneath the bench, retrieves my new ID and Holly's car keys. Looks at the picture, then holds the card and keys out to me. "Here you go."

Holly grabs them before I can react. "We appreciate that, Irene." The woman's name is on her badge. "We've always been happy with your company. Thanks again. I'll write a note to your supervisor, tell her what a help you were." I've got to get her out of here; she's trying to stuff everything into the pocket of her shorts, but they're on backwards.

"You were lucky," Irene repeats. "God was looking out for you tonight."

Saved a wretch like me. I need to get my giddy self out of here, too; the giggles overtake me once again. "Good night, Irene," I say, then wish I hadn't. Holly's hand tightens on my shoulder, and we head to the nearest door.

The Sick Girl
by Teresa Cooper

Before that day, I had never actually seen her walk. She was always sitting on the same bench in the park, paying no mind to the people walking by with their bags, dogs, and carts. I smiled at her a few times, but she never smiled back. Sometimes I'd stand behind one of the wide tree trunks and watch her while my dog was taking a dump. Her hair was short, dyed red, thin, and straight. But her hair was the only thing about her that looked straight. She was beautiful. And I was dying for some recognition out of all that aloofness.

The first day I saw her walking, I was on my way to an interview, my portfolio tucked into my armpit. I had sucked up to the bitchiest queens to get my foot in the door for this one. It was between me and this other illustrator, whose work I knew from around town. He did more ads, whereas I stuck to magazines, but his drawings were all angles; you could tell he read too many Japanese comics and ripped them off in all his work. So I thought my style was better-suited for this safe-sex campaign, and I'd actually be in the running to see my work plastered all over the subways of New York, Boston, and D.C. It would be a huge break for me to get away from publishing and into ads, but this guy had the experience.

I had actually dressed up in slacks and a silk shirt (from

my girlfriend Alison's business-girl wardrobe), walked the dog, and then left to catch the cross-town bus on 14th Street. As I was heading up Avenue A, I saw the girl from the bench walking toward me. She limped, dragging a cane off to her right. It didn't seem to be helping her walk; it was more like a slurred afterthought to stumbling. I'd never focused on anything but her face before; her limp surprised me, made me want to follow her. I stopped to inspect a few waxy green apples while she passed. Then I trailed her for five blocks in the opposite direction from my interview. I had ten minutes to spare.

She walked faster than I'd expect someone with such a limp to walk. Her left leg seemed to be the source of the limp. With every step it kicked out slightly ahead before settling onto the sidewalk; there was only a hint of uncontrollable impulse there, but enough so the left foot rarely landed where you'd expect it.

She approached the shattered glass door of an apartment building above a bodega. She rang the second buzzer from the bottom and waited, looking up at the building, or maybe the sky. I couldn't tell because her wire-rimmed mirrored sunglasses were in the way. She swiveled around on the good foot, replacing the cane in front of her, resting both palms on the handle.

I kept walking slowly toward the curb; I was afraid she'd notice if I just stood there. But it didn't look like she was noticing anything. Then she lunged at the buzzer and pressed it again, this time pecking at it three or four times. When no one answered she backed away from the door, bumping into a woman walking by. She didn't excuse herself. In fact, I don't think she even knew she'd run into anybody. But then I think she noticed me staring at her. It felt like she could see right into me, that my hand was revealed, and she'd have the upper one. But in reality she was looking right through me, seeing nothing.

She immediately turned and headed up the block, continuing that fast pace, and turning back once to see if I was still in tow. I saw a break in traffic and headed across the street, keeping an eye on her while walking up the other side of the street.

I remembered my interview, which distracted me long enough to gaze up the street toward 14th. I couldn't keep my eyes off of her, though. Walking with my head turned in her direction, I smacked into a messenger's Spandexed ass. Before I could apologize he hissed "Fucking dyke" and slung his bag over his shoulder. And I thought I looked all nice and femmed-up for my interview. But I couldn't be bothered to swear back.

After I eschewed what would've been, on any other day, a serious tangle with the messenger, I looked across the street thinking I'd lost her. But she was a couple of buildings behind, resting her elbows on a bent parking meter. She just stood there, leaning against the meter, head hanging down. I assumed she was crying, because a few people turned their heads to stare as they passed her. I looked at my watch: twenty-five minutes until the interview, maybe a twenty-minute bus ride at that hour. I stayed across the street a while longer, ducking my head back and forth as cars passed and parked, so I could see her. If she fell, I'd run and get her. But she didn't.

I started stressing out about getting there. I started up the block but then stopped again, whispering "Fuck" to myself, loud enough for the hairy guy walking next to me to hear. I crossed against the light and went up to her. She was crying. Her baggy jeans seemed to wrinkle under the weight of each sob.

"Hey," I started, almost touching her shoulder with my hand. I was afraid to put it there, thinking it wasn't my place, even though I felt like I knew her. "You seem pretty upset. I just wanted to see if you were OK. Can I—"

"I'm fine, thanks, I'm fine," she said, inhaling quickly through her nose and wiping the tears with her thumb knuckle.

"Are you gonna be OK?" I asked, touching her shoulder, encouraged by her response. She didn't recoil but still wouldn't look at me. "Do you want to sit down for a second or something?"

"No." She turned to head up the block, toward the park where I'd always seen her sitting. I stood there, switching my beat-up leather portfolio from my left arm to my right. The zipper caught the skin of my palm and tore it as she limped away. I sucked on my palm and recognized the taste of blood. After a few seconds I headed up the block as well, because the bus was in that direction anyway.

But when she got to 7th, I noticed she headed into the park, toward her bench. I looked at my watch again; the interview was in fifteen minutes. Maybe I could take a cab. I followed her into the park, past the dirty guys sitting around the chess tables without playing pieces. If I were dressed in my usual dingy dog-walking attire, they would've nodded at me, but I cruised by them unrecognized and approached her.

She slowed down and turned around. "Why are you following me?"

"I don't know. I guess I just wanted to see—want to sit down on your bench for a while?" I pointed toward it.

"What do you mean, *my* bench?"

"Well, I've, uh, seen you there so many times. I usually walk a brown and white dog. I thought you might've seen me a couple of times."

"I don't remember," she said.

I sat on the bench next to her regular one, and after thinking about it she followed, landing hard and bouncing against the wooden slats next to me.

"Are you a dyke?" she asked after a few seconds.

"Well, yes I am," I answered, laughing, although she remained serious. She was probably thrown off by my corporate clothes. "Are you?"

"Yeah." She pulled her leg away from mine, dragging it awkwardly over her right. Her version of crossing her legs. I felt the hairs on the nape of my neck rise. Her skin was so, I don't know, *barely there* that I kept watching it as she moved her arms and head. It looked soft, made my stomach twitch.

We sat in silence for what seemed like minutes. She reached to take her sunglasses off, but she missed, grasping instead at her ear. I felt like I had to say something.

"Well, I guess—I guess I've just wanted to talk to you for a while now, and today seemed like a good time since it seemed like you might need to talk to someone."

She didn't say anything.

"You know, because you were crying—I wanted to see if I could help or something."

"Why?"

"Because I feel, I don't know why, because I kind of feel *bad*—" She turned her head to look over her shoulder, seemingly interested in anything but what was in front of her. In the blinking shadows of the leaves above us, her skin looked transparent. I could make out blue veins cradling her jaw on both sides. I had to say something to salvage that last remark. "I don't know, not bad for you or anything, just like empathy of sorts, you know what I mean?"

"Sort of." She was giving me a little. I could tell there was something in her that wanted to—like she hadn't in a while. She turned back to look at me. Her green eyes were as translucent as her skin. "What's 'empathy of sorts' supposed to mean?" She wasn't going to give much.

"I'm Justin," I said, reaching my hand out to shake hers. She grasped it loosely. "What's your name?"

"Zeke," she answered, rearranging her weight from her left side to her right, which put her a little closer to me. "Justin...that's a guy's name."

"It was Justine. I axed the 'e,'" I said, relieved she actually acknowledged something beyond my pity. Her voice resonated, low and hollow; I wanted to hear it again. "Yours is too."

"What?"

"A guy's name."

"Oh, yeah."

"So, what's going on?" I asked, after another excruciating silence.

"What do you mean?"

"I mean what's upsetting you, who was in that building, what's—"

"You mean what am I sick with?"

"I guess that too."

"I have MS."

"I'm sorry, I—"

"Don't," she interrupted me.

"My cousin's had it for eight years, so I sort of know what it's like," I offered after a few seconds.

69

"How is she?"

"Honestly?"

"No, lie."

"She's in a wheelchair," I said, looking away from Zeke.

"Then I guess I don't need to hear anymore." She swung her legs as best she could, but they didn't move fluidly.

"That's fair. What do you want to hear about then?" I asked, slipping comfortably into flirt mode.

"Almost anything else."

"How about that I've been watching you for the last few months now, but I was always afraid to talk to you."

"I guess I'd listen to that," she said, barely smiling and leaning back against the bench.

❧   ❧   ❧

Needless to say I completely bricked the interview. I stayed there talking to Zeke for another hour, my arm brushing against hers a few times. Her skin was cold, but every time we touched I'd forget what I was saying and feel the sweat dripping from my armpits into Alison's blouse. Zeke asked me so much about myself, it seemed like she forgot what she was sad about. Nobody I'd met in a long time actually listened to my answers to their questions. But she seemed genuinely interested. I kept wondering when she'd tell me she had to go. Every time there was a pause in our conversation, I'd ask her something about herself to keep it going.

"What kind of music did you guys play?" I tried, referring to her brief mention of the band she used to be in. She quit shortly after the diagnosis.

"Mostly punk-funk, kind of thrashy," she said. For the first time since the street, her voice cracked with what might've been crying.

"I think I might've heard you once," I lied, wanting to make her feel substantial. "Do you have a tape?"

"No, I don't have anything," she said quickly. "My ex— she's the one who lives in that building on A—she has all the tapes and posters and reviews and stuff."

"Oh, I'm sorry. Did you just break up?" Was I feeling a twinge of jealousy? I had no right, but I was.

"She started sleeping with someone else after I found out I was sick. Then we broke up, and I moved out. Haven't talked to her since."

"Who's helping you out?"

"What do you mean?"

"You know, like at home. Are you fine with everything; are your folks around, helping out or anything?"

"I haven't talked to them since I told them I was a dyke," she said. "Like eight years ago."

I swung my legs. Then she added, "No, seven," like it made a difference.

A fight broke out in the dog run. By instinct I craned my neck to see if I knew anyone involved. I didn't have anything else to say to Zeke. I would've kissed her if I thought she'd let me. I was thinking about what it would be like, how my darker flushed skin would look against hers.

"I have to go," she said suddenly, as though she knew what I was thinking about.

"Why? I mean, can I take you where you're going or something?"

"No, you look busy."

"No, I'm not at all, I was just heading home, I—"

"I really have to go," she said. "But it's been nice, really."

"Can I get your number?"

"You don't quit, do you?"

I smiled. "Can I?"

"I can't do this. It's not like that...." she trailed off.

"What? It's not like what? Because you're sick?"

"Yeah, because I'm sick, OK?"

"I'm sorry, I just really want to—"

"I know, me too," she said, looking at the ground. "And normally I would, but—" It seemed like she wanted to stay with me, but something in her was sending out defensive forces by the truckload. She knew I was in an open relationship; she was cool with that. Or so I thought. I tried to mention MS as little as possible. But maybe even once was too much. She climbed up her cane to a standing position. I sat there quickly sifting through what she'd said; I thought there was some interest there.

"Will you take my number then?" I asked, a little too desperately. She shook her head no, but I pushed it, acting like I was just talking out loud to myself. "Last name's Wax. I live on 3rd Street. I'm listed." I said it again—and again. She actually laughed.

"I'm sorry," she started after a couple of seconds of smiling at me, definitely thinking I could be cute (I fancied). "But you need to know this is nothing. Really." She squeezed her right hand with her left on the handle of the cane. Her knuckles looked like they were about to push through the paper-thin skin. I wondered if she was left-handed.

"What do you mean?" I asked.

"I mean this, you, all this. It's not what you think."

"How do you know what I think?" It was the first time I challenged anything she had said. "I'm sorry, I just—"

"Why are you sorry?" she asked. She looked like she'd been missing something for a while but just noticed it was lost.

"I know you have to go," I said, and reached to hug her. She jerked slightly, and we negotiated clumsily which side to put our heads. When we touched, my lips brushed up against her neck. She smelled mostly clean, but there was something else too, like bleach.

ã   ã   ã

I lost the chance even to show my safe-sex drawings to the ad company. That queen wouldn't even let me messenger them over that afternoon. But I got reassigned a job at *Family Circle* that the week before I had declined to get ready for safe sex. The pouty art director faxed over the article. It was about kids who like strangers too much. I came up with an idea: a kid in a shopping basket, reaching out to an old lady squeezing peaches while the kid's mom is down the aisle getting apples. In a couple of hours there were roughs scattered everywhere beneath my desk. The dog stepped on them, pissing me off as usual, even though they were just roughs.

It took me two more days to pick the best drawing and scan it. I was entranced by the high-pitched whine of the scan. It had been three days since I met Zeke, and I'd gotten one drawing done since. She was all I thought about. And there was something just off about the drawings I eventually turned in, a day late: One of the old lady's legs was shorter than the other, the kid's diaper was too yellow, the perspective of the grocery aisle skewed.

Abandoning revising the drawings yet another time, I walked the dog in hopes of running into Zeke. But she wasn't anywhere I had spotted her before. The street was clean from rain, smelling like gasoline and gravel. The dirty chess guys in the park nodded at me as I made my way to Zeke's bench. I looked all around, gave up finding her, and sat down. I tried to remember the things I said to her. I shouldn't have pressed her about her phone number. I should've told her flat-out I was attracted to her. She knew. Maybe I shouldn't have told her about Alison. But she didn't seem to mind. I didn't know what I should've done.

I knew I'd said some things right but fucked up others. I wanted to take back the sloppy comments, replace them with new smooth ones, giving her a reason to try letting someone in again. Or at least me. What did she like hearing? What had I said to make it like we were just two girls flirting—not a sick one and me trying not to fuck up. The more I worried, the more I wanted to get in bed with her, like then she'd see it would be OK. Thinking of her skin made me feel that if I jumped awake from sleep, she'd be there next to me, all worried why.

When I got home from the last long dog walk without a Zeke sighting, Alison was just getting back from work. I asked her if she wanted to have dinner at home, but she said she had another meeting and could we do it tomorrow. On the way to the closet to change clothes, Alison brushed my cheek with the back of her hand. She stopped at my desk.

"These are great," she said, shuffling through my drawings.

"Oh, those—those didn't turn out so good."

"No, I like them. What's the story? Taking kids on errands?"

"No. Kids who go to strangers too easily," I said, sitting

on the couch, thinking about sex. "They didn't like it, though." I always wanted to have sex with Al when she was going somewhere, when her mind was focused on the next thing in her life—about the only time she couldn't be persuaded to get into bed with me.

"Well, I think it's good. I like the wrinkles on the old lady's neck. Nice," she said, finally freeing the back of her earring. She disappeared into the bedroom, yelling from the closet, muffled, "What are you going to do for dinner?"

"I don't know. I'll find something."

She came back out. "Want me to pick you up something on the way home?"

"No." I clicked on the TV. Local news—a five-alarm fire. "I think your tax refund came today. It's on the counter."

"Thanks," she said, dressed down in jeans and a T-shirt. She kissed my cheek, and I pulled away, hoping to pull it off as a joke, but I also really didn't want her touching me right then. "You're such a baby," she said. And then I kissed her on the lips.

The dog spun in his ceremonial *I'm being left* circles when Alison closed the door behind her—as did my head. If she didn't come home every day, I wouldn't know what to gauge life by.

In the morning I rolled over and ran my palms over Alison's thighs. She was surprised but jumped right in, following my lead. We did things we hadn't done in years. Al knew something was up.

"Who is she?" she asked, post orgasm.

"Who?" I said, rolling a pillow under my armpit.

"Who are you screwing? I can tell."

"It's nobody, Al."

She peeled the sheet from between her thighs and sat on

the edge of the bed with her spine to me. I closed my eyes. She got up, and the next thing I heard was a groan from the shower pipes. I did feel Zeke there; I'd been wondering about how I'd make her come. Alison wasn't stupid.

Al had never asked me who I was seeing, and I didn't ask her—a tacit understanding. But this time something was different. Maybe my hands were more insistent, my desire to control her surpassing my desire to be controlled. I wondered how to call Zeke. Just once, to tell her what I'd been thinking.

Alison came back into the bedroom fully dressed, with her satchel strapped across her chest. She leaned down and kissed my head. "I fed the dog," she said.

"Al, it's no one."

But then "no one" called in the middle of the next day, when I was drawing some preliminary sketches for a *Seventeen* article about best friends who can't be trusted with your deepest secrets. I started with a girl on the phone to her friend who was listening and covering up the receiver to tell someone else in the room what she was hearing. I was just about to fax it to the assistant art director when the phone rang. I thought it would be a long distance company asking to speak to whoever is responsible for the phone bill—like whoever that person is would be home in the middle of the day. But it was a familiar voice, pleasant.

"Hi, Justin; it's Zeke."

"Oh, yeah, hi!" Too exuberant. "How are you doing?" I switched to the cordless phone and sat on the couch. My stomach felt knotted all over again.

"Fine, thanks. I just called to say—I hope it's not a bad time—are you busy drawing?"

"No, no, I'm glad you called. I didn't think you would," I said, thinking of a way to show how happy I was that she looked up my number. "I've been thinking about you."

"Really? Why? I mean, what's to think about?" She laughed and then waited for me to have nothing to say. "Well, anyway, do you want to get a cup of coffee this afternoon?"

"I'd love to. I'll meet you at Cups at three—is that OK?"

As I sat in the coffee shop with Zeke, my legs shook, and it wasn't from the coffee. She brushed up against me a few times as we talked about silly things—nervous small talk from my perspective. But it seemed as though she really enjoyed being with someone, interacting. She occasionally put her hand on my leg to emphasize a point, but when she touched me inadvertently while shakily reaching for her tea with both hands, my skin tingled. I thought to myself repeatedly, *What the fuck am I doing here?* But I wanted to stay next to her so badly I couldn't sit still.

I saw her look down at my legs a couple of times. Once I caught her eyes, and I think I saw her smile.

"What?" I asked.

"Nothing."

"What are you looking at?"

"Your legs are shaking."

"I know."

"Why?"

"I don't know. I just can't—I don't know."

"What do you mean?"

"This. You. Whatever." I shook my head and reached for my coffee. She put her hand on my forearm—bare skin. I saw her notice the little bit of hair that stood up from her touch.

"Would you be so hot for me if I weren't sick?"

"What? I don't know."

"Why not? Why don't you know?" She took her hand away. "What made you think you could follow me in the first place?"

"I thought you were beautiful."

"There are tons of beautiful women on Avenue A."

I switched my legs back and forth over each other to stop the shaking. She followed my movements, taking stock of the positions that made me most uncomfortable.

"I mean, did you think I would *need* you or something?"

"I guess you could call it profound sadness...I couldn't leave you alone without talking to you."

"Profound sadness. I see," she shook her head like in the cartoons, but slower. "What the fuck is *profound sadness*?"

I didn't say anything.

"I was just wondering, because it's the same reason someone else left me—"

"What do you mean, being sick?"

"Yeah, being sick. I mean, it's why she left me, why you won't leave me alone." Her deep voice was climbing octaves. "I guess you could say I'm a little confused, that's all."

≈ ≈ ≈

I didn't talk to Zeke for three more days. I called to apologize.

"For what?"

"I don't know, you seemed upset after coffee."

"I'm not upset," she offered coolly. "Do I seem upset?"

"I don't know you; how would I know if you're upset?"

"What's that supposed to mean?"

"I don't know."

"Do you know *anything*?" She waited for a moment, catching her breath. "This is ridiculous," she laughed, drawing each syllable out. "I have to go."

She hung up. I looked around my desk, adding up the hours I'd need to get caught up with all of my fucking magazine assignments: a husband turned off by his wife's pregnant body, handling your wretched drill-sergeant boss, five easy steps to healthy hands. It would have to wait another day; I decided to call Zeke back.

When she answered I just said, "Can I come over?"

As I was pulling Alison's old college sweatshirt over my head, Alison opened the apartment door, bumping into me. "Oh, I didn't know you were standing there. You leaving?"

"I gotta go somewhere," I said, not looking up at her. "I have to see someone who's sick." I patted furiously at my pockets for the keys.

"Here, take mine," she offered, holding out her key chain. "Unless you haven't walked the dog; then I'll need them."

"No, he went out about an hour ago."

"So take them," she offered, but I just stood there. "The flu?"

"What?" I asked, looking up at her and taking the dangling keys.

"Your friend—you said she's sick."

79

"Oh, not like that. She's...got MS or something."

Alison looked at me for a few seconds. "*This* is the one you're screwing?" she asked, putting her fingertips to her forehead, like I'm sure she does to exaggerate dissatisfaction in the board room.

"I'm not *screwing* her; I just—"

"What the fuck are you doing, Justin?" Alison's hand dropped to her side for emphasis. "What're you doing with this girl? Is she *sick* with it?"

"I have to go," I said, pushing past Alison. "I just have to go," I said again, softly, and closed the apartment door behind me.

ﾞ▲   ﾞ▲   ﾞ▲

I could tell Zeke was staring at me for a few seconds through the peephole before unbolting the various locks. I shifted my weight from left to right, then back again, put my hands on my waist. I pictured her there, on the other side of the steel door, self-consciously breathing, standing as still as her body would allow.

Zeke let me in. She looked embarrassed. So I kissed her neck, slowly leaning around the corner of her face and inhaling the sterile scent. She turned her head slightly, giving me a broader view of the transparent skin of her neck that poorly concealed her veins. I kissed her a few more times gently in the same place on her neck. I thought I heard her whine, but it might have been my exhaling.

She started limping toward the bedroom. But without her cane, her muscles jerked even more than they did on the street that first day I saw her walking. She sat on her bed, trying to look calm, but she had a self-consciousness I couldn't interpret. So I ignored it, deciding to show her how much I wanted her. I sat next to her. Her chest heaved; she was breathing irregularly.

She wore a white ribbed men's tank top, smeared across her right breast with something greasy and brown. Her shoulders rolled out of the tank top and hunched over to catch her weight as she lay on her side. She looked up at me, surprised and scared.

I took off my shirt and lay next to her, as close as possible without putting any weight on her.

"You won't break me," she whispered.

I took off her shirt, and she fell over as soon as she had to support her own weight. She laughed nervously. I put my finger to her lips. They parted as I reached my other hand around her waist and pulled her toward me. Her torso didn't come with the rest of her; it was like I had to move her in two parts.

As I tucked the tips of my fingers into the waist of her jeans, I felt her stomach contract against the back of my hand. An extra layer of something crackled between her skin and jeans. I realized she was wearing some type of diaper, but as I thought about it I couldn't remember the term for adult diapers. I knew there was one.

Zeke tried to maneuver her hips away from me, to direct my attention elsewhere. Her weight fell awkwardly. I kissed her on the lips for the first time. Her chest heaved again, and a tear fell into the web of my hand.

"Why are you crying?" I asked. "You're beautiful." She didn't stop.

She surprised me by pulling my face toward her with both hands clasped onto the hair behind my ears. She kissed me sloppily, making her way down my neck, my chest, and then rested her cheek there. It was wet. I rubbed my hands over her back, which bulged in places other girls' didn't, where Alison's didn't. Where mine didn't. I heard the crinkling of plastic when she slowly moved down to kiss my stomach.

I looked up at the ceiling, cracked from the center of the room almost to the window. I followed the light outside, and my pupils ached at the brightness. When I looked back down, Zeke had already made a decision to trust me with something. She pulled at my belt with both hands, her elbows poking into the mattress on either side of my hips. Her arms looked thin and pale, bleached even. She stopped her fumbling around my waist and looked at me.

I looked back up at the ceiling. She saw. We lay there for forty-eight more minutes. I timed it by the green digital clock by the bed.

A Butch, a Femme, and a T-Bird
by Bree Coven

How's this for role play, baby? It's just like I'm 16 and I'm sneaking out of my father's house to meet my mysterious older lover, only it's not so farfetched, because even though I'm almost 24, I am about to sneak out of my father's quiet and well-alarmed house to meet you—just a bit older and terribly handsome, if not so mysterious. I've promised to show you the '57 convertible T-Bird my father is selling so that you know it's real and not just another grand plan to seduce you (like you need seducing), and you won't let me near your sweet mouth to kiss you until I've delivered— until I have furtively set free the garage door with stolen keys and led you to the car, fumbling in the dark, my bare arm bumping against the crotch of your Levi's as I pretend to search for the flashlight. But first, before I can show you what you have come all this way to see (and maybe, I'm hoping, just a little more), before I can reveal this fantastic car I am praying is still tucked safely into the garage, before that, I have to crawl out my bedroom window in the high heels I always insist upon wearing, however impractical the circumstances, whenever you come to visit. I feel your arms on the other side of the window, waiting in the warm night air. It's hard to maneuver this in a lady-like fashion, and my dress gets caught on the window partition, pulling it up over

83

my thighs. I laugh as you free the material with your teeth, since your arms are full with me, and then you push your mouth over mine to hush me, throwing your head back and administering a very stern Daddy-look to remind me that my parents' room is just a few feet away. I don't stop to remind you that you've already broken your "No kisses for you, girl, 'til you show me this car" rule. I just smile as though I haven't planned this whole thing all along.

It's absurd, sneaking out like this. I could have just informed my parents in a very adult tone that I would be going out late, but they'd inquire where. "To your shed to fuck in an open T-bird by the light of the moon" is not, I fear, an acceptable answer, even if you and I think it's a great idea. Besides, it's more fun this way; it heightens the, mmm, tension. It's a challenge—I am a prize to be won, the sneaking is a puzzle to be solved, and you, my darling, are a prince to be charmed. They always say the way to a butch's heart is a car, and I wonder briefly if you've really come for the car or for me, then brush off those worries like an evening mosquito because I'm damned near delirious with happiness just to have you here, and I can't see why you shouldn't be able to have everything you want. That means the girl and the car, if I can manage it.

But first things first: Before I can begin my demonstrations of *101 Reasons Why You Should Run Away With Me*, I have to find that damned shed, and in this darkness and with your warm breath against my face distracting me, I am off to a less-than-stellar start. To my rescue, having succeeded in pulling me from the window frame and untangling my body and dress, you take my hand and lead me toward the clay path. We start down the hill, darting between trees to hide from the loud geese that might give us away. I am suddenly scared because I remember there are bobcats, and I hold on to you tightly and wonder what a city kid like me is doing visiting here. I don't know if there are bobcats where you're from, but one look at your amused, almost-cocky profile and I am convinced you would know what to do if one should appear. You smile at how ridiculous I am and are amazed yourself that you are here, and that's when I remember my task and why I wouldn't be anywhere else but where you are. Tonight you have come to where I am, or more accurately where the T-bird is, and for the time being you hold fast to your resolve not to lay a hand on me until I can be laid down properly, across the hood of what is to be, if only for the evening, your brand new toy.

We rush down the hill like children, biting our lips to keep from laughing out loud at how outrageous we are. I breathed in your shirt when you plucked me from the window, and already I want you so much that I am damp from more than the humidity hovering in the air. Even in this darkness you seem to know this, the way you always know what I want before I do, and I seriously contemplate staging a fall over a rock so I can be on the ground in front of you and have some semi-valid excuse for pulling you on top of me. But I don't. I'm trying very, very hard to be good. I know I will be rewarded. You never disappoint me.

Finally we reach the garage, and you hold the flashlight as I fumble with the keys in the same nervous, excited, I-don't-know-what-the-hell-I'm-doing-but-please-love-me-anyway manner in which I fumbled with your buttons that first time. I can never be cool around you. For reasons that escape me but for which I am nevertheless grateful, you find this quality endearing, and I remind myself that I really must marry you someday. The T-bird would make a nice engagement gift, I think. The garage door opens at last, and your breath quickens as your flashlight scans the area. I make a game of standing in front of you, blocking your view, but you are all business now and push me away. I take the flashlight from you, leading you to the other side of the garage.

You can see the car's outline, trace her curves beneath the sheet. I lift the corner of it to allow you a peek at her body. It's a pure, creamy, silky white as though no one has touched her since 1957. "So white," you murmur through pursed lips, your hand over mine, urging me to pull the sheet back farther. "She's a beauty." I pull the sheet away in one grand movement, sing-songing "Ta-da!" with a flourish. But you are silent, your eyes fixed upon her. You are breathless. I don't think I've ever seen you breathless before. Nervous, I start to rattle off everything I have learned about her, hoping to impress you with the knowledge I've amassed, precious knowledge to which you will now be privy.

"She's a Model E with factory dual four-barrel carbs. Three-speed manual transmission. Fully restored."

You say nothing—you still haven't moved. Mesmerized, your body is perfectly still, unblinking. The only hint that you are, in fact, still breathing, is the subtle stir of the fabric above your sternum—it participates in the tiniest rise and fall. I start to feel as if I am interrupting something. I feel awkward; this moment is no longer a special gift for me to share with you. It has become something private.

"Well, she's only $19,995," I offer, to get the conversation rolling again. It doesn't. "She rides real well, very smooth." Only a nod. "The paint hasn't even needed a touch-up since—"

"Shh—" you tell me, gently. I feel as if I am in church and have hiccuped. I'm interfering with the sacred. "Can't you feel it?" you whisper finally. But I don't feel much of anything except a little stupid in this dress with my makeup just right when it's clear I'm not the one you're admiring. Then it dawns on me—I'm jealous.

"I feel jealous!" I blurt, angry at you for making me state the obvious embarrassing truth. You laugh, low and growly. You laugh, sure and strong. You look at me in amazement, shake your gorgeous head, and laugh some more.

"Jealous?" You repeat, still laughing between breaths.

"Yeah…" I admit sheepishly, my face flushing.

"Baby, it's a *car*," you remind me, picking me up by the waist and sitting my butt on the hood. This is more like it.

"Yeah, well…" I mumble, tucking a strand of hair behind my ear. I too am laughing now, reluctantly.

"Well, what?" Your nose nuzzles mine.

"I dunno," I revert to baby mode. I can't help it. You know what that nose nuzzle does to me.

"Sure you do." You start to tickle me. I am defenseless against tickling, and I am really laughing now.

"Nothing!" I gasp between giggles. "Ah! Nothing, I swear!"

"Go on—go on, say it—" you coax, tickling my sensitive sides, my warm belly, the insides of my arms, my shoulders. I convulse in laughter, incapable of saying anything. "Tell me," you demand, your lips tickling my throat, fingertips fluttering, tickling my breast. My breath draws itself in sharply. I kick my feet so that you have to restrain them, pinning each ankle to a separate corner of the hood, so that my legs span the entire surface. Your knee presses hard between them. "C'mon angel." Your tickles turn to caresses, turn to tugs at my dress. Flutters turn to wings beating against my tender flesh. Your hands turn rough, urgent, insistent. I feel want pouring out of me, soaking the silk spread beneath me. I whimper as you run your hand along the edge of my panties and no farther. I struggle to place more of myself within your reach.

"Uh-uh-ah," you chide softly, the tips of your teeth teasing my neck back behind the ear. "What do you have to say for yourself?"

"I—I'm a very silly girl, very silly, ludicrous really—" The words tumble out of me.

"Mmm?" You want more.

"I'm very silly to be jealous—and of a car, for Pete's sake—Oh! Oh, I'm...um...I'm sorry, Daddy, really I am." I must be getting warmer, because you certainly are. Your fingers slide beneath my underwear to the soft, soft skin, and you begin to stroke me like a kitten, while I open up for you and my own fingers stroke your back, massaging your shoulders, pushing you tighter against me.

"What else, baby?" I don't know what else to say. I don't even remember the conversation we were or weren't having, but the words keep coming: "I'm sorry, Daddy...yes, Daddy...please, oh, please, I'll be so good now, yes I will...." Promises pour from my lips like rain, your fingertips pressing between my lips like bold rays of sunshine, no, *lightning*, as you enter me and I push my hips against you, fierce. But you keep me talking; you won't let up. Your hand pushes inside, relentless, and as I'm straining and falling into that delicious nothingness of my bottomspace, your words slap me back into consciousness, keep me from going anywhere, hold me tight—ow!—almost painfully tight against, around you, and as you're fucking me you're still asking me those words: "Whatcha got for me, angel?" And I'm crying and begging —"I'm sorry, Daddy"—though I don't know exactly for what. But I would apologize right now to you for every time I was ever jealous, even before you, and then I would say no, no, no, there was *nothing* before you—nothing existed before this, right now, nothing worth remembering. And your hands rock into me, and the breath blows out of me, and my fingers become claws tearing at your back, and I'm howling like a cat, screaming like a baby, crying like I mean it, which I do, and I know I'd do anything, say anything for you right now when you've got yourself latched onto me like this. And soon I'm coming, and the words keep coming, "Daddy, Daddy," and I could apologize right now for the depletion of the ozone layer and mean it, mean anything, give you everything, only please, please, please don't stop fucking me. I come all over your hand, and I cry all over your shirt, and you don't even care, because you're so wonderful, and I am so overwhelmed that I cry and come again and then tell you I love you. You look at me, and I tell you again, "I love you." I tell you over and over, and suddenly you believe me. I love you, and this isn't just a hot cheap fuck but a hot cheap fuck you could have every night of your life with breakfast afterward, and I wouldn't be scared or run away; I'd love you for it and never leave you, an "I love you" always on the tip of my tongue solid and real as the streaks on your hand that make you even hornier.

You throw me back against the car, because that was just the beginning. That was an appetizer, and my butch is still hungry. Now the car is nothing but a prop, a convenient one at a convenient height, just right for setting me against as you pull your dick out, which is rock hard from all those salty orgasms you inspired. Now it's your turn to get off, and you want more, and I want more. I grab your cock before you can even offer it. You stiffen against my palm, and it's so real you can feel it as I tug lightly and then stroke you, rougher, like your hand against me. Your breath shudders out, and I jump off the car throne, knees on the gravely floor of the garage. You don't even protest—I'm a big girl, I know what I want, I know what you want.

You lean almost casually against the car door. I kick the flashlight. It shines to your crotch like a movie camera, spotlighting your magnificent hard-on caught between my sweet stroking thumb and tightening palm. This would almost be vulgar if I hadn't already said my "I love you"s, but I have, and now I want to show you, and you want my lips wrapped around you, tight, so that's where they go. You're so hot with wanting and waiting and making your little girl come that each touch is magnified, and watching my open pink mouth envelop you almost makes you slam into me. But you're kind; you go gentle, not wanting to scare me. But I am tougher than you know and invite your roughness, taking you into my throat, sweet and gentle, then sucking hard and butting my head against your pelvis.

It's your turn to make unintelligible sounds, which eventually you do, easing into the rhythm as I circle the tip of your dick, tracing your cockhead so lightly, like a whisper, then throw myself into you, full-throttle, as you barrel down my throat, past all restrictive muscle. There is nothing barring your entrance—you shove that dick into me like my face is a pussy, your hands gripping my hair tight. "You belong to me— me!" you remind me, as if I need reminding, thrusting yourself in and out of my mouth with terrible urgency. It's for you—all for you. You own this mouth, and you know it as you feel it tighten around you, lips gripping the ridges, rocking back and slamming forth. I close my teeth down around you— not hard, just more pressure—and it's like a cooker. I've got myself wrapped around you so hard you've got to explode. Licking, circling, sucking, nibbling, pulling, slamming, taking, taking, taking. I take your whole cock, the entire length, into my throat, savoring each precious delicate firm taste. My head bounces as my mouth moves along you furiously. I want to draw out your come, suck you like a straw. I'm blind, only a baby sucking for dear life. You're rigid, strong against my lips, batting against my tongue, your dick an extension of yourself, and I would lick and stroke and suck your entire body like this if you'd let me. Your breath staggers, and you heave what would be your last breath into me; you shove and strain, and still I take more, more—that's it…all.

I could go at you like this for hours, but you come into my mouth fiercely, drawing breath sharp as a knife, and before I know it you've pulled yourself from me, slammed my bare ass hard against the cold white hood, and you're shoving into me, pumping again, wild and frenzied, into my cunt this time, my saliva your only lube. You're big, but it doesn't hurt until you want it to, until your hands pummel my chest as you yell for me to take it, give it—give it to you, now; I slam my head against the car, and your free hands twist puckered nipple flesh, and my mouth devours your lips, hungry, biting as you slap at me, pull my hair, groaning as you start to lose control. Your dick sears into me, pins me down, and you support your weight with your hands on either side of me as you bear down with such force I'm sure you'll tear me open. I rise. You pump, groan, throw yourself into me—fast and furious, like our lives depend on it, which, at this very moment, they do. You fuck me harder than you mean to, but it's OK, because I'm with you. I'm with you, I'm so with you, baby, taking you every bit of the way. I holler at you for more, and you deliver—you deliver me, your hardness pushing practically out my back. I'm so full, so full with you, of you, of love for you. I think I've got to come, but I won't, not 'til I feel you about to go off inside me. You grunt and strain, and your cock beats me from the inside, pummeling, slapping, slamming, finally crashing against my cervix. We scream and I yelp and you shudder and I bear down. My cunt clutches you like a fist, threatening not to release you, ever, and your orgasm shudders in my ear—sputters, stutters like a car engine. My own howl rings above and around you, and I pull you tighter, closer. We've come together, but not ever like this. This fierce fucking feels so good it hurts. Each coming wails inside me, and I come again, tasting pleasure in the pain. It's a ripple effect: When my muscles pulse around you, it sets you off again, and like an alarm—like a bomb—you explode inside, on top of me. You shudder into me full-force, sounds coming from your throat, deep from your chest, that surpass even my own pornographic imagination. Lightning bolts flash through us, melding our slick sweaty skins together. You breathe heavily, your head pressed tight against my breast. I hold you to me with all the tenderness I've ever felt.

"Nothing," you sigh, your breath grazing my skin like a breeze. "Nothing could make me happier than I am right now." I grin widely, knowing you to be wrong and hoping you'll forgive me for proving so.

"Honey?" I coo into your ear gently, almost casually.

"Mm-mm?" you murmur in post-orgasm contentment.

"One more thing—the car? Did I mention? It's already yours." I pull the papers from underneath me, point to your name. You look at the papers, the car, and back at me, and you come again.

Eye of the Hurricane
by tatiana de la tierra

It was the 23rd of August, 1992, and they had second-row center seats for Ana Gabriel's concert that evening. It would be Ana Gabriel's first concert in Miami, right on the eve of Sirena and Julieta's two-year anniversary.

They had planned their special date far in advance. Sirena would call for Julieta at six P.M. sharp, as if they were on one of those dates they used to have when they were courting. Dinner at the Rusty Pelican in Coconut Grove. A leisurely walk around Bayside. The James L. Knight Center, where Ana Gabriel would be sure to entrance them with her husky voice. Afterwards they would go to the oceanfront hotel room they had reserved, have a few drinks at the bar, maybe play a game of pretending to meet for the first time, and head for their room. By then Sirena would have trans- formed the hotel room into their private sex chamber, though it was hard to say what she would conjure. Would she wear the honey leather saddle on her back and make Julieta ride her across the room? Blindfold and strip her woman immediately upon entering? Paint her skin cobalt blue before bondage? Immerse her, fully clothed, in the apple-scented warm waters in the bathtub and then peel off her street wear, article by article, in the candlelight? Any scenario would do, because it would all lead to fucking, which in their relationship was all that mattered and just about the only thing the two had in common.

"Look toward me but not at me." Julieta turned her face a bit to the left and focused just beyond her lover's figure. She held a huge Dominican papaya in her hands, as if she were offering it to the goddess of cunts. The fruit was sliced down the middle, revealing the vaginal form of the glistening black seeds on the reddish orange flesh. "Así, mi amor, that's right." Sirena was painting her nude fruit-bearing lover on their bayside balcony, as she had done every morning the week prior to their anniversary celebration. In the daylight Sirena saw details of her lover's body she missed in their lights-out lovemaking. An abundance of black hairs over astonishingly white legs. The caramel mark on her thigh that seemed like a country that belonged in an atlas. A sprinkling of freckles and stretch marks over her belly. The way each breast had its own personality. The aquamarine veins that bulged on her wrist from the weight of the papaya. Sirena was an artist, and Julieta was her model as well as her woman.

"Are you almost done?" Julieta was just a little impatient. She wanted to go shopping again. Every day she thought of something else to add to her attire for their date.

"Ya casi. Shush." It was warm out and windy. Sirena highlighted the glint of the morning sun over the rolling surface current of the bay. The little curl that moved slightly in the breeze. Bumpy black papaya seeds. The openness and tranquillity on Julieta's face. Just a few more sessions and the painting would be complete. "Ahora sí," she told her lover, covering the paints, placing the brushes in solvent, taking off the splattered overshirt. Julieta carried the papaya into the kitchen to wrap it in cellophane as Sirena stood in the doorway, gazing at her from behind. "Give me some papaya."

"I'm going to the mall." Burdine's was having a lingerie sale that day.

"I said give me some papaya." Sirena didn't like having to repeat herself, and Julieta knew this. She also knew that when Sirena was born, her parents had named her Isabel Caridad, *Isabel* as a tribute to the maternal grandmother and *Caridad* in reverence to la Virgen de la Caridad. But before she was baptized, the infant amazed the household and nearby neighbors with her piercing wails whenever she had needs to be attended to. "Where is that siren coming from?" asked a visitor who had been passing by during one of the baby's tenacious displays of lung power. The fitting name became hers. Sirena always had to have her way.

"And which papaya would you like?" Julieta wasn't sure. The fruit? The flesh?

"Give me some papaya." Sirena liked confusing her lover. She waited for her on the rocking chair in the living room.

Julieta brought out a plate of papaya sliced in lengthwise chunks, wet with lime juice, and offered it to Sirena, who took the plate, without a word, and placed it on the floor. She stood up, motioned Julieta to the chair, and when Julieta was seated, still naked and warm from the modeling session, Sirena rocked the chair and straddled her. "My woman doesn't know the papaya of my desire?"

"I do know."

"Well?"

"It's just that I want to go shopping."

"You can go shopping after you give me my papaya," said Sirena, sucking Julieta's neck, fingering her nipples. Julieta whimpered just a little, enough for both of them to know that, yes, she would give Sirena her papaya, and then Julieta would go shopping.

"Ay, I just feel so exposed," said Julieta, who always seemed to be naked in the daylight these days.

"The more I see, the more I want," said Sirena. "I want you exposed. It's the only way I'll have you."

"Well, then...Ay...Aaaaaayhh." Sirena had Julieta's body in a buzz again. Was there no end to this, getting turned on, late mornings, late evenings? Julieta wasn't sure if it was just a physical response, like water that automatically comes out with the turn of the faucet, or an emotional one, like loving that leads to constant cuntal wetness.

Whatever the cause, her papaya was ripe. She could smell it, ready to be picked and peeled and eaten, or maybe just picked and bitten through the flesh, raw. She felt her ass being pinched by the round pattern of the wicker seat as Sirena spread her lips open and inhaled her thick scent before licking. She felt the yank on her scalp from the lock of hair that got caught in the corner of the chair when she thrashed her head to one side. She felt the pull at the small of her back as she raised her feet to Sirena's shoulders, the splinter that entered her palm as she gripped the oak arm-rest. She heard the hollow scream that flew from her throat, the panting that became a song they had both just written together. The orgasmic release, her leche being delivered directly into her lover's mouth. And then she felt her feet plop on the floor, her lover fall into her lap, and the slight rocking of the chair as they interlaced hands and closed their eyes.

Sex when you least expect it. Nasty word games in bed, crying from being tenderly sucked, getting fucked over and over like waves that repeatedly lunge at the shore as if eternally yearning to land. That was why, even though Sirena was domineering, anal retentive, and unreasonable, Julieta loved her like crazy.

Before meeting her Julieta had thought all artists were funky and liberal. But Sirena was meticulously clean, orderly, and conservative. It was as if the bread crumbs knew not to fall on the kitchen counter. The pillows on the bed had to be fluffed up just so, the shoes cleaned each evening and arranged in matching pairs. She applauded Ronald Reagan's foreign policy, George Bush's oratory skills. Sirena was from the old order of lesbianism, Cuban style, a butch who created all the rules, made all the decisions, owned and pleased her woman thoroughly, and didn't let herself be eaten or penetrated or otherwise mauled. Julieta, on the other hand, was a hippie Democrat who wore wrinkled mismatched clothes and took the trash out in her bare feet. She liked to eat and fuck women, travel to Disney World on a whim, let the cobwebs take over a corner of each room. Of course, she didn't dare do these things with Sirena in the picture, though sometimes she yearned to. The two of them were different enough to make living together a challenge yet passionate enough to be in a committed relationship.

Julieta bought a black lace negligee that afternoon, one with snaps at the crotch so that her papaya could easily be devoured. Then she came home and put on Ana Gabriel's latest CD, *Silueta,* so she could have the new tunes fresh in her mind for the concert. Her devotion to Ana Gabriel went beyond the singer's rough rocky voice or the way she wrote love songs like a coconut flan recipe, and even beyond her Chinese eyes, the suggestive lips, and the widespread rumors that she was a dyke. Ana Gabriel's music made

Julieta weak because one of her songs had healed her relationship with Sirena on a night they were both certain it was over.

Julieta remembered the tension in the stony silence after they had returned from a weekend in Houston. They had gone to a conference together and had ended up at a party in someone's hotel room on their last night. Julieta had downed one tequila after the next. When they got back to their room, she had stripped off her clothes and gotten in bed with Sirena, nuzzling into her and letting the alcohol rule her sex. She tried to suck Sirena's nipples and was promptly brushed off. But when Julieta tried to bury her tongue in the center of Sirena's papaya, they both knew she had transgressed the holiest unspoken rule between them. Sirena was not to be touched, tongued, or penetrated, ever, and no amount of alcohol would excuse the attempt. Sirena had gotten out of bed, packed her bags, and left the room at four o'clock in the morning. The next day they sat next to each other on the airplane on their way home, neither of them saying a word. They took separate taxis home.

That night, Julieta had sat on the balcony, her bags still at the entrance of their apartment. She overheard Sirena making plans to go clubbing. She knew what she had done was unforgivable. She felt her heart frozen, the desire barely a memory. And then, pivoted by an unknown force, she had walked to the stereo and hit play on the CD player. Ana Gabriel's voice had filled the room, accompanied by guitars, mariachis, and the exact dimension of Julieta's emotions. The voice passionately sang about carrying the taste of her lover within, the sensation of being near her beloved, and the great love born between the two of them. Julieta reached for Sirena and wept with anguish until arms encircled her with love. For the rest of the night, as they explored each other's familiar bodies, Ana Gabriel's raw voice spoke for them both.

By Friday morning Sirena and Julieta were completely ready for Ana Gabriel's passionate rancheras and the ensuing sexy anniversary celebration at the Fountainbleu Hotel. Sirena had finished touching up the papaya painting of her lover and had made arrangements to check into the hotel in the early afternoon so she could design the sex scene and get dressed while Julieta prepared herself at home. Julieta had finished shopping, finally. Perfectly ironed, her outfit hung in the closet, the new shoes and underclothes stacked neatly on the shelf above. Clothes for the following day were packed in an overnight bag, along with favorite sex toys, a zip-lock baggy of marijuana, and a bottle of vermouth. Then, for that inevitable pause that almost always took place around three A.M., she had bought a jar of black olives stuffed with garlic, a small mesh bag of baby goudas, and a box of stone-ground crackers. And for lounging around in the morning, a cobalt kimono for her and a red velvet bathrobe for Sirena. There was nothing they weren't prepared for.

Except the hurricane. Julieta had heard about it first on Friday morning when she was driving, running errands, listening to the radio. Right in the midst of Daniela Romo's hit song, an emergency broadcast blasted the news of a storm brewing over the Bahamas. Hurricane Andrew was heading for Miami and was expected to hit land Saturday night.

Julieta rushed home and called the James L. Knight Center. "Is the concert still on?" She was frantic. *Please, please, don't let this ruin our plans.*

"As far as we know," responded a kind lady from the

administrative offices. Julieta was relieved. It didn't occur to her to consider mass destruction, homelessness, power outages, gasoline rationing, or the National Guard. Sirena came home later that day, equally unfazed. They went to Miami Beach with a few friends and hung out on the sand, talking and drinking rum and Cokes. The water was choppy; the wind rushed ferociously through Julieta's hair, hummed high in the night sky.

"Ooh…it's coming," said one of their friends.

"I've been here twenty-one years and have never been in a hurricane," Julieta snapped.

"Pssst. Come here," said Sirena. Julieta leaned her head into her lover's shoulder and closed her eyes, wiggled her toes in the sand, and tuned out the rest of the conversation.

Saturday morning she awoke to the sound of hammering. In the living room Sirena was nailing a two-by-four into the wall that crisscrossed the sliding glass doors. Each window was marked with a huge masking tape X.

"Oh no…What's happening?" Julieta was aghast.

"I'm sorry, I didn't want to wake you, but this is for real."

"But it can't be! We have plans!"

"We *had* plans. Now we have to make other plans."

In those next few hours of scrambling to secure whatever they could before evacuating, the possibility of a hurricane became very real. The Ana Gabriel concert, as well as any other scheduled event in the city, was canceled. The hotel, which was on the beach, had to be evacuated, along with all businesses and residencies within three miles of water. Tens of thousands of people were going to spend the night at public schools that would serve as shelters.

Julieta and Sirena would go to a friend's empty house in Leisure City, south of Miami. Julieta disconnected the stereo and the computer and plunked them in the bath-room, covering the equipment with black plastic bags. She packed jewelry, a video camera, and a strange mixture of objects in a duffel bag: perfumed powder, an anthology of British literature from the 18th century, her women's almanac, a music box, yarn, chocolates, and a bunch of 100% cotton Indian skirts that she hadn't worn in years. Oh, and some Ana Gabriel CDs and the overnight bag that was ready to go. What in the world was essential for a hurricane? She just didn't know.

Sirena, meanwhile, filled the gas tank, checked the engine's fluids, and bought gallons of water, candles, duct tape, rope, plastic, and bubble gum. She packed a color-coordinated outfit, watercolors, a sketch pad, and Infante's *Tres Tristes Tigres*, the book she had almost finished reading. She protected the fresh papaya painting with plastic and placed it on a top shelf in the bedroom closet. Meanwhile, the water from the bay was splashing high on the concrete wall that was just twenty feet from their apartment.

"You get ready while I pack the car," said Sirena, who had a stain of sweat in the middle of her back. It was a humid and hot summer day, and she had been hammering and moving furniture away from the windows for hours. She hadn't wanted to get caught up in the hurricane warn-ings, but it was hard to avoid the hysteria. Julieta took a shower and quickly put on khaki pants, a polo shirt, and her favorite sandals. "You're going like that?" Sirena looked at her in shock.

"But it's a hurricane!"

"I will not be with a woman who is not dressed like a woman!"

"You're insane! Our lives are on the line, and all you

can think about is how I'm dressed?"

"That is my point precisely. If this is our last time together, do you think I want to spend it with you looking like a preppy?"

Julieta had to laugh at how ridiculous it all was. "OK, OK, I'll get ready." She locked herself in the bedroom while she put on the outfit she had prepared for their anniversary. Silky black undergarments. An ankle-length taffeta skirt with red roses imprinted on the shiny black background. The matching crimson blouse, very simple, over which she wore chunky silver chains. A rose in her hair. Studded bracelets and black soft-leather calf-boots, zippered on the side, made in Italy. And then, of course, the brunelle lip liner, matte red lipstick, and blood-red nails. If Sirena wanted her as planned, she would have her, all right.

Julieta unlocked the door, black velvet purse in hand. "At your service, madam."

"That is how I like my woman," said Sirena, who had also showered and dressed elegantly. She took Julieta by the arm, and they headed for their shelter right at six P.M., the time their date was to commence.

They settled into their friend's three-bedroom house. Winds were traveling at seventy-seven miles per hour right around when Sirena and Julieta would have been in their second-row seats at Ana Gabriel's concert. That's also when they heard on the radio that the eye of the hurricane was destined for South Dade, where Leisure City was located, right where they were. But it was too late to go anywhere by then. A city full of panicked people had created mayhem in the streets, and Mother Nature was whipping trees and power lines around as easily as little girls jumped rope on the sidewalk after school.

By midnight Sirena and Julieta had finished securing their friend's house as best they could and had polished off the bottle of vermouth. Ana Gabriel sang hopeful love songs with a funky Brazilian bass. The wind hammered at the glass on the window panes. Walls rattled. Papers from the study flew throughout the house. Porcelain cups bounced on the shelf. A glass crashed on the terrazzo floor. A dog howled and barked somewhere on the block. Sirens wailed in the distance. Suddenly Ana Gabriel's voice stopped in mid song, and all the lights went out.

"We're going to die!" Julieta had stopped trying to calm herself with long deep breaths. It was fruitless. She threw herself in Sirena's arms. Sirena rocked her, patted her head, and stroked her back until she was calm.

"Happy anniversary, mi amor," Sirena whispered in her ear. "If this is the end of the world, I'm glad we're together to celebrate."

"You always say the right things," said Julieta. "You make me feel safe, even in a hurricane."

"You inspire me to say the right things, even in a hurricane." Sirena kissed Julieta on the mouth like a teenager in the back seat on Lover's Lane. Long and hungry, young with excitement. "Is there ever a moment that you're not mine?"

"Never."

"Is there anything you won't do to please me?"

"No. That's all I want, to please you."

"That's why I love you, you know?"

Julieta knew. Who could understand it? Maybe all love was without reason. Maybe there was just nothing better to do as the winds picked up to ninety-eight miles per hour. Maybe it was the stress, the uncertainty, the distinct feeling they were truly in danger and powerless. The long black night. The thunder and lightning. The adrenaline. The horniness amid a natural disaster.

Sirena bound Julieta's wrists above her head, spread her legs, and secured each ankle to the bedposts. Bit her breasts through the silk blouse, choked her neck with the heavy silver chains long enough to make her gasp for breath, waited for her to recover. Kissed and soothed her. Pulled up the long taffeta skirt, pinched her ass, and gripped her inner thighs hard enough to leave a mark. Ripped her fingers through the pantyhose, fucked her in the ass first of all. Slapped her across the face while she tamed her restless pelvis. Said, "papayona," as she greeted her cunt, stroking the fine pubic hairs. Teased her wet crica before entering. Said, "Ay mami, qué papaya más rica." Asked, "¿A quién le pertenece esta papaya?" Waited for a response that affirmed her ownership before fucking Julieta with all her fingers, ramming her.

Meanwhile, a pine tree fell swiftly on top of the roof in the patio. Long fluorescent bulbs crashed in the kitchen. Windows shattered. The ceiling cracked in the living room. Wind howled; objects flew. And Julieta screamed from being fucked all the while, and Sirena ground herself into Julieta's thigh. Then, there was a stillness, absolute silence as the eye of the hurricane positioned itself at three A.M. Sirena undressed herself and for the first time ever, with Julieta bound beneath her, offered her papaya to her woman's mouth.

Uncommon Janitors in Lust
by Lisa Gonzales

I swear the fucking mop handle would do. Every night for the last two weeks, we've shown up around 7:15, and the little hot mami I lust after is still in her cubicle working hard for her money. Working so hard to keep her skirt and top still closet-fresh and her hair newly primped and fragranced. She drives me crazy and makes me so horny when she goes through her drawn-out motion to say hello.

It's a slow pan to the right and then the left, and then her dimples start to form a smile, but first she completes the head lift, directs her dark brown eyes, and then *bam*! She shoots me a flirtatious grin. Last Wednesday I thought I saw her curve her smile as if she were saying "ooouuuh." She looks like the girl in the Doritos commercial, like Hope from *Days of Our Lives*. Need I say more?

The other lesbian janitor thinks I'm imagining all this shit. But a girl knows when there is a vibe going. I definitely do. Oh, and I definitely want to do her. I have this fantasy about meeting her in her boss's office and telling her how much I want her, and then gently setting her on her boss's desk to begin the feast and eat her sweet shrimp sushi slowly, tail and all. Man, I can't wait.

"Stop your fucking daydreaming, Marie, and help me with the trash," says Evy.

"Hey, man, look at her breasts. It's gotta happen. Maybe I should go talk to her."

"We've got two more buildings to clean tonight, and I want to go home and get laid too, so hurry up." Evy starts to laugh, then continues, "Look, you're fucking making me horny too, damn it. Well, go see if she's even a little interested—I doubt it, though. But don't take too long. I mean, be back here quick, man."

"I wonder if she likes poetry," I say softly, staring at the voluptuous woman.

"Dude, don't even start your shit. You always do that when you meet someone. Poems, candy, teddy bears. Girls don't want that anymore. They fucking want you to have a car and an apartment and pay their bills. Lesbian expectations are getting more and more like straight women's."

"Ah, save the drama for your mama! I'm going in."

"Fine, I'll meet you on the second floor. I'll give you some pri-va-cy," Evy says with a smirk.

"Wait," I say. "Give me one of the trash cans. That's my ticket. See ya."

I begin to throw trash in the area most remote from the girl. I keep thinking of her name, Gina. It's so good for sex! It's so pretty on its own. I start to throw trash closer and closer to her; then I stop to see her through the partitions. She's so into her work. *Oh, my precious smart little woman,* I think. Her brain and her job dedication are so sexy. I don't know if she'll know I want her, so I decide to go really butch on this one to get it clearly across.

Most straight girls expect a dyke to look like a dyke, but not really, not in Los Angeles. So my long hair won't hurt me. Still I think I'll go in a little rough and tough. Talk about football and cars and shit and impress her. I hope she knows less than I do. I duck into the bathroom to check my look. I have on a navy blue company T-shirt and some chinos from the Gap. My pants are a little wrinkled in the thigh area; I wonder if she likes the grunge look. But I think I look all right at 5-foot-4, 139 pounds with dark hair up in a ponytail, and deep dark eyes. I still have on my makeup from my day job at the clinic, so I look fine. Hopefully she is Latina and at least into her own kind, 'cause that's me.

Maybe I'm making a mistake. What if I'm her fantasy? Her sex toy? Toys are always outgrown. I want more. What if she wants me because I'm supposed to be the lowly and savage janitor? What if she wants me in a carnal way like housewives want their landscapers and plumbers? I'd be degrading myself, participating in the social stigma of the working class, but then again...I'd be getting laid!

I start to exit the bathroom, and she walks in. Right past me! She didn't even flinch. Completely dumbfounded, I instinctively walk out of the room. All my planning, shattered. I can't go back in there. I panic and run to the elevator, which takes me to the second floor, to Evy.

"Hey, man, what happened?" With a bottle of disinfectant in hand, Evy rushes to me as the elevator opens.

"Nothing," I declare with frustration. "Shit! I was working myself up to it, you know, thinking about what I would say, and then I didn't notice her, and she walked right by me in the bathroom and said dick."

"She dissed you? Well, so much for that vibe you two had going, huh?"

"Fuck you, Evy."

"Sorry, man," Evy replies.

"Just go back upstairs and get the rest of the trash. I'll finish here and then let's go. I don't want to talk right now, so leave." I turn away, then look back at Evy and yell, "And don't talk to her!"

The next day at the women's clinic where I do pre- and post-test counseling for HIV, I can hardly concentrate. It's a Friday, and I'd rather not start another weekend with an evening alone. Actually, I've started to get used to being alone since I broke up with my ex three months ago, but today feels especially cold. I try to shrug it off. I call Gina every fucking name in the book 'til I feel like a reckless Don Juan son of a bitch. But then the rejection resets itself upon me. Around two o'clock, I call Evy to make sure she'll be at my house by five, so we can eat and buy some supplies at Clean Source before going to work. I still have three hours to go at this job, and although I'm well-booked, I tell the head nurse to let me see patients on a walk-in basis.

At home, I have two messages on my machine: one from my cariñosa mom and one from my dentist. I call my mom quickly and get her answering machine: "Marie, if it's you, call me in the morning, and don't be out too late. I went to church with your Tia Esmeralda. Voy a resar por ti, mijita."

That's just what I need—a prayer. I quickly start to change clothes, then hear a knock at the door. It's Evy. "Hey, what's up? It's fucking cold outside." She pats me on the back. "Hey, man, thanks for the defrosting yesterday."

"What?" I say with quick anger.

"That chick, and you talking about doing her? Whoa, I went home and got some good shit!"

"Yeah? Well, good for you. Too bad you make your girl sound like weed."

"Ah, don't be mad. I'm just fucking with you. She was

asleep like always when I got home."

"Let me finish getting dressed, and we'll get going."

Evy nods and sits down. She turns on the TV and starts flipping channels. Before long we're heading out to eat and on to our first building—Gina's.

A lot of cars are still in the parking lot at the Bravo Corp. when we arrive. I look up to the third floor as we walk from the visitors' parking lot. Most of the lights are still on. Although I hate Gina right now, I really hope she didn't mean to walk by me in the bathroom yesterday. Maybe she'll still smile at me.

"Hi, George," I greet the security guard.

"Hey, Marie. Hey, Evy."

"Is there a party going on?" Evy asks. "Why are there so many people still here?"

"They're throwing a party for one of the executives who is transferring to a field office," George answers.

"Do we have to wait to start working?" I ask.

"No, go ahead and start on the top floors. By the time you guys work your way back down, most of them should be gone."

"All right. Evy, grab the supply cart and the trash cans. I'm gonna inspect for vacuuming."

"Yeah, sure. I'll take my time, " Evy says to me with a suspicious eye.

I don't know what's gotten into me, but I have the irresistible urge to see if Gina is upstairs. I exit the elevator at floor three and pretend to inspect the carpet for spot vacuuming. I have to go through a hallway toward the west side of the building to squeeze between partitions and look for her. She isn't at her desk. Damn it. Maybe she's at the party downstairs. My shoulders give way to heavy disappointment, and I head for the elevator.

Before I round the corner to it, I hear the bell sound as someone is about to exit. I stop in my tracks and start inspecting the carpet again, but the person doesn't come my way. I peer through another angle, and I notice her legs. I notice her ass and her height and the back of her hair. My heart starts to race, and I lose sight of her. But I decide without question that I can't wimp out. Not tonight. Then the whole weekend will really suck.

"There you are," a cheerful voice says to me from behind.

It's her. She approaches with two slices of cake. "Hello, I'm Gina. Your friend Evy said you were up here. My boss invited her to have some food and cake, and she's down there with everyone. She said maybe you'd like some cake. She threw in some cherries, and the syrup is getting on my hands. Would you mind taking these from me for a minute while I wash up?" She hands me the plates, and I nod.

"My name is Marie. Nice to meet you. Is the person leaving an important person at the company?" I ask stupidly.

"Yeah, I know your name. It's my boss who's leaving, only she's not leaving the company. She got a promotion and has to transfer to our San Francisco office. My father owns this company and feels she's the best person to head up operations out there."

"San Francisco is the place to be," I declare.

"Why's that? Have you ever lived there?" Gina asks.

"No, I was just talking. I've never traveled there really. Have you?"

"I think the prettier people are in L.A. I think the 'call of the wild' is exponential here."

"The 'call of the wild,' what do you mean?" I start to fidget with my pockets and hair, but then slowly I calm myself down.

"Do you want to sit down? Come over to my boss's office. I can finish packing her things and talk to you at the same time, unless you have to get to work. Your friend Evy doesn't seem to want to rush into it, so why should you?" She asks this with those flirtatious eyes from before, and she turns toward the cubicle in the center of the room.

"Sure, I'll even help you if I can." Suddenly I decide to get butch and let her know that I am a woman-fucking woman.

She unlocks the office and lets herself in. I follow. She closes the door after me, grabs a box to the left of her, and proceeds to the bookshelf. I start to speak first. "This weekend I'm going over to watch football at my friend's house. We might get to fixing her car if the game is a blowout."

"Really, who's your favorite team? I like the Vikings myself. What's wrong with the car?" she asks.

I start to reply, astonished and turned on that she likes football and asks about some made-up car. "Well, I like the Broncos and the Dolphins, but I just like to watch any game as long as it's a tight game. As for the car, something's wrong with a cylinder or carburetor. We'll take it apart, put it back together. You know, the usual."

She keeps smiling and nodding as I go on talking bullshit about football and fishing and cars and things I think are butch. Every time I stop to get an acknowledgment from her, she smiles that knee-bending smile and reaches up for another book so that her skirt rises farther and farther up, since she refuses to use the stepladder next to her. I keep talking until finally I am so plugged into her ass and waist that I let the room fall silent, and she does too.

Finally, after grabbing the last book from the uppermost shelf and driving me completely insane, she says, "I love all that raw energy of contact between two people—like in football. In a tackle their adrenaline needs to knock the other guy's head apart, but after it's all said and done they say 'good game.' Know what I mean?"

She starts to walk toward me, with her hips swaying and that mischievous smile on her face—oh, this girl is so fucking sexy! I feel hot all over, and I have to sit down. Take me, please. "Yeah, I know what you mean. It's like their dick gets so hard for a good hit, and the more they play and the more tackles they make, the more they come and come and come. Whoa, sounds good, huh?" She stands over me. From my sitting position on the chair, my eyes meet her breasts.

"It does sound very good. Stand up, Marie," she firmly orders, guiding me upward. I stand slowly, shivering with sexual anticipation.

She looks at me like a lion ready to pounce on its prey. Her shrewd smile overpowers me, conveying she's going to get me no matter what. She softly bites her bottom lip, licks her lips, and comes forward to kiss me. Her tongue is soft and tough at once, and her rhythm is perfect.

"We don't have much time," she says breathlessly. "Come here." She talks to me like she's begging. I love her lust. I love her lust for me. While she presses her lips to mine, we start to remove clothes. She unbuckles my belt. I reach to grab her shirt, and she says, "No, this one is for you. I'll get mine, don't worry. Take off your shirt. Hurry. Do it now!"

Her panting and her commanding orders make my pussy totally wet. I quickly take my shirt off and help her take off my shoes. Next she asks me to get on the desk. She's like a sexual military commander. I want to disobey her so badly just so I can be punished; my clit is hard and throbbing and needy. I'm just about to drop my panties, but she presses my hands and says, "I'll do it. Lie back. Hurry. I want your pussy bad. You want me to fuck you? Tell me. Tell me, 'Gina, fuck me.' Come on, say it. Are you ready for me? Tell me!"

"Fuck me, Gina. I've been wanting you all day. You are so hot. You are so fucking fine. Suck me. Suck me right now." I say it and am trembling for it. Her passion is so overwhelming. I feel so desired, so absolutely completely desired.

She pulls up a stool and sits between my legs like an experienced nurse performing her one-millionth exam. Then she lifts my legs and places them on her biceps. She runs her fingers through her hair and out of her face—to free herself of distractions. Her hands come over my pelvic area to open my pussy lips for her tongue. She starts at my ass and works it up and down to my clit over and over again. A lick here. A suck there. I gasp and moan with every orgasm. My right leg keeps shaking, and I feel shy because I don't know why it's doing that. I tell her to stop. But she keeps insisting that I like it and that she isn't finished. I give in and put my head down on the now-disorganized memos that find their way to the floor. I'm relaxed yet sexually electrified. Every stroke is placing pleasure knots in my stomach.

Soon I can't take any more. My left leg begins to shudder too, and I'm feeling emotionally tied to a lover for the first time in a long while. I start to get up to tell her to stop again, but instead she stands up, puts her left hand behind my neck, and tilts my head to meet her gaze. "You look so beautiful when you're naked and vulnerable," she says softly. Then she surprises me and puts one finger slowly inside me. She fingers and kisses me, eyes open and sincere to settle me down. But instead, she brings me an emotionally deep orgasm, and I feel like crying. Again she moves my head back to look at her.

"Stop. Please stop, Gina. I can't take any more. Please stop."

"OK, OK. Shh. Calm down. Calm down," she says to me with affection and concern. "Are you OK? I'm sorry." She's a little out of breath as we embrace once more, Gina still standing with me propped on the desk.

"I'm fine. I just need to catch my breath. You are very good. I haven't felt this way…" I force my eyes shut to settle my tears.

Outside the door we hear the elevator bell. I scamper to find and jump into my clothes. Gina starts picking up all the memos and giggles softly.

"What's so funny?" I ask her.

"You have your shirt on backwards," she whispers. "You still look beautiful, though."

"Oh, you're so sweet," I reply. "Now help me find my other shoe." I start to laugh too.

As we trample around the office, I hear doors opening and closing down the hall. I know by the tone and rhythm that it's Evy throwing the trash. "Fuck! It's my coworker. Is there a way to lock the door?" I ask, still trying to put my pants and socks back on.

"Yeah, but she has the master key even if I lock it. You'd better hurry," Gina says holding my belt and taunting me with this naughty-girl look in her eye, like she's the cat that ate the canary. She approaches me quickly. "You tasted so good, by the way. I think you're too calm now for me to have seconds, but I'll have them later. Let's meet somewhere. Would you like that?"

"Of course. I didn't get to eat my cake," I say, a devilish look in my eye.

Just then the door opens, and Evy stands there staring at

the two of us. "There you are. Thanks a lot. I did the whole building practically," she says in a half-joking, half-whiny voice. I look at her with a devil-could-care look, and Evy says, "OK, then. I'll just wait downstairs. Everybody's gone now. Bye." Evy shuts the door.

Gina and I exchange numbers and promise to see each other later. She keeps apologizing for not saying hello in the bathroom, but I just feel silly and giddy about the whole thing. She walks me to the elevator and kisses me passionately. We're still smiling at each other as the doors begin to shut. She says "good game," to which I respond in kind before descending.

When I meet Evy on the first floor, a big grin spreads across her face, and I put my arm around her shoulder. "Don't say a word 'til we get outside," I demand. We turn to exit through the automatic doors. She is near explosion and finally says, "Now I really got to get home and get some. Look at you. She turned you out, huh? You're fucking glowing! Ooh! Take me home, please. Take me! I can't work like this, man. This is torture. I'm going on worker's comp, seriously."

I just smile at her and say, "That girl is wicked. Wicked. Wicked. Wicked. Mmm. Mmm. Mmm."

"Think this is going to work out for you?"

"Yeah." I smile. "I'm meeting her later. Come on, get in the car. I'll tell you about it."

Evy jumps in the driver's seat. I look up to the third floor. She's standing there. Her silhouette so amazing. So aesthetic. So romantic, staring out the window waving good-bye. I lift my hand to greet hers. My heart melts, and my pussy rests up for the second half. And who knows, possibly a whole new season.

An Anatomy Lesson for Mary Margaret
by Margaret Granite

Mary Margaret hesitantly opened the creaky door to the bar. A string of bells around the door knob jingled, and she tried not to flinch with self-conscious surprise at inadvertently announcing her own entrance. Two weathered butches in leather looked up from their game of pool and openly cruised her. Mary Margaret blushed and cast her eyes down.

"Over here!" A familiar voice called from somewhere through the smoke. Finally, Mary Margaret spotted Rose at a table in a corner. Rose took a long drag off an Export A with one hand and ushered Mary Margaret toward her with the other. Mary Margaret, with her wave of shiny black hair, intense blue eyes, and 21-year-old innocence, captured the gaze of the leather dykes as she walked past the pool table.

When she saw Rose's face light up, just for her, Mary Margaret's heart stumbled all over itself. She went to sit down on garish purple cushions next to Rose but then balked at what looked like a fresh spill of Coke.

"Ew," she said, crinkling up her nose.

"Oh," said Rose, laughing, "It's not exactly the cleanest place, is it?" She arranged some paper napkins over the offensive spot. "All better?"

Mary Margaret sat down, inwardly wincing but not wanting to make a fuss.

"Hello, Mary Margaret." Mary Margaret looked up, a little startled. She had been so tortured trying to decide how much of Rose's smile she could bear to take in that she hadn't noticed Lynn and Janet. They were Rose's coworkers, fellow nurses, and they were sitting a yard away.

"Hello," said Mary Margaret.

"How was your day?" said Rose, riveting Mary Margaret's attention by stroking her hair, which fell over her generous breasts, hidden beneath a bulky sweater.

"Good. I gave a paper on camp and drag in my Theorizing Identity class. I think the professor liked it."

"You're a prodigy, honey." Rose turned to Lynn and Janet. "Did you know Mary Margaret is the youngest person in her graduate program?" It was true, but Mary Margaret didn't like attention called to the fact.

"Drag, that's like drag queens, but how exactly do you define camp?" asked Janet.

"Well, that depends on what point you are in the historical debate about camp. Susan Sontag defined it as—"

"Look!" said Lynn, tugging on Janet's sleeve. "Those two ladies are finally done with the pool table."

"Let's get over there!" exclaimed Janet. "The blonds at the bar are eyeing the table." Lynn and Janet hurried to rack up before all was lost.

Rose put a finger on Mary Margaret's chin. "Kiss me," she breathed, turning Mary Margaret's face toward her own.

Mary Margaret hesitated. She'd never kissed in public before.

"Kiss me," Rose insisted, leaning forward to claim Mary Margaret's lips. The tidal wave of the kiss washed the room away. Somebody's breath quickened. A caress melted into a thigh. A hot flush rose from Mary Margaret's chest up into the roots of her hair. She felt an impulse to wrap her arms around Rose's waist but quelled it by planting her hands into the sticky seat cushions instead.

Finally, Rose drew back and smiled. Her dark brown eyes, almost black, now sparkled mischievously. She was Mary Margaret's first girlfriend, her first love. Her hair was close-cropped and red, and she always wore earrings and traffic-stopping lipstick, which she reapplied frequently. She was svelte. She talked like Marilyn Monroe, yet her voice was husky from smoking nearly a pack of cigarettes a day. Her facial features presented an almost comical cross between Boy George and David Bowie. She was one of the sexiest women Mary Margaret would ever meet in her life.

"I need a drink," said Mary Margaret.

ea   ea   ea

After rapidly siphoning a sloe-gin fizz, a concoction Rose had introduced her to, Mary Margaret felt more at ease in her surroundings.

Rose was the belle of every bar she frequented. She made everyone laugh with her hospital stories.

"Guess what he had up his butt? Just try to guess. I defy you."

"I dunno," said Janet, blasé. "A hamster?"

"No, that wouldn't be terribly original, would it?"

Mary Margaret blanched. Why would somebody have a hamster up his butt? She didn't get it.

"An Easter egg," Rose said, deadpan. "One of the real ones they put chocolate in, however they manage that. The chocolate had melted, and the shell broke!"

"Eeeeaah!" exclaimed Lynn.

Mary Margaret was appalled. She could imagine an Easter egg. She could imagine an Easter egg with chocolate inside. She could imagine an Easter egg with chocolate inside, broken into parts. But…a wedge of apprehension inserted itself between these images and the human anatomy.

"Doesn't surprise me," said Janet.

"The great thing is, there really isn't any excuse," continued Rose, gesturing with her cigarette. "I mean, one guy came in with a shampoo bottle up his butt once, and even though the fags in E.R. knew full well he didn't slip in the shower, at least he could have claimed that he did with some sort of plausibility!"

Rose went on to talk about how she'd determined her cat was gay, because he enjoyed getting his temperature taken rectally.

"I changed his name from Buddy to Fabulous Buddy," she told the now-small crowd of an audience, an assortment of hospital staff come to pay court to her during happy hour. She proceeded to impersonate her cat receiving this particular form of pleasure by wiggling her ass deeper into the seat cushions and caterwauling. Almost everyone burst out laughing, except Mary Margaret, who was pleased that Rose was so popular but uncomfortable about the subject of her performance.

"I have to go to the rest room," she said, close to Rose's ear.

"OK, doll." Rose stroked her lover's arm.

The touch lingered all the way to the bathroom stall, where Mary Margaret carefully arranged sheets of toilet paper over the seat. The lock on the stall door was broken, and she leaned forward, awkwardly trying to keep it shut while she went to the bathroom. She tried to relax. Sometimes she got stage fright. If she could just go before someone interrupted. A few drops came out. What if one of those butches walked in? The stream abruptly stopped before it could begin.

"Yoo-hoo!" Rose burst in and stooped down to address Mary Margaret's feet. "Darling, I freshened your drink!"

"Almost done!" Mary Margaret decided to forgo the effort and zipped up the pleated black skirt she'd worn especially for Rose, who'd said she liked it on her.

"Here, take a sip," said Rose, plying her with the drink. Mary Margaret obeyed then Rose whisked the drink away and set it precariously on a sink top. She removed the cherry from the glass and backed Mary Margaret up against the sink.

"Eat this for me, will you?" Rose more or less commanded.

Before Mary Margaret could swallow, Rose's tongue was in her mouth, mixing and swapping maraschino cherry bits around.

"Wait!" said Mary Margaret. She swallowed. "There." She pulled Rose forward by the belt buckle and kissed her passionately. Rose groaned. Mary Margaret felt a surge of excitement and power at turning the tables on Rose, if only for a moment, and getting her to respond so intensely. She felt Rose's thighs press against her own—Rose's hands impatiently working their way under her sweater to her bare skin...caresses on either side of her spine...fingers journeying up the vertebrae...her bra unfastening.

"Not...here..." panted Mary Margaret into their kiss.

Rose slid her hands around to Mary Margaret's breasts and gently pushed them together. "You have such beautiful breasts...I'm one of the few people in the world who really knows." Rose pressed the lushness against her face and urgently dragged one cheek, her nose, the other cheek, against Mary Margaret's breasts through a now-maddening barrier of wool sweater. Mary Margaret caught her breath, closed her eyes. Rose imprinted Mary Margaret's neck with a kiss, then another, and another, until Mary Margaret couldn't refrain from grabbing her lover's sweet ass. So tantalizing, it came to view in Mary Margaret's mind as she'd seen it the week before, in the hospital elevator, where she'd been flooded with stymied desire while rediscovering its full curves in khaki pants. The doors opened onto the hospital cafeteria; Mary Margaret gripped harder.

Rose put a hand on Mary Margaret's thigh, then slid it up to the crotch of her tights. "Oh, honey," she murmured.

Mary Margaret suddenly remembered where they were. "We...we can't...I want...to be in bed with you," she managed.

"You're very wet," Rose breathed. "I can tell."

"Oh, Rose, not here!"

"I've always wanted to do it in this bathroom."

"Rose!" Mary Margaret grabbed Rose by the wrists to keep her hands out of trouble. Rose rolled her eyes and smiled. She handed Mary Margaret her second sloe-gin fizz. "Drink up, sweetheart."

One of the leather dykes walked in when there wasn't much to walk in on anymore. She smiled warmly at the two girls. "Ah, to be young and in love," she said before disappearing into a stall. Mary Margaret felt flustered and looked down at Rose's stylish half-boots. Rose squeezed her hand and led her out of the bar.

It was a surprisingly warm night in San Francisco, almost balmy. They sailed down 18th Street, past rows of Victorians, on Rose's scooter. They rode without helmets. With her hands clasped around Rose's waist, Mary Margaret got whiffs of hair gel and Aussie shampoo mingled with the cheap men's cologne Rose liked to wear, Eau Sauvage. It was a divine smell. Utterly divine. Mary Margaret wished she could loosen up and meet Rose's spirit, but she was too painfully and awkwardly in love. How she would have liked to tease Rose the way Rose sometimes teased her. *Oh, nurse Rose, take my pulse! Nurse Rose, my forehead is burning up. Feel! Nurse Rose, I craaave your attention.* It was hopeless…you couldn't rehearse in your head how to tease someone, how to flirt with them. You just did it, spontaneously, as Rose seemed to do everything.

❧   ❧   ❧

Back at Rose's apartment, with the tap water running, Mary Margaret managed to empty her bladder. She breathed a sigh of relief and gazed up past the bunched-up tights around her ankles to take in the sights of the bathroom with pleasure. On the sink top, Rose kept a ceramic dish filled with soap in the shape of little scallops. Next to the soap dish was a glass jar filled with brightly colored bath beads, and a basket overflowing with toiletries. Mary Margaret was fond of the tile, robin's egg blue. There was a large old-fashioned tub with claw feet, where she had taken baths with Rose, who sometimes shaved her legs for her. "Trust me," said Rose, the first time. "I won't cut you."

"Sister Mary Margaret! Come to bed!"

Rose had taken off her clothes and lay propped up on one

elbow. Mary Margaret stopped when she came in the room, uncertain whether to take off her clothes first or just get into bed. The graceful curve of Rose's hip fixed her gaze.

"Undress," said Rose. Mary Margaret unzipped her skirt, folded it, and placed it on the seat of a chair. She likewise removed her tights and sweater and folded them. She tried to concentrate on folding. She made a neat pile of clothes on the chair.

"Look at me," said Rose. Her eyes were shining with desire.

Mary Margaret unhooked her bra and slowly took it off. Rose took a sharp intake of breath as Mary Margaret's breasts came into view.

"Come here," said Rose, who with one swift movement sat up on the edge of the bed and held out her arms. Mary Margaret walked into them, and Rose, making a sound somewhere between a sigh of satisfaction and a groan of impatience, kissed her hungrily on the inside of her left breast. Mary Margaret could remember this. Rose slid her fingers beneath the elastic of Mary Margaret's cotton under-wear. For a moment, everything became a teasing touch at some magical juncture between spine and ass.

Mary Margaret's breath came quickly as Rose cupped her lover's breasts together and circled her tongue around and around the pink nipples, surprisingly small and delicate, like an adolescent's. Through half-closed eyes, Mary Margaret watched her lover kiss and suck the treasure kept hidden beneath bulky sweaters. Their swell, their heft, their soft generosity all seemed meant for this. The hunger welled up hot into her pussy, surged into her fingertips.

Rose pulled Mary Margaret onto the bed and shifted to her preferred place on top. Now, finally, for Mary Margaret, Rose's weight, the length of the woman was fully upon her. She entwined a leg around Rose's and gripped Rose's ass, each finger claiming its own indentation. Rose gently sunk her teeth into Mary Margaret's shoulder, gripped her ass tight in return, and began to bump and grind. The first time Rose introduced her to this motion, Mary Margaret had been a little taken aback. But now she met Rose's thrusts with her own, angling for the tantalizing brush of pelvic bone against clit, a special challenge through underwear. A neighbor might have heard the sound of dueling girlish moans and sighs through the bedroom wall, mounting in volume and intensity, but neither Rose nor Mary Margaret cared.

Yes, Rose liked to be on top, but Mary Margaret felt impatient to kiss from that vantage. She shifted her weight out from underneath Rose, and they wrestled a little for dominance. Mary Margaret gained victory and straddled her lover, pinned her wrists to the bed. Rose looked up at her with longing. "I want you," she breathed. "I can't stand it."

Mary Margaret slowly leaned down, pressing her nipples against Rose's. "Unmmmh!" someone exclaimed. Mary Margaret kissed Rose lightly, then drew back as Rose tried to kiss her back. She kissed Rose again, flicking her tongue briefly into the corner of Rose's lips. She drew away. She kissed Rose lightly again, then caught her lower lip and sucked, let go. Rose groaned, plunged her hands in Mary Margaret's hair, and drew her down for a long fierce kiss that left both breathing like sprinters. As they kissed more gently, Rose worked her hand between their bodies and into Mary Margaret's panties.

"Mmm, what are these doing on?" Rose murmured.

Before Mary Margaret could decide whether to reply, Rose had melted her fingers into the luscious folds of Mary

Margaret's pussy, which greedily took in the attention. Mary Margaret cried out. Rose lightly stroked Mary Margaret's clit with one hand while making caressing circles on her ass with the other. "Say yes," Rose urged. "Tell me yes." Mary Margaret kissed Rose's cheek, her neck, breathed yes into her ear.

At first with just a dip, Rose entered Mary Margaret. Then came a very shallow rapid fucking until Mary Margaret couldn't refrain from thrusting forward to try to take in more of Rose's finger. Rose withheld it, and her lover, straining in frustration, felt a finger travel gingerly down the crack of her ass and then stop at the entrance no one's finger had ever come near. Rose continued to teasingly fuck her lover to distraction with one hand, then experimentally worked her middle finger into Mary Margaret's anus.

Mary Margaret drew away. "No, not that!" she exclaimed.

"What?" Rose asked with mock innocence.

"You know," insisted Mary Margaret. Really, it was unthinkable.

"OK, honey," said Rose gently, flipping Mary Margaret onto her back, taking her face between her hands, and softly kissing her. She kissed her way down between Mary Margaret's breasts, briefly delved her tongue into Mary Margaret's belly button, then impatiently pulled off the panties and threw them into a corner. Rose traveled along the inside of Mary Margaret's thighs, grazing them with her lips. She burrowed her fingers into Mary Margaret's pubic hair and traced around its perimeter with precise brush strokes of the tongue.

Mary Margaret relaxed and sighed, whimpered as Rose's tongue finally made its way into the secrets of her cunt, then began teasing her clit, flicking it back and forth. The heat fanned out in waves from Rose's tongue, coursing through Mary Margaret's veins. Rose gripped her lover's hips and felt them thrust forward, ever so slightly now. Mary Margaret's moans, like caresses on a much-neglected expanse of flesh, made Rose even wetter. As Rose started slowly fucking Mary Margaret with a finger, she humped the bed a little, never ceasing the movements of her avid tongue.

Mary Margaret felt she was melting into a molten pool of pleasure. Her pelvis shuddered once, strained. Rose started finger-fucking her swiftly now. Mary Margaret moaned over and over. As wave upon wave of hot pleasure crested near the high-water mark of complete ecstasy, Rose worked another finger into Mary Margaret's asshole and began to move it in and out slowly. Mary Margaret bucked with orgasm, plunging Rose's finger deeper into her ass with the motion. But oh how she wanted her ass worked now. How good it was! Her cunt and ass filled and overflowed with an overwhelming satisfaction that blotted out everything but itself.

Rose knew well enough to remove the otherwise marauding finger just as Mary Margaret began sliding down the slope of her climax into quiescence. When Mary Margaret lay on her back still and panting, Rose kissed her stomach, then caressed it. Mary Margaret's hairline was wet with sweat. She sighed, opened her eyes, and turned on her side to smile at Rose. She felt an urge to put the giddy euphoria into words.

She couldn't. The feeling turned back on itself and lodged in her chest. Trapped there, it made her want Rose badly, so much that she could cry.

"How was that?" asked Rose.

"That was...not what I'd expected," said Mary Margaret.

Rose threw her head back and laughed, an intoxication. "The best things are never what we'd expect," she said. Mary Margaret pulled Rose to her. Her mouth descended on Rose's breasts, which in contrast to hers were small, like a Grecian statue's. Rose surprised her by evading her grasp and jumping out of bed. "Always wash your hands!" she exclaimed.

"Oh," said Mary Margaret, embarrassed.

Mary Margaret waited impatiently as the water in the bathroom ran. She thought about what she might say—teasing, clever things—if only she were the playful somebody else she kept locked up inside herself.

ﻙﻙﻙ ﻙﻙﻙ ﻙﻙﻙ

The next evening Rose came home from work to find the bed she had reluctantly left at dawn—then disordered, harboring a sleeping lover—now carefully made. This came as no surprise, but the note she discovered on top of the pillows did. "Nurse Rose," she read, "Thank you for the lovely anatomy lesson. Love, Mary Margaret." As she laughed and laughed with delight and dialed the phone, Rose had no idea how many crumpled-up, scratched-out, ripped-apart drafts had been removed from the site of composition, nor did she know how eagerly, and with what suspense, the author awaited a response to the final draft.

Burning Zozobra
by Renee Hawkins

We may be setting Old Man Gloom on fire tonight, I told myself, but if I'm not careful, I'll get burned right along with that overgrown puppet. I shook my head and wondered what was going to happen.

I was driving from Albuquerque to Santa Fe, on my way to meet the girls at Fort Marcy Park. Tonight was the burning of Zozobra, or "Old Man Gloom," as he was affectionately called. Zozobra is a larger-than-life papier-mâché marionette. Every year he is burned at the stake as part of Fiestas de Santa Fe, a time-honored New Mexican tradition celebrating the anniversary of the city's settlement. Burning Zozobra is also a great excuse for a party.

Normally I would be in the best of moods. Zozobra meant the beginning of autumn, my favorite time of year, but right then I was not up for the celebration. My head was in a permanent fog, for all I could do was think about my friend Sharon. I don't know how, but it happened. Suddenly I had a crush on her.

The past few months had been hell. I agonized about telling her, weighing the cost. What if I revealed my feelings and lost her as a friend? I went crazy every time I was around her and even crazier when I wasn't. I told myself that if it didn't work out, I'd just forget about her.

I wasn't sure how I was going to accomplish that, especially since we all hung out together. We called ourselves Sisters in Black, the SiBs. We were all African-American, all lesbian, and we were inseparable. We went to the movies, shopping, the bar. We'd have breakfast, lunch, and dinner together. Tonight it was an excursion to Santa Fe. It would be Sharon's first Fiesta, and we couldn't wait to show her what it was all about.

Sharon had been in town almost a year. She was in the military, stationed in Albuquerque at Kirtland Air Force Base. I had seen her in uniform only a couple of times, but that was enough for me. I had fantasies about making her scream. We made love on my imaginary movie set—on the kitchen table, out camping, in the bathtub, and on the hood of my car. Hot nasty fantasies that left me wet, no matter where I was or what I was doing. I played them over and over in my mind until I could think about nothing else.

I couldn't stand it anymore. I was losing sleep and was sick of worrying about losing my friends. These women were my support system, my family. If I told Sharon I had feelings for her and it didn't work out, what would happen to the dynamics of our group? Fuck that. *What about the dynamics of my life?* I asked myself.

For the past two weeks, I had stayed close to home, trying to figure things out, and it got me nowhere. I missed everyone, especially Sharon.

Then came the phone call last night. I thought it would be Gina, one of the SiBs, calling to firm up plans for Zozobra.

"Hello?"

"Hey, girl, what's up?"

It was Sharon! "Where you been? Why haven't we seen you lately?" she asked.

It took several minutes and some of my best acting, but I finally convinced her I was just "laying low." When she was satisfied there was nothing wrong with me and that I would still be going to Santa Fe with the group, the interrogation took an unexpected turn.

"Let me ask you a question. How come you haven't settled down with anyone yet?" she asked.

"I don't know."

"That's all you gonna say?"

"Why you all in my business? I could ask the same thing about you," I said, feeling defensive.

"Don't get upset. Just answer the question."

"Girl, I'm too busy worrying about me."

"Why is that?" Sharon asked. "As long as I've known you, you've never been with anybody."

Because all I can do is think about you. "You haven't known me all that long," I said.

"Answer the question."

"OK! Hell, I don't know. They say you find the one you're supposed to be with when you aren't looking. And what about you?" I asked. "Why haven't you found the right one?"

"I guess I'm picky."

"About?"

"Mainly about the sex."

"Sex? I guess that's honest."

"Hey," she said, "I know you need to be friends and work on a relationship and all that, but good sex is just as important. To get with me, you gotta be special."

I could hear the smile in her voice. Sharon could be mischievous, and that's part of the reason I was so attracted to her. I relaxed, since the focus was off me. "Special," I said. "You sounding pretty bold, girl."

"I speak from experience."

"Oh, really?"

"Hey, it's all good."

Yeah, I knew it would be, if I'd only speak up. I wondered what Sharon was wearing right then. I pictured her on the couch in just a T-shirt, legs propped on the coffee table. I leaned back on my own couch and closed my eyes. "So what makes for good sex?" I asked.

"It has to be memorable."

"What does that mean?"

She laughed. "Honey, I want the kind of coochie you can call up from memory like the taste of your mama's peach cobbler."

I laughed too. "You don't know anything about my mom's peach cobbler."

"Yeah, I do. I likes to get all in it, have it all over me."

"The cobbler or the coochie?"

There was a pause. "Well, to tell you the truth," Sharon's voice dropped low, "I've been thinking a helluva lot about pussy."

The word jarred me. Maybe because I couldn't remember the last time I'd heard it said like that. Or maybe because I'd never heard her say anything like that. I cleared my throat. "Go on."

"Hey, you know, I've been single a long time," she said.

"Yeah. And of course your last girlfriend was the bomb in bed, huh?"

"Oh, yeah, we had mad sex, bumpin' pussies like bunnies."

"And what made it so good?" I asked.

"My girl put me through a lot of shit but knew some

things in bed. She could make me come just by playing with my nipples. Have you ever been that sensitive? With someone just sucking on them?"

"No, I–I can't say I have," I stammered. I could think of nothing else to say, but she had my attention. Every bit of it.

Her voice grew sexier, more intimate. "Don't you love it when you put your head between a woman's legs and she's already wetter than your tongue could make her?"

"Well–"

"And it's not just all over your mouth. It's on your cheeks and chin and eyelashes too."

I couldn't believe what I was hearing. "Eyelashes?" I said.

"Mm hmm."

I laughed. "You're crazy."

"I miss working my tongue on a woman's clit and looking up and watching her titties heave up and down."

Did she really say that? Suddenly, I realized my clit was asking for attention. This pillow talk was getting to me. I couldn't help it–my hand found its way between my legs. Damn, I was wet! I let out a small groan. Did she catch it? I swiveled the phone's mouthpiece to the top of my head to keep her from hearing what I was doing.

"What gets you excited?" she asked.

It took a second to get out the answer. My hand was feverishly working on my cunt, and I could barely keep my voice even. "Me?" I managed to say.

"Yeah, you. Tell me what you like." I heard rustling on the line. Did Sharon just switch ears, or was she getting as comfortable as I was?

"I forget."

"What kinda answer is that? Come on," she coaxed, "give it up, girl."

Was it my imagination? Or was her breathing a little errat-ic too? My hand slowed, but it didn't stop. "All right," I final-ly said. "I like it outdoors, OK? Especially when I'm camp-ing. You can be as naked as you want, and nobody's around."

"Outdoors, huh? I stop when the pavement does. Camping is not for me."

"But you're the big bad army girl. Don't they make you go out on maneuvers or whatever it's called?"

"Yeah, and that's part of the reason I don't like being out there unless I have to," she said.

"Well, one day you should try it out there."

"Well, maybe one day I'll get the opportunity. Tell me how wild it gets when you go camping."

Just then my call-waiting clicked in. Not now! The only person I knew who would call this late was Gina. As usual, her timing was the worst. Maybe it was a wrong number and I could just ignore it. The phone beeped again. It had to be her; I'd bet my last dollar on it. "Sharon, I have to get the other line," I said. "I'm sure it's Gina."

"No, you don't. Get on with the camping story."

"You know how she is. We won't get any peace."

Sharon sighed. "Let her call back!"

"It'll just take a minute."

"Look—"

"Hang on," I interrupted, and clicked over to the other line. Sure enough, it was Gina, wanting to finalize our Santa Fe plans. Since I was working so late, I'd join the group later. We would check out Zozobra, then head to the bar and go dancing. I quickly worked out the details with Gina and went back to Sharon.

"Well, that was convenient," she said.

"Hey, I didn't do it on purpose. I haven't talked to Gina

all week, and we needed to figure out where we should all hook up tomorrow."

"I forgive you. Now finish."

"Finish what?"

"Don't let me hang like this! You owe me a story!"

"I'll finish the story tomorrow," I said.

"Oh, hell no!" Sharon wailed. "Finish what you started!"

Gina's interruption had definitely changed my mood. And the reflection in the mirror with my shorts around my ankles didn't help either. "Girl, it's late. I'm going to bed."

"I can't believe you're gonna hang up!" Sharon protested.

"I'll tell you tomorrow, I promise. In fact, I have a lot to tell you."

"Tell me now!"

My mind was made up. I was done for the night. "You can wait one day," I told her.

"No, I can't."

"Well, you have to. I'm hanging up."

All day, I obsessed about our conversation. Over and over I wondered what would have happened if we hadn't been interrupted, although I had no way of knowing whether our little chat had affected her the same way it had me. Sharon was used to getting her way and definitely knew what she wanted. The question was, would she want me? I was making myself crazy. I had to make that move, and it had to be tonight. *This shit's gone too far*, I told myself. *If she kicks me to the curb, so be it.*

The plan was to meet the girls just inside the main entrance at Fort Marcy Park, then settle in to watch the burning of Zozobra. Fort Marcy could hold about 20,000 bodies, but it sorely lacked parking space. Most people left their vehicles downtown on the Plaza and hiked the mile or so to the celebration. I took a chance and looked for something closer. I finally found a road on a hill above the park that ended in a new cul-de-sac. There were several houses under construction and a few cars on the street. I thought it would be safe enough. I could even see Fort Marcy below.

I got out of my Honda and hesitated. On the one hand, I couldn't wait to see Sharon. On the other, I was afraid of what was going to happen when I did. *Just don't freak her out,* I told myself. How I was going to accomplish that was beyond me. I was freaked out. For a moment, I thought about just staying put and watching the fireworks from my car, but I forced myself to begin the trek to the park.

The entrance teemed with people trying to get through the gate at the same time. Many young children were dressed as little "glooms," racing through the crowd in ghost-like costumes and makeup, playing pranks as part of the festivities. There were souvenir and food booths, a mariachi band, and, of course, Zozobra.

He stood silent for now but would later come alive, moaning and thrashing about at the bidding of his puppeteers, then become engulfed in flames until there was nothing left of him. And there was a lot to burn. Old Man Gloom towered more than fifty feet. He was dressed in his usual bright red gown, buttoned from head to toe. On top of his long body sat an oversized head with saucer-like eyes that were supposed to look scary, but his wide mouth, crooked nose, and cauliflower ears made him appear comical. I smiled, forgetting about my queasy stomach.

"Hey, girl!" Gina pulled me from my thoughts. She, along with Tami, Vida, Janelle, and Sharon, was waiting just inside the gate, food and beverages in hand.

"Y'all couldn't even get a drink for me?" I asked.

"You just mad 'cause you gotta catch up," said Vida.

Sharon offered me some of her beer. "You ready to get into a little somethin'-somethin'?"

"Oh yeah!" I sang.

At least we were speaking. After the way I got off the phone last night, I wasn't sure how she would act around me.

Sharon was actually in a great mood, laughing and joking as always. I couldn't help checking her out. Her short curly hair was pulled tightly back in a ponytail, with bangs above her almond eyes. She was wearing jeans and a yellow sweatshirt that set off her mahogany skin. Her jacket was tied around her waist, outlining that sweet ass of hers. Damn she looked good. I had to stop staring at her, so I craned my neck upward and took another look at Zozobra.

Sharon stood next to me and looked up too. "I didn't think he'd be that big. Tell me about this shit."

"I will as soon as I get something to eat," I told her. Instinctively, I reached for my fanny pack and realized I had left it on my dashboard. I was so nervous about Sharon, it was a wonder I'd made it to the park at all. "Damn! I gotta go back to my car, y'all."

I felt like an idiot in front of Sharon. What would she think of me now? My friends chided me, but there was no way I could enjoy myself wondering if someone was gonna walk off with my shit, especially since I had left the invitation of cash and credit cards in plain view.

"I'll go back with you," Sharon offered. "Then you can tell me about Zozobra."

I didn't know what to say. And I was so surprised she volunteered to leave with me, I had to think hard about exactly where I'd left my car.

Sharon took charge and suggested everyone meet later at

the bar. It was obvious we wouldn't be able to find each other again in the sea of people, especially after the sun went down. We said our good-byes and began the long walk back to the cul-de-sac.

I was grateful to be alone with Sharon, although I couldn't stop my stomach from churning. I quickly began telling her about Fiestas de Santa Fe to hide my nervousness. "Back in the late 1600s, a Conquistador named De Vargas conquered this part of New Mexico. Folks have been celebrating ever since."

"I bet not everybody wanted to celebrate."

"I hear ya. But there's a Fiesta anyway."

"And Zozobra?"

"Invented to help with the party. They set Old Man Gloom on fire every year," I said.

"So what does he have to do with anything?"

"Part of Fiesta is letting go of past bullshit. And the way to do that is to burn Zozobra."

"I don't get it," Sharon said.

"The official story is he's been running around all year spreading doom and gloom. We put a stop to him and start fresh. A new beginning."

"But why burn the man? Can't they just tell him to lighten the fuck up?"

"Hey, he was actin' a fool all year. He had his chance to chill."

"So it's death by fire."

"Zozobra's the bogeyman. You gotta burn him. Besides, how else are they gonna light all the fireworks?"

"I get fireworks with this too? Viva la Fiesta!"

I laughed. Sharon's mood was light, but something was not quite right. She seemed preoccupied. Maybe it was my imagination. And after last night's conversation I couldn't find the courage to bring anything up. I had no idea when or how I was going to tell her how I felt. "We'd better hurry," I said. "It's gonna be dark soon."

"Damn, girl, where'd you park? Egypt?"

"We're almost there."

My little Honda was right where I had left it, valuables still inside. A few more cars had found their way to my secret parking spot, but no one else was in sight. I grabbed my fanny pack, extracted a couple of twenties, then shoved the bag under the seat. "Let's hit it," I told her.

Sharon didn't move. "You know, you got off the phone at a bad time last night," she said.

My stomach did a back flip. "Yeah, why is that?"

"'Cause we were just getting started. I couldn't believe you wanted to get off—the phone, that is." With a knowing smile on her face, she moved toward me.

She took my hand and leaned in to kiss me. I had always pictured our first liplock as sweet and sensual, but this was neither. We were rough and hungry as we explored each other. I finally pulled away. "I've wanted this for a long time, but I wasn't sure."

She kissed my collarbone, and as she moved up my neck, I felt a surge of electricity concentrated in the small of my back. "I wanted you too," she breathed in my ear, "but I wasn't sure either. And after last night...you got off the phone so quick."

All my fear and doubt melted away. I lightly brushed my lips on her face, then parted her mouth with my tongue. Finally! I turned her against the car, grinding my crotch against hers. My hands wouldn't keep still. I touched her everywhere at once.

Wanting more than just her clothes rubbing against me, I

moved her hand to the top of my jeans, and she yanked at the buttons. I leaned against the car and supported myself with both hands but continued to explore her mouth.

Sharon's hands slipped inside my panties, and I felt them slide down my thighs, exposing my skin to the night air. I felt the warm breeze against my wetness and across my ass, making me even hotter.

I finally pulled away from her mouth and looked into her eyes. I couldn't explain what I was searching for, but with the look she returned I somehow got the right answer.

She held my gaze while continuing to tease me. My clit now had a pulse of its own, the blood simmering just below boil. "Touch me," I pleaded. I concentrated on the feel of her hands, needing more.

In response, she ran her finger the full length of my crack but stopped just short, taking her hand away. "Tell me what you want," she said.

"Why you makin' me beg? You're driving me crazy."

"That's the idea."

I moved my hips, trying to catch up to her hands, but she kept one step ahead. "I can't take much more of this."

"Gimme some tittie," she said.

I took a step back to open my shirt and unhook the front of my bra. I was just the right height to feed Sharon one of my swollen nipples.

My breath caught in my throat as she put her mouth on me. She took in as much of my breast as she could and greedily began sucking. I felt a jolt as her hand finally gave me the release I needed. She slid her fingers in and began to move inside me. I thought my knees would buckle, but her other hand moved around my waist and held me tightly.

My moist cunt made noises as I fucked her hand, hips

moving along with my ragged breathing. I was surprised at how quickly I came, the orgasm rolling over me in wave after wave.

It took me a minute to recover, but I wanted to make love to her as much as I had needed her touch. "Your turn," I told her.

I took Sharon's jacket from around her waist and put it on the hood of the car. I turned back to her and kissed her long and hard while I unbuckled her belt.

"God, you feel good," she whispered.

"You too." With trembling hands I fumbled with her jeans. They did not come down as easily as mine, but I finally managed to get them over her ass. I picked her up and put her on the car. We locked eyes as she moved the jacket underneath her.

I kissed her again as I pushed her backward. I took one of the legs of her jeans and pulled it all the way off. To my delight, Sharon wasn't wearing any underwear. She lay back against the windshield, head cradled in her arm. "Come here," she said.

I put a knee between her legs and leaned over to kiss her. Taking her tongue in my mouth, I sucked gently as my hand wandered across her belly, then down to her thighs.

My mouth moved from her lips to her chin, then selfishly lingered on her throat. I wanted to explore every inch of her, to know this was real, not just another one of my fantasies.

I pushed her small breasts together and tongued a figure eight between them. Moaning, she put her hands on my head and aimlessly played with my hair. I blew on her wet nipples, then began kneading them between my thumb and forefingers. As I continued the motion, I used my tongue to make a wet trail on her torso. Every so often I retraced the pattern and blew on her skin, raising goose bumps.

I licked her belly and followed a thin line of fuzz down to the tight patch of short curly hair between her legs.

"Hurry, baby," she whispered.

Sharon arched up to find my mouth, and I obliged her. I inhaled deeply, taking in every bit of her. Her strong legs wrapped around my shoulders, and I was pulled into her salty moist box. My tongue flickered over her clit, and occasionally darted inside as far as it could go. She tightened her grip on my hair and undulated against my face. I continued working on her little button and roughly put two fingers inside her.

Her belt buckle played an urgent rhythm on the hood of my car, and I knew it wouldn't be long before she came. Sharon was more vocal than I had been, although I couldn't make out much of what she was saying.

Finally her body began to shudder. She cried out so loudly as she came that I was sure the entire neighborhood had heard.

I took her in my arms and held her. "I guess we'll have to head to the bar soon."

"We might not get there," she replied.

Fireworks began to fill the night sky. Zozobra was going up in flames for another year, marking a new beginning.

The Alley Below
by Karleen Pendleton Jiménez

I can't stop rubbing my hands together. The grooves in my skin make a muted high-pitched sound like a whistle. I watch the fingers fall off each other. The pink and warmth of the rubbing fade immediately. Beyond them gray water drips along the middle of the concrete. Cigarette butts, potato chip bags, and used condoms interrupt the stream.

I am squatting in an alley. The glare of red neon blinks on and off from the sign of The Flame. The bar is still open, and inside lesbians are smothering each other in drama and dance, but it does nothing for me but make me miss you more.

All right. I've gotta fess up. I left you, not the other way around. Everyone would be more comfortable with that. You, the married bisexual. You had no intentions of giving me up. But I left you the moment my ex popped back into my life.

I hadn't anticipated her return, I swear. She just called me up one day after three years of heartbreak and evasive tactics and told me "I'm ready," and so what could I do? You had come into my life only months earlier.

You, ever so proper. "I'm calling from the *Gay and Lesbian Times*," you cleared your throat, "I'm doing an article on the

142

word *queer*, and apparently you are one of the few activists in the city using this language." All straightforward and decent. Without any other motivations, except a meager paycheck.

I answered all your questions and suggested we should sit down and write together sometime. As a conscientious Canadian immigrant, you had already discovered the Southern California penchant for making imaginary plans. You tossed off my invitation as San Diego small talk. To be honest I often say I want to do things like coffee and lunch and never do them. It is usually enough for both parties to imagine them happening and smile at the possibility.

But with writing I am dead serious, and I will pretty much do it with anyone. I am a writing whore.

Months later we ran into each other at the front desk of The Center, and I said, "Hey, you never called me to write," and you said, "Oh, I wasn't sure if you were serious," and then a week later we met in The Living Room coffeehouse on University Avenue. I was ten minutes late. You had already figured I wouldn't show, as is typical local custom, when I walked in with my journal and pen. I sat down and took out a brown paper bag full of cat's-eye marbles. I reached in and grabbed a handful of the smooth cool drops of glass and rolled them into your fingers. You smiled first and then scrunched your eyebrows for a question. I like doing this, causing a subtle physical response followed by a bit of uncertainty. With methods no more complicated than this, I spend most of my time teaching writing to university students and community groups. I search secondhand stores, toy stores, parks, beaches, and the garage full of generations of my family's stuff for anything that looks interesting, that might trigger a memory or at least catch a person off guard when they see or touch it. And then I look out for a line to start with on a bus, a billboard, newspapers, television, or even what people mutter when they walk along the street. And somehow when I present the exercise I've come up with, people tend to trust me and start to write. "I gotta line," I tell them. "Just follow it, and don't think too much...."

You nodded, opened your laptop, and waited for my words. I began, "If you could see through to the other side of a marble...." You picked up a cat's eye and focused intently inside. When you found something there, you laid it back down and began typing. I rolled a marble around in my pocket and thought about the tiny air bubbles trapped inside. I wrote about smashing it open so that I could get to them but how, if I did that, I would just end up with blood and cut fingers. You took my line and went into beautiful prose, a bit of metaphor and some creepy little story about cobalt blue marbles and an ex-boyfriend drug dealer. It was perfect.

We kept meeting this way. I had the line, and you had the story, and afterward I told you about my sexual adventures with her on the beach and her with the mango and tamales and another her and a particular blanket.

I would never have told you so much had I known you were interested, had I known you frowned at the flirting happening between me and the assistant manager at the coffeehouse. She was cute, you gotta admit, but I was just having fun, and I had no idea about the eyes you were making at the end of our dark cherrywood table.

Then I would have understood why you invited me to the more private balcony beside your apartment. I gave you the line "You know, I didn't really want to kiss you" so that I could write about my anguish over recently kissing another ex. After ten minutes of frustrated scribbling, I'd adequately exorcised the memory from my skin. I looked up and saw that your eyes were rounder than usual. They had that five-year-old kid quality that comes over people when they're a little more vulnerable than they'd planned. Before I could ask, you told me to read first. I started pouring out the story of my ex using our abscessed cat as a reason for me to come over to her house. After I had rubbed the scab from his neck, she pulled out the tequila and seduced me with a careful combination of guilt and charm. I felt peaceful reading you the story, but when I raised my head off the paper I saw that kid look again.

"I'm going to read now, but I'm a little nervous," you explained, your face totally drained of color.

"It's OK if you don't want to read or if you just want to share what you're comfortable with." I immediately went into care-taking role, imagining you must have remembered some horrible nonconsensual encounter.

"You know, I didn't really want to kiss you, but thank you for this opening," you began with a shaky voice because you had forgotten to breathe in enough. I thought about how effective the use of second person can be, and how it really makes the listener feel like the writer is talking to her specifically. "I was telling you the other day about Maia, the first woman I had a crush on," you continued. "Wednesdays I'd have dinner with her before choir practice. She played in the orchestra, and I used to maneuver, as musicians filled my table, so that she would just naturally end up next to me or across the way. I saved up my best stories to entertain her, but I never told her she was keeping me awake at night. You asked me if at least I kissed her, and I said, 'No.' "

I nodded thoughtfully as I listened, and then blood shot into my ears. The shaky voice, the gratitude for the beginning...I began to feel uneasy about where this might be leading. My ears were getting hot, and I knew immediately they had become bright red, making my concern obvious. I hate that my body betrays me like this when I get nervous. "All that strategy, the lack of sleep, the dreams (making love to her in the back of a speeding taxi), for a year, maybe more, and not even a kiss. God, I should have kissed her." Relieved that you were only expanding further on this Maia lady, I scribbled in my notebook, "Nice imagery—I love the taxicab—what kind of seats were you on?" and thought about what it was like when I made out once with a woman in a San Francisco cab on vinyl seats that we kept getting stuck to.

After a deep breath you stopped my daydreaming with your conclusion, "It seems I'm still eating meals with women I want to kiss and not doing it. It's not because I don't want to kiss you. That's not a question. What I'm trying to do is use the prompt you give me to tell you something other than my best story."

And I learned immediately that wanting to write with someone is hardly a platonic arrangement. I focused on my toe wedging itself into the brick in the terrace. I sat there turning red and finding images like the speeding taxicab to pick out and compliment. And then I was the one who couldn't breathe. I made the mistake of raising my head for an instant in the middle of this looking down and spotted your heavy blue eyes. My professional critiquing went down the drain with the hunger I saw. You flipped your hand gently to offer it to me, and I reached and covered it with my own. My skin was so clammy that

I got even more embarrassed that our first touch had to be with my cold sweaty hand. And so I did kiss you because I couldn't go on sweating a puddle into your skin and forgetting to breathe. Besides, I thought it would make more sense to kiss you since you were pretty and all, even if I hadn't thought of it before.

The thing is, you told me you were married. And for a long time you hadn't mentioned a certain nonmonogamous aspect of the marriage. But more importantly you weren't my type. A sophisticated lady with silver golden curls—long magazine legs, plump breasts, pouty ass all covered in milky skin. You look like a portrait of an aristocrat displayed on a museum wall. I still hear someone whispering "Don't touch" when I reach for you. You look like what walked elegantly in big lights across the giant screens at the movie theater when I was growing up. I knew how to love only brown women. My mother with her arms around me in bed, pushing her fingers through my hair. My baby-sitter with a warm pink washcloth wiping the blood from my face when I hurt myself. I could stand on the corner of the street where I grew up and never see a white person. When you wrote about kissing me, I was as shocked as if you had poked your head out of my TV screen and invited me in. And so I followed in curiosity and astonishment.

I didn't know my ex would come back two weeks later. I swear. You were suspicious of a simple lunch date I had with her. And as is usually the case with femmes, I didn't know I would leave you for her as soon as you did.

Did you smell her on my skin the last time I came over? Did you feel it in my desperate biting? I devoured your neck. I dug my fingers into the long sweet curls and yanked your head back. Your tender throat was exposed, and I lunged for it. You let me bite you hard. You whimpered and screamed, but when I stopped, you only raised the raw skin back up to me for more. We had done a lot of this messing around. I made out with you every weekday while your husband was at work. You kept the bedroom doors shut. We never left the living room. Not so dangerous there. The high ceiling and shiny hardwood floors where antique furniture rested. It felt both luxurious and innocuous to me, like I had come upon a maiden in a castle high up above the city streets. I could corrupt you, but only to a certain point. Like the fairy tales. Besides, the couch was narrow with big clunky pillows. I couldn't just lay you out and fuck. Kissing and biting and rubbing would have to do. I pinched your nipples until they bruised and swelled. I shoved my thigh into your crotch. I wrestled my fingers past your zipper and pulled your panties up between your legs as you sat. I jerked them into your pussy as deeply as I could and heard you moan and shiver, but I couldn't reach what I really needed—the long hard strokes of my hand or my dick contained completely inside you, the act that would make us possess each other in some way forever. I am quite aware this is a heterosexual myth, but I still can't seem to shake it. So I wasn't through yet.

I had kissed my ex already. The night before. She had made it clear that I could expect something serious this time, that the only thing I should have been doing with you that afternoon was breaking it off. She and I hadn't made any promises yet. I thought I could at least have this one more thing before I left you. Then I would be OK. I wouldn't be so distracted while trying to be faithful to my new relationship. I could get it out of my system before things went any further so I wouldn't have to feel guilty about it. I think of your reading these words and cringing. The months of anger and sadness that have followed for you. It was pretty fucking selfish of me. I had thought I was a caring person. Women used to say they liked me because of my honesty, my straightforward approach to wanting them. And then somewhere along the line, I began needing them to want me back—to continue the wanting long after I had left the affair—to run into them months or years later at the supermarket and still see it all over their glassy eyes. To this day it makes me crazy to think that any of my former lovers could have stopped the wanting and gone on to someone else. It's a desperate part of me, as elusive to my understanding as the famine I feel when a woman jerks her body around two or three of my moving fingers.

I packed a sock above my harness. I carried the dildo in my book bag. I walked along the wide blocks of Park Boulevard to your apartment. I kissed you after we slid open the heavy metal doors of the ancient elevator. You asked about my lunch engagement, and I answered after a slight hesitation, "It was fine. It was nice to see her. She's happy with her new job." Everything simple and vague. You heard and understood it all immediately in what was not said. I might as well have told you we were eloping in Las Vegas the next day. You led me to the bedroom.

I started grabbing and tearing at your breasts. I slapped your ass with my other hand. I moved to your pants and began yanking them off you. You reached underneath me, attempted to grab my pussy to slow me down a bit, to balance out the power. All you got was a handful of bulge, and you understood what I'd come for. I tried to apologize. I don't know what you'll think of me. I'm never sure with lovers how they'll look at me again when I admit how necessary a thick pad of sock or silicon packed under my jeans is. How I feel more whole all of a sudden just walking with it down the street. How I'm on top of the world if I can then slip a condom and lube over a molded head sticking out from my harness and push in. I wanted to tell you I was sorry about wanting this from you.

"Get it ready." You answered my racing eyes and started stroking my thigh.

"Are you sure? Because really it's OK. I mean if you're not into it, I totally understand, and…." My shaky voice spilled out the words.

"Now," you said brusquely, squeezing it firmly. I started to pant.

I returned to you ten minutes later, after wrestling with leather straps and looking at my face and body from every possible angle in the bathroom just to make sure everything was right before we did this important intimate act together. You were frantic, biting gouges into your fingernails. "What took so long?"

I skipped a breath, and then I was a superhero flying over to the bed, climbing on and into you. I plunged. I have dived out an airplane into the warm soft clouds and fallen farther. I thought they would hold me there in the sun, so much brighter than what you find down in the city. But of course it's an illusion. I knew this when I jumped. I wanted to pretend otherwise. I fell instead into this wet dangerous place that burns and bleeds. Our bodies fractured upon impact. Our bones and organs crushed, and I kept beating on and looking down at the pain squinted across your eyes. "Fuck, fuck, fuck, what the fuck have we gotten ourselves into…." There are too many other people involved in our hearts. We were doing something irreparable. What the fuck were we thinking?

The next day I told you no more of this messing around, I had a wife to take care of now, a family to create. Then I spent the year flirting instead.

I met you for lunch and imagined through a polite carne asada burrito what it would feel like to jam my fingers inside you. I watched your pink lips tear at the tortilla. And the whole time we both chewed on the meat and rice, you saw it all over me—what I want. I need your trembling under me. It's essential that I run my nails along your back until the skin rises into plump red lines. I don't have to mention again about the neck and how we kidded around about the desperation of that guy in *The English Patient.* I won't be able to survive unless I wrap my hand around your ass and down the deep curve that leads into your waist. I need to tug at the long smooth hair covering your pussy. Baby, I'm gonna die if I can't lick the strong saltiness that sticks to my fingers just once more.

That's when the phone calls started. If you'd just let me say a few dirty things in your ear. If you'd let me talk about what I'd do to your body if I didn't have this girlfriend. Was it cheating when through plastic and wires I could hear the rustling of your body tensing and twisting until you came? My body shook too, and you knew it. I wouldn't give over my skin, but my eyes and words were yours. That only worsened your hunger. Why couldn't I just go away, since I had replaced my body and yours from the picture with my marriage to her instead? It pissed you off. And I don't really have an answer to that. You were supposed to have been doing the needing, not me. But I've never been too good at following the rules, especially when I make them. Absolutely no touching, right? And that's when I started burning.

That's when you took me home and took the dollar out. The crumpled bill that fell out of my pocket that very last time we fucked. You kept moving it from place to place in your apartment, trying to put me somewhere that wouldn't make you crazy. Only I kept getting closer, all the while telling you nothing could happen and succeeded instead in making you insane. So the next time you invited me up in your apartment, you led me to the balcony with the dollar bill, the Pyrex, and a box of matches. You wanted us to burn the money together and be rid of the memory cluttering your room. You were torturing me. I wanted to cry or fuck you to make you stop. You wanted me to do both so you could be sure you hadn't mistaken my interest as a childish game. In the end you let me take the dollar away in my wallet, and I thought I'd saved the situation, when really the thing meant nothing in my hand. It meant something only when you couldn't let it go.

We can't breathe enough to talk or even finish our meals. We are too restless to sleep. You lie awake, sweating in your marriage bed. I sit a hundred feet below you, rocking my body against the wall. Lesbians have begun to spill out of The Flame and are suddenly everywhere. It is two A.M., curfew time, and bodies are wobbling and sneaking and laughing too loud to remember there is a neighborhood around them trying to sleep. Young dykes with shaved heads and reflecting vests direct them to their cars and ask them futilely to keep the noise down. A couple has found its way to my alley. One of the women is in a black velvet dress that endearingly wraps around her chubby stomach. She pushes her boydyke, another young woman in a suit and tie with short black hair, against the wall twenty feet from me. They are kissing and rubbing in a frenzy, and I am sure they don't know I am watching. You always smile when I tell you about the alley fantasies I've had ever since I read a poem about two dykes making it in an alley somewhere in Chicago. I admit to you how I wait down here sometimes, hoping I'll catch you taking the trash out or getting something from the car. We would be the ones smashing against this wall in the night. My fingers would be warm and safe inside you.

I pull the dollar bill from my wallet. I rub my fingers along the creases. I try to remember every movement from that one afternoon for each crumpled line through the president. It's too simple to blame that single day. If it hadn't been the fucking, it would have been the imagining of the fucking. It started maybe with the interview, maybe with the kiss. It won't end until we have devoured each other, torn out every vein, dug deep into the source of each other's blood. There won't be anything left when it's over. And that will be the biggest joke of the whole thing. We will have destroyed our marriages for a mess of our corpses laid out on the beautiful hardwood floors of the penthouse apartment. Your husband will be bitter cleaning us up; my girl-friend might be so angry that she would miss my funeral. But you would not have to worry about the enormous sighs keeping you up every night. And I would not be stuck lurking in trashy alleys, grabbing pathetically at the crotch of my jeans and your shadow through the blinking red lights.

Somebody Famous

by Lauren Johnson

I slept with somebody famous. I won't tell you who it is because she wouldn't like it, and you probably wouldn't believe me anyway. It's true, though, and she was so perfect, perfect, from her feet with extraordinarily long toes ("I never let my feet show on camera." She laughed when she said it.) to her slate-blue eyes. I write poetry, you know, so I can say things like "slate-blue eyes" and get away with it, but if you had been me at just 18, you would have found the words to describe her eyes. Yeah. You would have.

She tapped me on the shoulder at the coffee cart at the studio. I could say I didn't recognize her at first, but you know that would be a lie. She wasn't supposed to arrive for two more days, and I was so shocked I almost dropped the cream pitcher.

"Hi." She introduced herself, needlessly, and I managed to respond by telling her my name. She nodded at it, not really listening, and then inexplicably reached out and touched the collar of my shirt as her eyes flicked over my body.

"The costume designer, Marla, have you met her?" I shook my head. I had no idea where this was going.

"No? Well, she spotted your shirt and necklace, and she

got a wild hair to try them in the apartment scene. I told her I'd ask you." She didn't smile.

"For you? For you to wear?"

"Yeah, but don't feel pressured. You don't have to say yes." She smiled at my confusion.

"No...I mean sure, no problem. I don't mind at all."

"Really? Great." She seemed relieved. As if she was used to people telling her no. About anything. As if I wouldn't have taken the shirt off right there and then and handed it to her. Not because of who she was. Just because of her. This is an important point, and I want this clear. I was not mesmerized by her fame or any of that crap. I've been on sets since I was a kid, and I've met lots of actors and famous types, and a lot of them are nothing, I mean nothing, special. My uncle, he's a producer, and he's always trying to get me to write screenplays, like I know anything about anything but poetry. But he's the reason I was there in the first place. He was producing the thing. But I don't think she knew that. I mean, I don't think she knew I was his niece. Not right then.

"OK, you want them now?" Stupid me.

She laughed. "Sure, shed 'em. We'll switch." A sudden gleam flashed in those slate blues. I could see she was half serious.

"You wouldn't." I didn't mean it as a challenge. I just thought she wouldn't.

"Wanna bet?" She was ready.

Well, hell, I wasn't going to let myself be shown up by some half-grown child-prodigy starlet type, even one who was pretty damn good at what she did and had those eyes. She was only four years older than me (four? five?), but she was already a woman, and I was just a kid wanting what she had, wanting it bad. Not the fame. Not the money. Just the knowing.

"I will if you will." She'll say no, I reasoned.

"Ready?" She was grinning like crazy, and all I could think was, *Jesus, when was the last time I shaved my armpits?*

"Go!" Off came both of our shirts, and my necklace, a heavy silver ball with golden imprints on a black cord, and any ounce of propriety I had known thus far. People on the set stopped to gape. I caught only the slightest glimpse of her body—black bra on lightly tanned smooth skin. She tossed her shirt to me, but our hands brushed lightly as I handed mine over. I felt my face go hot and every pore of my skin open up. It was like stepping into a cold shower. I blushed, and my nipples went hard. I struggled with the shirt—I wanted it on before she saw. My shirt slid over her body as if it belonged there and settled on her shoulders like snowfall. Her shirt (Oh, god! Her smell!) caught on my arm, and, now giggling hysterically, she helped me untangle myself from my new garb. She gave me a quick squeeze.

"You've got a bit of exhibitionist in you. I'm impressed."

"Your idea." I was flushed, but with embarrassment?

"Right. I've gotta go." She grinned jauntily at the gawkers and disappeared around the tailgate of a trailer. I tried to walk nonchalantly the other way, but my legs were wobbly, and my flush was growing.

At six o'clock the next morning, my Uncle Dana accosted me as I came down the stairs for breakfast.

"What the hell is this I'm hearing? Are you trying to give me an ulcer?"

I was staying with him for the summer with my parents' reluctant approval. Uncle Dana knew I was a little dyke because he himself was as gay as boys come, although you'd never know it to look at him. He was thick-shouldered and hard-headed, with a quick temper and a generous nature. I

adored him. Tony, his lover, put a plate of pancakes in front
of me and snickered.

"We knew you started early, Janie, but please!" Tony
chuckled. He was amused. He shot me a smile and a "go for
it" look over Uncle Dana's head.

"Don't encourage her!" Uncle Dana whacked the table
with his hand. He was my mother's baby brother, and she
adored him, respected him, coddled him, and was just plain
afraid of him, with his wild ways.

"It was completely her idea." No way was I taking all the
blame for this. I defended myself hotly. "She just came up
to me, and next thing I knew...."

"What next? That girl already has a reputation as a wild
ass, and I see she's living up to it. I'm sure she has no idea
you are jailbait."

"I am not any such thing! I've been 18 for three months!"
Sometimes Dana really pissed me off.

"Does that law even apply to two girls?" Tony interjected
diplomatically. He poured more coffee for Dana.

"That and other laws, I'm sure. Now I mean it, Janie, keep
me out of the tabloids, would you? Stay away from her.
Don't be following her around and stuff."

That made me mad. I don't like starfuckers, if you'll par-
don the expression.

"I didn't! I didn't even know she was there! She just..."

"All right, all right. I believe you. Just keep your mind
on being an intern, not a budding lesbian. Your mother's
going to blame me for the rest of my life as it is. I don't
need you getting some for the first time on the job I set
you up in." He touched Tony's arm as he passed him the
bagels. They'd been together ten years that March. I
watched in envy.

"What do you mean the first time?" The implication of his remark had just registered. Tony jumped in immediately.

"You mean you've already…"

"All right, all right!" Uncle Dana stood up and threw his napkin on the table for emphasis. "I want to know nothing about it, you hear me? That way when her mother injects me with truth serum I'm safe. Come on, we've got to be there by 7:30. Love you." He kissed Tony quickly.

Uncle Dana said nothing on the way to the shoot, but as he parked and I rolled out of the passenger door he grabbed my sleeve.

"Keep your shirt on today, will ya?"

I couldn't help looking for her on the way to the production office. It was unlikely she would be out wandering, but I looked anyway. My stomach shifted uncomfortably. I felt an electric current running from about mid thigh up to my brain. Looking back, you might call it an attack of teenage lust. Then it felt like an illness.

I was on time to work, if you could call it that, and the unit production manager, Dave, nodded in my direction to acknowledge me. My "job" as an intern was a joke, and I knew it. Uncle Dana thought it would be fun for me to hang around the set, and it was for the first twenty hours. After that it was boring, boring, boring. I tried to work on my newest poem, but my mind was wandering. Someone tapped me on the head from behind.

"Hey, kid, your uncle wants to know if you want to give me a hand today." It was Nora, the second or third assistant director, an energetic round-hipped girl with a good smile. "You know anything about props?" I shook my head, and she looked heavenward with a "Why me?" expression, softened by the punch she gave me on the arm.

"That's OK. I can always keep you busy getting me coffee."

The apartment scene was being shot first today on Sound Stage 12. She was already there, in the center of a group of her friends and I guess her "people." Pretty, very pretty, the girls she kept around her. Nora glanced over.

"The entourage," she mumbled. "Over here, Janie, and quit staring." My head snapped around. She hadn't seen me, but she was wearing my shirt. Just for a second, I imagined her in my other clothes, putting on my jeans after climbing out of my bed after a night of...

"Hey, Janie. Hello!" Nora waved her hand in front of my face. "What's the matter with you, kid? Maybe I should get *you* some coffee."

Nora put me to work. I was grateful for the distraction. Uncle Dana ambled in, acknowledged her and the ladies-in-waiting, and took a second to give me an appraising glance. He seemed satisfied that I was suitably distracted. About half an hour later, Nora crooked her finger in my direction.

"Dean says you can stay on the set and watch the takes." Her look said I should be honored, or surprised, or both.

"Who's Dean?"

"The director!" Nora rolled her eyes again. "But she usually closes the set. So stay out of the way and maybe you'll slide by." The warm crawl from my throat to my stomach told me it wasn't Dean who had said I could stay and watch. I glanced over at her. She was looking in my direction. Her eyes flickered at me; I knew they had, but I held myself still and gave no sign until she let a smile play across her lips.

I was taken. I was too young to be coy. I smiled for all I was worth. She laughed and tapped her watch. I had no idea what she was saying, but I nodded and grinned and agreed to it, whatever it was.

I could tell you the shooting was breathtaking, her performance incredible, that she dazzled me with her intensity and talent, and you would buy it all, because you know her from the screen, and all these things are true at times, when you watch her work. But the truth is being there is slow, irritating, repetitive, and mechanical. Unless you're standing behind the monitor, you can't see the performance, and I was stashed over by what had to be a broom closet. Every once in a while when the crowd of grips and assistants shifted, I saw a glimpse of her face or my shirt. If you can be bored and riveted at the same time, that's what I was as I watched for a flash of that shirt or the body inside it.

I felt a sudden tug on my arm. It was Dana, with his finger over his lips to indicate I should say nothing. Since they had called for quiet on the set, I was screwed. I had to follow him out with nary a protest. Angrily, I trailed him to his so-called office, really a borrowed trailer he was using during the shoot.

"Sorry to distract you from your obsession." Dana teased me good-naturedly as he punched in his message code on the office phone. "I thought we'd head home early today and...Mother of God." Dana sighed and wrote down the phone number someone was rattling off in his ear. "Jerry, get me a reservation at Vincente. Promise that snotty door whore whatever you have to." Jerry, my uncle's secretary, flipped open his over-used cell phone. "But for God's sake keep it under a hundred bucks. It wasn't the only restaurant in Los Angeles last time I checked."

"What's the matter?" I shifted my pencil to the other useless hand and looked at him.

"I've got to take this guy's family to dinner tonight. Important possibility, you know the drill." I did; Dana was always taking people to dinner because they said maybe to something. "It's going to be early. Do you think you can stay here until I get back? Watch TV or something? Driving all the way back to the Valley would be a hassle."

I shrugged. I was used to this. Things constantly came up that I was not invited to. I didn't mind; sitting through the dinners was far more excruciating than being excluded from them. The few times I had gone, there was usually some 20-year-old son slobbering on me or asking me to go into the bathroom for some blow. I wasn't into it—the guys or the blow. Better to be here, with the bunk bed and the television. The trailer was equipped with both of these things plus a small kitchenette and a bathroom. It was used for location shooting, but Dana always managed to wrangle the use of it whenever he wanted. He was a convincing guy.

I woke up to a distinct tapping on the trailer door. The TV was on. I was disoriented. I didn't remember falling asleep. Tap, tap, stop. Tap, tap, stop. I sat up on the little bunk, but before I could stand the door squeaked open and the blue eyes swung over my jeans (on the floor) and my white T-shirt (on my body) to my face.

"Napping? Not bored, are you?" I didn't—couldn't—respond right away. I reached for my jeans.

"Don't on my account. I just brought your stuff back. Can I come in?" She was already in, but I nodded anyway.

"Where's your uncle?" So she did know.

"At some dinner."

"Business, no doubt." I nodded again. She was very close to me now. It was a small trailer. Her long-fingered hand reached for the TV remote and flipped the channel to the football game.

"Do you mind? I'm a UCLA fan." And that's how I

remember it. Play by play, with whistles and cheering in the background. She is golden-haired all over and smooth and sweet. She put her hands in my black hair first and murmured softly about how thick and soft it was. Her hand crept around to my mouth, and I kissed her fingers first, kissed them and then took them in my mouth before she slid them to my back and turned me over, over on the bunk bed to face her.

"You're so young."

"So are you." I was bolder now that my hands were under her shirt and there was no resistance.

"I'm a lot older than I look. Let me see that body again." Effortlessly she slid my shirt from my shoulders and pushed me down gently. Her mouth brushed my breast in an almost kiss, and her hand slid down to my embarrassingly pristine white cotton panties. But she did not seem embarrassed by them as she pushed her hand inside and touched me gently.

"You've been with a girl before, yes?" I nodded, unable to speak as her fingers stroked me into silence. "You started early." It was only a partial lie. I had kissed a girl—several, actually—but I had never…done what she was doing to me now. Abruptly she took her hand away and stood.

"What time is it?" I managed to gasp. She locked the trailer door and turned to me with a half grin—now a very famous half grin—and returned to the bed.

"You have somewhere to go?"

"No…my uncle…"

"Not to worry, sweetheart. Jerry told me he'll be tied up until at least ten."

Lying beside her, almost beneath her, on the narrow bunk, I traced the outline of the stubborn chin with my finger as she kissed the soft line from my belly to my crotch.

Gently she urged my knees apart and up, and I gasped when her mouth closed on me and her tongue arched upward. She explored me as if we had all the time in the world; in fact, she gave me all the time, taking me to the edge and then pulling back playfully to ply my soaking-wet pussy with only gentle teasing kisses until she had me slowed down, then flicking my clit with her tongue again and again until I cried for her to stop. When she pushed inside me with her fingers, I pulled her shoulders to me and kissed the top of her head as I came. I was awkward, I know now, returning the caresses, returning the pleasure, but not so awkward that I didn't find the place where my tongue made her cry out and press me closer, and not so awkward that I couldn't turn her on her stomach and push into her from behind at her urging. My fingers slid in and out of her. She was wet and slick and hot on my hand. I was gentle at first. Too gentle. She turned and looked at me.

"It's all right. Go ahead and fuck me." My eyes must have gone wide, because she laughed and grabbed my wrist, shoving me inside her. I put aside whatever fear there was and took her like I wanted to—fast and hard, 'til she collapsed, panting and trembling. Seconds ticked by. Then she reached for me, slid my hand up to her breasts, and held it there until the trembling stopped.

We both jumped at a soft knock on the door. I recognized Jerry's voice.

"He just called. He's on his way." She got up then, smiled at me, and reached for her clothes.

"I do like this shirt," she said, tossing it at me. "Thanks again for the loan."

"Keep it." I tossed it back at her. "I'd like for you to have it." She caught it and gave me that half grin. After a second's reflection she tossed me her shirt—a UCLA jersey that had seen a few washings.

"It's a trade." I touched her thigh as she buttoned her jeans. She pushed my hair out of my face and kissed me again on the mouth.

"You'll be around?" she asked.

I shook my head. "I go home in a week."

"I only have two more days here. Then I'm flying to Japan." She touched me again. I kissed her fingers, and she slipped out of the trailer.

And that's it. Don't ask me to tell you who it is, 'cause I won't, but you can use your imagination. And don't ask me if I ever saw her again, because I didn't, except that I own a very special copy of a certain movie, and every once in a while when my lover isn't home and I'm feeling like remembering, I'll put on a very old UCLA jersey and pop the tape in the VCR. Then when Sharon gets back, I'll take her to bed in the middle of the day, much to her surprise and pleasure.

"What's gotten into you?" she asks as she strips off her shirt, showing me her beautiful full breasts and strong shoulders. I smile, but I don't tell, not the whole story, not ever. It's something you should keep to yourself, I think, when you've slept with somebody famous.

Diesel Donuts
by Ilsa Jule

Part I

As Lu and Dee peered at the huge selection of donuts, Dee leaned back, resting most of her weight into the heel of her boot, playfully crushing Lu's toes. "Ow, ouch, you're killing me," Lu deadpanned. "Don't the donuts look glamorous? I always thought fluorescent lighting made things look dead. Those donuts could come to life and hurt me."

Dee turned so that her cheek brushed Lu's and said, "There are so many of them, I can't decide which one I want."

Lu leaned hard into Dee and draped her arms over Dee's shoulders. She pointed at the donuts and said, "That cruller looks good."

Dee thought it was odd seeing Lu's fingers instead of feeling them inside her. She gazed at the hand hungrily and thought perhaps they should have stayed in bed.

Lu added, "Looks good enough to stick in your ear."

Dee replied dreamily, her hair against Lu's face, "I suppose the only way to find out is to buy it and—"

Lu cut the sentence short by rubbing her fingertip first along Dee's lower lip and then inserting it into Dee's mouth and stroking her tongue.

Dee bit down on the finger, and Lu felt herself get a hard-on instantly. Lu wondered if the donut thing was going to work out. *We probably should have just stayed in bed. Getting dressed is such a hassle. Of course there is the undressing to look forward to.*

They were in the donut shop at Dee's insistence. Lu, being a gentleman, allowed breaks for meals, although she herself would never let anything like hunger get in the way of fucking. Lu predicted that the remark about the ear would get to Dee. It referred to their first night together some weeks ago when Dee still had a boyfriend. Lu had never fucked anybody in the ear before, but their first time together required all the resourcefulness Lu had acquired through decades of pleasing women.

They had ended up on Dee's couch, which, as luck would have it, converted into a bed—and wasn't the only thing that was converted that night. Lu was propped on her elbows, lying on top of Dee. They were giving each other small kisses, wondering what it was the other might like. The lights were off.

Lu had felt Dee tense up when she reached over her to tug the little pull chain turning off the lamp.

"Are you OK?" Lu asked.

"Umm, not really," Dee said, biting her lower lip.

"Do you want me to turn the light back on?" She watched Dee's expression in the fluorescent glow from the streetlight.

Lu thought to herself, *It's that damn boyfriend getting in the way. How serious can she be about a guy she won't live with anyway?*

Lu felt responsible for the outcome of their first date, since it was Lu's experience that Dee was counting on. Even though Dee had been the one to devise the evening. After months of flirting over the phone, she'd invited Lu over when her roommate went away for the weekend.

Lu ached to fuck Dee. She moved so that they weren't so mashed up into each other. "What's up?" asked Lu, not ready to give up on this mission.

"I'm way past bending the rules," Dee said forlornly, invoking *his* presence with the small sentence. Lu had assumed they were past bending the rules when Dee had lifted up Lu's shirt and started kissing her breasts. That was all the way back in sitting position.

"Look, I'm not going to fuck you, so don't worry about it," Lu said firmly.

This seemed to be what Dee wanted to hear. She relaxed, reached up, and pulled Lu's face back down to hers. Lu was kissing her and contemplating the fucking-while-not-fucking angle. The dyke in her knew it could be done. She undid Dee's bra one-handed, and Dee remarked, "You're very good at that." Lu laughed, pressing her face between Dee's shoulder and neck. With a mouthful of shirt, she muttered something about "years of practice," and Dee laughed also. Lu looked up to catch her smiling and saw the light reflect off the small even teeth.

In the weeks that led up to that first night, Dee had expressed unhappiness about having a boyfriend. She said she yearned for a girlfriend but wasn't sure how to go about getting one. Lu knew Dee meant "female lover," not "girlfriend." She and Dee would have a short-lived fierce sex life, and Lu would have to leave, as her cultivated dyke desires could not be wholly satisfied by Dee's eager but inexperienced newfound lesbian identity. This did not discourage Lu from kissing her; Dee's mouth became softer with each kiss.

Dee pulled Lu into the fullness of her breasts. "Your skin is so soft," said Dee, a note of surprise in her voice as she ran a hand along Lu's back, "softer than mine." Lu's hands caressed Dee's waist and eagerly awaited a visa for *down there*.

"Don't mark me," Dee implored, pulling away as Lu nibbled on her neck.

Looking her in the eye and pressing her pelvis with force into Dee's, Lu reassured her, "I won't fuck you, and I won't mark you."

Lu's nipples got hard as Dee lifted her head from the cushion and bit into her. She added, "But you can mark *me*." As Dee sucked harder, Lu was glad to be the first, and not the last, woman Dee would leave a mark on.

Nibbling Dee's lips kindly, Lu ran her hands across Dee's breast's, pinching the nipples—she wondered what color they would be in daylight. She continued to ponder the fucking-while-not-fucking thing. Lu ran the tip of her tongue along Dee's ear, then jabbed her tongue inside the ear and tasted the bitter wax. Dee drew her breath in sharply.

Lu realized she could fuck Dee without actually fucking her. She pressed the tip of her index finger into the opening of the ear canal. As Dee's breathing got heavier, Lu noticed that *he* was no longer in the room. There hadn't been enough room for the three of them on that small couch. As she pressed her fingertip into Dee's ear, she whispered into the other one, "I'm not going to fuck you." Dee lifted her pelvis and groaned. She grabbed Lu's hands, pulled them to her waist, and guided them down her stomach and inside her pants. Lu resisted the urge to put her hands *down there* as she felt Dee's soft stomach. Her fingertips hazarded the elastic waistband of Dee's bikini underwear.

While it is true that the pussy is usually located below the waist, Lu knew it could be found in other places. She had once located it in the fold of skin below the armpit.

Dee started moaning softly, and Lu realized Dee knew when she'd said "I'm not going to fuck you" that she was playing a game that all schoolchildren play called "Opposites." Dee's back started to arch, and she was grinding her pelvis into Lu's. Dee rubbed the tip of her index finger back and forth along the short hair at the base of Lu's neck. Where the electric razor of the barber scolded biweekly, Dee's touch now assuaged any hard feelings.

Lu thrust her pelvis into Dee's, returned her fingertip to Dee's ear canal, and cleared her mind of all thought. With her free hand she grabbed the frame of the couch, sand-wiching Dee between her and the cushions. Their hips moved together, and they had a small joint celebration called an orgasm.

When one considers that months of flirting over the phone and being attracted to someone does not guarantee against disaster or disappointment, one small orgasm can be classified as quite an achievement.

Lu opened her eyes, her heart racing, and Dee said, "Did you know this couch turns into a bed?"

Lu laughed, stood up, pulled Dee to her feet, then stated, "Then I think it's time we got in bed."

It became clear to both women that the boyfriend's tenure was up, and Lu's time had just begun.

Part II

That big ol' butch Lu wants you to think she's clever, that

we ended up on my couch and then in my bed and that this was all her doing. As if.

It's true that those huge hands reshaped my way of thinking. While she was caressing me, a portion of the credo of the arts and crafts movement of the 19th century I had memorized for an art history class popped into my mind. "A hand-crafted object is inherently more desirable, beautiful, and worthy of human endeavor than anything made by machine." I had seen objects made by hand and by machine and could tell they were different, but I had never quite known the difference. I realized through my experience with Lu that the hand imparts an ineffable quality. I wanted her to mold me. I am not sure if this means that lesbianism, rather than art history, needs to be added to curricula.

Lu left out the part she doesn't know about. The part where I was riding the bus to go window shopping downtown, then I saw her and decided I could wait on a wardrobe I couldn't afford anyway.

Sure, she got me into the sack, but she didn't do it with a phrase or a touch; she did it on the bus, just by the way she was standing there. The way the back of her neck, fresh from the barber, presented itself like an engraved invitation cordially requesting my presence at a gala event. Her neck was graceful, contrasting the hardness of the rest of her.

Upon seeing her I felt struck by a Sapphic thunderbolt. I am not the only who experiences this. She stirs desire in people. I have noticed even men take a liking to her. That's a waste of their time. She's just a closed-minded butch. Not that she doesn't have good reason to be closed-minded.

For me, I prefer open-mindedness. If I didn't have a sense of options, I never would have annoyed the bus driver as I jumped through the closing doors. He barked at me, "Lady, ya tryin' ta get yasself killed or what?" I laughed, fell a few paces behind, and tailed her. I watched her feet, big in men's shoes, looking like men's feet, as they owned the pavement. I liked how she filled the shape of her overcoat. I thought it was a joke, that a woman looked handsome.

I hoped she wasn't on her way to meet someone. When she stepped into the supermarket parking lot, I felt relief. She ignored a group of giggling teenage girls leaning against a car. As I passed this same group, I overheard one of them say, "I want to marry a man like that." I couldn't be sure she wasn't referring to Lu. Her appearance spoke in ideals.

I noticed her hands as she pulled out a shopping cart. They were enormous. I was glad she didn't look around, that she seemed caught up in her own sense of being. She didn't need me. Yet.

I grabbed one of the blue plastic baskets and wondered if I could play a woman the way I could a man. I stepped near her in aisle five, reached right in front of her, and grabbed a jar of spaghetti sauce. She looked up, disregarded me, and moved along.

I came close to frisking her. I wanted to pickpocket her, to glean personal details: Where did she live? Whose photo did she carry? Was she into herbal tea and cats? Black coffee and a dog? Or ginseng tonic and a bird?

She continued to walk the aisles, brooding, with a tendency to bump into other people's carts. She was completely oblivious to small children. She had the standard bachelor diet: frozen entrees and sports drinks. It wasn't until we passed the pastries and she selected a box of chocolate eclairs that it occurred to me she might have a girlfriend.

I was determined, even though she might be married, to

at least speak to her. She was heading to the checkout, and I knew if I didn't act fast, I would lose my nerve. I grabbed for something, anything, and when I reached her I said, "Excuse me, sir, I think you dropped this." She looked at me, figured out I was the woman in the spaghetti aisle, and asked churlishly, "What?"

I raised my hand and laughed when I noticed I was holding a box of maxi pads. At this she started to smile and then laughed. When she smiled she didn't look like a man at all. She had pretty teeth, and the shape of her eyes changed. She appeared powerful in a way she would use to make you feel happy, not sad.

Once the thrill of the maxi pads dimmed, I asked for her phone number. She said "You can call me at work" and handed me her card.

è   è   è

A few weeks later, I felt the scratchy wool cuff of her overcoat as we stood next to each other. We had decided to go to the only store open this late on a Sunday night, the 24-hour bakery that was a short bus ride from bed. Lu was standing behind me, leaning into me. I liked when we both agreed that holding hands was just too conventional, and so we'd stand close, pressed into each other.

Men and women want her. I want to laugh at the men who smile at me when she and I walk down the street as a couple. As if I would ever consider their brief proposals. If they could feel her lips (and no man ever has or will), they would know in an instant just how stupid the idea that I would ever let them touch me was. Her kisses have the feel of a nice afternoon in grade school. I like that she has the heart of a woman and the body of a man (sort of). Her knees get pink during sex. Afterward, I rub lotion into the abraded skin. Who knew cotton sheets could be so brutal?

As we stood at the counter, I looked out the window, and a bus went by, sending snowflakes from a drift into the street, like a small ghost. I cleared my throat and said loudly "Excuse me" in the direction of the counter woman, who continued to ignore us. Lu took a napkin off the counter, crumpled it up, and threw it toward the woman. It wasn't supposed to hit her, but it bounced off the hot-chocolate machine and landed in the fold of the newspaper she was reading. She looked up and glared. We both suppressed a laugh. She walked up to us, "Yeah, what do you want?"

In a friendly voice, Lu said, "We'll take two of the choco-late-creme donuts, please."

The counter woman looked puzzled and said, "You're a woman?"

"Kind of," answered Lu.

Part III

Lu and Dee waited in the bus shelter, Lu holding Dee and the bag of donuts. Lu, who is in the habit of horsing around in public, of speaking her opinions loudly and not caring what others think of her, started jostling Dee. Dee laughed it off, and then as Lu pushed with more force, Dee implored, "Baby, please stop. That man just mouthed, 'Are you all right?' to me."

Lu stopped messing around. Something in Dee's tone Lu had not heard before. It hinted at conclusions.

Lu contented herself with placing her arm around Dee's

shoulders. She liked the way Dee's neck fit perfectly in the crook of her elbow. As if Lu were meant to hold her that way. Not like a headlock from one butch to another but with a sense of comfort and security. Lu pulled Dee close and sniffed her sweet hairline.

When they got back to Dee's, as soon as they were in the door, the cool night air still fresh on their clothes, Dee turned and, with a bright look in her eye and a sharpness in her voice, commanded, "Don't you ever shove me in public again."

Lu felt sucker punched. She resisted an urge to shout back. Instead she stood frozen, as if her feet weighed thirty pounds each. She was puzzled as to why Dee had waited so long to reprimand her. And why was it she felt she needed to reprimand her? Couldn't she just have easily asked her not to do it? Lu was unable to gauge how much of a threat the words posed. And did it mean that Lu was free to hit Dee in the privacy of her home?

"I'm sorry," Lu said, clearly not used to taking orders.

Dee sensed that the way in which she spoke had carried more meaning than the words. She said quietly, dropping her coat onto the couch, "I just don't want people to think it's OK for a man to hit a woman. That's all."

Lu stood in place feeling as if her heart had stopped and then said defensively, "Oh, right, I forgot I'm a man."

"People think you are. You owe it to yourself as a person, and to other women as a lesbian, to be the one man who sets an example of decency."

"I was just horsing around. I didn't mean anything by it."

Dee raised her arms and said, "Baby." As soon as Lu was in Dee's embrace, the tiff passed, and the fear that had bristled Lu subsided.

They slowly fell to the couch. Dee took one of Lu's fingers

and started to suck it, pushing it slowly in and out of her mouth.

"I know you're a woman; that's why I love you. It's just hard for me sometimes."

Lu kept her head in Dee's lap while Dee continued to suck her finger, Dee's mouth feeling more like a pussy. "Why is it I can't be an unconventional woman?" Lu asked.

Dee lifted Lu's head out of her lap, stood up, dropped her pants, and then straddled Lu. "You cannot be an unconventional woman, my dear, as long as you remain a conventional man," said Dee.

Lu laughed out loud, "Now there's some logic for you."

Dee took Lu's face in her hands, gently rocking her hips, and covered Lu's face with tiny passionate kisses.

"I thought you were hungry," Lu said, ignoring the effect the kisses were having on her. Lu reached over, pulled one of the donuts out, and licked off some of the chocolate filling.

"Baby, please," begged Dee, pressing into Lu, feeling the wool pants against the inside of her bare thighs. Dee reached to take the donut from her.

Lu swung her arm away and held the donut out of reach.

"Honey, I really think you should eat. You're going to need all your strength," said Lu, who then took a big bite out of the donut.

"I don't want to eat right now," sulked Dee.

With Dee still sitting on her lap, Lu continued to eat the donut. "This is a really tasty donut," said Lu.

"I can think of something else that's tasty," said Dee.

"Really?" said Lu.

"Yeah, and it also starts with the letter *d*."

"Hmm," Lu closed her eyes, chewed, then swallowed.

"Let's see, *pussy* doesn't start with the letter *d*, nor does *finger* or *fist*."

Dee slapped Lu's face. Lu smiled.

"Aren't you going to eat your donut?" asked Lu, her hand loudly rummaging in the bag.

"I don't give a fuck what happens to that donut," said Dee, who moved to stand.

Lu encircled Dee's waist with her free arm and pulled her back down to her lap.

Neither of them spoke. Lu started to eat the second donut. Dee looked out the window, with Lu in her peripheral vision.

After finishing the last bite, Lu smacked her lips loudly. She licked her fingers in an exaggerated fashion. Knowing Dee could see her every move, she shoved three fingers into her mouth. She took her time pulling them back out. "Mmm."

While Dee continued to look out the window, Lu lifted Dee's ass slightly with one hand, and with the fingers that had been in her mouth she pushed past the underwear and buried two fingers into Dee's wet pussy.

Dee closed her eyes, drew in her breath, and Lu said, "Tasty."

"Indeed," said Dee, adjusting her hips so that Lu's fingers were at home.

"You know, there's something I never told you," said Dee.

"I'm sure there are lots of things you haven't told me."

Dee opened her eyes, "I'm being serious."

"Oh, right," Lu made a serious face, then asked, "What is it?"

"You remember that first night we were here?"

"Uh-huh," said Lu.

"Well, I was worried that if we fucked in my bed, Don would smell it. I figured two women being together would smell a lot different than a man and a woman."

"Fortunately, I am not familiar with the difference," Lu said smugly.

"Anyway," Dee continued, "after you left, your scent was on the cushions. I flipped them over when I put them back. One night when I was missing you, I went and got one of them and took it to bed with me. The smell of your pomade made me feel close to you."

"Mmm," Lu said, considering the turn of events in her favor. "Now you get to take me to bed," she concluded.

Dee lifted her shirt, stretched out her arms, and pressed her hands against the wall behind Lu, her bare stomach close to Lu's face.

Lu reached over to pull the chain on the lamp. As the light went out, she felt Dee begin to melt. Now in the dark, whether they are in bed or on the couch, they know exactly how to find each other.

subway ride 4 play
by Rosalind Christine Lloyd

It was a Friday, approximately 5:45 P.M., and I was about to be held captive on the New York City IRT number two train. By the time I would board the train at Chambers Street after work, dreams of a seat would be considered delusional even by your less-seasoned strap hanger. With strangers of every persuasion imaginable pushing, shoving, cramming, breathing on me, and, God forbid, touching me, it is the absolute worst part of every day. The experience is a horrific assault on the senses. The sights: homeless, hopeless, and hungry people (whom I can't help even though I want to) inhabiting the system; dirt and pollution everywhere—cigarette butts, candy wrappers, remnants of fast-food cartons, discarded newspapers, filth; the visual abuse of the ugliness of an architecturally uninspired transportation system. The smells: body odor, sweat, urine, halitosis, vomit, gas, trash, loud perfumes, and aftershaves. The sounds: the loud roar and screeching of aging equipment; boisterous, angry, and often-violent arguments; a potpourri of languages and accents attempting to out-talk everyone else against an already-annoying background of noise pollution. Strange cumbersome bodies monopolizing space, sharp-edged briefcases, smelly underarms, spiked heels threatening toes, all in war for a minimal amount of elbow room. And the perverts: the ones who consider the tightness of the crammed subway cars as more-than-suitable carnivals to soothe their carnal cravings for flesh; their infractions can destroy the illusion of innocence of any day.

On this particular evening, I stood in my usual spot about midway down the platform for the perfect position so that when the train came into the station the door of the sixth car would open right in front of me. When I'd arrive at my stop, I would be directly in front of my exit for an easy escape. A ritual I am a bit embarrassed to admit, but a necessary behavior.

It was a hellish week at work. Logging in unwanted hours of overtime, I looked to the upcoming weekend as dead time to relax and unwind. The subway platform was somewhat festive. This is usually the case on Fridays. Couples looking forward to dates; yuppies slinging weekend bags over their shoulders; white- and blue-collar workers rushing to their favorite hot spots to tie one or more on; teenagers and coeds jubilant about parties. All I could think about was going home, showering the week off my tired body, and diving into a good book. Luckily, within two minutes a dull red train in all its urban glory came barreling into the station symbolizing my departure from 9-to-5 hell to deliver me to my safe haven uptown.

As usual the subway car was jammed with bodies, but I managed to squeeze in and arrange myself in an excellent position close to the door at the opposite end of the car where the doors would not open for about four express stops. This spot would allow a minimal amount of contact with people coming into the train. I would make the five stops to 110th Street with minimal crush-factor—quite a coup for a Friday.

After the exchange of outgoing and incoming bodies at Chambers Street was complete, the doors closed. At this point I tend to shut down, closing my eyes, lulling myself into this fake sense of serenity, blocking out the negativity that can permeate New York City air. On this day, however, I was compelled to open my eyes due to some unpredictable mystic vibration inside the train. Through the crowd, halfway to the other end of the car, I could see the thickest poutiest lips and the largest most magnificent eyes—eyes blacker than a moonless night. The owner of those lips and eyes had skin the color of warm toasty waffles and bushy hair sprinkled with natural twists and spirals the color of raspberry preserves. The subtlety of the woman's beauty was resounding as certain men stole opportunities to leer at her, fighting over one another to give her their seats. Her reaction to them was, in a word, oblivion. I couldn't take my eyes off her and strained for a better look. She was styling a small vintage leather jacket the color of a fine cognac. It seemed tailored to fit her tiny statuesque frame. A cream-colored turtleneck stretched across her tiny bosom, while overly confident nipples, fat and edible, poked out without shame. Obviously she wasn't wearing underwear (well, at least not a bra as far as I could tell). Yes, I managed to see all of this through the crowd. I'll never forget those brown plaid boot-cut slacks, so tight I could almost feel the outline of the soft *w* between her legs.

I stared at her as the men did, only harder.

The train left Chambers Street picking up speed as it entered the tunnel. She started to fidget while preparing to get off at the next stop. Clearing a path was no small feat as the train was crammed, wall to wall, shoulder to shoulder, but the crowd parted for her as if she were royalty. Without even looking at me, she squeezed past me before maneuvering her back directly to me. She was so close I could smell her shampoo and conditioner, which saturated her kinky hair—something sweet and nutty. The heat of her back was flammable, threatening to torch me. I couldn't believe how easy it was for me to become aroused by this absolutely beautiful stranger. As I enjoyed her warmth and her smell, the train careened wildly through the tunnel. The car started to buck and jolt from the high speeds, hurling Ms. Honey into me. Her back and legs flung against me violently, but it was her bottom, now pinned against me, that sent powerful impulses to my brain (not to mention other body parts). It seemed she decided for us both that it was a good idea for her ass to remain where it was, crushed right against my pussy.

I was near the door, and I couldn't move. A large woman with far too many bags wedged her thick shoulder deep into the small of my back while the beautiful stranger held herself against me, persistently pressing her hot ass deep into my hard clit. The train bolted to a stop.

Fourteenth Street station: The car barely thinned out. There were more than enough people on the train to camouflage what was happening. My stranger was still pressing against me as I tried to appear unaware of her immediate proximity. Had the train been near-empty, I felt she would have done exactly the same thing she was doing at that very moment. When the doors closed and the train moved on, she began to move against me very slowly, rotating provocatively.

Riding a perfect stranger on the subway was completely unexpected and quite enticing, but my clit needed more as it rubbed the backside of this wondrous beauty. My nipples were so hard they hurt, and I knew I needed to do something to partake in the lusty moment she had initiated. With my right hand tightly gripping the strap above, I steadied myself against her. The leather backpack I wore gave me balance. I eased my left hand near my thighs closer to her, where a swirling circle of clit-numbing heat lay just under her ass. She moved against my hand, and as she rubbed I slid my finger slowly along the fabric of her slacks, down the crack of her ass and between her legs. Suddenly she stopped moving, almost as if she were holding something in. Slowly I began to stroke her, moving my finger in and out of the space between the voluptuous cheeks of that phenomenal ass swathed in those plaid slacks until she moved with me. At this point I felt pairs of eyes lightly brushing over us, but I knew I couldn't stop—the embarrassment too weak, the will too strong.

My finger moved like a pencil in a sharpener as if it had a mind of its own. My fingers curled into a fist as I began to gently apply pressure underneath her. Each of us took deep breaths. I was loose and liquid; my thighs felt as if they were melting. She started to move 'round and 'round against my fist as I sunk myself into her as far as I could go with her fully clothed. My eyes darted nervously to confirm that no one was looking. I didn't want to be noticed. Weekend anxiety levels filled the car like bad air; these commuters didn't give a damn about anything but getting to their next destination. It got so intense, I thought she'd burn my fist off as I continued to bury it deep into her inferno.

The doors opened abruptly. We had come into Penn Station, and it seemed there was some interruption in service on a train in front of ours. In a variety of verbal and non-verbal ways, those with a view of the platform expressed their displeasure in the sea of commuters eager to board. Some exhaled, others spewed profanity, some even attempted to block doors. My stranger craned her lovely caramel neck, straining for a better look out the window to view the platform. The temptation to kiss her neck, to taste the caramel, to wrap my tongue around her slick loveliness, was stretching my case. With my fist fitting snugly between her hot thighs, she squeezed around me as if it were meant to be. I started to sweat. My heart beat strangely and irregularly. The unruly crowd on the platform, pissed off and armed with bad attitudes, did not allow the departing passengers a clear path out of the train. Those entering tumbled in like crazed testosterone-driven football players prepared to get on the already-filled train at all costs. I could have sworn the train sighed as the incoming bodies joined ours and formed an ugly sculpture of human flesh. I felt mangled and manipulated when suddenly I realized my stranger was now facing me. She didn't dare meet my gaze but turned her eyes away. A subtle hint of her scent lingered in the air. I blushed. We ignored the other bodies crammed against us: bodies contorted in strange angles, some holding onto the ceiling to steady themselves. A commuter mosh pit.

She was perfectly still at first. Then the train picked up speed, accelerating through the dark cavernous tunnels deep in the belly of the city, the cars rocking wildly, gripping themselves against the silvery slippery tracks, fueled by the energy of the dangerous third rail. We allowed our bodies to absorb, merge, dissolve, and exchange the very essence of our now-frontal collective body heat and hungry aimless desire. Breasts were hot, pressing together, nipples stinging; our heavily breathing stomachs danced, the expanse of womanly hips on such a slender body laid flat against mine. Then thighs, hers, started a slow roll against me. Catching her breath I rolled my bigger more muscular thighs deeper. Pushing, swirling gently, we slowly humped each other with as much subtlety as we could stand. The train's rocking added to the feminine rhythm we so courageously developed in this public place. Thighs rolled slowly then quickly against each other, sometimes in synchronicity, sometimes deliberately out of sync, her gaze as far away from me and from us as possible. Her hips rose to meet mine, and I thought I was going crazy.

When I felt the grip of her tiny hand with their long painted nails on my waist, I could wait no longer. The train was moving fast; bodies swayed everywhere around us with lights inside each of the cars blinking on again, off again. Slipping my hand between us, I nervously unzipped her slacks and eased my finger inside. A moan escaped from her cranberry lips, but it was swallowed in the sound of the train. I dug deeper in my search and discovered she had skipped the underwear entirely—just as I suspected. Instantly I felt the soft heat of her downy bush. Her scent was even stronger now, so strong it made my mouth water. I felt her raise her hips toward me, spreading her legs so I could get my finger in. With an abrupt rock of the car, my finger became submerged in a curly womb of hot wet heat. Her entrance was hot and slippery. She wiggled her hips with a slow but intense rhythm while my middle finger worked itself deeper between her soft-smooth-slick-silky lips. Her grip was so tight around my waist it pinched. As the train shook wildly, she moved toward me while I jammed my finger in her as hard and as far as I could. She was melting around my finger like chocolate on a hot summer day as her very soul started to tremble in the palm of my hand in a pelvic dance, not a belly dance— my anonymous Nubian princess.

As 72nd Street approached, she pushed her large leather bag in between us (to hide her now-open plaid slacks) and pushed through the crowd, almost running as she neared the doors. She stepped out. She did not look back. All I could do was catch my breath in an attempt to convince myself this had not been a dream. To confirm what had happened, I took a seat and raised my left hand to caress my face. Instantly I inhaled the banks of the Nile River after a torrential downpour.

That's What Friends Are For

by Nilaja Montgomery-Akalu

Women suck! I hate them. They're good-for-nothing low-down dirty dogs. Actually, that's a harsh thing to say, considering I am a woman and dogs are faithful. If I had any kind of sense, I'd be straight. Naw. That wouldn't work. I can't stand that whole leaving-up-the-toilet-seat thing. So now it's back to women.

Why do they piss me off? I shouldn't even say *them*. It's more like *her*. Rahiema Walker. My ex-girlfriend. Correction, make that ex-fiancée. Why is she my ex? Because she's a playaette and tried to play the wrong woman. I wasn't havin' it. You would think that after three years you could trust a bitch. But no, that hoochie was fuckin' some barely legal tramp at the high school around the corner from my apartment building. So I dumped her. And yes, I kept the ring. It's worth at least a couple of hundred. I wasn't about to walk away empty-handed. Not after all the bullshit I put up with from that worthless piece of human flesh.

So here I was, two months later, alone in my apartment getting drunk on chocolate fudge cookies, rainbow sherbet, and Oprah. Rahiema may have treated me wrong, but I was missin' her with a fierce passion. OK, I was missin' the sex.

It had been all that and a bag of chips with dip and then

some. Feel me? That woman could work me over with just her pinkie finger and those juicy kissable lips. Damn, Rahiema was one of the finest sistas I had ever laid my eyes on. She was a darker version of Toni Braxton (another woman I would give my kidney for) and twice as fine. Rahiema had skin the color of dark plums and was just as sweet when she wanted to be. That's how I prefer my women. You know the saying: The blacker the berry, the sweeter the juice. I'm surprised all my teeth didn't fall right outta my head.

I was heading for the kitchen for another refill of rainbow sherbet when my doorbell rang.

"Hey, skank. You can't call nobody?" Araina Hill, one of my three best friends, said as she came barging into my apartment. My other two friends, Daire Grant and Joi Darling, followed behind.

"We thought you done crawled up and died in this mug," Daire said. I hadn't spoken to my friends or anyone in weeks since the break-up.

"Hey, love," Joi said in her heavy British accent. She was the only black person I had ever met who had been born and raised in England. "How are you?" she asked, hugging me.

"I'm OK." I shrugged.

"You look like shit warmed over," Araina said, smacking her gum like the tramp we all knew she was. Araina was decked out in her usual skeezuh gear: halter top and a skirt so short it showed things only a gynecologist should see. She was right, though. My apartment hadn't been cleaned in weeks. The dishes were piling up in the sink. I couldn't have even imagined what I looked like standing there in an oversized sweatshirt, cutoff jeans, and hair tied back in a ponytail.

"Leave T.T. alone," Daire said. T.T. was short for Tilo Thomas. Me.

"Thank you, Daire," I said, hugging her round body. She was the only person who called me T.T. Daire was what we called *healthy*. She had meat on her bones. She wasn't really fat, just kinda big. Like Queen Latifah. Daire gave the best hugs and was like the mother of the four of us. She was also affectionately known as Big Momma D.

"So how are you doing, Ms. Tilo?" Araina asked, plopping herself onto my couch.

"I'm hangin'." I sat between her and Joi. Daire sat on the arm of my couch.

"Have you heard from Rahiema?" Joi asked.

"No, I haven't," I said wrinkling my nose. "And I don't wanna hear from her or about her."

"Then I guess you wouldn't be interested in hearing the dish on Ms. Rahiema," Araina said.

"What dish?"

"Thought you wasn't interested."

"Bitch, you workin' a nerve."

"You must not be gettin' any," Araina said, sucking her teeth. "You hella grumpy."

"What about Rahiema?"

"The high school tramp dumped her…for a man."

"Serves her right," Joi said. "I never did like her."

"I'm not finished," Araina said, holding up a newly manicured hand. "Anyway, I was out at Zami's, you know gettin' my groove on with a fine-ass piece of woman. I go to the bathroom, do my thing, and your ex corners me just as I'm coming out."

"What did she want?"

"She wanted to know what was up with you and if you

were seein' anybody," Araina said. "She wants back in."

"She has got her nerve," Daire said. "After the way she treated my girl."

"What did you tell her?" Joi asked.

"I told her you were dating this fine-ass piece of woman and had moved on," Araina said. "What could I say? That you were locked in yo' apartment cryin' over her?"

"Thank you, Araina." I hugged her. "You slut." I added.

"You my girl. I gotcha back, baby." Araina grinned. "That ain't all. So after I tell her you was taken, bitch starts hittin' on me."

"No!" Joi's eyes bugged out.

"Yes!"

"No!" Daire said.

"Yes, dammit! Y'all need to clean the wax out ya ears so you can hear a sista."

Araina looked at them in disgust.

"That is foul," Daire said. "T.T., I got peeps who will take care of Rahiema for you."

"You always got peeps you gon' get to take care of somebody," Araina said.

"That won't be necessary, D," I said.

"I should think not," Joi said. "Violence doesn't solve anything."

"Shut up, Ms. Prim and Proper," Araina said. "Violence doesn't solve anything," she said, imitating Joi's thick accent.

"Fuck you, slut." Joi gave Araina the finger.

"Speakin' of fuckin'," Daire said before Araina could come back with some flippant remark, "you gettin' any lately, T.T.?"

"No, I haven't," I said. "And I'm not interested in gettin' any."

"Oh, bullshit on me," Araina said, rolling her hazel eyes. "It's been two months, and you mean tell us you ain't went out and snagged you some fish tacos?"

"We all ain't nymphos like you, Araina," I said. "Some of us have class."

"Class my ass," Araina said. "You need to put on one of the hoochie-mama skirts we all know you got in your closet, go out to the club, and get that punanny stroked, baby!"

"Do you always hafta be so vulgar?" I said, even though I knew she was right. It had been a while, and I was horny as fuck.

"Two months is a long time, T.T.," Daire said. "Even Joi got hooked up last week. You know what a prude she is."

"Hello. I'm sitting right here," Joi said. "And I am not a prude. I have taste, and I have standards."

"I appreciate all of your concern," I said. "I'm just not really looking to start dating anyone right now. It's too soon."

"Who the hell mentioned anything about dating?" Araina said. "I'm talkin' pure raw sex. No commitment."

"The story of Araina's life," Joi said.

"Bitch!"

"Slut!"

"Shut up, both you," Daire said. "Now let's get back to T.T.'s problem."

"What problem?"

"Your lack of a sex life, baby." Daire stood up. "We're takin' you out tonight. You gon' eat somethin' besides chocolate fudge cookies. Let's go find somethin' for you to wear."

"Didn't I let you borrow this?" Araina asked, holding up a black sheer blouse. Daire, Joi, and me were sittin' on my bed watching Araina go through my closet.

"No, that's mine."

"Can I borrow it?" Araina asked as she took off her halter top. "I got a date tomorrow. This is perfect." As usual, Araina wore no bra. There was a 99.99% chance she wasn't wearin' panties either.

"You are straight hoochie, Araina," Daire said, flipping through the latest issue of *Essence*, with Toni Braxton on the cover.

"Ya mama."

"I don't think so. But I do believe it was yo' mama callin' out my name last night." Daire laughed and tossed the magazine aside.

"Bitch, please," Araina rolled her eyes. "My mama's got way betta taste."

"Too bad she lost out on the looks," Joi joined in. "Look at you."

"Don't you even try comin' for me," Araina threw up her hand. "You will get dissed." She twirled around. "This is 115% supreme fineness, baby." Her hands rested on her hips. "Besides," Araina continued, "y'all got nerve callin' me hoochie. I'm not the one with the mirror over my bed." She pointed a long finger at me.

We looked up at the large square glass that covered half of my ceiling. That had been Rahiema's idea, her reason being, "I like to watch." My ex had been kinky.

"Someone was into the freaky-deaky," Araina said.

"Eat me," I said.

"At least you'll be able to watch," Daire said.

"Yeah," said Joi. "Instant replay."

"You and Ms. Rahiema musta had some good times up in here," Araina said. "What other nasty stuff you guys was doin'?"

"Fuck you bitches." I rolled my eyes.

"Is that an invitation?" Joi asked. Araina, Daire, and I all looked at her, shocked. "What? The British girl can't have a dirty thought?"

"We just don't expect it, prude," Araina said.

"Skank!"

"Ice princess."

"Are you two fuckin' or what?" I said. "Y'all argue like some old married-ass couple."

"You ain't got no business talkin' about somebody fuckin'," Araina said. "We know you ain't get any."

"I gets mine."

"If your lover needs double 'A' batteries, you aren't getting any," Joi said.

"Leave my girl alone," Daire said. "She can't help it if her shit's done dried up and died." She, Joi, and Araina all broke out laughing.

"My shit is still all good." I gave them the finger. "Don't make me whip it out and give you a taste."

"That definitely sounds like an invitation to me," Araina said.

"Sounds like one to me," Joi agreed. "What about you, Daire?"

"Sounds like we're gettin' invited to a party."

"I…I was just joking." I stuttered. "Y'all betta stop lookin' at me like that." I said, my friends looking like hungry horny hyenas.

"Shut up, Tilo," Araina said, pushing me onto my back. She climbed on top. "This is what you get for always havin' a big mouth."

"Besides, if you can't fuck your friends, who can you fuck?" Daire grinned.

"That's what friends are for," Joi said.

"Oh, good Goddess," I said as Araina brought her mouth down hard on mine.

ঌ   ঌ   ঌ

That's what started it. Soon Araina was giving me kisses on the back of my neck. I shivered at the cool wetness her saliva left on my skin. Her tongue made circular motions as she crept down my back, undoing my clothes as she went. Joi soon caught on. She took my nipple in her mouth and sucked like a baby. Daire was stroking my hair. The muscle in my rectum contracted when Araina ran her tongue between my ass cheeks. She gave me a sly grin.

"Turn around." Daire whispered in my ear. I did as I was told, turning so that her chest pressed against my back. With her left hand, Daire squeezed and played with my left tit while Joi continued sucking on my other nipple. Daire reached around my waist and ran a finger over my clit. I shivered again. She stuck the pussy-drenched finger in Araina's mouth. Araina licked it dry.

"Good." Araina licked her lips.

I pulled my knees up, giving her a clear view of a wet cunt. "You know what I want now," I said, fingering myself. Araina gave me that slick grin again. I knew that when it came to sex Araina Dawson liked it rough. I laid down on my back. Daire, who had undressed herself at some point, had her crotch bumping up against my head. Joi had stripped out of her clothes too and was sitting cross-legged, playing with herself. Araina grabbed both of my legs and forcefully spread them. She rubbed her hands together like a mad scientist about to bring her greatest creation to life. I could barely stand the wait. Araina grabbed my buttocks in her hands.

"Now, Araina," I said praying I wouldn't come right there before she even got inside. "I want it now." Squeezing my ass, she plunged. Involuntarily I sucked in a large breath as her hand curled into a ball and slammed against the walls of my cunt. I lubricated her as she fucked deeper, and I wrapped my legs around her back, pushing her farther in.

"Hey," Joi whined, "what about me? I wanna taste." Daire, Araina, and I broke out laughin'. I had never had a woman whine about not tasting my pussy.

With Daire's fingers, I spread my labia open. "Get down there, girl."

If I had known Joi Darling could work me over with just a tongue, I would have gotten it on with her years ago. My God, that woman could eat some punanny. She was lightly dancing her tongue over my clit, teasing me. I grabbed her head and tried to push her farther into me. Daire was still playing with my tit, and Araina was working her mouth on my other tit. She bit me hard enough to bring a sharp pleasure gasp from my mouth. I made her kneel so that her cunt was right in front of me. I was right: She was wearing no panties under that short skirt. I slipped my finger inside her, working that little bud between her chocolate thighs. Araina worked her hips back and forth in time with the finger fucking. My room, hell, my entire apartment, filled with the sounds of sex. After a while I had lost track of who was doing what to whom. First there was Joi eating me, then Araina, then Daire, back to Araina while Daire and Joi got it on with each other. I looked up at the mirror on my ceiling. We were like beautiful black vines entwined with one another.

My friends fucked, made love, and had sex with me that day. At one point they had me on all fours doing a train on me. Each got her chance to fuck my ass and cunt. Araina even had the nerve to fuck my snatch with my own dildo! That bitch! It was fabulous. I came and came and came and came and came all over again.

After sex we curled up under the blankets. Our bodies warmed one another. As Araina, Daire, and Joi all drifted off to sleep, I kissed each one good night. This is what life was about. Friends. They were always there to lift a gal's spirit. Hey, that's what friends are for.

All the Modern Conveniences
by G.L. Morrison

There's something about summer. Maybe it's the deca-
dent lifestyle of underemployment we've chosen to live.
Chosen in the kind of religious way God or a particular
career puts her hand on your forehead and says, "Do something meaningful with your life." In smaller print are the
words "Don't expect to ever buy a sports car" and "In
exchange I will give you summers." Long golden summers.
I went straight—more accurately, I went gaily—from being a
student at my hometown university to teaching at a local
community college. Directly from student summer breaks to
teacher summer escapes. A litany of exquisite summers. It
was at the university that I met June. Maybe it was June's
hand on my forehead, and not God's, that convinced me to
become a teacher. She was so passionate about it, about
everything. I needed something to be passionate about. I
needed June. I knew the minute I saw her with her wide
hips and even wider smile. I was delighted when it turned
out she needed me too. (I have that "knew it the minute I
saw it" feeling about a hundred things I never get a shot at.)

Even her name delighted me. *June.* I told her I could
never love a woman named April. "April is the cruelest
month," I said. And she laughed. She had a rare sense of

humor about her name. She displayed none of the scars of childhood name-calling. She put that strategic humor to good use in the classroom. It made her a more durable angel than some of the other do-gooders who had also felt a calling to teach at her inner city high school. June teaches high school English. I teach Spanish 101 to indifferent business majors required to submit to me.

June's parents had a sense of humor about names too. June's sister was named May. Her mother must have shared my bias against April, but since she had only two daughters we'll never know for sure. June's brothers were the oddballs: Justin, Mark, and Zeke. Not an Augustus among them. At 15, May became Maya, with a clenched fist that dared anyone to say it had ever been otherwise. June wore her name less like a badge of honor than an embroidered logo on an expensive sweat suit. You knew how much she'd paid for it, but she wore it because it was comfortable, because it fit her. (June had one of those rare happy childhoods you read about. It made me jealous and glad.)

At the university we started to fill our summers with each other. She would look for excuses not to go home to her parents during summer break. I would stop pretending to look for a summer job. We spent all those lazy grantless months making love inside my refrigerated dorm room. I warmed her chilled skin with my mouth. The utilities were included, so I ran the air conditioner even in the winter because I grew used to the reassuring sound of it and the nipple-chilling air. We lived on pizza and beer with the money we'd gotten by selling back our books. In spite of the crimp it put in our lovemaking schedule, we were always glad to get back to our studies and the Pell grants, student loans, and regular meals that came with September. With the fall also came my dormmate and the thermostat wars. After a few number-crunching pop-quizzing weeks (in which the most energy June and I would have for sex was discreet petting on the sofa in study hall), we'd pine for summer to return. It always did.

After all these years June and I still live for summer. Since we don't have a lot of money, fucking is our favorite entertainment. It's cheap and accessible. The next time you're searching under the sofa cushions, hoping to scrape up enough change to see a movie or the band playing at a nearby bar, stop and think: *Why not stay home and fuck?* June and I have decided this would be an effective anti-consumer campaign. The library could run it along with their Turn-Off-Your-TV week. Under the sign WHY NOT STAY HOME AND FUCK? they could have a shelf of sex manuals and erotic classics such as *Lady Chatterley's Lover*. A campaign like that would entice me to renew my library card.

        28.   28.   28.

Something about summer makes me sleep until noon. When I wake up I reach across the wrinkled sheets. I notice June isn't there.

"June?"

The air conditioner answers me, *thumpa thumpa*. I can barely hear myself above its asthmatic rasping, *thumpa thumpa*. I lie back down.

"June?" I ask the ceiling. I start to fall asleep.

From the corner of my half-closed eye, I see June coming back. She pushes the bedroom door open with her butt, because her hands are full. She is carrying breakfast for two on a tray—well, on a cookie sheet. Precariously, she balances a bowl of sliced peaches, a plate of jam and toast, and a single cup of tea. I smell the hot tea from across the room. Apple cinnamon. The smell props me up. I take the cookie sheet from her, and she slides in beside me.

With guilt I bite into the first peach slice. Breakfast in bed? Is this some special day I've forgotten? I rack my brain for anniversaries, birthdays, or holidays. I smile a knowing smile. I feed her a peach slice. She licks the juice off my fingers. Finally, I confess.

"Is today a special day?"

"Yes."

I sigh. "I don't remember."

"You don't remember?"

A sheepish "No."

"It's a very special day," she says.

I squirm.

Lips against my ear, she whispers softly. "It's Thursday."

I pounce on her. The bed shakes, and tea sloshes out of the cup onto the cookie tray.

"Careful," June warns.

I chew her neck in response.

June giggles. She stuffs my mouth with peach and licks her own fingers. I swallow quickly and go back to her neck with more gentle, less toothy kisses. I push her hair aside to kiss her neck and ear. I kiss the exposed part of her shoulder, then push aside the spaghetti strap of her nightgown to kiss the one-eighth of an inch of shoulder the pink silk had covered. June sips her tea.

"Careful," she says sternly when my shoulder-kissing jostles her elbow. "This tea is hot."

"Sorry."

I munch on a piece of toast while I wait for her to put her

cup down. It's so good; I have another. I tear off a small piece of toast and feed it to June, the way you might feed a bird or a deer at the zoo. She accepts bites between sips. Her mouth is warm from the tea. She chews each bite, then pulls my hand back to her to suck the thick marionberry jam off my fingers. She holds my fingers in her mouth long after any trace of jam is left. I swoon and nearly drop my toast. Careful of the teacup she is holding, I kiss her mouth and—by necessity and accident—my own fingers. I pull my fingers out slowly. Her hands are busy with the teacup. She has placed one hand over the mouth of the cup to prevent it from spilling; the other hand holds the cup handle. While I kiss her she cannot see to put the cup down. I like this unplanned helplessness and kiss her more fiercely. By the stiff way she returns my kisses, I can tell she finds her accidental bondage more annoying than erotic. I take the tea from her. I drink it in one gulp and set the cup aside. Then we lean in for such a swift passionate kiss that we bump foreheads.

"Ouch!" June moans.

I reprogram my mouth for the boo-boo kisses I plant on her forehead softly while my own head smarts. Hoping to rewind to a previous moment of mounting passion, I tear off a piece of toast and offer it to my bird/lover. She stares at me in horror.

"You're getting crumbs all over the bed."

I eat the guilty toast and shoo the crumbs off the edge of the bed. I hold up a peach slice expectantly. June nods. It is an acceptable substitute. The peach bit wobbles between my fingers, wet and orange. I bite the slice and eat half. I feed June the other half; her mouth is slick with peach juice. She reaches into the bowl and feeds me a slice. Her fingers taste bitter and salty. I pull them into my mouth and suck the sweet pulp and juice off her fingers. I hold a slice to her. June opens her wet mouth expectantly. Pinched, the peach pulp squishes, drops onto her. With apology I lick it off her silk nightie. June wriggles out of the loose pink silk, then tosses it under the bed. I squeeze peach on her intentionally, drawing a path of juicy curlicues around her wrinkling nipple; then I kiss it off.

The air conditioner goes *thumpa thumpa*, and my kisses start to shimmy to the regular beat of its music. June's breath comes quicker. My hair keeps falling in my face, mingling with my kisses. I push it aside. I stop kissing her to pull a hair from my mouth. Her nipple softens while it waits, like ice cream melting in the sun. I harden it under my tongue. I hear June's sharp intake of breath. She tries to make as little noise as possible. She is surprised by the sounds I squeeze out of her when we are making rough love. The indelicate gasps and groans don't fall in line with her image of herself. She is one of the few women I know who uses the word *ladies* even when she's not looking for a rest room. She is a terra cotta vase, bone china, the polished wood of a virtuoso's cello. A Lady. She doesn't make funny excited noises. She smells of baby powder or some faint, mysterious, and expensive cologne. She never swears or spits and rarely sweats. But right now my hair is damp with sweat, hers and mine. Sweat pours off both of us. The smell of June, the smell of her excitement, her sweat and wet cunt, is intoxicating. A subtle rain pours off us. Sex in this heat is delicious and painful. I wipe the stinging sweat from my eyes with peach-stained fingers.

"Ow! Ow! Wait a minute." I sit up and rub my burning eyes on the bed sheet.

June laughs. "Are you OK?"

"No, dammit!" I lick my fingers, rub my eyes. Lick the sheet, rub my eyes. She was right; bread crumbs are everywhere.

She rubs my back sympathetically. When it appears I'll survive, she asks, "Would you turn up the air conditioner?"

Dutifully and somewhat grudgingly, I turn the knob as high as it will go. I am rewarded with a hissing rattle and cool blast of air. *Thumpa thumpa.* I come back to bed and grab June by the shoulders, pulling her to me. *Thumpa thumpa.* I taste her mouth from the inside. Still peachy. We twist tongue tips. The *thumpa thumpa* grows faster and louder; the air conditioner is humping the wall.

"Can't you do something about that?"

I get up again and scowl at the air conditioner. This has no effect on it. In spite of all evidence to the contrary, June is convinced that being butch is somehow connected with being mechanical. Not wanting to disappoint her, I give the air conditioner a good swat. No effect. I hit it with a wrench that rests above it for just this purpose. This makes it angry. *Thumpa thumpa* is joined by a sound like whistling bees. I smile wanly at June. She grins back encouragement. She has eaten the last slice of peach. I fidget with knobs. No effect. It is now stuck on high cool and high thump. A third swat quiets it. Completely. There is a deadly stillness. I can't get it started again. After many minutes of swatting, prayer, and profanity, the whistling bees return. *Thumpa thumpa.* The Proud Conqueror, I return to June. She has fallen asleep.

A restless sleeper, she has rolled over so that her hand is lying in the toast. I lick the jam off her fingers. She smiles in her sleep. I place the food and dishes on the floor. I kiss her shoulder and neck, traveling up to nibble her ear. She wriggles. Is this a sexy Sleeping Beauty game? Shall I awaken her with kisses? She answers me with an indelicate snore. She really is asleep. I spoon behind her and fall asleep to the *thumpa thumpa* lullaby.

&a. &a. &a.

When I wake up, June is gone and the room is eerily quiet. I step around the dishes on the floor. No amount of banging, cursing, or pleading will resurrect the air conditioner.

"June!" I call out, wanting to be consoled and forgiven.

I wander naked through all the rooms of the house, but I don't find her in any of them. An oversized T-shirt hangs over a chair where I left it. It slides loosely over my head and covers me to just above the knee, graciously concealing the parts of me most likely to offend (or arouse) the neighbors. As long as I don't bend over too far, I can pass as dressed. I step onto the porch.

I call softly. "Darling?"

No answer.

"June!" I bellow.

"Out here, Ward," she yells from the backyard. That's her favorite joke. My name is Sharon. *Ward, would you have a talk with the Beaver?*

I follow the sound of her voice. She is hanging laundry on the line with oh-my-god-are-those-clothespins? Where did she find clothespins in this era? I remember clothespins as a particular torture of my grandmother.

I sprawl on a lawn chair that she's pulled into the shade of the neighbor's hedge.

"Mrs. Cleaver," I report, "the air conditioner is broken."

"What isn't broken?" June sighs. "The air conditioner, the

dryer. I shudder to think what's next. Married life isn't what it looked like in the brochure, Mr. Cleaver."

"It's much cooler out here. Watching someone else work always relaxes me anyway."

June smiles. "Get off your beautiful lazy ass and help me."

I pick up a clothespin, mesmerized by the wood and wire contraption. Snap. It bites my finger.

"Whatever shall we do with these?" I snap the clothespin at her, revealing its hungry alligator jaws.

June leans languidly toward me. In her most seductive Scarlet O'Hara voice, she murmurs, "Frankly, my dear, we're going to pin up the laundry."

I pin up one side of a wet sheet. With the row of laundry in front of us and the neighbor's privacy hedge behind us, we are screened in. I remember how as a child I dragged all the blankets into the yard to make forts and castles. I flash my gorgeous fortmate a mischievous smirk, but she isn't looking. June struggles with a wet dress whose slippery strap has slid out of her hand but that she caught just before the clean wet laundry hit the dirty ground. She unwads it, pins it purposefully.

While her attention and her hands are filled, I slide behind her. Brushing her dark hair aside, I kiss her shoulder and neck and that ticklish place in between that is not quite shoulder, not quite neck but begs and begs for kissing. Her skin delights my lips with goose bumps. I mouth obscenities into her neck, into her hair. Just lips without sound making the words: saying how I want her, what I will do, where I will touch her next. Though I know she can't hear me, her whole body is taut listening to my moving lips. I put a little teeth into my kisses. She moves in surprise—but not far. I put my arms around her waist, push my hands under her shirt. A soft moan escapes her like steam as my fingers twist her nipples, adjust the pressure. June holds onto the clothesline. With her arms raised I am free to explore her body.

"Oh." She relaxes under my hands. "Oh, yes."

My hands linger over each full delicious curve. Starting below her knees, I stroke up. One hand on each bare leg. My hand is a boat on the river of her leg, moved across the still dark water of her skin by quick and unseen currents. My fingers dangle, tickle the hair on her unshaven legs. My hand is a leaf on that same river; it gets caught in the eddies and the still thoughtful places where her leg muscle ripples. My leaf/hand is moved as much by the quick breathing I hear escaping her as by the compelling river/flesh; it is easily blown off course, lifts and drops, listening to the ripples in June's breathing. I blow on her leg in cool curlicues. I lay kisses into the invisible concentric circles I've drawn. My thumbs stroke in the often forgotten place behind her knees, tickling and pressing lightly. June squirms.

A slight breeze blows the wet sheet toward her where it clings lecherously, wetting the front of her shirt. I continue my slow ascent up her legs, pushing up her loose skirt as she goes. Even in this heat, June shivers.

The clothesline bends under the pressure as I travel by kisses and fingertips up June's legs. The wet sheet in front of her is cool on her fingers, wetting her clothes and cooling her off while the afternoon sun and I overheat her.

Her skin produces goose bumps under my traveling hands and the light tickling scratch of my short nails. My hand rounds her thigh. Then her hip. I am surprised not to be stopped by the border patrol of her silky panties.

"You wanton woman. You're not wearing any underwear!"

"It was too hot." June blushes.

June turns to face me. Her nipples jut through her wet shirt. She grabs my crotch unceremoniously, half under, half through the oversized T-shirt that is all I am wearing.

"You're not wearing any either, my slutty sweet." June leers at me while her finger has slipped into my cunt, unannounced.

"Madam," I gasp. "You have your finger in my cunt."

"The better to fuck you with, my dear."

I spasm under the delightful shock of her slender finger's probing. So June will not have the upper hand, I reach blindly, pulling her toward me, finding my way under her skirt more quickly than before, slipping my own finger into the dewy depths of her. She tilts, sliding into my approaching finger. With her tilt she slams her own finger deep into me. We gasp in unison. Slower now, I mirror every motion her finger makes, anticipating even, the way mimes mirror each other, so that we touch each other exactly and simultaneously. She is wetter than I am, and so my finger slides where hers is slowed. But I feel my juices quickening.

A breeze passes, blowing off the clean laundry, cooling the air and filling it with the lemony smell of soap and the musky smell of June. Although we are mostly if not completely dressed and screened from view, I feel more naked than I ever remember being.

June's finger and my finger continue their dance as some internal drumbeat gets faster, harder in rhythm with our pounding clits. Her wet cunt squeezes my finger as I slide in and out of her. Dizzying in the heat and the sea of feeling her and being felt by her, I lose track of where she leaves off and I start. No one is following anyone anymore; we move in unison, puppets of the same hungry thought. Our two fingers slide over our each other's clit in wide regular swoops, feathering until we stroke the edge of the crowning clit. The heat is drawn out of the air around us and centered in my clit. Heat that breaks in waves, like the air melting; a fire demanding to be put out, the burning air wetted with even the mirage of water. The oceans swelling in us, lapping at the shore of my burning cunt, overtake my finger-teased clit, and I come. And June comes. Our dams burst at the same impossible moment; waves, real or miraged, spill over us. The wet laundry flaps around us, echoing our satisfied sighs.

A Femme in the Hand

by Lesléa Newman

The first time I saw her, I got weak in the knees, I swear to God. She was a beauty all right, but *beautiful* doesn't begin to describe her. Try *strong. Powerful. Built.* I stared at her until my eyeballs ached and something else ached, too: that sweet place between my legs that butches like me don't talk about very much. But that's where I wanted her, and frankly, the sooner the better. In other words, ladies and gentledykes, in case I'm not making myself perfectly clear, I had it *bad.*

I guess I've been out of circulation longer than I thought, because for a good twenty minutes I felt I had no bones in my legs. They just wouldn't budge even though I kept telling them to move. I mean, as much as I wanted to I couldn't just stand there all day staring at the vision of love-liness before me; I had to take action. So even though I was scared shitless, I strutted right over to the man standing next to her like I knew what I was doing, cleared my throat, prayed my voice wouldn't crack, and asked, "How much?" The price was fair, so I whipped out my checkbook, scrawled the amount, and in a flick of my Bic, she was mine.

Now let me tell you something. I know I'm nothing special. Just an average butch. Average height, average weight, average smarts, average looks. But with this baby between my legs, I'd be way above average. I'd be brave. I'd be bold. I'd be bulletproof. You know what they say, right? Clothes make the man? Well, let me tell you what I say: The bike makes the butch.

I swung my leg over my prize and dropped my weight onto the seat. A deep sigh of pure pleasure escaped my lips, and my bones settled inside my skin in a different way than they ever had. Have you ever felt that all was right with the world, even though you know that babies are crying all over the planet, and we've made a total mess of the environment, and somewhere right that very second some asshole of a man is making a woman do something she doesn't want to do, and you've got job troubles and girlfriend troubles and family troubles, but still you're amazed at the miracle of your own heart beating inside your chest and your breath coming in and out of your nostrils without any noticeable effort, and your muscles move a certain way just because you want them to, and hey, you're alive, and the sky is blue and absolutely nothing else matters? That's how I felt the first time I started up that bike.

My hands were shaking as I inserted the key, but she turned right over, my baby, my darling, my Harley. I still couldn't believe she was mine as I walked her back a few steps to turn her around and point her in the right direction. Then I gave her some gas and picked up my feet, and before you could say *Moving Violations* we were out of that tired old parking lot and out on the street.

Now in case you've never been on a bike—and if you haven't, I feel mighty sorry for you—let me explain why it's so different from riding in a car. It's like the first time I got glasses. I didn't even know the world was as blurry as an out-of-focus movie until my mother hauled me in to see old Dr. Norton, who took one look at me and pronounced me blind as a little bat. Not to worry, though; my vision was nothing lenses thick as Coke bottles couldn't fix. My mother and I started fighting immediately right in the office over my frames: She wanted me to wear these light-blue glittery cat's-eye monstrosities, and I, being a baby butch even then, had already picked out a cool pair of square black frames that made me look like a miniature Clark Kent. Of course my mother won in the end—after all, she was the one with the checkbook—and I was so pissed I vowed never to let those spectacles within a foot of my face. But when the doctor hooked my new glasses around my eight-year-old ears, the world was so sharp, so bright, so crystal-clear, I pushed my butch ego aside and put up with looking like a girly-girl (and an ugly one at that) because I just couldn't believe my eyes. It was like I had been transported to another planet. And that's just what riding a bike is like. If you're not Nancy Nearsighted like I am, the only other way I can describe it is through *The Wizard of Oz*. Remember when Dorothy lands in Munchkinland and all of a sudden the world isn't a drab, dull, black-and-white affair; the world's an amazing, sparkling, dazzling show of Technicolor? That's what life is like on a bike. Everything's in ultramegafocus. That's because there's nothing between you and the world. You're a part of it, and it's a part of you.

See, when you're out on the road, the air unzips to let you by as you and your bike slice through it, and once in a while a warm pocket of air surprises you, like when you're swimming in a lake and you hit a warm spot of water (which hopefully isn't pee). Smells come and go: the sweet smell of burning leaves in autumn, the even sweeter smell of lilacs and honeysuckle in the spring. If it rains, you get wet; if the sun's out, you get burned. But you don't complain. You're a kid again. Ever hear a kid complain about the weather? Me neither. If it's snowing, a kid makes snow angels. If it's raining, a kid goes stomping in puddles. If it's ninety degrees, a kid heads for the nearest swimming hole. Kids are very Zen; they're right there in the moment, which is how I am on my bike. Whatever comes my way is what I deal with. If there's a fallen tree in the middle of the road, I figure out how to get around it. If there's a scumbag trying to pass me on the right, I figure out how to lose him. If there's a babe on my backseat, I figure out how to give her the best ride of her life. And speaking of babes, I was definitely in the mood to pick one up. It was just about Miller time, so I headed for my favorite hangout, a beer dive called Where the Girls Are. And truer words were never spoken. Especially on a Friday night.

I zoomed into the parking lot and took a space right out front. Separation anxiety hit as soon as I was about two feet from my bike, but I made myself not look back. She'll be all right, I told myself. And besides, this is my moment, the moment I'd been waiting for my whole life: to walk into a bar with my hair all flattened out on one side and my helmet dangling from its strap off my arm, feeling like the coolest dyke in the world. I swaggered past the dance floor and the pool table and swung my leg over a bar stool the same way I had swung it over my bike a few hours ago, just knowing I was God's gift to women. But that illusion was shattered two seconds later when I ordered a club soda. I mean, how dorky can you get? The bartender, a pretty gal named Fuzzy, raised one perfectly tweezed eyebrow at me, as if to say, *Oh, Jamie, don't tell me you've gone AA on me too?*

especially since I usually down a glass of whatever's on tap pretty quickly and immediately snap my fingers for another. But I wasn't taking any chances tonight, not when there was nothing between me and the hard cold concrete but my reflexes and a four-pound helmet. Pretty funny when you think about it. Many a woman's tried to straighten me out, so to speak, but it took a bike to keep me sober. At least for tonight.

I leaned against the bar and chugged my club like a dyke who had it made. If that bike isn't a babe magnet, I told myself, I'll eat my jockey shorts. I was sure that by the time I finished my soda and sauntered back outside, there'd be a beautiful broad standing by my Harley, tapping her foot with her hands on her hips, all ready to be my one and only biker chick. Or maybe there'd be a crowd of girls, each one of them sure they deserved the first ride. Maybe there'd even be some pushing and shoving. A cat fight. Wouldn't that be something? Just the thought of it raised me off my bar stool and propelled me back to the parking lot. And believe it or not, there was a crowd of girls standing around my bike, much to my amazement and delight. Better yet, as soon as I got near them, they were all over me. "Hey, man, nice bike. Where'd you get it?" "How much did it set you back?" "What's it cost to fill?" "How big's the engine?"

Christ, was I disappointed. Why, you ask? Because these are not femme questions, now are they? No, they are not. My rehearsed *Ladies, ladies, one at a time, please. Everyone will get a ride* stuck in my throat because the mass of females swarming around my bike wasn't exactly a hen party. It was just a bunch of jealous butches, one admiring the chrome, one stroking the leather seat, one fitting her greasy paws around the handlebars....

"Outta my way," I said, and with a wave of my hand I parted the crowd like the Red Sea, claimed what was mine, and left them all in the dust. Though the truth is, they left me in the dust by a mile, because I knew most of those girls, and I knew they had femmes to go home to. Terry had Susie, Sal had Rita, Ronnie had Clara, Riki had Buffy. All I had was me, myself, and I. And even though none of those femmes were exactly my type and I loved riding solo, I knew after a while I'd get tired of feeling the wind at my back. I wanted to feel a girl at my back, with her arms around my waist and her legs snuggled up to my thighs, her helmet clinking against mine every once in a while as she leaned up close to whisper something in my ear. The girl had to be out there, but the question was, *where?*

The problem with this town, though, is it's smaller than most people's high schools, and I'd already gone through most of the femmes in this county and the next one over. And even so, I had yet to find what I was looking for. I wanted a girl with style. A girl all powdered and puffed who wore lipstick and lace. High heels even. A girl who was no stranger to hairspray. A girl who smelled like my mama. I know those kind of girls live in big cities mostly, but I had moved here to escape the rat race, and if I had done it, wasn't there a chance my femme counterpart had done so too? You know what they say, right, anything's possible, so I wasn't giving up hope. A friend told me I should put a personal ad in a lesbo paper with a wide circulation, which I thought a fine suggestion. Until I sat down to write it. I never sweated so much over ten little words in my life. Finally I came up with something I thought sounded clever: "Well-equipped butch with bike looking for high femme to ride." That says it pretty well, don't you think? I thought so too, until the calls starting coming in.

One woman actually said, "Do I bring my own pot?"

What, is she planning on moving in already? As I've told you, I'm not the quickest horse in the race, so I'm thinking, Pot…pot…what can she possibly be talking about here, chicken soup, beef stew?

"See," she went on, "I didn't know if you wanted me to get stoned first or wait until you picked me up…."

Oh, *high* femme. I get it. See what I mean about the dykes around here? "Never mind," I told her. "The bike's in the shop. Maybe some other time."

And that was just the first call. The others aren't even worth mentioning. Except, for what it's worth, let me give you gals out there a few pointers, OK? There are certain things you do not say to a butch about her bike. Number one: "It's nice, but it's not as big as my boyfriend's in college." Number two: "Does it have to be so noisy?" Number three: "Can I drive?" I met some lulus, let me tell you, but they say you have to kiss a lot of frogs before you find your princess. I tell you, I was getting so desperate, even a frog was beginning to look good to me, but you know, it's always darkest before the light or calmest before the storm or something like that, because just when I was going to bring my extra helmet back to see if I could get a refund (hey, those babies aren't cheap), I got a phone call, and I knew as soon as I heard her voice that this one was different. You've heard of love at first sight, right? This was love at first sound.

"So, you're the butch with the bike?" she said, like she was issuing me a challenge.

"Yep, that's me," I said, in what I hoped was a deep, mature, Marlon Brando kind of voice.

"What color is it?"

"Black with white hub caps and a dash of red. Why?"

"Because," her tone was impatient, like she already thought I was a fool, "I don't want it to clash with my outfit."

"Great," I said, hoping she couldn't hear me grinning like an idiot. "I'll see you on Saturday."

Saturday didn't come a moment too soon. I spent a good part of the morning fussing with my hair (all two inches of it) even though I knew by the time I got to Valerie's house it would be a total helmet-shaped wreck. I put on my best riding outfit: black leather pants, black leather jacket, black leather boots, black leather gloves. Thank God it was one of those glorious autumn days with just a few wispy clouds in a blue-as-the-sea sky, the air as crisp as the first bite of a perfectly ripened Macintosh apple. Otherwise I'd have sweated to death. Though even if it was ninety-eight degrees outside, I still would have dressed in black leather from head to toe. I could tell from Valerie's voice that she expected it. And I could also tell this was not a woman you'd want to disappoint.

I picked her up at high noon, and I have to say, she looked gorgeous. I'd gotten up extra early to shine up my bike, and boy did she shine. You know the way the sun glints off the ocean so it looks like there are hundreds of little diamonds shimmering up and down with the waves? That's just how sparkly my bike looked, from chrome to shining chrome. And Valerie wasn't exactly hard on the eyes either. When I roared into her driveway, she was standing there wearing jeans so tight, I wondered how the hell she was going to get her leg up over the seat of my bike, but hey, that wasn't my problem. Her T-shirt was even tighter than her Levi's, and she looked so fine I almost broke my own rule and let her ride without a jacket, but I wouldn't be able to live with myself if anything happened to those pretty little arms. She was all in black like me, except for these sweet little red boots that damn near broke my heart. Femmes—I swear to God I'm like putty in their hands. Make that Silly Putty, because if you want to know the truth I was already half in love with Valerie and totally in lust with her, and she hadn't even opened her mouth or set foot on the bike yet. But I played it cool. I said hi, and she said hi, and then the fog I was in lifted slightly, and I noticed that instead of carrying a pocketbook she was clutching an enormous yellow balloon that I hoped to hell she wasn't going to ask me to tie onto the back of the bike.

"What's with the overgrown lemon?" I asked, handing her a helmet.

"Oh, P.J. has this rule," she said, rolling her eyes.

"P.J." I stopped dead in my tracks. "Who's P.J.?"

"Oh, did I forget to mention P.J.?" she asked, all innocence.

"Yeah, I guess you did," I answered, already removing my helmet. A girl like this was bound to have a butch who would turn me into chopped liver if I came within two inches of her chick's aura. But who was I more afraid of? P.J., who was nowhere in sight, or Valerie, who was standing there with this are-you-a-butch-or-a-mouse look in her eye that said, *Listen, sister, you promised me a ride, and you damn well better give me one?*

I sighed. "What's P.J.'s rule?" I asked, already tucking my head back inside my helmet.

"P.J. said it was all right for me to go riding with you as long as we keep this between us." She bonked me lightly on the arm with the balloon.

"And how do you figure we're going to manage that?"

Valerie shook her head like she was saying, *You poor butch, you have no imagination,* and unzipped her jacket. She reached down under her T-shirt where the sun don't shine and came back up with a safety pin. "Will you do the honor?" she asked, holding out the balloon and the pin. I popped that sucker while Valerie covered her ears.

"Oh, it broke. Isn't that too bad?" Valerie curled her bottom lip into an adorable pout, looking sad as a little kid at a county fair whose ice cream cone had just dropped to the ground. For a second, anyway. Then she put the safety pin back from whence it came and dangled the bit of deflated rubber in front of me. "Problem solved, sugar. So are we going to spend the whole afternoon standing in the driveway or what?"

"Let's go." I put my helmet back on and started up the bike. I knew Valerie was danger with a capital *d,* but I figured what the hell. I also knew from bike riding that danger and excitement go hand in hand, and I was excited all right. So excited, I could have wrung out my BVDs like a sponge. I practically gushed a geyser when Valerie hopped on behind me and leaned up against my back to put that dead-as-a-doorknob balloon between us and keep it there. Then she said the five words I've been waiting forever and a day to hear: "Where should I hold on?"

I sighed like a butch in paradise and gave her my well-practiced reply: "Anywhere you'd like."

We took off, and let me tell you, P.J. was one hell of a lucky woman because Valerie knew exactly how to ride. She stayed with me the whole time, through every curve, turn, and bump of the road, not letting an inch of air come between her chest and the back of my jacket. You know what it's like riding with a gorgeous chick on the back of your bike? It's like the first time I got contact lenses. I already told you how my world changed 360 degrees when I got my glasses, right? Well, I didn't know things could get any better until the doc handed me my contacts. I popped those pieces of plastic onto my eyeballs and the world, which I thought looked fine as could be, grew so sharp, it was absolutely breathtaking. I felt like Rip Van Winkle—isn't he the one who fell asleep for a hundred years? That's how I felt with Valerie on the bike: Something inside me that had been dead to the world had just woken up, and boy was it great to say good morning.

We rode for a good hour before my butt began to ache, which of course I couldn't admit, so I asked Valerie if she was ready to take a rest.

"Hell, no," she yelled over the roar of the bike.

"Aren't your legs tired?" I yelled back.

"No," she answered. "I'm used to keeping them spread like this."

Christ almighty, this girl was really something else. I mean, who was taking who for a ride here? I picked up the speed, and off we went, across highways and byways, over hill, over dale, winding our way around beautiful country roads with nothing but that bit of busted balloon between us and not a cloud in the sky. It took every ounce of strength I had not to reach down and squeeze one of Valerie's pretty little hands or reach behind me to stroke one of her sleek denim-covered thighs. I was in butch heaven and butch hell at the same time, let me tell you, with such a knockout of a lady a hair's breadth behind me, her hands holding fast to my love handles, her legs pressed up against my quivering thighs. This was more action than I'd had in longer than I care to admit, and I was getting mighty worked up, but hey, I'm no home wrecker. There was no way I was going to do anything naughty—unless, of course, Valerie made the first move. And what the hell, maybe Valerie and P.J. were non-monogamous. It was pretty weird that P.J. would let her chick ride off into the sunset with a butch she'd never even met before. What the hell was wrong with her? And even if she didn't give a damn about what I looked like, any butch worth her weight in chainsaws would have at least come down to check out the bike.

Well, it looked like I wasn't going to ask, and Valerie wasn't going to tell. It was hard to talk on the bike anyway, and even though I have an intercom system I don't like to use it. I'm not that much of a talker, especially when I'm on a bike. It's too distracting. I like to just feel when I'm riding, and right then I was feeling pretty fine. So fine, in fact, it didn't even matter what happened between me and Valerie once I took her home and we got off the bike. Just seeing her drop-dead gorgeous face grinning in my rearview mirror was enough for me. Well, almost, anyway. Someday I'd have a femme of my own to ride with, a femme who'd throw her arms around my neck and press her breasts against my back as we rode off into the sunset to live happily ever after, at least for a week or two.

Well, you know what they say, right: All good things must come to an end. The day was fading fast, so I started heading back toward Valerie's place. We'd put in a good couple of hours, and I hoped she'd gotten what she came for. When we pulled up into her driveway, I killed the engine and thanked her for the ride.

"Thank *you*," she said, shaking her head like a horse tossing its mane as she handed me back my helmet. "Why don't you come up for something tasty?" she asked in a voice that wasn't about to take no for an answer.

"Uh...OK," I said, hanging both helmets onto the bike. I followed her inside, and then halfway up the steps I couldn't help myself. "Um, where's P.J.?" I asked.

"Who knows?" Valerie lifted her hands and shrugged her shoulders. "She could be anywhere."

Anywhere? Like in the bedroom with a shotgun? Even though warning bells loud as sirens were going off in my ears, I kept following Valerie, whose jean-clad ass was pulling me along like a magnet.

She sat me down at her kitchen table and disappeared into the bathroom. I counted silently—one, two, three—and then right on cue Valerie shrieked like I knew she would, "Oh, my God, my hair!" She came out freshly fluffed a few minutes later and tossed her jacket over the back of a kitchen chair. I tried not to stare at her breasts, but I was like a deer caught in the headlights. And Valerie came closer and closer until she swung her leg over my lap and plopped herself down, her face only an inch from mine.

"Wanna take me for another ride sometime?" she asked in a husky voice.

"Uh, sure," I stammered. "How about next Saturday?"

"How about right now?" Valerie leaned even closer and whispered in my ear.

"Um, I think I'm out of gas," I said weakly.

"We don't have to go very far." Valerie punctuated her sentence with a flick of her tongue against the side of my neck. "The bedroom's right in there."

I knew I would be a fool to say yes but even a bigger fool to say no. I knew I should think with my head here, not my crotch, but they were having one hell of an argument. My head was saying, *Now, Jamie, don't do anything foolish. You'll have a femme of your own someday.* And my crotch was saying, *The hell with someday. You know what they say, Jamie: A femme in the hand is worth two in the...*and as soon as the word *bush* entered my mind, I knew I was a goner. And so I was, for I didn't even attempt to protest as Valerie interlaced her fingers with mine and led me toward her bedroom over the threshold into Paradise.

Valerie plumped up some pillows and lay back on the bed as if she had all the time in the world. She smiled at me, and my heart just turned over because nothing does it to me like a femme fatale all ripe for the taking. *The hell with P.J.,* I thought as I knelt before Valerie and removed her sweet little boots. I took off her socks too and kissed each red-painted toe. Somehow, tight as they were, Valerie's jeans came off pretty damn quick, as did her T-shirt, black lace bra, and matching bikini underpants. I was practically on fire as I kissed her everywhere—her neck, her breasts, her belly, her thighs, the palms of her hands, the soles of her feet.

I inched my way back up the bed until her head was right next to mine. "I've got a surprise for you," I whispered into her velvety ear.

"I *love* surprises," Valerie whispered back. "Lay it on me, sugar."

Without a word I took her hand and guided it down between us until it landed on my crotch. "Feel that?" I asked as I unzipped my zipper.

Valerie's eyes widened. "I should have known, you naughty girl," she said, her lips spreading into a grin as her legs spread wide as well. "Well-equipped, indeed."

"Hey, no one can accuse me of false advertising," I said as I rolled on top of her and slid the dildo inside. Valerie gasped a short sweet intake of breath, which to me is the most beautiful sound in the world.

We moved slowly at first, getting used to each other and finding our rhythm, and we were just getting into a groove with our lips and hips locked together and Valerie's finger-nails digging ditches down my back when all of a sudden I felt her stiffen.

"I'm coming," Valerie yelled, turning her head to the side.

"Come on, baby," I said, raising myself up on my elbows to move faster inside her. But Valerie pushed me away.

"I'm coming," she yelled again, clamoring out of bed. "Just a minute, P.J."

"P.J.!" I sat up and tried to get my tool back into my pants, which was easier said than done because my hands were more than shaking. Even all zipped up I was in a heap of trouble, as the air was thick with the smell of sex, the bed looked like a hurricane had hit it, and Valerie, for some reason, had gone to the back door in nothing but her birthday suit. I didn't know if I should head for the closet, jump out the window, or dive under the bed, but before I could move a muscle I heard Valerie's voice, and her words froze me to the spot.

"P.J., where have you been all day? I missed you. C'mon, baby, there's someone in the bedroom I want you to meet."

Oh, my God! Was Valerie psycho? Was this a lesbian remake of *Fatal Attraction*? And what the hell was I sup-posed to say to P.J.? "Pleased to meet you? How do you do?" Before I could decide Valerie came back into the bed-room, and the sight of her, naked as the day she was born, undid me all over again. "P.J.'s here," she announced, all smiles, like now her day was really complete. "C'mon in, P.J.; don't be shy," Valerie coaxed. She took my hand, and we stood there waiting, Valerie's bare skin rippling in the breeze and me sweating like hell inside my leather jacket, my heart pounding so hard, I was sure my chest would be covered with black and blue marks in the morning. It felt like we stood there for hours, but I'm sure it wasn't more than a minute before P.J. gathered up her courage and strode into the room.

"Isn't she amazing?" Valerie bent down to scoop up the biggest, hairiest, fluffiest black-and-white cat I'd ever seen. I didn't know whether to kiss Valerie or kill her, I was so relieved. "This is P.J." Valerie extended one of P.J.'s paws for me to shake. P.J. started to purr, and Valerie lowered her head until her ear was next to P.J.'s neck.

"What'd you say, P.J.? Oh, yes, we kept the balloon between us the whole time, didn't we, Jamie?"

"We sure did," I said, relaxing a little and petting P.J.'s head. "So this is the famous P.J., huh?"

"This is my girl." Valerie scratched the cat under the chin.

"And she's the one who makes the rules around here?"

Valerie looked a little sheepish. "Well, I had to bring the balloon with me, Jamie. I mean, what if you turned out to be a dog?"

"And did I?"

Valerie grinned. "I'd say, sugar, you're more of a wolf."

That made me grin in my boots, let me tell you. We were both standing there rubbing P.J.'s fur, and each time our fingertips touched, my snatch shuddered, and I could tell from her breathing that Valerie's did too.

"So what does "P.J." stand for anyway?" I asked her.

"Pussy Junior."

I laughed. "Is there a Pussy Senior?"

Valerie gave me a look that was already becoming dear to me and batted her big brown eyes. "Does a femme wear mascara?"

I took that to mean yes. "So when do I get to meet her?"

"You already have." Valerie reached for my hand again and led me back to the bed. "And I think it's high time you two got better acquainted."

"Sounds good to me," I said, but before I could lay Valerie down, P.J. leapt onto the bed, turned around in a circle three times, and plopped down right in the center of the sheets. "I wasn't talking about you," Valerie said, picking up her pet. "Why don't you go into the kitchen for a while?" She shooed the cat out, and before she shut the bedroom door I had already unzipped my zipper. We hit the bed flying and resumed right where we had left off, and believe me it wasn't long before all three of us, Valerie, P.J., and I, were yowling to beat the band.

Every Lesbian's Fantasy
by Debra Olson

Part I: Introduction

I had been given two days to interview her. Two days seems like enough time to get the facts on another person, but it isn't. You follow her to a photo shoot or go on location with her and spend an enormous amount of time sitting around waiting. During this time you grab a few minutes here and there to talk to her. Mostly you just watch and use what you see as background when writing the piece.

The woman I am in Amsterdam to interview isn't involved in a new film. I have no idea whether she is well-known in this country. I've seen her most recent movie, but that's it. I've heard rumors about her, but isn't everyone in Amsterdam that way?

Yesterday had been a nightmare. We met at her agent's office. I asked questions, and she answered through an interpreter, a sallow, humorless fellow with curly red hair. I had never interviewed through an interpreter before.

"I really appreciate your meeting with me on such short notice," I said to her, at which point the interpreter started his interpreting. After hearing my words put into Dutch, she turned to me and answered with this guy's interpretation coming at the same time. Needless to say, five minutes into the interview I was a confused mess.

"Was your most recent film hard to prepare for?" I stumbled as I looked directly at the interpreter. She quickly said something in Dutch, and they both laughed.

"She's sitting right next to you," he said smirking. "Why don't you talk to her?"

᷈᷈   ᷈᷈   ᷈᷈

As she does know some English, I am hoping today's session can be sans interpreter. I'd rather fumble through lunch in broken English than do a repeat of yesterday. I felt humiliated.

I was so down last night I called home. It was good to hear my girl's voice even though we agreed not to run up huge trans-Atlantic phone bills.

"Has she put the moves on you yet?" she asked enthusiastically. A true lesbian.

"She's probably not gay," I responded. "Otherwise…" I heard my girlfriend's throaty chuckle across the miles. I couldn't wait to get home.

The first thing I see when I walk into the pub today is that damn red hair. I resolve to try to get along with the guy. She gives me a smile as I ask the interpreter to help out only if things get really confusing. He takes it in a manly fashion, and now I can look at her when I speak. I don't know why, but it makes me uncomfortable. I suppose we got off to a bad start.

"Hi," I say as I look down.

"Hello," she says. She glances briefly at the pencil I am rapidly tapping on the table.

"So, uh, let's begin." I look her in the eye and can't quite find my voice. "When we were talking yesterday about your most recent film, I didn't find out if it was difficult for you to play a lesbian."

Throughout this question she has been staring at me and nodding her head. Now she frowns, furrowing her eyebrows, but says nothing. I look at the interpreter, but it is obvious he is enjoying my discomfort.

"I don't know, um, 'a lesbian.'" She gazes out the window, frowning for a long time, then turns back to me. "I don't think I understand." I know the interpreter wants to laugh, but I decide not to give him the pleasure.

"I think it's going well, don't you?" I say to him with a smile.

Actually, it does go well, and by the time I'm finished with all my prepared questions things are kind of cozy. I ask her if there is anything else she wants me to know about her. She turns to Bozo and speaks rapidly in Dutch. The look on his face is the most animated thing I've seen on him in forty-eight hours, like seeing a corpse come to life. Grotesque! He doesn't appear pleased with what she had said. From the tone of their exchanges, I fear they are going to start fighting right in front of me.

"She wonders if you would care to go for a walk," he says angrily. I am stunned. I look toward her and see she is smiling at me. The smile is electrifying. I agree to the walk. We leave Mr. Happy to his own devices and exit the pub. She pauses outside the door and openly looks at me. She seems pleased.

We walk along water. Ocean or river, who knows. Amsterdam is like that. The morning mist is fading, and light reflects the gold of leaves on the water's surface. Our awkward attempts at conversation usually end with both of us laughing. We walk on and on for what seems like hours. Finally we pause and watch an old man take his spot on a bench. He is immediately surrounded by a bunch of squawking ducks.

She turns and motions as if it is time to go. I point in the direction I must walk. In parting we embrace, kissing European style, first one cheek and then the…

Quickly our eyes meet and then, slowly, our mouths. I know we are both surprised. We kiss again, and the old man looks bored. Amsterdam is like that. After a while she links her arm through mine, and we walk.

"I thought you had to go," I say to no one in particular. Her eyes tell me I have misunderstood and that this may be interesting. We walk down a cobbled street. My calves hurt like hell. I can't get used to these European surfaces. She turns at a gate onto a flagstone drive. We stroll along the drive to a hotel. Like the one in her movie, it is perfect for this moment.

Once in her room, I can see the water from the window. It is one of the three rivers that converge in this city. I sense the old man down there somewhere by its bank. She stands beside me, and we touch in the changing light. Fingers to lips, hand to cheek, mouth to throat. Our clothed layers of autumn fall away, and we sink to the floor.

She is turned away from me, and I embrace her from behind. My hands stroke her ribs and butt and legs while I kiss her neck and shoulders and back. I trace my fingers along the inside of her thigh, find the wetness, and slowly draw my fingers upward. Her hips move, and she arches. As her head falls back onto my shoulder, our mouths again meet.

One hand moves on her as I tease her breasts with the other. My own nipples ache and strain against her back. I meant this only as a prelude, but she wishes to finish. Her hips move, and I take my hand from her breast and enter her. All parts find the ancient rhythm, and after some time she shudders and whispers something in Dutch. I like the way it sounds. We fall sideways, and she rolls on top of me.

We smile and look at each other in a kindly way, I think. We kiss for hours. I feel her slip down my body, pausing here and there, but I'm still surprised when her tongue finds me. I gasp and say something—I don't know what—and I feel her breath on my thigh as she laughs.

I wonder after all my years of interviewing why, this time, this is the outcome. I suppose, after learning about her, all those facts about her childhood dreams, her frustrations and successes, her dog and two birds, that I feel I know the person. I feel close to her...so close. I ride her soft surface until I cry out, showing my complete self, the sum and total. Together we float, while the man feeds the ducks and the light below—such incredible light—glitters over the liquid surfaces of Amsterdam.

Part II: Coda

The long-distance phone lines crackled like something from an old movie.

"Four hours!" the heavily accented voice screeched. "That is all the time she will have available for the interview."

Now, two weeks after the phone conversation, I find myself in Amsterdam. I had a hell of a time finding this restaurant. Unlike most of the writers at the magazine where I work, I have never been to this city. I have never been to Europe. This restaurant, The Rookies, is a funky little art deco coffeehouse. Of course, the object of the interview is late. Typical movie star. Now we will have only three hours and forty-five minutes.

I recognize her when she enters the room and advances toward the maître d'. She speaks with him, and he is visibly delighted to have someone so famous in his establishment. He leads her to where I sit.

"I am sorry I am so late," she says as we shake hands. She has a strong accent. I can't hide the surprise on my face. "What?" she says mockingly. "Did you expect my English to be so awful I would have to bring an interpreter with curly red hair?" I blink and look down. Honestly, her English is not perfect, but I decide to keep quiet. She reaches into her bag, withdraws a narrow volume, and lays it on the table between us.

"I figured," she continues, "since you got a bio on me before the interview I should get one on you." She looks at the book. "Your writing." The volume on the table is my first, a collection of short stories. She moves an elegant unadorned hand to a marker and flips open the pages. *Every Lesbian's Fantasy* is circled in red. I look up and meet her eyes. We smile at each other, but I say nothing. She calmly points to the book. "Am I your fantasy?"

I shake my head, grab the book, and open to the front page. "This book was printed seven years ago. That's an awfully long time for a fantasy."

"Just what is this lesbian fantasy?" she asks. I look at her a moment and try to figure out if she is pissing me off or not.

"I'm supposed to be interviewing you," I say. She screws up her mouth like she did in her movie and smiles.

"Please," she says, "indulge me for a moment. I don't want to be interviewed by a psychopath." I wince and lean forward on my elbows. She leans back.

"It's a lesbian fantasy," I begin, "because whether you, the star, are gay or straight, you were, for two hours on the silver screen, a lesbian. You acted it well, convincingly." I pause and look at her. "In that sense you become a fantasy."

"Am I your fantasy?" she again asks.

"You're the fantasy of lesbians who see you play the part. They really want you to be gay." She looks doubtful as I continue. "The character you played was strong and independent. She found a man, got pregnant, had the child, fell in love with a woman, and lived happily ever after." She smirks and looks at her coffee cup. When she speaks, her voice is heavy with sarcasm.

"And that's a lesbian fantasy? Yuck!"

I wonder if she still thinks I'm a psychopath. "Well, no," I say. "Maybe some lesbians fantasize having a girl in every port."

"Or every interview," she says and locks eyes with mine.

I return her gaze. "No, my fantasy is the first. Only I was an idiot and had a husband briefly before I got the child."

She laughs. "And you fell in love with a woman and now live happily ever after?"

"We're trying to live happily ever after," I say, and our eyes meet again. She asks me to sign my book. We proceed with the interview. She is candid, funny, and utterly charming, but I still sense her distrust. I am busy afterward packing up the recorder, rolling cords, and collecting my hundreds of pencils when she speaks in my ear. "Would you like to go for a walk?" I freeze.

My heart pounds, and I cannot meet her gaze. I decide to stay busy. "I thought you had only four hours."

She takes in the room, but I feel her eyes rest on me. "That's what my agent always says. I think a walk would be more," she pauses, "interesting."

We walk along the water. A canal called Prinsengracht. She pronounces it as she looks over my shoulder at the guidebook. Amsterdam has so many canals. She links her arm through mine, and we say nothing. We walk through thick trees to the water. We stop in the center of a green bower with dark velvety grass. A bench sits near the bank. I look at it. "Where's the old man?" I ask.

She shrugs her shoulders and points. "But look, there's a duck." We laugh as she pushes me against a tree. We kiss for what seems like hours with our hands under each other's sweaters. Her lips are on mine, and she speaks into my mouth. "Am I your girl in this port?"

"No," I answer.

She moves down my body with her mouth, scattering light kisses on my breasts, ribs, and belly. My pants go down with her. I grab her by the elbows, but she continues until her tongue finds me. She opens me like an orange. I gasp. "This—" I begin.

Her breath is on my thigh as she speaks. "—is *my* fantasy. You didn't write this," she says. I arch and feel the rough bark against my scalp. I feel...so...close. Nearby a bell rings. Two bells, then three more begin their chimes. I look up and see sky and dappled sun through leaves the color of blood. The bells are loud, thunderous and I cry out. I...

Part III: Finis

...feel rhythmic contractions between my legs. My eyes open and see a face so familiar, I smile.

"Good morning, lover," my girlfriend whispers. I feel her hand between my legs. She blushes. "I just wanted to start your day right. I want to send you off to your interview feeling well, calm."

Our hotel room is a lot like the one in the movie. Last night we dined at a table set out on a broad green lawn. She stretches and jumps from the bed, wanders to the window, and looks down at the water.

"I hope you're not gone more than four hours," she says. "There are so many places and things I want to see. I want our first trip here to be absolutely perfect." She turns from the window and smiles at me.

"I think you are absolutely perfect," I say. She rushes on, pausing briefly to acknowledge my declared love.

"I think I'll walk around and take in some of the nearby sites." She glances at me with a wicked gleam in her eyes. "I hear she's a lesbian, so be careful she doesn't put the moves on you."

I walk up behind her and slide my arms around her waist. Bells ring out from a church. We stand together by the window and silently watch an old man sit down on a bench and begin to feed the ducks.

Desert Ride Songs
by Gina Ranalli

When Jill Casper left the Albuquerque city limits, traveling North on I-25, the western sky was still smudged with the lavender-gray bruises of a January dawn. Determined to beat the Friday morning rush hour, she'd managed to make it out of her condo, luggage and all, by 7:30. In the ten minutes she'd been on the road, she'd seen only a smattering of other vehicles, most of which were 18-wheelers.

She turned the Ford Expedition's heater on full blast to drive the chill from the air and melt the frost that lay over the windshield in sparkling crystal patterns. Dressed in Nikes, jeans, and a favorite old blue corduroy shirt over a black tank top, Jill felt comfortable and ready to conquer the looming majestic force that was Taos Mountain. She planned on skiing all day and possibly hitting a casino at night. She was also interested in exploring several museums, but the main plan was to break in all the shiny new ski equipment that lay in the back of the truck. She'd resolved to get out of her own head for a couple of days, to exhaust herself with physical exertion, and to put the stress of everyday life on the back burner for a while.

Who are you trying to kid, Casper? A voice inside her head asked. *It's Rachel you want to forget, Rachel and all the crap she spewed at you that last day a month ago.*

"That's bullshit," she said aloud. "I couldn't care less about her or her misguided opinions."

But she knew part of her wondered if perhaps the things Rachel had said were true. Was she dull? Unimaginative? Unadventurous? She didn't care to recall the half dozen other adjectives that had been thrown at her that day, cruel words that bit into her with deadly sharp fangs.

Maybe that's what this little excursion is all about, the inner voice suggested. *You want to show yourself you are able to have fun. That you're not some stick-in-the-mud, unwilling to ever try anything new or different. That the only reason you're taking this trip and taking it alone is so there will be no witnesses if you fail.*

With a grimace she glanced at her reflection in the rearview mirror. Her brown eyes gazed back at her, cloudy with the painful memory of Rachel and their abrupt ending. Though she knew most people considered her pretty, Jill could barely see it for herself. She thought of herself as average; her nose was too big, her eyes too small, her figure more pear-shaped than hourglass-perfect. Plus a few strands of gray had recently appeared at her temples and crown, though she'd only just turned 30. They stood out in defiant contrast against the rest of the long chestnut hair that fell to her shoulders in lush waves.

"Argh," she growled, bringing her stare back to the road. Since when was she so concerned with her looks anyway? Women seemed to like her just fine; she had a successful career as an attorney in Albuquerque, a city she adored; and she was about to drive up to Taos for what was going to be an adventurous weekend of skiing and who knew what else. The world was her oyster, and Jill intended to take full advantage of it. *Screw Rachel,* she thought. *She didn't know what she was talking about when she dumped me, and it's her loss!*

Maybe it's her loss, the pessimistic half of her mind retorted. *But maybe it's her gain. Because if you're really as boring as she says you are....*

Jill sighed and clicked on the radio in a futile attempt to silence the little traitor nestled in the back of her brain. Sheryl Crow was singing cheerfully about winding roads and feeling fine. Jill turned the heater down to low to hear the song better and even forced herself to hum along for a bit. Eventually, though, her thoughts turned back to her failed relationship, and she was forced to question yet again whether the things Rachel had accused her of were true.

Rachel hadn't been the first person to say such things about Jill, although she'd surely been the only one to say them with such ferocious venom in her voice. Prior to her it had been pointed out to Jill mostly in a joking manner, coworkers making remarks about "all work and no play" or friends commenting on her unwillingness to alter plans, to be spontaneous and free.

"I just don't like surprises," she muttered as the song ended and a new one began. "Lots of people don't. It doesn't make me a criminal. It just means I like to be organized. What the hell is wrong with that?"

She knew there was such a thing as being organized to a fault; she'd read about obsessive-compulsive disorders just like everyone else had, but those were extreme cases, and she displayed none of their symptoms. And just because she didn't live her life in a wild uncontrolled fashion certainly didn't imply she was inhibited. She cherished that she was methodical and orderly while she watched so much of the rest of the world fall to chaos, disarray, and confusion.

Turning the radio's volume up another notch, Jill tried once more to ignore the self-doubt that now danced in her mind with cruel smirking glee. She reminded herself that she never had difficulty getting a date or even holding onto a woman, so she knew it was ridiculous to worry about one woman's criticisms.

Forget about it, she thought. *Once and for all, forget about it.*

She decided instead to concentrate on the scenery. The interstate was quiet; she shared the road with only a few other cars and took the opportunity to admire the deep pinks and gentle browns of the desert landscape. The sky had bloomed into a cloudless intense blue, and she was suddenly filled with a soft contentment, secure in the knowledge that she was home, traveling through her beloved New Mexico. The terrain was nothing like the Pacific Northwest where she'd grown up. Where Washington was trees and rain, New Mexico was desert and sun.

Jill suddenly found herself smiling as she reached forward and snapped off the heater just as the Rolling Stones kicked hard into a song about where to get your kicks. She began singing along in her most robust voice, feeling genuinely good for the first time all morning.

Looking east across an impassive umber mesa, Jill saw white in the shadows where the sun had not yet ventured, drifts of snow cloaked in the shade of overhanging rocks. The sight made her crave the aura and magnetism of the mountain and of Taos. She gave the Expedition a little more gas.

About 500 feet ahead, a canary-yellow VW was pulled

over on the side of the highway, smoke churning out of it toward the radiant blue sky like a spirit finally unbound from the earth and sailing gratefully toward heaven. Jill could clearly make out the figure leaning against the crippled vehicle, and she instinctively slowed down as she approached.

"That's a bummer," she uttered just as she was passing the breakdown, noting with interest the rainbow decal in the Bug's rear window. She also saw that the stranded motorist was a woman: young and slim with short dark hair, dressed in jeans and a black leather jacket.

Driving on, Jill frowned, suddenly unsure of what to do. Naturally she was reluctant to stop, as anyone in her right mind would be. On the other hand, the woman appeared to be alone, and she was apparently a sister. The Beetle clearly wasn't going anywhere anytime soon, and Jill knew that she herself would hate to be stuck out on I-25 in the middle of nowhere.

A highway patrolman will be along to help her, Jill reassured herself. *Don't worry about it. You have your own plans, remember?*

The guilt-ridden part of her argued, *Who knows when a cop could be along? It could be hours. And what if someone else stops? It could be a very dangerous situation for her, a woman alone... You could offer her your cell phone if nothing else.*

"Good grief," she said to herself as she watched the VW receding in her rearview mirror. "What the hell is wrong with you? I can't believe you're even debating this foolishness. Since when would you even consider doing something so reckless?"

The words had barely slipped from her lips when Jill's eyes widened with realization, and she hit the brakes.

Without another thought she swung the Expedition around and headed back the way she had come. A moment later she was passing the breakdown in the southbound lane, and then with another U-turn she eased over to the side of the road and pulled the truck in behind the Bug.

The woman in the motorcycle jacket was eyeing the Ford with undisguised suspicion and seemed hesitant to come over.

Jill rolled down her window and called out, "I have a cell phone if you need it."

After a pause the woman reluctantly approached the truck, her black cowboy boots crunching over desert sand. She stopped a couple of feet from Jill's window. "I was just gonna wait for a cop." Her clear blue eyes shifted warily past Jill's face and into the truck, then back again. Evidently she had gathered that Jill was alone in the vehicle and came a step closer. "Thanks anyway."

Somewhat taken aback by the woman's attractiveness, Jill couldn't help staring. The stranger was probably in her mid 20s with full sumptuous lips and a complexion made rosy by the brisk morning air. "Are you sure?" Jill asked when she finally found her voice. "You don't want to call a tow? Or maybe a friend?"

"Nah, I'm just gonna leave it for now, I think. It's a piece of shit anyway. Probably older than me." She laughed, an open earthy sound.

"I could call the police for you, at least."

"You know what? I may even just start hoofing it." The young woman was looking north up the interstate, her face contemplative.

Jill was quiet for a moment, considering. She followed the stranger's gaze with her own and saw nothing but empty highway and emptier desert. Could this woman be pulling some kind of scam? Could she be dangerous? *Damn right she could be*, the careful side of her brain replied. *She could be a murderer for all you know*. Jill's mind was suddenly assaulted by a vision of Rachel rolling her eyes at her as she so often had. Jill growled inwardly and turned back to the woman. "Why don't you let me give you a lift? It's cold, and frankly walking sounds like a pretty dumb idea."

The woman looked back at her with what looked like amusement. "Didn't anyone ever tell you not to offer rides to strangers?"

Jill thought about it, then answered, "Yes. Which is why I'm offering you one."

There was a second when Jill thought she'd made a mistake; the woman peered dubiously at her for an uncomfortable tick of time, but then she broke into an amazing spellbinding grin and announced, "I guess it's my lucky day. I'm just gonna go grab my shit, OK?"

Jill could only nod. She felt as though she'd had the breath punched out of her and knew without a doubt that this stranger could break a heart in less time than it takes to watch a shooting star. She released a heavy sigh as she watched the woman leaning into the backseat of the VW to gather her belongings. *You're completely insane*, she thought to herself. *You could get yourself killed!*

"Maybe," she mumbled. "Maybe not."

She leaned over the passenger seat to unlock the door when the woman returned carrying a canvas army-green duffel bag in one arm and a six-inch plastic statuette of Jesus in the other. Jill marveled at the latter, wondering if she'd just offered a ride to a born-again. She thought that would be the one thing worse than offering a ride to a murderer. Please, anything but that!

Her new traveling companion opened the door and heaved the bag onto the backseat, carelessly pitching the inexpensive icon in after it before climbing into the truck herself. When she saw Jill's worried eyes on the plastic Jesus, she laughed and said, "Don't look so scared. I just had it glued to my dashboard 'cause I thought it was funny. I guess you could say I'm a little on the sarcastic side."

Jill raised an eyebrow but said nothing. Instead, she checked for traffic and pulled the Expedition back onto the road.

"I can't thank you enough for this," the woman continued. "It's not often that you come across good Samaritans these days."

"I know that if I were in that position, I'd certainly want someone to help me out."

"Ah. So you're one of those karma folks, huh?"

Jill shrugged. "Maybe. I've never thought about it, I guess."

The woman seemed to ponder this for a moment before volunteering, "By the way, my name is Izzy, in case you were wondering."

After introducing herself, Jill said, "Wow. Izzy. That's an unusual name."

"It's short for Isabel. My dad thought it was an amusing nickname when I was a kid. I don't think he expected it to stick."

Jill smiled. "You're lucky to have a name that stands out. Try being a Jill some time."

"Lots of Jack jokes, huh?"

"A few." Jill rolled her eyes, and it was Izzy's turn to laugh.

Nearly a full minute of silence passed before Izzy asked, "So where are we headed anyway?"

Jill gave her a sidelong glance. "I assumed you were going to tell me."

"I guess any place will do." She turned her head to gaze out the window, seeming to appraise the azure sky. "I think I'm kinda screwed. I'm a long way from home; I sort of doubt anyone is going to want to come all the way down here to get me."

"Where do you live?"

"Taos."

Jill gaped at her, somewhat startled, but the surprise was quickly replaced with an undeniable surge of pleased anticipation. Izzy didn't notice, her eyes still focused on the passing desert. When Jill finally spoke, the words came out softly. "I'm going to Taos."

Izzy looked back at her. "I figured."

"You did?" Jill was stunned. She laughed and asked, "Do you have ESP or something?"

"Nope, I just knew."

"But…" Jill stammered, and then realization came to her. She immediately felt her face burning with embarrassment. "Oh, the skis in the back."

"Bingo." Izzy flashed her flawless grin.

Jill's belly turned another cartwheel at the sight of that smile, and she quickly returned her attention to the road, praying Izzy hadn't noticed her reddening cheeks. To distract Izzy she quickly asked, "What were you doing in Albuquerque?"

"I had an art show," Izzy told her nonchalantly. "Ever hear of the Moon Song Gallery?"

Jill shook her head. "You're an artist?"

242

Izzy laughed. "Don't sound so surprised. What's the matter, you've never met one before?"

"It's not that. It's just…" she trailed off.

"Oh, I get it. You're wondering about the shitbox car, right? It was my first show. Well, my first real show. And congratulations are in order because I actually sold a few pieces, which is why I don't give a shit about the Bug. I figured I'd reward myself by taking a trip to Santa Fe next week and buying a better car, maybe one that's only half as old as me. Eleven years old is practically brand new compared to that clunker back there." She laughed her earthy laugh again.

"You're only 22?" Jill balked.

"Jeez, why do you say it like that? It's not like I'm 12. Besides, I'm actually 23."

"I see. Yeah, that's a big difference. I apologize." She tried to conceal her smile by glancing out the side window.

"Do I sense a note of sarcasm?"

"No, of course not!" Jill did her best to sound appalled.

Izzy began pulling off her leather jacket to reveal the black cable knit sweater she wore beneath it. As she flung it back on top of her duffel bag, she said, "Cool. You're a wise ass. I like that."

Jill was mysteriously tickled by being called a wise ass. She didn't think it had ever happened before. After a moment she said, "Aren't you curious about my age?"

Shrugging, Izzy asked, "Why? Will I be shocked?"

"Maybe," Jill giggled. She couldn't believe how comfortable she was with this young woman who less than thirty minutes ago had been a total stranger.

"Nah, I doubt it. Besides, it's not important to me how old someone is. You gave me a ride; you're a good shit. Period."

She paused, as if she were debating on speaking her mind. "I'm a pretty good judge of character too, a good observer. I guess it's because I'm a painter. You spend a lot of time just staring at things, seeing what other people can't."

"Don't they say that about most artists? Writers and actors or whatever?"

"Probably. But it's not hard to guess certain things about people based solely on observation. For example, judging by this fat-ass truck, you have a great white-collar job, making lots of money, and you probably live in one of those mod new condos downtown."

Jill was silent, staring at the road ahead.

"And," Izzy continued, "you probably don't have a girlfriend, or why else would you be going on a skiing trip alone? Unless you're meeting someone, which doesn't seem likely."

"Girlfriend?" Jill's mouth fell open. "How do you know I'm gay?"

"Oh, please," Izzy laughed and went back to looking out the window.

Disconcerted, Jill began to speak and immediately stopped when she realized she had no idea how to respond. She didn't consider herself closeted; her family, close friends, and even a few professional colleagues knew she was a lesbian, but to have someone mention it first was unheard of.

"People don't usually guess that about me," Jill said finally. "Not even other lesbians."

"I'm not just a lesbian," Izzy told her. "I'm a painter. It's true what they say about the eyes, you know."

"Is that so?"

"Windows of the soul, and I'll tell you what: I can see

right down to the bottom of yours."

Jill let out a nervous laugh. "And what do you think you see?"

"I don't think I see—I do see a beautiful but lonely woman who's been mistreated and could seriously use a little caring. You remind me of a flower that hasn't been watered in a long-ass time, you know?"

Suddenly, Jill felt a twinge of chilly fear creep up the back of her neck—not a fear of physical danger but a fear of being abruptly and unwillingly exposed. *How much can this woman really see?* she wondered apprehensively. *Anyone could guess I make good money, but...* Her mind halted, afraid to continue. She told herself she was being foolish to let a lucky guess or two frighten her. So what if no one, not even past lovers, had ever seemed to really know her. Maybe they just never tried.

But Jill knew that wasn't so; they all had tried to one degree or another. She'd always just assumed she was unknowable. But now she wasn't as convinced of that as she had been. Out of the corner of her eye she caught a glimpse of Izzy staring at her, and when she turned her head to return her gaze, Jill knew her fear wasn't completely pure: It was mixed with fierce, quivering excitement.

She quickly faced front again, fidgeting in her seat. "I don't think we need to discuss your theories about me, Izzy. We just met, for God's sake."

Izzy shrugged her shoulders and stretched her long legs out as far as she could. "You asked."

For the next twenty minutes, neither woman spoke. They passed Santa Fe and switched over to Route 285, still blessed with little traffic. A jackrabbit hopped through the desert beside the highway, darting from one sagebrush to another while the Indigo Girls crooned energetically about Suzanne calling from Boston.

Drumming her fingers against the steering wheel, Jill dared an indirect peek at her passenger. Out of the corner of her eye, she scanned the length of Izzy's body, beginning with the flawless ivory skin of her face. She imagined what it would be like to trail her tongue over the tender hollow of that throat, to place her lips on the beautifully delicate curve between the collarbone and the shoulder, or to feel the supple warmth of the breasts protruding like an invitation from beneath that sweater.

"Hey," Izzy said.

Jill cringed as if she'd been slapped, quickly snapping her eyes back to the highway, but it was too late. She knew she'd been busted. Reluctantly, she turned to Izzy, her face flushed with guilt.

"You look like you've seen a ghost," Izzy said, her voice low. She peered intently at Jill, her blue eyes as steady and endless as the New Mexico sky. "Are you afraid I'll touch you?" She smiled her ache-inducing smile again. "Or that I won't?"

An electric current instantly slammed its way through every nerve of Jill's body, beginning between her legs and shooting off in all directions like the branches of an immense and ancient tree bursting into flame. The truck veered dangerously toward the curb, and she struggled to rectify it, her hands damp on the wheel. Her mind reeled, and the first coherent thought it produced flew out of her mouth. "Am I dreaming?"

The question was answered when she felt Izzy's right hand brush lightly against her cheek, softly caressing it. Jill jumped at the touch but fought the instinct to pull away. She swallowed hard, staring straight ahead.

"Are you OK?" Izzy asked, leaning farther over the console that separated their seats. "Did I misread the vibes?"

Jill slowly shook her head and then shocked herself by turning her face quickly into Izzy's hand, kissing her palm and giving it a brief nibble before turning back to the business of keeping the car on the road.

Izzy responded by plunging her hand into Jill's chestnut hair, propping an elbow onto the console for balance, and bringing her lips to Jill's neck, where she gently began to kiss and trace figure eights with her delightfully warm tongue.

Trembling, Jill moaned weakly as she fought the urge to close her eyes and lean her head back. Instead, she tilted it to the side, giving Izzy better access.

Izzy took advantage of the position by sucking in tiny spurts up the length of Jill's neck. She made her way to Jill's earlobe, taking it into her mouth and teasing it with the strategic tongue of an expert. Pleased with Jill's sigh of pleasure, Izzy removed her hand from Jill's hair and brought it down to cup her breast, her thumb circling over the hardening nipple beneath the open corduroy shirt.

What are you doing? the rational part of Jill's brain shrieked. *You don't know this woman! You're in a moving vehicle, for God's sake! Have you completely lost your mind?*

It was in that moment that Jill nearly regained her sterile sensibilities. She almost pushed Izzy away, almost yelled for her to stop. But a fraction of a second before she could do either, two things happened. The first was that the vision of Rachel that had plagued her all morning came to her once more; Rachel's sneering expression and hostile words, her insistence that Jill was nothing but a dullard, afraid of her own shadow and unwilling to ever cut loose and enjoy a spur-of-the-moment adventure. The second was Izzy unexpectedly pinching her nipple and giving it a slight tug. Jill gasped in thrilled surprise and knew that despite her better judgment this was what she wanted, what she needed. This was a way to make herself forget everything Rachel had said and help her feel adequate again.

To convince herself she was doing what was right for her, Jill pulled away from Izzy just enough to turn and face her. She took one hand off the steering wheel and placed it beneath Izzy's chin, tilting the beautiful young face up into her own. Looking into those radiant eyes so dark with hunger, Jill saw herself reflected there and recognized the desperation for what it was. She leaned forward, meeting Izzy halfway, and they kissed with a rabid need, tongues lusciously intertwining in yearning exploration. Someone growled deeply, a low animal noise, but Jill couldn't be sure if she or Izzy had made the sound. She reached for Izzy's hand and guided it under her tank top, back to her breast. Reluctantly breaking the kiss Jill forced herself to face forward again, glancing down at the speedometer to ensure they were not breaking any speed limits, since they were quite clearly breaking some other law.

"Mmm, you feel nice," Izzy breathed hard into Jill's ear as she found her way beneath a designer sports bra. "I think we should pull over."

"No," Jill said at once. She didn't know why, but she knew she wanted to keep moving. Nearly panting, she added, "I want to feel dangerous."

Instead of protesting as Jill suspected she might, Izzy darted her tongue into Jill's ear and groaned a sound of approval. Her fingers squeezed the rock-hard nipple to the edge of pain, and Jill cried out, gripping the steering wheel with white-knuckled tension. The waves of desire burning between her legs had already become nearly intolerable, and she tried to shift slightly in her seat, but to no avail. She knew there was only one thing to ease the discomfort building there.

Izzy, sensing Jill's need, murmured into her neck, "Not yet, baby. Not 'til I say so." And then, as if to prove her adamancy on the matter, she pulled both Jill's tank top and her bra up, exposing her small pretty breasts, the pale pink nipples instantly erect from the chilly air inside the truck.

"Izzy, don't. Someone will see...." Jill trailed off as Izzy bent to flick her tongue delicately across one stiff bud, pausing every so often to cover the entire swell of the breast with tender kisses, her lips as soft as smoke.

Jill pressed Izzy's face firmly to her, no longer caring if anyone saw, her hips rocking involuntarily and her breath coming out in tiny snatching gasps. "Please," she begged in a hoarse whisper. "I can't take this." She heard Izzy snicker against her, and she wanted to howl in frustration. Outside the truck the world rolled by in a blur, all open land, empty but for the blanketing sage. They passed a sign informing them they were thirty miles south of Taos.

"Traffic will be picking up soon," Jill said just as Izzy's hand began creeping down her torso and into her lap, where it rested for several seconds like a wilted flower. Eventually Izzy began stroking Jill's inner thigh, easing her hand with agonizing slowness up to the sultry V that was the prize.

"I'd love to paint you." Izzy's voice was muffled, her mouth still wrapped around Jill's breast, busily licking and sucking. "I'd turn you into a sunset, use reds and yellows, orange for your skin, crimson for your nipples...set you on fire."

Although Izzy continued to speak, Jill was no longer listening. She pulled Izzy's hand to the button of her jeans and pleaded, "I can't wait, Izzy. Please...."

"OK, baby." Izzy told her with a mischievous smirk. "But you're going to have to help me."

"Yes, I will," Jill whined, lifting her ass a few inches off the seat. "Just hurry." Izzy obliged her, quickly ripping open the jeans to reveal the plain white waistband of Jill's panties. But to Jill's dismay and confusion, Izzy only tugged at the jeans instead of slipping her hand inside them as expected. A moment passed, each woman waiting for something the other didn't understand. Finally, Izzy said, "Help me take them down, baby. Come on." She pulled at the open flap of Jill's jeans.

"Wha...what?" Jill stammered, bewildered. "I can't take them down!"

Izzy grinned. "You can, and you will." She gave the jeans another yank.

Jill couldn't believe it; she gave Izzy a torn helpless look. "But..."

"But my ass. You're wasting time. Soon we'll be surrounded by other cars."

Jill knew it was true; they'd been extremely lucky so far, but that was all about to change with their approach to Taos. She glanced in the rearview mirror, then the side mirrors.

"Look," Izzy sighed. "If you don't want to, it's fine by me. We won't do anything you're not comfortable with. But you're the one who said you wanted to feel dangerous."

That reminder was all it took. Jill immediately began fighting with her jeans, trying to get them down at least to her mid thighs while trying to keep her foot on the gas pedal. Izzy laughed, doing her best to assist but somehow managing once again to become preoccupied with Jill's breasts. She was clearly enjoying making the entire escapade as challenging for Jill as possible.

Feeling teeth close exquisitely around her aching nipple, Jill felt a wave of heat flow through her body just as she and Izzy succeeded in lowering the stubborn Levi's.

"God, you're beautiful," Izzy whispered as she combed her fingers through the thick reddish-brown bush, her cheek resting against Jill's chest. "Really gorgeous."

Jill let out a tiny whimper of need, her hips reflexively jerking up at the touch. The fabric of the bucket seat felt rough and scratchy against her ass, and she was astonished to discover she actually liked the feeling.

Izzy continued to play down there in an almost absent-minded way until Jill thought she would scream. The teasing fingers slowly parted her lips and tentatively stroked the dripping opening, sliding over the silken folds with excruciating expertise. They lingered just below Jill's throbbing clit, seeking out every crease before traveling back down and slipping deliciously inside her aching vagina. Jill groaned loudly as Izzy inserted first two fingers and then a third, gliding in and out with increasing speed. Jill's entire body began rocking to match the thrusts; she held the steering wheel so tightly that her hands began to cramp around it. She spread her legs as far apart as she could, her pelvis rising and falling, grinding down on Izzy's fingers with all her might, eager to take in as much as she could. Izzy increased the rhythm and slid her thumb up to the sweet swollen clit. Jill cried out at the touch, urging Izzy to flick her faster, rub her, coax her over the edge, and then at last she froze. With a swift intake of air, she became silent, a shudder building within her like a distant peal of thunder, rolling closer, reverberating through every nerve in her body until finally she imploded with a colossal earth-shattering crack. Jill nearly screamed with the power of the orgasm that shook her, her hips jerking and bucking like a spooked mare caught in a tempest. Izzy did her best to hold on and ride out the violent gale until Jill unknowingly slammed the gas pedal to the floor. The vehicle lurched forward with a roar, weaving erratically toward the center divider before Izzy was able to grab the wheel and correct their course.

Aware only of the landscape whizzing by the window, Jill settled back into her seat, exhausted and blinking, as if she'd just awakened from a long restful sleep. She was dimly aware of the beautiful voice of R.E.M.'s lead singer hauntingly advising kids to rock 'n' roll. Before her, the highway stretched far into the distance and disappeared over the crest of a gently sloping hill.

"I guess this means you're giving me a ride home?"

Jill glanced to her right with bleary eyes. Izzy sat beside her wearing a smile to tempt the devil. "Yes, I guess it does," Jill answered, her face splitting into a wide grin. And with those few simple words, she felt all of Rachel's painful accusations become nothing more than harmless wisps of smoke dissolving into the crisp desert air.

That Summer
by Robin St. John

I wondered at Sarah's wildness. I always knew it was there, crouching like a waiting animal in a cave, and its many faces, the many things that delighted her, astonished me. I released her, at last gave her permission to be, and while we were together she dragged me along with her by the hand, the two of us like children running down a hill in sunlight.

I remember that long-ago day, the peculiar hot smell of it and the summer sounds: They live in my mind and body as clearly as this morning. Sometimes on these hot days, I sit in the tall grass by the pond, where the water moccasins sometimes race across the water and new generations of grasshoppers leap around my feet. At such times I remember Sarah, feel her wildness running like blood against my bones, taste her salt in my own sweaty skin, and sitting in the shade of the chinaberry tree, its branches now spread far across the surface of the pond, I am taken back to her. I wonder where she is, what she is doing, wonder if she ever thinks of that day.

ॐ   ॐ   ॐ

In the stillness of the sultry afternoon, the air heavy, hot, and damp, ringing with the buzz of insects in the trees, we walk together out behind the farmhouse. Everyone has gone to town for the day; there is no one here but Sarah and me and a few lazy sun-drugged cows huddled together under the sparse shade of the cottonwood trees near the pond. In the tall grass, grasshoppers leap, and occasionally the still surface of the water is split by the razor-thin line of a water moccasin streaking across the pond like a shooting star across the sky. Because of the snakes we cannot swim in the pond. We are allowed to fish there, baiting our hooks with ripe fat grasshoppers that we pluck from the grass with our hands and hurl into the water, hooked but still kicking, or worms, still wriggling, that we dig from the moist ground at the pond's edge. Dragonflies soar over the pond like small aircraft, darting, sunlight catching flashes of blue and green.

We sit on the bank, shooing a cow away; she stands chewing grass, looking at us stupidly, and moves slowly. We search the ground, checking for snakes, cow pies, patches of thistle that dot the ground here and there, then sit. I lean back against the tree trunk, feeling its roughness through my thin shirt. My skin, where it touches itself, is covered with a fine sheen of sweat: The boundaries between my body and the air have ceased to exist. I close my eyes for a minute, hearing only the silence of the still air, the noise of the insects, the cow's quiet chewing, Sarah's breathing. Sarah, sitting a few feet away, moves, and without opening my eyes I feel her suddenly closer to me.

I am 19; Sarah is 18. We have grown up together, as close as sisters. We have been inseparable for as long as we can both remember; our mothers grew up here too, best friends on adjacent farms. There was never a time when we did not know each other, born of a shared life and common dreams, sprung from the same dusty earth as surely as the new cottonwood trees along the bank of the pond. We go for minutes, hours sometimes on these endless summer afternoons without speaking. We run out of things to say, lose the volition to communicate except by desultory movement, grunted assent; we move like a herd of two, one following the other like migrating birds, as if some invisible cord binds us together.

I can smell Sarah, her scent familiar to me as that of grass and dust and somehow distinguishable. I hear her moving again and open my eyes, finally, to see what she is doing.

She has taken off her T-shirt and is sitting there with nothing on but her shorts, her long tanned legs stretched in front of her, her small pointed breasts raised to the air like the masthead of a ship; she is leaning backward on her hands, and her eyes are closed.

"Sarah," I say. "Are you crazy? What if somebody sees?"

"Oh," she says. "This feels so good. I'm so hot. Don't be such a worry wart. There's nobody for miles around." She is right, of course. Her parents will not be back until dinnertime, and the road to town is a good half mile away, too far for anyone driving by to see us.

Sarah's eyes are still closed, and I look at her again, at her bare brown shoulders, the white skin of her breasts, her firm nipples the color of rust, and I feel something stir in me and quickly take my eyes away.

I hear her laugh, the sound ringing into the still air like glass breaking delicately, and I look at her. She is laughing at me.

"What's the matter?" she asks.

I scowl at her. "Nothing's the matter."

"Why don't you take yours off too?"

"No, I don't think so." I feel my face burning. My breasts are not small and compact like Sarah's; they are large, so large that when I wear a T-shirt that fits the rest of my body, the cloth strains across the front of me like a fitted sheet over a bed. Most of the time my breasts embarrass me. I hate the looks men give me, the low guttural sounds, the wolf whistles. If I could trade them for a pair like Sarah's, I would in a minute.

"You shouldn't be so embarrassed about your body," Sarah says.

I sigh. We have had this discussion before. "Yeah, well, that's easy for you to say," I tell her. This is a tape we have played over and over, and I am willing to engage in it now only because there is nothing else to do. I am bored, and the awareness of her sitting next to me half naked has unaccountably muddled my thinking. All I can do is repeat words already said, covering familiar ground because it feels safer than anything else I might let myself say.

She lies down in the grass, stretching luxuriously like a cat preparing for a nap, and when she is on her back her breasts go almost flat, disappearing into the thin frame of her body as if they have gone under water, leaving only the nipples above like small buoys.

I feel a tickle on my arm, and thinking it's a bug crawling on me I twitch and slap at it.

"Hey!" she says. "Take it easy." I look at Sarah, see her grinning, and realize it was her fingertips running over my skin in that sensitive area at the back of my arm, just above the elbow. She continues, and I don't slap her hand, but I feel like I should. She keeps it up, stroking lightly, and in spite of how hot it is, how hot the air is, how hot my skin is,

I feel the heat of her hand against me like a small flame.

"Sarah," I say, "cut it out." I pull my arm out of her reach and turn around, then stretch out beside her on my stomach, leaning on my elbows. I watch a trail of ants move up one side of the tree and back down again, across a bare patch of dusty ground to their nest a few feet away.

My sweaty thighs are sticking to the grass underneath me, and I shift slightly to move my elbow off something prickly.

"It is just too damn hot to live," I say.

Sarah opens her eyes and turns her head to look at me.

"Take off your shirt," she says.

"Sarah—"

She cuts me off. "I want to see you."

I look at her now, astonished at her words, searching her face for a clue. There is a new and dangerous look in her eyes, and it scares me. I feel my face getting hot again.

"What do you mean, you want to see me?" I snort a little. "You've seen me plenty of times."

She gazes at me, her clear green eyes echoing the hue of the tall grass, and says, seriously, "But I don't think I ever really looked."

I throw her an incredulous scowl. "We have got to find something to do, Sarah. Maybe we should walk into town and go to the library or something. Or go to the drugstore and get a slush."

She laughs again. "Am I making you nervous, Lani?"

"Yes, you are. I think the heat has gone straight to your brain."

She doesn't answer me, just smiles, keeping her eyes on mine until I am forced to look away again.

She reaches a hand over and traces a line around my lips with her finger.

It has always been this way. Sarah is younger, but she has always been brave and foolish, and I have always been powerless to resist her. She has got us into more scrapes and mischief over the years than I can recount; left to my own devices I would lead a tame and dull life. Perhaps it is my own painful awareness of this that leaves me vulnerable to her.

I can smell the scent of summer on her hand, and I have that feeling I so often have with her, of being caught in a current, being swept downstream. I know from experience that with Sarah there comes a point when it is futile to argue, when I might as well save my breath. I know, despite my confusion, despite the sudden warmth that has lain over the already hot day like an extra blanket, that if I don't do something fast it will be too late. She will have me hooked like one of the small perch in the pond, and I will hang there, dangling helplessly, while she stands laughing at me. "Let's go swimming," I say, getting up.

"We can't go swimming," she says. "The pond is full of snakes."

"Oh, now who's chicken?" I ask, challenging her. I start unbuttoning my shirt, toss it into the grass, and reach around to unhook my bra.

I strip off the bra, feeling the delicious release of my breasts from the damp confinement, and then pull down my shorts. I don't let myself think about my too-pale skin that burns so easily that I have to stay out of the sun; I don't let myself notice the ponderous weight of my breasts; I refuse to allow myself to consider the roundness of my belly, the folds of flesh Sarah doesn't have, the thickness of my thighs. I take off my cotton panties and throw them onto the pile of clothes and stand there naked, defiant, looking at her.

She is sitting up now, watching me, a small amused grin on her face.

"What in the world has gotten into you, girl?" she asks.

           *   *   *

What has gotten into me is that in that moment when she touched my lips with her finger, it all became too much, and if I hadn't gotten up, stood up, done something, I would have ceased to be able to breathe. I would have lain in the grass and smothered to death under the weight of Sarah's odd words, her disconcerting behavior, the oppressive damp heat, the suddenly unbearable feel of wet cloth against my skin. I would have died, and in that moment of realization I decided to live. Snakes or no snakes, I needed to feel the shock of cool water against my skin, needed to wash off the sweat, to wet myself and shake Sarah off me like a dog shaking off water after running in the rain.

"Are you coming?" I say to her and turn, before I can talk myself out of it, before I can tell myself what a stupid idea this is and how this is the kind of thing Sarah would do, not me. I resist the tide of words, the cautionary voices in my head, as if I am pushing away hands reaching for me, and I am at edge of the pond. Then I am running out onto the dry splintered surface of the tiny dock, and I hurl myself off the end of it, feel my body enter the water, feel it embrace me in its murky depths. My feet don't find bottom, which surprises me; I seem to go down and down for a minute. I open my eyes, look upward, and see bubbles, green and white, rising, and the sparkle of the sunlight on the surface of the water several feet above me. The water is cool but not cold, and I see plants growing, waving in the disturbance caused by my entry. I kick and swim upward, bursting out of the water, gasping for breath. Sarah has taken off the rest of her clothes and is sitting on the edge of the dock, one leg hanging off, one knee raised, so that I can see clearly the patch of dark hair between her legs. I swim over and throw handfuls of water at her, but before she reaches down I dive below the surface. I see her hand break the water, and I grab it. She is instantly off-balance, and I pull her easily into the water, shrieking, gasping, fighting me. Sarah is wiry and tough, but I am heavier and taller, and I pull her easily under the water, where we both open our eyes, cheeks puffed like strange fish. Her eyes are the color of the water, and when she laughs the sound rolls out thickly, sharply, through the water, bubbling upward. I hang onto her for a minute, holding her down, but then both of us are desperate for air, so I let go of her and kick forcefully. We shoot toward the surface in a tangle of thrashing limbs and streaming hair.

Sarah is laughing, pushing her dripping hair out of her eyes. She takes a deep breath and blows it out, and we just hang there in the water, treading, looking at each other, smiling. Uncle Sammy always says no one really knows how deep this pond is, but I always figured he was kidding, making sure no kids went for a swim with the moccasins. Remembering the moccasins now, I look around, hoping that what I feel moving around my feet, far down in the water, is plant life and not snakes. I am surprised that even here, close to the dock pilings, I cannot feel the bottom. Out of breath, I reach for the edge of the dock over my head, moving into the shade underneath it.

Sarah follows me, and we hang there, suspended in the cool water, the silence. "Want to swim across?" she asks suddenly.

"Across the pond?"

"Yes, silly. What do you think, the Atlantic Ocean?"

I look across to the far side of the pond, about a hundred yards away. On the bank are the ruins of an old bunkhouse, left over from the days when this was a cattle ranch, and where Sarah and I had played childhood games of pretend, heedless of the black widow spiders and rattlesnakes.

I don't answer but place my foot quietly against the dock piling and look at her as if I am mulling it over. Suddenly I shove off with my foot, gaining a good body length or two on her before she has time to react. I shout over my shoulder, "Beat you!"

I know this is not true; Sarah is lean and lithe in the water, her movements fluid and graceful. As a sophomore she was the best swimmer on our high school team. But I have a substantial lead, and I give it my all, knowing but not caring that she will overtake me easily and leave me with a face full of rippling swelling water as she glides by me. I roll over on my back because I am fastest that way, and I watch her as she gains on me, then moves past. My ears are in the water, and I can hear the sounds our bodies make as we swim. Overhead I see the deep blue summer sky with one or two pillowy white clouds. I have forgotten the heat, forgotten the slow syrupy feel of the day, forgotten everything but the delicious sensation of being supported in the cool spring-fed water of the pond.

I am about ten yards from the shore. I cannot see her because I am still swimming backward, slowly now, almost just floating and kicking slightly, but I know Sarah is already on the bank, watching me, probably laughing and shaking her head at my easy relinquishment of victory to her. In the same second as I think of her watching me, I become aware of my bare breasts bobbing along above the surface of the pond, nipples firm from the cool water. Instantly I turn over and start to dog-paddle the rest of the way, a kind of swimming that Sarah despises as beneath anyone but poodles and three-year-olds. Sure enough I see her standing there, her arms wrapped across her chest. She shakes her head in mute testimony to my being a lost cause, but she is smiling.

I smile back, continuing my leisurely progress, and suddenly, when I am about fifteen feet from the bank, I see her expression change.

Her features shift into slow motion: Her smile moves inward from the sides of her mouth, until her mouth forms an O; her chin drops, her eyebrows rise, and her hands reach for me. As if I can read her thoughts and see with her eyes, I know before she manages to scream out the words what it is she sees.

"Lani, there's a snake! Swim!"

I do. I have no idea where the snake is, if it is coming at me, if it is coming from the side. I move as if electrified, my limbs feeling heavy and clumsy in the churning water, my feet reaching desperately for the feel of solid ground beneath them, finding only deep water and long tubular things I am now certain are not plants but writhing masses of snakes. Horror rises in my throat like bile, and I hear my own heart pounding in my head, the sound of my ragged breath like the whine of a saw. Finally I grab the grass at the edge of the pond and then Sarah's hand. At last I fall gasping on the bank, looking wildly back at the water.

I don't see a snake. "Where did it go?" I ask her when I get my breath back a little, and then I see she has her hand over her mouth, her shoulders shaking.

I leap to my feet. "Damn you, Sarah!" She does not try to hide her laughter now but is almost hysterical, tears running down her face. She looks at me, still dripping, and I start for her. She leaps away, and I chase her, although running is just like swimming; she can almost always beat me. But I am fueled by a combination of anger, terror, and outrage, so I catch her this time as she scrambles up a small embankment at the back of the cabin. I throw my full weight on her, pinning her to the ground, my belly against the hard roundness of her butt, my breasts pressed against her bare back. We lie there for a minute, Sarah still choking with laughter, and I feel my anger and fear start to subside. Then, even though I desperately don't want to, I feel myself giggle too, feel laughter well up like water bubbling from a faucet. I roll off her, and we both lie helpless with laughter for several long minutes. One of us stops, breathes, wipes tears away, then the other does, and just when we are almost calmed, the hysteria hits us again. I can't remember ever laughing so hard, so hard I know the muscles in my belly, around my ribs, are going to be sore. We shriek and whoop, lying in the dust. Finally, exhausted, all I can do is lie back and look at the sky through the trees, waiting to be caught in the next wave. But finally it calms, I calm, and I turn to look at Sarah, who has also grown quieter. She has turned over on her back, and her whole front is covered with the dust of the embankment where I pushed her down; it has caked in places, and rivulets of sweat have run down her skin, making small trails across her pale breasts. Her damp hair is full of dust and bits of grass, and looking at her I almost start laughing again. She looks like a four-year-old coming in at the end of a summer evening, happy, gloriously dirty, and blissfully unaware.

"You are just a mess, girl," I tell her. She turns those clear green eyes on me, and suddenly a truth of which I must have had an awareness long unarticulated, bursts upon me like sunlight through an east window in morning: how I love this girl, my playmate, my sister, my friend.

Sarah smiles at me, and I reach out and brush some of the dust off her skin. I brush her belly, her shoulders, the small mounds of her breasts, her firm compact body so different from my own and yet so much a part of myself. Together we have bathed, slept, played, studied, fished, fought, cried, and even run away once when Sarah was in third grade and hated her teacher. Of course it was her idea, and of course I went along.

I smile, remembering these things. She lies still under my hand as I work the drying dust from her skin. I accidentally (*Was it accidental?* I would ask myself later) brush one of her nipples with my hand, and I feel it stiffen under my touch. Sarah places her hand on mine, pressing it to her breast. I look at her, startled; she looks at me intently, a kind of challenge in her eyes, mixed with something else, some new emotion. I struggle to read it, to make sense of it. She takes my hand and moves it slowly over her breast, over the stiffened small nipple. I feel my body come alive with a kind of humming, as if some strange energy is coursing through me. She reaches for my nipple, explores it with her fingers as if she is trying to read some message hidden there. I stop thinking—I am unable to think—and moving slowly, deliberately, I take my hand away and take her breast in my mouth, feel her fingers in my hair, feel her back arching as she meets my movement.

Her skin tastes of salt and dust and lavender soap and pond water and the grass that grows under us and grasshoppers and the acrid smell of snakes. She tastes of earth, and I eat as if coming home, feeling the amazing nub under my tongue. My hands seem suddenly to have a will of their own. I am helpless to stop them. I watch as if from a distance while they move over her belly, her thighs, feel her swimming-hard muscles ripple under their touch. Her hands are on me too, and it is almost too much, this river of sensation. I feel as though I am being swept down, losing my footing, water closing over my head.

Our mouths find each other, our tongues like two long-lost friends, and I take her like food, like water, like long-awaited sustenance I did not know I needed. Her usual wiry resistance is gone, and she melts under me, becomes some-one new, someone I have been waiting for since before I had life, since before I had breath.

My fingers find the soft patch of hair. I feel her legs open slightly, like a door, and I step through into the land-scape of her, into this region we have not until now explored together. There on the dusty bank, in the deep-ening afternoon shadow cast by the ruined walls of the old bunkhouse, I taste her, taste earth and salt and water and air, taste our whole lives contained in the pungent sting of her juice against my chin, taste the solid containment of everything we have lived together there in the firm swelling of her. Not knowing what it is I do, driven not by thought but by some instinct deeper than hunger, deeper than thirst, deeper than sleeping and waking and being born and dying, I love her with my mouth, my hands, my bursting heart until she shudders, crying out in the dust. Afterward we lay for a long time, my head resting on the warm surface of her belly, her hands caressing my hair, until finally we see the lights of Uncle Sammy's car turning in from the highway in the dusk and a few minutes later hear him shouting for us.

We do not speak but get up, brushing bits of leaves and grass from ourselves. The pond has grown dark and brooding as the sun has fallen lower in the sky, and there is no thought of swimming back across. We walk around the pond, picking our way carefully with our bare feet; I stumble against a rock, and Sarah puts out her hand to steady me. I take it, holding on until finally we are back under the chinaberry tree, gathering our scattered clothing. We dress, the feel of the cloth warm and clean and comforting against our spent skin, and we walk back to the house.

Uncle Sammy and Aunt Vi look at our dusty faces, our disheveled hair but don't say much.

"You girls get cleaned up," Sarah's mother says, shaking her head at us. "Supper's about ready." The smells of meat frying, of black-eyed peas boiling, of cabbage cooking fill the warm kitchen. The room glows with a yellow light, and all my senses seem more acute: colors are brighter, more intense; smells seem to enter me, fill me, filter through me until I can feel them in the pit of my belly.

Showered, our wet hair still smelling of shampoo, we sit at the table. I don't remember ever being so hungry in my life.

"What did you girls do today?" Uncle Sammy asks.

Sarah and I look at each other.

"Oh, you know there isn't much to do around here, Daddy," she says, finally. "We just hung around the pond."

She looks at me across the table, our eyes meeting, and she smiles at me, almost shyly. I take a sip of iced tea, and it becomes pond water, becomes her, becomes all our collective summers condensed into one day, one deeply satisfying moment.

⁂

The last time I saw Sarah was at her father's funeral. She stood at the graveside between her husband, Scott, and her mother. She was still beautiful, but something, some freshness perhaps, was gone from her face. She looked tired. I watched her while she looked, distracted and dreamy, at her two tall sons, awkward and hot in their unaccustomed suits. Once she glanced over at me, and our eyes met. I smiled at her, and she seemed to study me as if trying to remember who I was, her face quizzical, slightly pained. Some recollection, maybe, brought on by the peculiar familiarity of the damp hot air, the smell of growing things, the buzz of insects in the quiet cemetery grass? I would never know.

Great chasms of time, uncrossable canyons of experience had separated us from each other and from that single summer day when all of life shifted. For me, it never shifted back. We did not play by the pond again.

Bridal Party
by Anne Seale

Debs and Kirsten are getting married this afternoon, and they've asked my lover, Selah, to be maid of honor. She's been in the bathroom for forty minutes trying to get her hair to fluff up around a floral headpiece. Every so often I hear her cuss.

I'm dressed and standing in the kitchen eating a bologna sandwich. Selah has ordered me not to sit down because it would make creases in my tuxedo trousers that were designed for a man with no butt. (He didn't have 44-D breasts either.)

I'm not in the wedding, but Selah insisted I rent a tux. She said it would look funny, her in a fancy long gown and me in my chinos. I protested, but she wore me down.

Debs and Selah were once lovers. They parted several years ago and have been best friends ever since, something I've never been able to pull off. Selah, therefore, has been very involved in the nuptial plans, which is good because if she sticks with me she'll never have a wedding of her own. I don't make commitments.

Selah runs into the kitchen, turns her back, and says to zip her up before I leave to pick up Kirsten. I've been assigned the task of driving Kirsten to the church to keep

Debs from seeing her in her gown before the ceremony. Debs, in turn, is coming to pick up Selah a little later, and they are stopping on the way for ice cream and half-and-half for the reception coffee.

As I pull on the zipper, it keeps catching in the lacy fabric. Finally I give a great tug, and it closes, but a two-inch length of purple thread now hangs from one of the snags. I try to break it off, but it won't break. To distract Selah, I say "Hey, your hair looks great!" as I fumble in the tight tux pocket for my key-ring jackknife. She grunts and heads back to the bathroom, the thread trailing in her wake. I decide to let it go (she's stressed enough).

Since the Saturday traffic is light, I'm a little early getting to Kirsten's mother's suburban home. Kirsten isn't ready, so I have to sit and chat with her mom like a high school kid picking up a date for the prom. She offers me coffee, but I say no. All I need is a brown stain on my starched white shelf.

Just when I'm wondering what time it's getting to be, Kirsten floats down the stairs. I catch my breath. She's gorgeous in a cloud of net over pure white satin. Her red hair curls around a halo of tiny flowers and ribbons. I've always liked red hair. For a moment, I wish I were that high school kid.

Kirsten's mother rushes to gather her train, and after a great deal of arranging we get her settled on the bench seat of my S-10. I can't see the rearview mirror on the passenger side for all the skirt.

"Don't be late, Mama," Kirsten tells her.

"Don't you worry, honey, I'll be there in that front pew when you walk down the aisle." She kisses Kirsten through the open window. "And Nana will be there with me, and Aunt Bern and Uncle Jack."

It makes me wonder who from my family would come if I were to marry Selah or anyone, goddess forbid. My cousin Jimmy might show up—I've had suspicions about him for years.

"Nervous?" I ask Kirsten as I back out the driveway.

"A little," she says. "I hate being the center of attention."

"What I meant is, aren't you nervous about promising to stay with someone the rest of your life? Through sickness and poverty and all that? I'd be petrified."

"You're right," she says softly. "It's a big step to take."

I mentally kick myself. What am I doing, frightening the poor woman with my paranoid feelings about commitment? I change the subject. "Hey, that Debs! Ain't she a great gal?"

"She's wonderful. How long have you known her, Tammy?"

"As long as I've known Selah, about eight years, I guess. They were already broke up by then."

"Oh."

We ride in silence for a few miles; then Kirsten says, "Do you by any chance know why they broke up, Selah and Debs?"

"No, I don't. Why?"

"Oh, no reason."

After a couple of more blocks, she says, "Was Debs faithful to Selah, do you know, when they were together?"

We're in the city now, stopped at a red light. I look at her. "Of course she was. Selah never told me she wasn't, at least. What's this all about, Kirsten? Do you think Debs is running around on you?"

"No, no," she says, patting my arm with a white-gloved hand. "She's just gone a lot, that's all. Like she says, she's a very busy woman. But I never really thought...'til lately...."

She laughs a self-conscious little laugh. "Oh, it's nothing, Tammy. Forget it. Wedding-day jitters."

I can't stop looking at her. I've seen Kirsten a lot in the months she and Debs have been going together, and I've always considered her nice-looking. Today, however, seeing her in that, well, *virginal* wedding gown, I just want to lean over and…

A car behind me honks its brains out, and I see the light has turned green. I cross the intersection, pull into the church lot, and park next to Debs's Honda. After delivering Kirsten to something called a "Bride's Room" off the church lobby and suppressing the urge to kiss her good-bye, I go off in search of Selah.

It's still forty-five minutes until the ceremony, but a few people are already seated in the pews when I peek in. A woman from our euchre club spies me and runs over, and I have to listen to a description of her wedding—she calls it a "union"—many years ago. She provides me with detailed descriptions of her gown, her attendants' gowns, and all the flower arrangements. When I ask about her spouse, it turns out the union didn't last much longer than the flowers. I excuse myself and take the stairs to the basement where the reception is going to be. Maybe Selah is helping set up.

No one is in sight, but there are lots of folding tables covered with pink plastic, one of which holds a four-tiered wedding cake with a nauseatingly heterosexual bride and groom standing stiffly on top. Geez! I look around to make sure I'm alone, then carefully lift them off, placing the gardenia from my lapel over the bare spot. Much better!

Now, what to do with Mr. and Mrs. Hetero? There's no wastebasket in sight, so I cross to a swinging door marked KITCHEN. As I raise my hand to push it open, I hear a low husky voice from inside that I recognize as Debs's. The voice is saying, "Oh, baby, I want you so much." I freeze.

Kirsten was right—Debs is messing around with another woman! Since Kirsten shared her suspicions with me, I feel I owe it to her to find out for sure. It may save her from making a big mistake today. I crack the door and peek in.

There's a woman standing between Debs and me who is wearing a dress, a long purple dress. I can't see her head because of protruding cupboards, but I'd know that zipper anywhere. There are snags in the lace alongside of it, right where I snagged them, and the two-inch purple thread is still hanging.

Debs's left hand reaches around and begins pulling the zipper down. It doesn't catch even once. I watch transfixed as the dress opens and falls to the floor. The hand pushes the bra strap off the right shoulder, then moves over and does the same to the left. I can't help wonder what the other hand is doing. Debs's mouth enters my vision as it kisses its way down the side of the neck and in the general direction of what must be Selah's nipples.

I draw back, let the door close, and tiptoe back through the room and up the stairs, ditching the cake-top couple on the landing. When I reach the top, I lean against the wall, feeling dizzy. What was it Kirsten had told me? "I never really thought...'til lately...." I try to think if Selah's patterns have changed recently. Has she been spending more time with Debs than usual? Well, yes, but they've been working on wedding preparations...haven't they? Oh, what a fool I've been!

I have to tell Kirsten. But how can I tell her that it's my own Selah that Debs has been messing around with? How mortifying! But if I don't tell her, she'll go ahead and marry the dirty two-timer. I find the Bride's Room again and, after hesitating a long time, knock.

"Who is it?" It's Kristen's voice.

"It's Tammy. Can I come in?"

After a moment a latch turns, and the door opens. After I enter, Kirsten quickly shuts and locks it again. "Tammy, thank goodness. Where's Selah? She was supposed to meet me here a long time ago."

"Selah? She's...uh ...downstairs."

"Downstairs? What's she doing there? She's supposed to be here with me."

"Kirsten, honey, why don't you sit down?" I steer her to a gold brocade sofa and sit beside her, taking her white-gloved hand in mine. She looks so scared and vulnerable, I can hardly say it. "I'm afraid you were right, Kirsten; Debs does have someone else. I...I saw them."

Kirsten turns white. "You saw them? Debs and another woman? Who is it?"

When push comes to shove, I can't do it. "Her back was to me," I say. It's not a lie.

Kirsten bursts into sobs. "I knew it! I knew Debs had someone else. How could I ever have believed her? Oh, Tammy, you're so lucky to have a good woman like Selah. So lucky."

"Lucky," I say, picturing in my mind what's happening down in the church kitchen right about now. I see Debs and Selah writhing all over the purple dress, Debs's hands still very busy.

Kirsten rants on. "How could Debs do this to me? I thought we were happy together. I thought she loved me. And all the time she was running around with this...this hussy. She doesn't want me. Nobody wants me!"

I wipe a drip from her chin with my thumb. "Anybody who doesn't want you is brain-dead."

She takes my hand and presses the palm to her mouth. I feel her lips move against it as she says, "Do *you* want me, Tammy?"

She raises her face to mine and stops an inch away from my lips, staring into my eyes, daring me to close the gap. Her brazen manner starkly contrasts the implied innocence of the gown. Her cheeks are flushed, and arrested tears sparkle in her eyes.

Without thinking, I meet the dare—I lower my lips and use them to open hers. Our tongues meet and communicate as we shift until I am flat on the cushions. The wedding dress whispers as her body moves on mine.

I don't realize she has opened my fly until I feel a hand slip in and begin softly stroking. The seams on the fingers of the glove add a nubby dimension to the caress. My hands move to her breasts and squeeze them through the silky bodice. Her nipples stiffen against my palms. Everything I own stiffens in response.

Kirsten's lips suddenly abandon mine, leaving me gasping. She pushes herself up and unhooks my suspenders and everything else that's in her way. I feel a wetness on my exposed middle as she eases down, tracing my nakedness with her tongue until she finally gets where she wants to be. A medley of soft curls, ribbons, and silky veil plays on my thighs as she moves her head in concert with the tongue.

White-gloved hands shoot up, aiming for my breasts. I waylay the hands and pull the gloves off, crushing them against my nose and breathing through them. They smell hot and earthy. The now-bare fingers expertly unbutton my shirt and push under the cups of my bra, quickly scaling the heights and celebrating the summits.

My lower body begins moving, gliding against satin, and I find myself groaning. In case anyone is near, I stuff the gloves into my mouth and bite down, but my delighted tongue begins moving against their roughness, and instead of being muffled my groans increase in volume.

The mouth that has been working me begins to move in for the kill. "Not yet," I mumble around the fingers of the gloves, wanting the excruciatingly blissful anticipation to last forever. I am trying to pull away when the giant breakers hit. Tsunami! Kirsten's tongue keeps moving until the last tiny wave has ebbed.

She emerges grinning from the deeps, halo askew. "My turn," she says.

I tear the gloves from my mouth and fling them across the room. Pushing Kirsten back, I prop her against the sofa's arm, displacing the voluminous skirts until I find damp lacy panties. I don't remove them right away but use them to tease. I run my finger along the elastic, blow on the dampness, pull the crotch aside for a quick touch now and then, letting it snap back.

Kirsten arches her back, thrusting her mound up. "Tammy, please," she whispers.

I'm as ready as she is. Pulling the panties down, I dive into her slippery eelness. As I thrust with my tongue, Kirsten leans over, pulls up the back of my shirt, and rakes her nails across my back. I move my hand down to my own wetness and pace myself to explode when she does. Her scream is loud enough to be heard on the next block.

Wondering how long until someone comes to the door, I don the tux in one eighth the time it took me this morning while Kirsten slips on the panties, smoothes her skirts, and retrieves the gloves. "Tammy," she says, "you won't tell Debs, will you?"

I freeze in the middle of tying my tie. "You aren't still going to marry her, are you?"

"I don't know. I need to talk with her."

I can't believe it. "What was all this about, then?" I indicate the sofa, the scene of the crime.

"Guess I was…vulnerable."

"Vulnerable." I echo. "Yeah, guess I was vulnerable too." I unlock the door and leave, passing without a word the dozen or so who are gathered in the hall searching for the source of a scream.

I drive home, wondering where I'll go after I change and pack. As I cross the living room, Selah calls from the kitchen, "Is that you, Tammy?"

I look in and stare. She's wearing jeans and a T-shirt and is mixing something that looks like it's going to be meatloaf. "How'd you get home so fast?" I say.

"What do you mean? I never left home. Didn't Debs tell you what happened?"

"I didn't see Debs. Well, I *saw* her, but…where's the purple dress?"

"I took it off and threw it at her. Told her to let her paramour stand up for her—I wasn't going to have any part in that charade of a wedding!" She gives the meatloaf a good kneading.

"She told you she was having an affair?"

"Yes, she did, when she came to pick me up. There was a woman waiting for us in the car, and I asked who she was. 'That's my new girlfriend,' Debs told me. 'Your what?' I said. 'Just a little something on the side,' she said. Then she had the nerve to tell me, 'You should know better than anybody that one woman at a time isn't enough for me.' " Selah wipes at an angry tear, smearing ketchup on her cheek. "It brought back all the hurt and humiliation I felt when we were together and I found out she was cheating."

"Debs cheated on you? You never told me."

"I was ashamed. I blamed the breakup on myself. Debs said it was my fault, that I was a cold woman."

"Well, you're not!" I say indignantly.

Selah washes and dries her hands and cheek and crosses to me, putting her arms around me. "Thank you, Tammy," she whispers. "I needed that."

"Wait a minute, you took your dress off in front of Debs?" I say jealously, in spite of what I just bared to Kirsten.

"Right in this room! I threw it at her, like I said. She grabbed it and left."

"What a jerk!" I say.

Selah backs up and gives me a serious look. "You'd never do that to me, would you, Tammy? Cheat on me?"

"Absolutely not!" I say. "I promise to be true from this day forward."

She hugs me again, then says. "My goodness, honey, you look sexy in that tux! Wanna get married?"

"If we do, will you wear white?"

She's surprised at my answer. "Well, sure, if you like."

"Any time then."

She backs up and stares, not knowing whether to take me seriously. Finally, she goes back to her meatloaf. "We'll talk about it," she says. "So did Debs and Kirsten get married or not?"

"I have no idea. I didn't want to be there without you," I tell her and go to take off the tux, hoping Kirsten's fingernails had not drawn blood.

Infinity
by Gail Shepherd

"My love, you are gold-crested and sun-dazzled as a scree of buttercups," says Sally Mae. The morning light arcs in through the leaded window. It streaks across her lover's hipbone and illuminates the penumbra of damp cleavage from which Sally Mae has recently risen, as if from a long dream.

Making love is like meditation; it slows Sally Mae's heart, which otherwise threatens to burst through the taut flesh of her eloquent rib cage. Her heart is a caged bird with a yen for flight.

Sally Mae's lover smiles her kitty-cat smile. She is, *in puris naturalibus,* both golden and florally scented, as Sally Mae has remarked. She is long and lazy and closely shaven, so that the light falls too on her visible netherlips, translucent and mauve. These Sally Mae unabashedly worships. Like a pagan encountering an unfamiliar sea creature beached by the tides, she falls to her knees in wonder, time after time after time.

Her lover, named Therese after the ecstatic saint, rolls languidly over, and Sally Mae is enveloped again in the pure weight of clean and pliant flesh, abundantly distributed along the length of torso and belly and thigh. This torporous *soixante-neuf* embrace, which Sally Mae has always likened to the sign of Infinity, is as close to God as she is likely to get. It is here, heartfully engaged in committing the triple deadly sins of gluttony, lust, and sloth that Sally Mae feels herself approaching some absolute state of grace.

So the hours pass, and when they awaken again it is with a muted double headache and the sadness of evening.

There are showers to be taken and gin tonics to be mixed. There is the cold green salad curled and glistening in its wooden bowl. And the linen napkins that when pressed to the lips release a faint essence of lavender.

The air is scented with the sharp blue exhalations of jasmine.

On a terrace overlooking the sea, our two lovers are now as mournful as a pair of abandoned shoes. Even the wind in the Royal Palms seems to whisper conversations to which they are not privy. Somewhere life is going on without them, out beyond the thin scrawl of highway and the illuminated beach houses strung together like pearls.

They will rouse themselves and go indoors. Therese will, Sally Mae knows, dress herself with much sensual abandon, like an exotic dancer seen in slow-motion reverse time. She begins naked; then the necklace of bauxite clasped at the throat; the four gold rings slipped over fingers and thumb; the gray silk brassiere (she bends at the waist to capture each pendulous breast); the tiny black G-string (really entirely useless, Sally Mae thinks, except as a purely aesthetic experience) that covers only one tenth, perhaps, of her sweet-smelling and freshly oiled *Mons de Venus*; then the wisp of a dress that slithers enticingly over the shoulders to fall just above two sculptural knees; and finally a pair of satin pumps, balletic. Therese will struggle adorably with the spaghetti ankle straps of these shoes until Sally Mae longs to kneel and take the buckle between her teeth. But she will refrain.

Sally Mae knows too that perhaps fifteen or twenty minutes will be spent arranging the blond hair to fall in soft curls around her lover's neck, which even now, still with half a headache and a sense of unease, Sally Mae likens to the neck of a fawn. Or a faun?

Sally Mae ponders this, abstractly.

This faun-like quality had drawn her to Therese, her softness, her self-absorption, her naïveté. Therese will bristle at this description, however lovingly rendered, for she sees herself mostly as adept and powerful and brainy, a person to whom money and accolades flow as surely as rivers move inexorably toward the sea. And this too, Sally Mae thinks, is not inaccurate. But it is Therese's night-time quality of repose, like a lily pond glittering and lapping under a full moon, that Sally Mae knows she will remember when or if ever they are parted.

As for herself, her brown hair has streaked itself with gray, and she is given to dressing in loosely tailored linen with a simple silver pin fastened to one lapel. A silver pin, like a sidelong figure eight, in the shape of Infinity.

And perhaps they pause for a minute at the door now, the clear blue eyes smiling into the dark brown ones, and perhaps a kiss is exchanged, just lingeringly enough that Sally Mae will feel again the suck and pull of love, how she is going under, turning over and over in the vortex, with the oceanic currents buoying her up again and out, out over the wide water into the unknown.

&.   &.   &.

"We have no future," says Sally Mae. "The future is an illusion." She is philosophical under the stars, curled in the leather lap of her vintage Triumph Spitfire. Trees whiz by, and Therese, in the passenger seat, holds one arm out into the open air as if she could stop time.

"Then marry me." Therese's words seem to come from a long distance, an overseas connection, through static. "We could go to Sweden," says Therese, the practical one. "I feel so energetic tonight."

But Sweden is far away, and they are headed toward the nearest city on the coast, which even now is tossing up a halo of reddish gold, the pot at the end of a rainbow.

"Marry me," she muses, "and I will never abandon you."

Sally Mae knows that "never" and "abandon" are two words rarely conjoined for long; they are like infinitives waiting to be split by the ungrammatical hand of Fate. Sally Mae feels loss in her body and blood; it is a part of her she can no more extricate than she can remove heart, spleen, ovary.

This thought makes her heart slow and her cunt wet, because it is always the knowledge of immanent loss that draws her toward (albeit impermanent) connection. She briefly considers pulling over on the soft shoulder of road above the city lights to bury her face between Therese's thighs, to moan *no, no, no* into the damp and luscious flower of her lover's sex, to mold her lover's body, tense and elastic between her hands as if she could sculpt this woman into some perfect semblance of bliss, permanent and everlasting.

But instead, Sally Mae says, "Marriage is a triumph of habit over hate."

"Says who?" Therese is annoyed.

"*Memoirs of an Amnesiac.*"

They are swooping down upon the city now, descending the circles of Hell. Sally Mae knows the night will be full of unexpected turns and that between them love will be lost and regained in a space of hours. They are a ship sailing the black void between continents, and the way is perilous, but the sailors rarely lose hope.

Along the empty avenues, past the row houses, the mortuary, the donut shop. Sweet wine spilled in a gutter. A shadow screwed to a lamppost.

❧   ❧   ❧

In the heart of the heart of the city is a basement. You are walking along the sidewalk, and as you step over an openwork grating you might happen to look down, and there is the pulse of humanity: a mad swirling devil dance of lust and liquor and bad talk and trouble. There is strife and flirtation and remorse and exhilaration.

Into this basement our lovers descend: Therese trippingly, light as a feather; Sally Mae half breathless and wondering, *What now, and why?*

Sally Mae lets go of her lover's hand, and Therese drifts into the whirl. The taste of gin in the back of her throat is bitter; she will have another to drown it. Therese is dancing already with an elegant man-woman in a black tuxedo. Their pelvises slide together; they are well-oiled machines. Sally Mae watches her lover's pretty dress slither up a length of cool blond thigh, watches as she grinds hard against her elegant androgyne. In a minute Therese will look to see if she is observed. She does. She is. She smiles at Sally Mae.

Sally Mae decides she will not purposefully avoid, tonight, the inevitable string of ex-lovers and embittered friends who will accost her, demanding and vengeful. Across the bar she spies one of this species, a large and grumpy and handsome woman. Sally Mae remembers that, somewhat against her better judgment, she once allowed this young woman to torture her with an open bottle of wine and a dildo modeled upon the genitalia of a famous male porn star. She remembers that her own apparent humiliation was fuel for this woman's fire.

Now, a couple of years later, this memory has not entirely lost its power to evoke the slippery and perilous descent into nothingness that Sally Mae had experienced during the act in question. There are times, Sally Mae knows, when one simply gives up, as if a spring in the soul has sprung, and the self unravels, peels; you find yourself floating above, say, a bed or a beach or a hammock, looking down upon yourself being made love to, down upon the churning sweating back of your lover over you, her hand bunched inside your cunt, or her tongue sliding down your throat, or her cock driving into you. *Then,* Sally Mae thinks, *is when you really understand how delicate any coupling is and how ephemeral, and you feel that death will overtake you surely sooner or later, and it will have no remorse.*

Therese has returned from the floor, leaving the androgyne gazing stupidly after her. She slides three damp fingers into Sally Mae's palm and rests her lips briefly and openly on Sally Mae's temple. The room fills suddenly with the scent of musk, her lover's breath blooming, a black flower, close to her ear.

Therese says, "You are the only woman I will ever love. There are no others, before or after."

This confession makes Sally Mae feel mournful and cruel. She squeezes her lover's fingers too tightly, watching her face register surprise, then pain, then resignation.

"In five years you'll be repeating those same words elsewhere," Sally Mae says. "And that's as it should be."

Therese appears unscathed by this meanness. She lifts her dress slightly to straddle Sally Mae's thigh. Behind her Sally Mae sees her large grumpy handsome ex-lover approaching.

Her ex-lover has come up behind Therese's back, which Sally Mae has wrapped both arms around out of habit and desire. But she is looking into the eyes of the bigger woman, remembering.

Her name, her name, Sally Mae is thinking. *How is it I've lost that and nothing else?*

She whirls through the Rolodex of memory, pausing at the letter "r." *Rhonda, Rea, Rebecca, Roberta, Romeo.* It had been a short-lived romance but meaningful. Sally Mae had learned much about herself through this interaction. *The name, the name,* she thinks. *How is it possible?*

Ravena? Or was that a city in the north of Italy she had visited with someone else entirely?

Sally Mae ditches this other memory with effort. She has a sudden flash of herself going down on an Armenian girl named Una in the deserted nave of a quaint Italian chapel. And the big handsome woman is opening her mouth to speak.

Therese turns and looks up into the woman's broad features. "Well, look who it is," she says. "Rae."

"Hello, Rae," says Sally Mae, relieved and exhilarated by this lucky twist. "You're looking healthy." And then, "You two know each other?"

Rae looks nonplussed and cagey. Sally Mae remembers this look well. It was the look that meant *I'm lying to you, but we both know it, and it doesn't make a helluva lot of difference in the long run.* Sally Mae remembers that Rae was somewhat fatalistic.

Rae says, "Yeah, I think we met once or twice over at the community center, didn't we?"

Therese just looks at her.

Sally Mae says, "Aren't you a counselor over there? For troubled youth?" Therese is leaning over the bar trying to catch the bartender's eye.

"They never get any less troubled," Rae says. She's looking at Therese's ass.

Sally Mae looks too. Then she puts a deliberate hand on the ass of her lover and gives it a slow squeeze.

Oh, it's all so predictable, Sally Mae thinks. *I'm a shopworn cliché.* In the space of the few minutes it took Rae to cross the room for this exchange, Sally Mae has transmuted from cynical woman of the world to a girl who just wants to be loved forever by the strikingly pretty blond whose ass now presses back meaningfully into her hand. The pressure of that ass means *Let me be yours.* It means *There are such things as permanence.*

And if Therese were now to turn, to begin to flirt with Rae—for it is clear they have known each other, and perhaps not entirely within the confines of the "community center"—known each other, it may well be, in the Biblical sense...Or even with the wine bottle? No, it is too much to imagine; Sally Mae's heart wants to burst with it.

"Still painting, are you?" Rae says this to Sally Mae, not taking her eyes from Therese. Sally had started Rae's portrait three years ago. Never finished it. Rae couldn't sit still enough, long enough. Her skin kept changing color: blue-black, purple, Davy's gray, the smear of ochre beneath the eyes shifting into impossible umbers. Sally had tired of chasing Rae's shadows. And finally sent her home abruptly.

"Yes, of course," Sally Mae says faintly. She is remembering their first encounter, how Rae did a simple thing, just walked up and sat down next to her on a bench in the park and shared her coffee because she had ordered a large. Sally Mae remembers the faint imprint of Rae's lips on the rim of the Styrofoam cup. And how later Rae had led her across the street, up the stairs to her pathetic apartment, pulling the Murphy bed down from the wall, hardly a word between them.

Afterward Sally Mae had said, "Will you come stay with me for a week? I want to paint you."

"You'll have to pay for it."

"Yes, of course."

They had both paid for it, hadn't they? Yes. Of course. Sally Mae doesn't want to let herself drift this way. Rae is talking now to Therese, her full lips close to the delicate whorl of Therese's ear. As from a long distance, Sally Mae hears Therese laugh her low laugh. That laugh. A private thing between them.

So many private things between them. She knows Therese will open slowly, like a flower opening, first one finger, then two, then Sally Mae's whole hand, how she relaxes when pushed, how she pushes back. Sally Mae has seen the look on her face, a kind of rushed concentration, holding on to something until the last minute, her mouth slightly open, cunt wrapped around her fist, holding on, holding on, as if they would never be parted, not ever. She knows the velvet insides of her ass and the bittersweet taste of the hollow of her throat and the feel of the heart beating when she holds her hand flat and hard against her lover's sex. Oh, such intimacy! Such sweet, sweet communion.

Sally Mae thinks she is not really seeing what she seems to be seeing, that Rae has in fact slid her hand between Therese's knees and that Therese is smiling into the big woman's eyes with that look. That look. It is as if, suddenly, Sally Mae is invisible. Ghostlike. Perhaps she is already dead, and Therese, as Sally Mae herself has said so many times, Therese has moved on. Trippingly, lightly. As she moves.

Sally Mae remembers saying, "I'm older than you. I'll die. There will be others."

Morbid! Sickening! Why can't she bring herself to just

live? To grab life by the throat, to grab this pretty girl and hold on? Will she, wonders Sally Mae, just stand here, idle and inevitable, older and wiser and jaded beyond repair? Already dead?

And she is overcome now with nostalgia for her lost youth and for perishable innocence that, like the remembered taste of pomegranate, is sharp and sour at the edge of her tongue.

She sees how she has always been letting go of anything that mattered, her hands falling open. And as if she can see the future, Technicolored and framed in close-up, she sees the body of her beloved intertwined with the bodies of others as the vine of the moonflower wraps itself, tendril by tendril, around camellia, gardenia, and rose.

For there is, in Therese, and Sally Mae knows this, an indelible desire for the real thing, for the taste and the rub and the human smell of being, for *jouissance*, which is joy and essence. One day perhaps, Therese will weep in the arms of Rae; she will dampen the cheek and the shoulder and the belly of Rae with salt tears of joy and release.

Sally Mae has no difficulty imagining this, having seen it before. She knows the soft cries of Therese—*lacrimis oculos suffusa nintentes*—who was the poet who said that? *Her shining eyes suffused with tears.* She knows the way the mouth opens, just enough for tongue to slide between lips and teeth, the taste of peppermint and cocoa. And the sanguine violets of the aureoles, the droplets of perspiration in the crook of an elbow. The crimes committed, the transgressions forgiven, all of it for her and her alone. Watching Therese laugh her low laugh into the eyes of Rae, Sally Mae wants to come up behind her, to lift her dress as she has so many times before, to thrust a finger beneath the art-for-art's-sake

G-string. She wants to bend her down like a sapling.

This way, Sally Mae feels for a moment the stirrings of immortality. She imagines taking the nipple, the nape of the neck, the middle finger between her teeth. The ecstasy of pain and then the deliverance.

From darkness we are born into light, she thinks, infantile, gasping, damp as kittens. In her lover's arms she is as an accidental relation of objects, one to another, a space, a voice around which horizons form and vanish and from which new languages emerge, heard only fleetingly, like whispers in other rooms.

It is this darkness interwoven with light, her appreciation for it, that makes Sally Mae the woman she is. The acute apprehension of time passing and the desolate grief that resides in the very core of pleasure. Therese's dress has slipped off one naked shoulder. *Oh, the allurement, the ambition, the idol, the lodestone, the fancy!* Has Rae unbuttoned her?

Sally Mae recalls those lips with a shudder. Kissing Rae was akin to suffocation, and knowing as she does how Therese sinks so willingly, how easily she abandons herself (she, who protests her steadfastness), her ravenousness and impulsiveness, Sally Mae doesn't doubt her lover is already half lost to her, lost in the whirl of fleshly improvidence, in the splendor of gin.

Sally Mae looks up at the openwork grating above their heads. A woman has positioned herself there, pantyless, remote as a goddess, legs spread.

And now Rae bends to place her lips, chivalrous and intrepid, upon the glossy bosom of Sally Mae's beloved.

☙   ☙   ☙

Recipe for happiness: Select the illusion that appeals to your temperament and embrace it with passion.

What is the shape of the infinite?

Her body has dissolved to atoms. Sally Mae has become primordial, and through the hours, which no longer run in a straight line from A to B but rather undulate or curve in fractal gyres, the hours that have become a snake swallowing its own tail, she feels herself expand and contract: She is her own beating heart. Imagine it, to go on forever!

There are worlds and worlds beyond this, she is thinking. And the body floats to the surface, breaks water, and breathes.

There is the face of Therese, angel of mercy, saint of ecstatic visions.

Through the leaded glass, an arc of sun descends. "I am in Heaven," says Sally Mae. And opens her mouth for the proffered cube of ice. Ice too on her forehead, ice to be drawn along jawline, cheek, and clavicle. Ice for the belly. Ice for the breasts. Lovingly circling right nipple, then left.

"To keep down the swelling," says Therese, the practical.

There will be forty hours of ice, another forty in bed. And then perhaps forty years more if she is provident?

"How brave you were," murmurs Therese, "to come to my defense."

Without a trace of irony! And utterly without irony too her tongue, working the cube of ice down and down between Sally Mae's thighs, apparently her only woundless region, somehow unbruised in the brawl. She is aching from stem to sternum.

"I thought you were a pacifist," considers Therese.

To the gods it seemed otherwise.

Animal Science
by Clara Thaler

The Doctor has finished today's surgeries—two routine spays, plus a Siamese with a four-inch segment of string threaded through his small intestine—and it is my job to clean the room and everything in it. She pulls off her sterile gloves and green surgical cap, tosses them in the garbage as I set aside the inventory list I was working on and move past her into the surgery room. Several bloody instruments are scattered on the steel table. The garbage can is filled with blood-stained gauze, stray ends of suture thread, and the detritus of surgery. I notice on the floor beside it a single cat ovary.

The Doctor unties her blue surgery gown and puts it in the hamper as I pull on latex gloves. Tom, who assisted with the surgeries, is already on the phone with a client. From what he is saying, I surmise that the client's cocker spaniel has been vomiting repeatedly for the past few hours. "Are you seeing pieces of dog food in the vomit?" Tom nods, scribbles something on a piece of paper towel. "Any grass or other solids, or is it mostly liquid?" He scribbles again. "No, ma'am, I'm not a doctor, I'm the technician. What's that?" Tom rolls his eyes. "Yeah, the vomit should wash right out of the fur on his ears." I catch the Doctor's smile out of the corner of my eye.

The bloody instruments go in a plastic tub filled with special instrument wash. The table gets wiped down with diluted disinfectant, as do the oxygen tank and anesthesia cart. I lift the stray ovary off the floor, wincing a bit as it sticks to the linoleum, and toss it into the garbage. If I turn my head to the left, I can see the Doctor standing in the hallway, flipping through a medical journal. Her head is down, her eyes moving rapidly as she skims an article; she lifts her arm and scratches the back of her neck. Through her sleeve I catch a glimpse of pink skin gathered in a soft fold beneath her upper arm.

I am here to learn, to gather information, so that I may then tell the career counselor at my college if I do indeed want to major in biology and go on to veterinary school. The counselor, Marie, was the one who suggested this internship. She brings her dachshund here, promised me the Doctor would be friendly and informative. "A good mentor," Marie assured me. "You can follow her around, soak up everything she shows you."

The scrub shirt the Doctor is wearing—size extra-large—is tight around her hips, tight enough for me to see the seams of her slacks. She yawns, turns the page. "Lynn," she calls, "there's an article here about that disorder that Abyssinian had, the one that was in last week. Compulsive grooming." She looks up at me. "Psychogenic alopecia is the official name."

"Oh," I say. I walk over to her carrying the heating pad from surgery.

She hands me the journal. "You can borrow it if you want to."

I thank her and slip the journal into my backpack by the door. The heating pad goes in the cabinet above the sink.

Although I spend only one day a week here, it has not taken me long to learn the rhythm of the days. The Doctor sees a few appointments in the morning, then performs the day's surgeries, then sees afternoon appointments for several hours. Between appointments, Tom jokes around with Mary Ann, the receptionist; Mary Ann reports on her 13-year-old son's latest misadventures; I ask everyone if they want coffee; I give the boarding animals fresh food and water; the Doctor asks me to mail something or wash something or straighten something up. Once when she saw me standing around doing nothing, she opened the broom closet and gestured at the broom. "There's always something that needs to be cleaned, Lynn," she said. "At any given moment some animal's cage is invariably dirty." I have detected an admonishing note in the Doctor's voice when she assigns a task to me, as if she were hoping I would have noticed on my own that it needed to be done. I have taken this to heart, vow repeatedly every Thursday to work harder, to please her.

"Vet school?" My mother's voice was shrill when I called her up and told her about the internship. "If you want to be a doctor, why not practice on people? That's where the money is. You think crazy old ladies with fifteen cats can pay their bills? Better yet, go to business school. Be an investment banker. Or maybe study computers." Then she asked me if I was growing my hair out yet. Before she could ask me if I had met any nice boys lately, I told her I had to get off the phone.

My mother was right about one thing: Old ladies with fifteen cats can't pay their bills. The Doctor warned me herself one afternoon, stopping by the dryer as I was folding clean towels, "You shouldn't go to vet school if you want to make a lot of money, you know. I've had this practice for almost ten years, and I'm still paying back student loans." I smiled, assured her the money wasn't my primary concern. The Doctor always chooses odd moments to give me advice; when she does, the admonishing tone is gone, and her voice grows warmer. I use these moments to ask her questions about herself: When did she decide to be a vet? What does she wish she knew before she got her degree? What dissatisfies her most about her career? When the Doctor answers my questions, she smiles, leans back on her heels. Once, mid answer, she absently reached into her shirt and hoisted up a bra strap.

"Pay attention to everything that goes on," said Marie, the career counselor. "Decide if you're interested in the day-to-day things the vet does."

    ❧   ❧   ❧

"We need to get some blood from Hercules," the Doctor calls to me. I go to the terrier's cage, open the door, stroke his wheat-colored forehead. He is resting on his towel, his eyelids drooping. He feels hot to my touch. The card on his cage tells me he is here for extensive blood work.

In the room that the Doctor calls her lab, I put Hercules on the table and hold him, his chin in the crook of my elbow. The Doctor swabs his hind leg with alcohol and slides the syringe into a vein. Hercules's muscles tense, but he doesn't struggle.

This room is tiny, its shelves crammed with bottles of pills, syringes of different sizes, glass vials stacked in boxes. There are no windows. As blood trickles into the syringe in the Doctor's hand, I feel the room growing warm. I am excruciatingly aware of the heat coming from the Doctor's body. I look at the top of her head, poised over her hands, her dark hair held back with a silver clip. I allow my eyes to drop down to her chest. Her shirt has fallen forward, exposing the cleavage between her large breasts. To my embarrassment—but not to my surprise—I begin to sweat. Hercules whimpers low in his throat. "It's OK, buddy, we're almost done," the Doctor says. She is concentrating on the syringe; her voice is patient, steady.

⁊⁊ ⁊⁊ ⁊⁊

It is February, my fifth month of college, the beginning of second semester. I have become friends with Eliza, the girl in the next room over. "The proverbial girl next door," she calls herself.

Eliza has a pierced eyebrow that she did herself with a needle and an ice cube. She was the first to bring up the subject. "I think you're a dyke," she said one rainy Sunday over our anthropology reading.

"If you're trying to come out to me, Eliza, you're supposed to say, 'I think *I'm* a dyke.' "

"Very funny. C'mon, I saw you staring at that cheerleader in the bookstore."

"Eliza!" I half grinned, half grimaced. "No way—she's not my type."

"So it's true? I mean, you are...?"

I looked at Eliza, trying to gauge her, hoping she was safe. My mouth moved before I had decided. "I tend to like older women. Smart ones."

"Really!" Eliza's pierced eyebrow arched. "Well, I'll keep my eyes open for you. Maybe a professor." She smiled wickedly. I took a deep breath. Smiled back.

I like the Doctor best when she doesn't know I'm watching her: when she's preparing medications and I'm cleaning litter pans at the sink; when she's reviewing a file and I'm putting towels in the washing machine; when she's near the reception desk and I'm checking the boarders' cages. Other times there is an edge to her, a hardness; but in these moments—when she's speaking to no one—her features soften, grow quiet. Once, in my car, I passed her going in the opposite direction. She had that same expression on her face, that lack of self-awareness. I thought I saw her mouth moving. Was she singing along with the radio?

Or perhaps was she eating?

The Doctor eats at work sometimes; this is when I watch her most closely. She eats her lunch in the back office—baggies filled with grapes or blueberries, halved apples, salads. Once she ate a pita filled with nothing but cucumber slices. When she brings sandwiches they are lean, two or three slices of turkey between dry wheat bread. On other days she leaves between appointments and returns with large greasy bags from McDonald's or Wendy's. I have seen her eat potato chips, putting one after the other into her mouth, not pausing to finish chewing between mouthfuls. When she chews her jaw moves quickly, efficiently.

My own body is nondescript, neither fat nor thin. My belly is round, my thighs loose and dimpled in a way that makes me want to hide them. My hips are wide—what my mother has called good birthing hips. But my naked body in the mirror, even in dim lighting, is neither here nor there, mildly disappointing, wholly average. My body and I are not enemies or friends; we are acquaintances.

But I wonder about the Doctor. About her boyfriend of twelve years, a man she met in college. Was she fat when she met him all those years ago? Did he watch her grow rounder with every passing year, her rib cage and hipbones becoming lost in a pillow of flesh? Did the Doctor grow fat in furtive shame and misery, in nightly binges balanced against the stress of med school? Or is it possible that she was always fat, was the fat kid growing up in New Jersey—and that her boyfriend has watched the same curves and roundness age, gain permanence? Does the Doctor binge-eat now? Does she hide it from her lover? Does she eat fruit and salad at work but ice cream, cookies, and chips at night by the light of the refrigerator? Does the Doctor like her body? Does she stand in front of a full-length mirror naked, holding the weight of first one, then the other breast in her hands? Does she turn loving patient eyes to the soft drooping skin of her stomach, to the rolls on her thighs? Does she use words like *succulent, voluptuous* to describe her body to herself? When she and her boyfriend make love, does she close her eyes and forget her weight, or does she watch him revel in the softness of her, delight in it? Did she outgrow all body shame? Does she eat and eat in the search for consolation, for comfort, for satisfaction?

ぶ　　　　ぶ　　　　ぶ

"Lynn." The Doctor's voice startles me. I am standing at the prep sink, scrubbing the dirty surgical instruments with what looks like a wire toothbrush. The Doctor is leaning out of the exam room. "Can you give me a hand in here? Tom is in the middle of a leukemia test."

In the exam room a slim blond is petting her springer spaniel. Being on the table makes the dog nervous; his legs are trembling, and small drops of drool speckle the table-top. "That's OK, Archie. Good dog, Archie. When we go home I'll give you a whole box of treats, OK?"

"He has some kind of cut by his left shoulder," the Doctor tells me. "We're going to shave a bit of fur away to see if it's a bite wound."

Archie drools freely on my arm as I hold him. The Doctor tilts her head as she guides the electric clippers around the wound. I can smell her shampoo. Does the blond notice I am watching the Doctor and not the dog?

"There it is—there's one puncture wound, and there's the other. Probably a tussle with a neighborhood cat, hopefully one that's had its rabies shot. We'll give him a rabies boost-er now and send him home with some amoxicillin."

If I ever do become a vet, I tell myself, I want to be as good with clients as the Doctor is. She never rushes anyone or rais-es her voice. I have seen her with suspicious clients, panicked clients, clients weeping because their cat has been hit by a car. In every case the Doctor remains steady and calm; she is firm but never abrupt. Around her clients she radiates confi-dence; and in the face of this, I find that I fall silent.

   🐸   🐸   🐸

It was the Doctor who taught me how to develop X-rays. In my mind I have rewritten that afternoon, those minutes, again and again. I have started with the facts but have sweetened them, allowing memory to intertwine with fantasy:

We are together in the darkroom, barely bigger than a closet. A narrow bulb casts a faint red glow, but my eyes have not yet adjusted to this light. "The film cartridge snaps open here and here," she says. "Do you see the film?"

I hear the two snaps but can make out only vague shapes. "Um," I mutter, running my hands along the table. I touch the open cartridge, find the thin sheet of film.

"Now clip it onto the metal bracket and hang it on the wall; then load the cartridge with fresh film." Wishing I had spent more time in this room with the light on, I reach above the sink, find the bracket. The clips that hold the film in place are tricky; seconds pass as I fumble with them. I can feel the Doctor waiting. She is standing only inches away from me, and in the dim light her gaze becomes almost palpable. At last I secure the film and hang it on the wall. "The box with fresh film is to the left of the sink," she tells me.

I manage to load the cartridge. Mercifully, my eyes are beginning to adjust to the darkness; I take the metal bracket back down from the wall and place it in the developer without a problem.

We become silent. I close my eyes and feel her next to me, the heat of her body, the weight of her presence.

I open my eyes. Reach out and touch her hand where it rests by her side. Her eyes jump from the floor to my face. "Lynn…" she begins.

"Please." My voice is barely a whisper. "Please, let me." I lift her hand to my face; she doesn't resist. I run her knuckles against my lips, spread her fingers, and kiss her palm. I cup her hand against my face, hold it there. "Touch me," I want to say. I want to beg her to touch me.

She brings her other hand to my face, runs her fingertips down my forehead, my cheek, my jawline. When she reaches my mouth, it is open. I scrape my bottom teeth against the pad of her index finger; she inhales sharply. Suddenly my hands are on her hips, and I am pressing her back against the X-ray table. "Doctor," I say, and it comes out like a plea. This is the word I repeat as I bite and kiss the soft skin of her neck; I whisper it into her ear, against her closed eyelids, I murmur it against her throat. "Doctor, please, Doctor."

         ஐ   ஐ   ஐ

The Doctor does not speak, but she is breathing hard, and I can feel her heart racing. Under her shirt the skin of her stomach is soft beneath my hands. She helps me lift the shirt up, pull it over her head. Everywhere I touch her she is soft, until I feel her teeth on my shoulder.

My fingers are pressing and kneading her hips. I rub my body against hers, angle my thigh against her crotch. I manage to remove her bra, and then I cover her breasts with long sucking kisses; I lift each to my mouth, taste her nipples, bite them gently. Her hands are in my hair, stroking, pulling. I raise my shirt to my armpits, rub my naked breasts against hers; the pleasure is so fierce I nearly stop breathing. My pussy is aching. Our bellies pressed tightly together, I lift my head and meet her eyes. Without a word she asks me to kiss her; her lips are unspeakably soft, her tongue delicate.

I wish the X-ray table were bigger, that I could lay her down. Instead, I sink to my knees, rub my head against her stomach, kiss the skin just above her slacks. Will she stop me from going further? I force my fingers to move slowly on the clasp. The Doctor tilts her pelvis toward me, spreads her legs a little farther apart. She is allowing me; she is *inviting* me. I unzip her slacks, pull them down over her hips, then pull down her underwear.

Her thighs are wide and smooth and soft, and my mouth adores them. She spreads her legs until I can lick the wetness from between her inner thighs. *I have wanted this for so long, Doctor. To bury my head between your legs. To smell you, to taste you on my tongue.* I nuzzle her pubic curls, spread her lips with two fingers, lap delicately at the head of her clit. The Doctor's breathing becomes jagged; her legs grow slack, then tighten. I'm practically coming as I lick circles around and over her clit, first lightly, then with increasing strength. I bring my hand up, trace the opening of her pussy, slide two fingers in. "Yes," she whispers, and again, "Yes." She presses against me; my face is slick, my hand wet to the wrist. My fingers move in and out, hard.

I want nothing but this, Doctor. Nothing but you.

She begins to shake against me, pushing my fingers deeper. Abruptly she stops, thrusts hard against me several times, stops, thrusts again. I don't think either of us is breathing as she rides out the staccato rhythm of her orgasm, my tongue still moving against her clit. Her motion stops; she exhales, long and shuddering.

She gathers me into her arms. Holds me against her breasts. In this fantasy I never come; I feel no frustration, only gratitude.

ဆာ   ဆာ   ဆာ

"If you decide not to go to vet school, what do you think you'll do instead?"

I do not answer right away. Beyond the car's window dark silhouettes of trees move by. The branches are tossed by the wind. It is raining steadily, and the Doctor is giving me a ride back to campus.

"I'm not sure...I mean, I wouldn't want to be any other kind of doctor. I'm taking this cool psychology class now. And my friend Eliza is trying to get me to major in anthropology. She thinks I'm a good observer."

The Doctor smiles. "Well, it *is* only your first year...I changed majors twice before I decided to be a vet. You have plenty of time to make up your mind."

I nod. She must think of me as a child. I focus on her dashboard, trying to memorize what it feels like riding beside her.

"And Nick didn't decide on architecture until after he got his bachelor's."

Nick is the boyfriend. "Oh," I say.

She makes a right turn off the highway. I look at her hands on the wheel; they seem both soft and strong. If I were brave, what would I tell her? That I hope she loves her body as much as I do? That my sole aspiration is to be as strong and beautiful as she is?

Maybe if she were single. Maybe if I were older.

"I think you'd make a good vet." Her comment surprises me; I sit up straighter.

"Really?"

"You ask a lot of questions—that shows you're willing to learn. And you're good with the animals."

I think I'm blushing. I feel touched, honored. We ride the rest of the way in silence until I point out my dorm on the right.

She pulls to the curb. "See you next week, Lynn?" My hand finds the door handle. I know this too is a moment I will reinvent in my mind, changing the script, revising the plot, dreaming what might have happened.

"Thanks for the ride," I tell her. Our eyes meet for the briefest second, and then I am out of the car, walking toward home.

Pas de Deux
by Leslie Kimiko Ward

K ate always leaves the bathroom with her pants undone.
I notice this time is no exception as she walks into the
kitchen, buttoning her fly and fastening her belt.

"Hey, what time do you want to leave for the bar?" she
asks.

"Was that really so important that it couldn't wait until
after you finished dressing?"

"Whatever, Madison—you're hilarious. Now just answer
my question."

Kate and I have such a loving relationship. We were each
other's first girlfriends almost four years ago in a completely
closeted dormitory affair. Now, thanks to the ever-mysterious
lesbian relationship process, Kate and I have evolved from
ex-girlfriends into best friends. All in all it's not such a raw
deal. Kate is the only person I can trust to give me a completely honest opinion whether I ask for it or not. Besides,
once you get to know someone as well as Kate and I know
each other, friendship is really no longer a choice. I mean, it's
not like I want someone with that much information about
me wandering freely through society. So for better or worse,
Kate and I are joined at the hip for all eternity, or at least
until one of us graduates and leaves Columbus.

It's been a lazy summer day, and Kate is obviously itching for some evening excitement. I, on the other hand, could comfortably lounge all night, chain-smoking on the front porch and watching the steady stream of deliciously underclothed sorority girls parade past my house.

I live up on Summit Avenue between the Greek houses and the campus bars. As far as I'm concerned, this is prime cruising territory. Every weekend hordes of fresh-faced effervescent young things make the brave journey down fraternity row toward the promised land of beer and brawn. Granted, most of the giggling coeds are straight as hell. And yes, most of them will probably spend the rest of their evenings fawning over flexing frat boys and grinding their precious little bodies against them on the dance floor, but I refuse to give up hope. Hey, a dyke can dream, can't she?

Kate doesn't see it the way I do. She's fed up with my overwhelming attraction to straight girls, and to be completely honest I can't say I blame her. Sometimes it seems that for every passionate evening I share with a girl I'm attracted to, there is a coinciding morning after where said girl sobers up and realizes what she's done. After that it usually takes another twenty-four hours for the novelty of her newfound sexual awakening to wear off completely. Inevitably, my *objet d'amour* quits returning my phone calls and spends the rest of the week sleeping with old boyfriends in a desperate attempt to convince herself she's "not really that way." The experience is never completely a waste, however; I get to spend one erotic night introducing a luscious hottie to the forbidden pleasures of Sapphic love. Afterwards the porn-schooled beefcakes of frat row learn of her lesbian liaison, and she becomes the hottest commodity on the frat circuit.

Kate has been on the receiving end of too many morning-after bitch sessions to take any more of my "relationships" seriously. And quite frankly, I don't know how many more times I can hear the phrase "If only you had a penis" before it really starts to affect my lesbian self-image.

"Is that what you're wearing tonight?" Kate asks, obviously trying to get things rolling.

"I don't know," I reply lazily. "Why don't you go home and change, and I'll call you when I'm ready to leave, like in about a half hour."

With Kate out the door, I manage to motivate myself off the kitchen chair and up the stairs to get ready. It's nights like these I'm grateful I was born butch. I don't have the time or energy tonight for any of those hair-curling, lipstick-applying, high-maintenance femme antics. I toss on a white crew neck T-shirt, my favorite pair of blue jeans, and a well-worn butter-soft black leather belt. I spend a little extra time making sure my shirt is evenly tucked all the way around and my rolled-up shirt sleeves aren't lopsided. Satisfied, I run a dollop of gel through my short dark hair, pleased when it settles into a nearly flawless wave. Not one to argue with perfection, I make a mental note to postpone my regular barber-shop appointment, determined to keep this good thing going as long as possible.

On my way to the door, I stop for one last look in the mirror. "Not bad." I smile to my reflection and pick up the cologne for a final spritz. Checking my watch I realize I'm ready a full fifteen minutes ahead of schedule. Kate would be so proud.

I pick up a Victoria's Secret catalog and plop down on the couch. No sense in heading to Kate's early; I wouldn't want her to expect it of me in the future. I think it's important to keep people's standards low. That's one of my secrets to being a successful underachiever. The way I see it, if you constantly attempt to impress people by going above and beyond the call of duty, pretty soon "above and beyond" is what they expect of you. Before you know it, you're busting ass 24/7 just to live up to their inflated expectations.

Like once upon a time my mom asked me to do the dishes. I broke a dish. My mom asked my sister to take over. My sister spent extra time scraping the lasagna off the casserole pan just to make Mom proud. A quick quiz: Which little Cinderella had to do the dishes every night for the rest of her childhood while the other left the table early to go play?

OK, enough stalling. I bid Tyra Banks and her bevy of lacy beauties *adieu* and head out the door to pick up my other half.

        🙰   🙰   🙰

Kate and I often joke that Wall Street Night Club, the only lesbian dance club in Columbus, is our default setting for Saturday nights. Tonight, however, I'm looking forward to going. Maybe it's because summer is almost over. Maybe it's because I'm having a good-hair night. Maybe it's because I haven't had any in a while and the thought of a bunch of gyrating sweaty dykes sounds mildly appealing. Whatever the reason there's definitely some sort of charge lingering in the air as we greet the bouncer and enter the club.

I stop dead in my tracks.

I stand transfixed.

Up on a platform a purple-red spotlight shines down from the ceiling and picks up the beads of sweat on her chest and shoulders. I stare at her glistening torso as it spirals and undulates to the pounding bass. My focus widens, and I am entranced watching her body twist and slide, her serpentine fluidity punctuated with syncopated contractions of her stomach and pelvis. My mind relinquishes control to my cunt, and I can't help connecting her staccato tremors with those that accompany only the best of orgasms.

"Drool much?" Kate observes. "Jesus, Madison, you might want to pick your jaw off the floor before it gets stepped on."

I break my gaze long enough to give Kate the finger and walk over to the bar where Fran, the bartender, greets me with her signature "Hey, girl" and a friendly smile. We dish the weekly gossip for a bit while she pours me a Rolling Rock.

"Go ahead and give me a glass of water too, Fran."

"Beer with a water chaser?" she asks, surprised. "Madison, you goin' soft?"

"Never. The beer's for me; the water's for her," I clarify, nodding in the direction of my fantasy on the platform. Fran winks and smiles knowingly as she hands me the beer and squeezes a lemon into the water. I take a swig from my pint glass and tell Fran to wish me luck.

"Good luck, hon," she says, whipping me a quick salute with two crossed fingers.

"Thanks," I reply, picking up the drinks and carrying them toward my wet dream come true on stage.

Standing at the base of the platform, level with the dancing girl's feet, my eyes begin a luxuriously slow pan up her gorgeous body. Toned and firm, she is every inch delicious. As I reach the top of my provocative inspection, I find myself inexplicably drawn to the expression on her face. Her half closed eyes, relaxed jaw, and parted lips convey a feeling of total absorption and absolute surrender. I try to burn this visage deep into my memory bank, hoping it will surface again in a future torrid context.

It takes her a minute to emerge from her reverie and notice me on the floor, a glass of well-deserved water in my outstretched hand. She grabs a bright yellow towel from the far end of the platform and kneels in front of me, patting her dripping forehead.

"Thanks, love," she pants, grateful and breathless. She downs the entire glass and hands it back with a wink. Tossing her towel into a yellow heap beside her, she holds my focus like a vice as she stands to continue dancing. It was, without a doubt, twenty of the most exciting seconds I have ever spent in my entire life.

We repeat this interchange several times throughout the evening. I make it my personal mission to keep this lady hydrated, and Fran begins referring to me jokingly as the "water lackey." Between hydrations I find myself a place at the bar with a clear view of the stage from across the dance floor.

Relaxing on my bar stool, enjoying my new view, I decide my three-dollar cover was well-spent. Her dark hair, pulled back with a headband, glistens in the light, and a few strands stick to her face and neck. She turns away from the dance floor, and I exhale audibly at the sight of her muscular back, chiseled and gleaming as she writhes against the music. Her back is bare except for the few tan strings of her halter, and the top of a small tattoo peeks out from above the waistline of her slim black pants. I wonder what it looks like in its entirety. I wonder what she looks like in *her* entirety, and I am just about to test my super-powers of X-ray vision when Kate sneaks up on me from behind my bar stool.

"How's the hunt, Romeo?" she interjects teasingly, "or are we still admiring from afar?"

"For God's sake, Kate. You scared the shit out of me. I almost fell off my bar stool."

"Too bad you didn't. That would have been hilarious. Listen, I'm going to snag a ride home with Kirsten," she offers, smiling mischievously. She winks and nudges me with her elbow in true fraternity-boy fashion. "I thought you might need a little extra room in the passenger seat."

I've got to hand it to Kate—she never misses a beat when it comes to the delicate art of cruising. And while I'm thankful for this opportunity, the reality begins to set in that at some point I will have to muster up enough nerve to ask this incredible woman to come home with me. My cool, calm, and collected butch demeanor vacates briefly, strangled by an overwhelming fear of rejection that shakes me right down to my Doc Martens.

I mentally run through my list of favorite pickup lines: *Hey, baby, what's your sign? What do you say, your place or mine?* I'm sure she's heard them all. *Where have you been all my life? She's my sister, not my wife.* I don't want to sound clichéd. Do I trust myself enough to wing it? Pray for a moment of improvisational brilliance? I suppose it's better than sounding scripted. All right. Here we go. Serendipity, don't fail me now.

I suck down the rest of my beer, for confidence's sake, and watch enraptured as the dancing girl finishes her set. She has jumped down from the platform and begun to towel off when I finally gather up the courage to walk over. I offer her yet another drink and, with as much sexual innuendo as I can muster, purr to her that I have some lovely bottled water back at my apartment should she be interested.

She laughs, amused at my choice of approach. Her confidence shakes me. I consider slinking back to my bar stool. I try to gauge her reaction; was she laughing at me, with me, or just near me? "I have some lovely bottled water back at my apartment?" Was that what I just said? Brilliant, Madison. Well, she didn't walk away or spit in my face; that must be a good sign. All right, Casanova, you're over here, you're talking to her; just keep going with it.

"So what do you say?" I propose, sounding much more brazen than I feel. "You, me, a little candlelight, and enough Evian to keep us drenched until morning?"

She flashes me a smoldering look that sends a river running down the leg of my jeans.

"How could I resist?" she breathes, stepping in closer to whisper her next thoughts into my ear. "It's not every night such a handsome woman offers to keep me wet for the rest of the evening."

Caught off-guard by her forward response, I struggle to maintain composure, grateful my lesbian status has saved me the embarrassment of what would surely have been a sequoia-sized hard-on.

"I guess there's no need for me to finish drying off," she remarks playfully, tossing me her towel. "Just give me a chance to collect everything, and then you and your bottled water can have my undivided attention for the rest of the night."

It's all I can do to keep from spiking her towel and breaking into a touchdown dance right here by the stage, but instead I simply smile quietly to myself and watch her ass swing as she walks away.

She disappears into a dressing room behind the stage and emerges moments later with a small duffel bag and a light jacket draped over her forearm. She walks over to Fran at the bar, and I see her gesture in my direction, whisper to Fran, and collect her money for the evening. Fran smiles in that omnipresent bartender way and lifts her head to catch my focus, tossing me a quick wink and an exaggerated thumbs up.

I tip my chin up and acknowledge Fran with my most confident dyke nod, trying not to unleash the maelstrom of butterflies swarming in my stomach. All tasks completed, the dancing girl saunters toward me, oblivious to the turned heads and whispers that follow her through the club.

"It's Sarah," she states matter-of-factly once she reaches earshot.

"What is?" I ask, slightly startled and confused.

"My name," she clarifies. "I don't believe we've been formally introduced. I'm sure I would have remembered."

Goddess, what a heel; I didn't even ask her name. "Madison." I stammer an apology. "It's a pleasure."

"Likewise. Well, Madison, shall we go check out that bottled water of yours?" Sarah grabs my hand to ensure I won't get lost, and together we manage to squeeze through the crowd and out the door.

୫   ୫   ୫

"So, what's it like working with kids all the time?" I ask after Sarah tells me she is a dance teacher. "I mean, don't they get annoying sometimes?"

"I have a frustrating day every now and then. Everyone does. But I really enjoy my students, and they have so much energy. They definitely keep me on my toes." Sarah laughs at her little pun. She continues talking, telling me an amusing

311

anecdote from one of her recent classes. I am only half listening, trying my best to nod and smile in all the appropriate places. Mostly, though, I am concentrating on the shape of her lips as she speaks, the way her eyes sparkle when she laughs, and how every time she wants to emphasize a point she reaches over and squeezes my thigh. We've been sitting in my living room drinking water and shooting the breeze for close to an hour now, and I'm finding myself more attracted to this girl by the minute.

"What do you want to do after you graduate?" she asks, turning the attention of the conversation back to me.

"Well, I…"

Sarah leans forward, shifting and settling into a more comfortable position on the couch. She tucks her slim legs under herself and leans sideways against the sofa back. She lets her arm fall forward lazily. Her hand brushes by my ear and then rests lightly on my shoulder. It isn't until she prompts me to continue that I realize I was the one who should have been talking. Completely engrossed watching her shift positions, I must have stopped speaking mid sentence. Great move, Madison. I don't even remember what I had started to say. Utter embarrassment threatens to set in unless I can finesse my way through this faux pas, and quickly.

"Madison…earth to Madison…you in there?" she inquires, waving a small hand in front of my face. "You were saying?"

"Whatever it was, it couldn't have been as important as this," I whisper, leaning into her and kissing her full on the mouth. My fears of rejection dissipate as she returns my kiss with all the electricity and tenderness I had hoped.

Yes, ladies, this is the stuff that daydreams are made of. I make a point to savor these precious initial moments, know-ing that tomorrow, in her absence, I will replay them like snapshots, reliving the excitement over and over.

Her skin is warm to the touch, and I bury my head into her neck, devouring her with kisses, drunk on her scent of musk and jasmine. Soft wet lips and satin-smooth hands, smaller and more delicate than my own, find their way to the most sensitive parts of my body, sending shockwaves through my skin.

With teenage eagerness we explore each other, kissing and caressing, tasting and touching. I sit back on the sofa and pull her body toward me. She swings her leg over my thighs and sits, straddling my lap with ease. My cunt con-tracts as I finally make the "dancer equals flexible equals incredible sexual potential" connection. Looking me dead in the eyes, she unties the strings of her halter top and lets the flimsy piece of fabric fall into my lap. Before I even have a chance to react, she leans over me, her breasts grazing my face. Reaching behind my shoulders she grabs handfuls of my shirt and pulls them over my head. In a moment of van-ity, I reach up to smooth out my hair, but she grabs my wrists, frowning, and points at the sports bra I am still wear-ing. Of course. I wriggle out of the sports bra, fling my arms open in an exaggerated gesture to display my toplessness, flick my wrists, and with no further interruptions run my fingers through my hair with all of the panache of the Fonz. Half naked and ready for business, I am understandably confused when Sarah suddenly climbs off my lap and stands in front of me.

She reaches for my hand. I look up at her with a puzzled expression and grasp her outstretched palm. She helps me gently off the sofa and leads me into the center of the room.

"Close your eyes," she whispers. I am hesitant and give her a sheepish smile.

"It's OK," she says soothingly. "I promise I won't bite."

Tentatively, I shut my eyes. I jump a little as her hands softly settle on my face and draw my head downward. Warm lips plant a kiss on my forehead. She turns my head gently, and I feel her breath hot in my ear; "Now just relax," she coos, her voice easy and seductive.

Without pulling away, she guides my head slowly back, dragging her cheek against mine. I feel the heat of her breath on my lips and lean into her, hoping to catch her mouth for a kiss, but her hands slip quickly to my shoulders and push me back with a tease.

I am about to whine in protest when she slides her hands through my hair to the back of my neck and slinks closer, brushing her bare breasts against mine. Instinctively I reach out and encircle my arms around her waist, drawing her toward me until we are pressed fully against each other, chest to chest, skin to skin. The contact is electrifying, and we both pause, awakened and aroused.

Then, imperceptibly at first, she begins to move in my arms. Slowly and fluidly, I feel her hips start a subtle rock from side to side. I stand, unable to move, overwhelmed by the sensation of her skin sliding over mine, her hips grinding against my pelvis. In the background Tori Amos makes mad love to her piano, alternately petting and pounding the keys into glorious harmonies and dissonances. Tori's music alone is usually enough to get me wet, but as Sarah continues to caress my body with hers in perfect rhythm I know I'll never hear this music the same way again.

Sarah's hands slip down my sides to rest on my hips, and with the slightest bit of pressure she initiates a small rock in my lower body. Tossing my hips between her hands, Sarah guides me into a dance, manipulating my movement to complement her own.

"Just feel me," she whispers. "Trust the movement, and let yourself flow."

Now I wouldn't consider myself the next Baryshnikov, but I've never been ashamed of my dancing abilities. I know I have a fairly good sense of rhythm, and I don't completely embarrass myself on the dance floor. I've even been told by a fair share of women that I am a reasonably good dancer, but standards are pretty low in the lesbian community. Most dykes at Wall Street suffer from what Kate and I have termed "White Girl Syndrome." It's a rampant epidemic in the lesbian bar scene, affecting almost every dyke of European descent over age 25, rendering them entirely incapable of moving rhythmically and cruising simultaneously. The result is usually a poor combination of the two, consisting of a haphazard, alternating, stiff-legged step-touch accompanied by a vacant stare and occasional scan of the surrounding crowd.

The preferred remedy for White Girl Syndrome seems to be the increased consumption of alcohol, which unfortunately only exacerbates an already pathetic situation. Luckily, WGS seems to have skipped a generation in my family, and I usually feel substantially comfortable out on the floor.

Tonight, however, is a different story. Sarah's obviously amazing abilities are terribly intimidating, and I feel myself moving joltingly, rigidly. A lumbering hippopotamus, I swear my feet have grown ten sizes bigger, and every step seems wrong. But Sarah is incredibly patient, comforting me with light touches and soothing words. Her soft voice echoes in my head, mingling with my own inner monologue until I can hardly distinguish the two. *That's it, Madison, just relax…Don't think ahead; the movement will come on its own…There are no mistakes, only choices.* Gradually, I feel myself let go of the nervous tension and frightened stiffness my body had been holding. I realize, breathlessly, that as aroused as I had become watching her perform at the club, it was nothing compared to the fire rising within me now, eyes closed, riding her dancing body, dipping and gliding, twisting and contracting, sliding and pulsing along the bassline of the music. Eyes shut, senses heightened, I surrender to her, to the music, to the dance. The dance builds like flames, and I open my eyes as we continue to move over each other with increasing ferocity. Her breast brushes mine. My elbow falls to rest in the palm of her hand, and she twists, wrapping my arm around her. I lean into her spiraled body, and my lips settle into the soft pocket between her neck and shoulder. Dipping and untwisting, she slides her arms around my waist, supporting me as I arch backward. Tori belts and wails, and we grasp at each other urgently, continuously, shifting and groping with impassioned fervor. The piano quiets, and we shift fluidly, luxuriously, sustaining and suspending contact, looking deep into each other's eyes. I lose my balance; she steadies me. She falls into me, and I absorb her weight like my own. She is no longer my leader; I am no longer her follower. The dance evolves spontaneously, develops independently, weaving in and out of the melodies and rhythms, carrying us along for the ride.

The music strains, then pauses between songs. We reach a stillness, standing only inches apart. I stare down at our bodies, my arms resting around her waist, our breasts brushing with each inhalation, our bellies sloping and curving into each other. This time I do not jump when Sarah clasps my face in both hands and draws my head up even with hers. I look into her eyes, sobered by the clarity I find in her gaze. I feel my walls collapse, the tension rushing from my face. A cloudy haze that I am aware of only in its absence dissolves from focus. I stand before her, completely exposed, intimately enlightened. Eyes unwavering, we absorb each other, potent and peaceful.

"You are a beautiful dancer, Madison," she whispers and covers my lips with hers. Overwhelmed with indescribable emotion, rivulets of tears escape and roll down my cheeks. The safety of her embrace, the electricity of her skin on mine, and the enormity of the experience we have just shared sends my mind reeling.

I convulse and sob in a release as powerful as orgasm. An emotional come. I hold her tightly, clinging to her naked back like a lost child.

And we dance. Exposed. Engulfed. Falling into each other like molasses. I lick salty tears from my lips and kiss them off her shoulder. My arm slides up her back, and I hold the soft spot behind her neck, tightening our embrace. The melody washes over us, surging and sustaining; my emotions rush along with the tumultuous cascade.

Amid the music, amid the movement, amid the intensity of feeling, she whispers to me, prophetic and comforting, "This is why, Madison…This is why we dance."

I understand completely.

And we dance…and dance…and dance.

Contributors' Notes

Aya is an African-American poet and fiction writer who lives in Philadelphia. Her work has been published in many feminist journals and anthologies. One of her stories recently appeared in *Nightshade: Gothic Tales by Women.*

Elizabeth Bachman works in health care. A native New Yorker, she lives in Atlanta with her partner and two sons. "Rebellious Streak" is her first published story.

J.L. Belrose attended the Ontario College of Art and Design and studied in London before settling down near Blue Mountain in Canada. Her fiction and poetry have most recently appeared in the journals *Lezzie Smut, Siren, Quota,* and *Church-Wellesley Review* as well as the anthologies *Queer View Mirror* and *Skin Deep.* She has just completed a novel.

Maureen Brady is the author of *Give Me Your Good Ear, The Question She Put to Herself,* and *Folly* as well as three nonfiction books. She teaches writing at New York University, The Writer's Voice, and The Peripatetic Writing Workshop. Recently her stories have been published in *Cabbage and Bones: Fiction by Irish American Women* and *Mom: Candid Memoirs by Lesbians About the First Woman in Their Life.* She and her partner, Martha, divide their time between New York City and their home in the Catskills.

Erin Brennan studied history and political science and worked as an advertising copywriter before embarking on a career in health care. Over the past twenty years, she has made her home on the prairies of Illinois, the high desert of New Mexico, and the low country of coastal Georgia—all with the same woman. "Anything for Her" is her first published story.

Bridget Bufford has had her work published in *The Coming Out Newsletter* and in the online publication *Erotasy* (www.erotasy.com). Her story "Working Out" is excerpted from *Minus One,* a novel in progress.

Teresa Cooper holds an MFA in fiction writing from Columbia University. Her fiction has appeared in *Best Lesbian Erotica 1999* and *Blithe House Quarterly.* In addition to being a freelance writer, she is the editor and publisher of a quarterly zine for dykes, *The Fish Tank,* which was awarded a 1999 Firecracker Alternative Book Award.

Bree Coven has had poetry, essays, short stories, and smut published in *The Femme Mystique, Best Lesbian Erotica 1997, Generation Q, Masquerade Journal,* and *Pucker Up, Princess.* She originated the Baby Dyke column at *Deneuve* (now *Curve*) and was a regular contributor there for three years. She lives in New York City, where she is finishing a book of nonfiction.

tatiana de la tierra is a bilingual, bicultural Colombian/ Miamian writer with an MFA in creative writing from the

University of Texas at El Paso. She is a former editor of the Latina lesbian publications *esto no tiene nombre, commoción,* and *el telaraña 30.* Her writing has appeared in *Chasing the American Dyke Dream, Miami Herald's Tropic* magazine, *Hot and Bothered, The Femme Mystique, Queer View Mirror, Perra!,* and *Ms.*

Lisa Gonzales is a 27-year-old Texas native who lives in California. She has received student scholarships to attend writing classes at the University of California, Los Angeles extension program.

Margaret Granite hopes that by the time this is printed she will no longer be a graduate student working on her dissertation, "Fleshing Out the Victorian Public Sphere of Letters." When she began her dissertation, she also began writing erotica. "An Anatomy Lesson for Mary Margaret" is her first adventure into this nonacademic genre.

Renee Hawkins is an award-winning radio personality who lives in Albuquerque, N.M. She attended New Mexico State University in Las Cruces and majored in journalism. An avid hot-air balloonist, Hawkins has been a pilot since 1983. She is also working on her first novel, a murder mystery with spiritual overtones. "Burning Zozobra" is her first published short story.

Karleen Pendleton Jiménez is a Chicana lesbian writer and teacher who resides in Toronto. She is the founder and former director of Queer Players, a creative writing and performance group for queer youth in the San Diego area. Her writing has been published in *Hers 3: Brilliant New Fiction* *by Lesbians, Early Embraces, Countering the Myths: Lesbians Write About the Men in Their Lives,* and *commoción* #3. She has just completed her first novel, *Not Everyone Turns Pink Under the Sun.*

Lauren Johnson, a native Texan, lives in California with her lover, a filmmaker. She has penned many plays, mostly for children, and like everyone else thinks she's a screenwriter. She received her MFA from the University of California, Los Angeles. "Somebody Famous" is her first published short story.

Ilsa Jule's essay "Your Mom Looks Like Superman" was published in the anthology *Lesbians Raising Sons.* She lives in New York City and is working on a novel.

Rosalind Christine Lloyd is a lesbian of color whose work has appeared in *On Our Backs* and local gay/lesbian publications in New York and Atlanta. She also writes a travel column for *Venus Magazine.* A native New Yorker, she lives in Harlem with her life partner, Pleshette, and their unruly cat.

Nilaja Montgomery-Akalu is a 20-something African-American aspiring filmmaker/writer/photographer. She resides in the San Francisco Bay area, where she is pursuing a certificate in American Sign Language. Her fiction has also appeared in the first volume of *Pillow Talk,* as well as *Lip Service: Alluring New Lesbian Erotica.*

G.L. Morrison defines herself as a "white, working-poor, righteous, leftist, omniverous, vitamin-deficient, cyber-Sapphist poet and mommy." Her writing has previously appeared in *Early Embraces 2, Burning Ambitions,* and *Mom: Candid Memoirs by Lesbians About the First Woman in Their Life.* An award-winning playwright and poet, she is poetry editor of *New Attitude (Fat Feminist Caucus)* and a member of the performance-art troupe Fierce Pussy Posse.

Debra Olson is a freelance writer who makes Salt Lake City her home.

Gina Ranalli lives and works in Portland, Ore.

Robin St. John has published both short fiction and nonfiction and is working on a novel. She lives in Sacramento, where she works as a legal assistant.

Anne Seale writes lesbian songs, stories, and plays. She has performed on many gay stages including the Lesbian National Conference, where she has sung tunes from her tape *Sex for Breakfast.* Her short fiction appeared in the first volume of *Pillow Talk* as well as *Love Shook My Heart, Hot and Bothered, The Ghost of Carmen Miranda, Lip Service, Touched by Adoption,* and the journals *Lesbian Short Fiction* and *The Journal of Lesbian Erotica.*

Gail Shepherd is a freelance journalist, poet, fiction writer, and editor. Her work has appeared in many anthologies and journals including *American Writing, The Yale Review, Poetry, The Iowa Review, Women on Women II,* and *Out/Look.* She published and edited *Red Herring,* a biweekly arts journal, from 1995 until 1998. Her awards include an Individual Artists Fellowship in Poetry. She lives in South Florida.

Clara Thaler is a writer and law student. Her work has most recently been published in *Friday the Rabbi Wore Lace: Jewish Lesbian Erotica.* She lives in Massachusetts.

Leslie Kimiko Ward recently received her BFA in Dance Performance and Choreography from Ohio State University. She teaches ballet, tap, jazz, and modern dance to students of all ages in Seattle.

About the Editor

Lesléa Newman is an author and editor whose thirty books for adults and children include *The Femme Mystique*, *The Little Butch Book*, *Out of the Closet and Nothing to Wear*, *In Every Laugh a Tear*, *Still Life With Buddy*, and *Heather Has Two Mommies*. Her writing has been published in a variety of magazines and journals, ranging from *Common Lives/Lesbian Lives* to *Seventeen Magazine*. Her latest books include a novella and short-story collection titled *Girls Will Be Girls*, and *Thea's Throw*, a children's book. Five of her books have been Lambda Literary Award finalists. She divides her time between Massachusetts and New York. Read more about her books at www.lesleanewman.com.

MARY VAZQUEZ